Eve at Peace
BY
Yvette Doolittle Herr

Copyright @ 2021 Yvette Doolittle Herr
TXu 2-268-770

All rights reserved. No part of this book may be reproduced, stored or transmitted by any means-whether auditory, graphics, mechanical, or electronic – without the written permission of both the publisher and author, except in the case of brief excerpts used in critical articles and reviews. Unauthorized reproduction of any part of this work is illegal and punishable by law

Cover Design
By
Linda Nichols

ISBN: 9798646415722
All characters are entirely fictitious and based on the imagination of the author. Any resemblances to person living, or dead, are purely coincidental and unintended.

KDP Publishing 2021

See also:
Ms. Magdalene's Halloween
The Lucky Two

DEDICATION

I began this novel in the spring of 2019, the first year of recovery from category five Hurricane Michael, which devastated Bay County, Florida, on October 10, 2018. The story was completed in the summer of 2020, when people all over the world were suffering through the multi-layered problems of a pandemic called COVID-19.

I dedicate this book to all God's children.

Mercy, Peace and Love be yours in abundance. (Jude 1:2)

Acknowledgments

Grateful appreciation to my husband, Travis, for collaborating, encouraging and editing this story. Without him I would be lost trying to pull it all together. It was fun to bring the city of Altoona, Pennsylvania, where he was born and raised, into the narrative. The railroad was central to the city's development, and the Pennsylvania Railroad was a strong economic force in the state. The famous Horseshoe Curve in Altoona is on the National Historic register.

Travis's recollections of the Altoona Lodge 102 of the BPOE as a child were very much a part of the dialogue. The Elks support for scouting, special needs children and scholarships remain a part of society, for those less fortunate.

Heartfelt thanks to my beautiful sister-in-law, Linda, for offering her special artistic talent.

Holy Bible scriptures are taken from the New International Version, copyright 1984.
Finally, many thanks to the people who read the first novel, The Lucky Two, and encouraged me to write another one.

Eve at Peace by Yvette Doolittle Herr

PROLOGUE:

Stories are sometimes rewritten with different endings, right?

When the details of a story become known, it's often easy to be perplexed about the outcome. Why did the story end in a certain way, and not another? Why did the worst possible outcome happen? Or, was it the best possible outcome? Why did the outcome seem to conflict with the facts within the story?

When someone is given a choice to do something that seems obvious to be in their best interest, why do they do something different?

Many factors are involved to explain the behavior of people, and animals, not the least being emotions, nature, or external circumstances beyond the control of anyone. These components cast a shadow on the history of any event, and blurs the view of anyone trying to fully understand the past. Oftentimes, to know the outcomes leads to more questions; questions that motivates even the least knowledgeable to continue to search for more answers. The truth is, some facts may never reveal the outcome expected.

To properly understand the outcomes of the past one must diligently assess each and every small detail. Even after all the scrutinizing, it's still easy to never completely understand, or accept, the results.

Finding peace with the past, and holding hope for the future, can be as easy as making the choice to look for love, which might be found in rainbows, painted skies at sunset, morning songbirds, butterflies, cool evening breezes, dolphins, or spiritual interference.

Chapter 1:   The Prison Visit
Chapter 2:   A New Breed
Chapter 3:   Sand Dunes And Sea Oats
Chapter 4:   The New Neighborhood
Chapter 5:   A Night Of Problems
Chapter 6:   Destined For Doom
Chapter 7:   Hidden Secrets
Chapter 8:   Birdies, Bugs And Butterflies
Chapter 9:   Sista's New Challenge
Chapter 10 Listen To Sista
Chapter 11 Not Gonna Be A Slave
Chapter 12 The Big Question
Chapter 13 Kings And Kittens
Chapter 14 Complicated Conversation
Chapter 15 Demon Cat At The Halloween Party
Chapter 16 Casey's Rebound
Chapter 17 Charles' Confession
Chapter 18 Showtime
Chapter 19 Romance And Revenge
Chapter 20 Dreamers
Chapter 21 Living On Another Planet
Chapter 22 Ricky's Request
Chapter 23 Eve Meets Charles
Chapter 24 Demon Dreams
Chapter 25 Dorinda's Departure
Chapter 26 Spiritual Advisor
Chapter 27 No Apologies
Chapter 28 Curiosity Kills The Cat
Chapter 29 Time For A Change
Chapter 30 Honor And Proper Burial
Chapter 31 Welcome Back Party
Chapter 32 Dinner At Smiths
Chapter 33 Chance Encounters
Chapter 34 Jonnie Mae
Chapter 35 Bombshell News
Chapter 36 Lucky Break

CHAPTER 1
THE PRISON VISIT

"He's in this room," the guard said, motioning with his hand. "You may go on inside. I'm right behind you."

Her heart was beating doubly fast when she placed her hand on the handle of her hope. She had waited many years since first hearing the story about the man she was about to meet. Finally, she was taking the first step to reach an opening in the mystery.

She slowly turned the round doorknob and gently pushed to open the thick, steel door. The door creaked with each inch it opened.

Taking two short steps into the small interrogation room, she came face-to-face with a freckle-faced man. He was sitting on a plain wood chair with his back firmly against the oakwood slats on the chairback. His face appeared freshly shaved and had a youthful look for being a man in his late forties.

Straightening his posture when he heard the door open, the man stared at her, wide-eyed. With a thin, closed-lip smile and, knowing the protocols, he placed his hands on top of the six-foot table that separated him and the woman. He watched her pull out a chair on the opposite side of the table and sit down. The guard, whose presence was mandatory, took a seat in the corner of the room.

Feeling confident that she would finally find the answers to many questions that intrigued her mind for years, the young woman was surprised by the man's friendly mannerisms.

The man she had been searching for didn't stop smiling at her with his bright, blinking, alert eyes after she sat down in a chair no different than his. Her first impression was he was eager to be with her. His body became animated as if invisible strings were pulling at his limbs. Both legs were bouncing up and down beneath the table, and his fingers fidgeted with something imaginary on top of the table. Finally, after a few minutes of merely looking at each other, he leaned forward, waved at her with one hand, and nodded his head, letting her know he was ready to begin.

She had written down the questions she wanted to ask. Still, she hesitated, distracted by the contrast of a warm, friendly face in the cold surroundings of the prison visitor interrogation room. Instinctively, she knew she must set aside her goals for the first visit and change her strategy.

Even though they were separated by a short distance across the table, she felt like she wanted to shake his hand, but that was impossible under the circumstances. He wore handcuffs.

"Hello," she spoke. "My name is Eve. I understand your name is Ricky. Am I correct?"

The man enthusiastically nodded his head up and down.

"I've been told that you cannot speak due to an accident, but you can answer questions if I ask you to nod your head yes, or no. Is that correct?"

He pressed his lips tightly together, forming them into a thin line. Then, with a solemn face nodded again, delicately tilting his head to one side as if to apologize for the inconvenience."

I've been allowed to come here to visit you after making a special request to the Department of Corrections. They have given me permission to talk to you to obtain information about your case as long as you agree to participate. So today, I plan to only ask you a few questions, get acquainted, and then you may decide how you feel about me continuing to visit you. Do you understand?"

He nodded his head, indicating he understood her question. His facial expression changed. His eyebrows furrowed together. Ricky was clearly not sure where this encounter would lead. He was wondering who this woman was and why was she interested in him?

Ricky remembered being surprised when the corrections facility staff asked if he would be willing to have a visitor. He had been in the Florida prison for a quarter-century and never once had a visitor come to see him other than the lawyer who met with him when he was initially booked into jail. His curiosity about why the visitor, a stranger, would want to see him won over his initial apprehension. He did not recognize the visitor's name, and no other information was given. He couldn't think of any long-lost friends or relatives who might be looking for him. Not even his mother had been in contact with him after he was incarcerated.

It took almost a year for Ricky to recover from the injury in his mouth.

It also took about a year for him to finally accept the loss of his best friend, Vince. He finally realized Vince was the impetus and the main reason he found himself in prison. Ricky wished he'd listened to his mother's advice about choosing friends wisely. Initially, he thought a lot about his mother, wishing he could see her again and apologize to her for being rebellious. However, Ricky knew his mother well enough to know she would not want to hear the details, nor accept them, of how he ended up in prison. If you ever get into trouble, don't expect me to visit you in prison, his mother once said to him. She lived by her words. Seven years after he was locked up, he received a letter, sent by the clerk of courts in Opp, Alabama, notifying him that his mother had died.

It took a few more years to adapt to the environment of his new life in prison. The memory of the frightening night before he ended up in prison lingered in his memory. He trained himself to be less fearful of the things he could not control, like the behavior of the other inmates, who sometimes taunted him for seeming to be meek and cowardly. The majority of the inmates, incarcerated for crimes involving drugs or robbery, had personalities similar to his old friend Vince, who seemed angry about anybody and everything. If there was one thing Vince taught Ricky, it was how to keep quiet when the flames of anger lit up Vince's eyes.

Ricky didn't argue or get into fights with anyone else. He couldn't since he couldn't talk. Eventually, no one else in prison bothered Ricky. Ricky was just another prisoner doing time for murder, only he couldn't speak with half a tongue missing.

When he consented to see the visitor, he signed an agreement saying that he would cooperate and share any new information the visitor discovered in the process of her interrogations. The agreement didn't worry him. But, on the other hand, what to expect from the visitor made him more nervous than being suspicious of her motives.

Who was this woman sitting in front of him, Ricky asked himself multiple times? Did she know his mother, he wondered?

"I bet you're wondering the reason why I am here," Eve said.

Ricky gently nodded his head to agree while thinking that the woman must have read his mind.

"I'm trying to find out more information about a person who died. The man named Earl Keith. The man you confessed to killing in 1986," she said without taking her eyes off Ricky.

Shocked by what she said, Ricky opened his eyes wide and locked them onto the blue eyes of the beautiful young woman sitting on the other side of the table. His heart began to pound inside his chest, and his mouth hung open. His breathing accelerated. The nervous habit of fanning his legs returned. He couldn't move his head to indicate how he felt about her statement. He didn't know what to feel.

"All these years later," Ricky thought, "and now here's this beautiful woman asking me about the murder of Earl. I only remember confessing to killing Earl after my lawyer told me that would be the best thing for me to do."

Neither person blinked for several seconds.

"Do you think you can write down answers?" she quickly asked, sensing Ricky's nervousness.

Ricky shrugged his shoulders and tilted his head close to one shoulder. He couldn't answer yes, or no, because he wasn't sure if he would know the answers to her questions.

Eve at Peace by Yvette Doolittle Herr

Unconsciously Ricky's thin legs continued to alternately fan and bounce beneath the table.

Not discouraged by his body language, Eve went on. "Can you write?"

Ricky reluctantly nodded yes. He knew his writing skills were weak, but he'd have to try.

"As I said, I just wanted to get acquainted today. I will be back to ask more specific questions which won't need to be answered in one single meeting. I will provide you with paper and a pencil. If you can't answer the questions while I'm visiting, I will come back on another day. You may need to take time to think about your answers. I will make the questions simple and write them down for you to think about if you want me to. Will you agree to do that? Please?" she eagerly asked, trying to hide her excitement.

Ricky calmed down and stopped fanning his legs.

He saw nothing in the girl's demeanor that gave him reason to distrust her. Instead, he suddenly realized he was curious to know a little more about Earl Keith himself.

Ricky nodded yes.

"Great!" Eve said, exhaling a sigh of relief.

Excited by his response, she talked faster. "I'll make plans to visit you probably once a week. I'll find out from the guards which day, and what time of day, is the best for you. Per prison regulations, we'll take no more than an hour on each visit. And, if at any time you want to stop my visits or can't answer any questions, you just let me know. Smile big if you think if this plan works for you."

Ricky's eyes, and smile, expressed his feelings. He certainly wasn't going anywhere else.

The years in prison changed him. He was thankful to wake up every morning in a place where he felt safe, had food, had shelter, and had no responsibilities besides following the rules of the prison guards.

Now he had something else to look forward to: it would be nice to have a pretty girl visiting him.

CHAPTER 2
A NEW BREED

"That cat's bitten into something seriously nasty," Big Joe, the head chef at Smith's Restaurant, mumbled to himself as he watched the cat convulse. Big Joe was sitting on his concrete bench, outside the back door of Smith's kitchen, taking a brief break.

A medium-sized cat, with black and white fur, was frothing at the mouth and convulsing on a patch of grass near the water's edge about twenty feet away, not far from where Big Joe's large feet were resting. The cat's head jerked up and down a few times, then tilted at an angle to let the spittle drain out the corner of his mouth before scampering away from Big Joe.

"So, what was that all about?" Joe remarked out loud to the cat as he watched it slowly trot down the ledge of the concrete seawall that separated the lagoon from the restaurant.

The cat stopped, sat down on its haunches, and turned his head to look back at Big Joe after hearing the sound of the human's voice. Its eyes glowed, but there was no hint of malice. The fur on its back spiked when a soft breeze blew across the lagoon. The cat recognized Big Joe as one of the friendly humans at the marina.

"Got a nasty taste of something, did you?" Big Joe asked the cat, who appeared to be interested in listening to what the human had to say.

The cat took advantage of the shared moment to lick his front paw, after which he curled the forepaw over his ear, face, and mouth. The long, nubby, pink tongue repeated the maneuver multiple times, all the while keeping an eye on Big Joe between every lick.

"How many times have I told all you cats to stay out of that dumpster," Big Joe laughed at his own question. He was aware that the cats frequently visited the garbage dumpster to search for something good to eat. The smells were too tantalizing for any animal to ignore.

The cat stood up, stretched out his front paws down and forward, and the hindquarters up high. After he finished stretching, the cat stood and shook his body like he was trying to shake off the distaste. Then he took off in a galloping run away from Big Joe sitting on the bench and toward the deep-sea charter boats tied to pilings in the slips.

After the category four hurricane named Louise made landfall near Panama City Beach, Big Joe grew fond of the gang of cats at Captain Anderson's Marina. He respected their resiliency in the aftermath, surviving despite the difficult odds they faced when there was almost nothing left at the marina. He became more curious about their behaviors and movement patterns, which helped to fuel his desire to stay working at Smith's. Like many people trying to help each other after the hurricane, Big Joe was a man devoted to staying and helping rebuild people's lives.

While other restaurants, gift shops, and charter boats at the marina were left in piles of rubble or bad disrepair after the hurricane, the damage to Smith's Restaurant was not as severe. The owners quickly reopened and got people back to work feeding people. Initially, construction workers and power line repair crews were the first hungry people to line up for a good, hot meal. Eventually, the tourists returned, hungry for a bit of paradise served on a plate.

Big Joe routinely sat on a bench close to the seawall outside the kitchen backdoor of the restaurant to take a fifteen-minute break before returning to the hot kitchen. His weight had become an increasing problem for his legs. They ached from the long hours of standing in front of a large open grill. Feeding hundreds of people on any given hot summer night was challenging his physical stamina.

There were many other restaurants Big Joe could have moved to with his expertise and chef skills. His request to add the bench for short respites during his long work shift was approved without any argument from the owner, who didn't want to lose a valuable employee. Big Joe told them he would be forced to quit his job unless he could add the bench and take brief respites.

"You need to supervise and train more," the owner kept telling Big Joe.

Those orders were too hard for Big Joe to follow. "I'm a hands-on chef," he told the owner, once more insisting he needed the bench. "You know how much I love working for you at Smith's, especially after all that we've been through together with the hurricane last October."

"Then I'll do whatever it takes to keep you here," the owner conceded to Big Joe. "Go find a bench and hire an extra sous chef to help you prep so that you're not standing on your legs for so many hours. The most important thing for me is making sure that the food comes out of the kitchen according to the standards we both expect."

Big Joe slowly lifted his body up from the bench with great effort and took one last look at the runaway cat.

"What's going on," Big Joe asked Geneva, who was standing at the kitchen door waiting for Big Joe to come back so she could ask him a question about menu specials for the night.

"*Dumb cat*, DC, is a good nickname for that stinkin' cat. It's about as dumb a cat as I've ever seen. It's even too dumb to know what's good to put in its mouth," she commented while holding the door open for Big Joe. "I was watching you from the kitchen door, waiting for you to come back, and saw that cat meander over near the bench. It probably jumped out of the dumpster. I thought it was going to puke all over you. So, you'd better be careful around it. No telling what happened that caused it to act that way," Geneva continued, following Big Joe as he lumbered past other employees busy at work in the kitchen.

"Something could have bit into him to make him froth at the mouth," she said. "Next thing you know it might bite you, or scratch you, and give you rabies, or cat scratch fever, or something worse."

"Well, I'd rather not comment on that nickname," Big Joe finally said when he stopped at the grill. "DC is a little different from the other cats loitering around the marina. Not many of them will come near me, but DC does. I'm not worried about DC hurting me. I'd be more concerned about DC hurting himself."

"Humpf! Any cat that chases its tail while cars are driving around in the parking lot, honking horns at it, is a dumb cat. I hope DC doesn't get killed one day," Geneva snorted. She returned to her station at the stainless-steel prep table in the salad room, busying her hands with food prep work.

This particular black and white cat witnessed by Big Joe suffering a traumatic, humiliating experience had been nicknamed DC by Geneva, the prep cook hired by Big Joe shortly after the bench arrived. She'd seen the cat hanging around the marina on many occasions.

A litter of four kittens, each with a thick coat of black fur and a triangular patch of white fur on their chest, were found by a boat captain in a storage box at the marina in the spring following hurricane Louise hitting the coastline in October 1986.

As they were affectionately nicknamed by cat-loving workers at the marina, the tuxedo cats turned into a small army of cats after a second litter was born in the summer. The cats had a shiny, thick, black coat of fur, with variations of white patches. All sported a white patch of fur on the chest below their chins, giving them a look of distinction when boldly strutting around with their fluffy tails held high and straight. Many in the new breed had four white paws, making them appear to be wearing booties. Some had only three white paws. All of the tuxedo cats were endowed with long white whiskers and eyebrows. A few had a thin, white mustache below the black nose, or at least a half mustache, or a dot of white fur on the tip of the nose. They scampered around the marina, sniffing and searching for food.

It was no surprise to the gang of cats at the marina to discover that the kittens' parents were Princess and King. What was surprising was the color of the kitten's eyes. The mother cat, Princess, was a solid white, fluffy Persian with green eyes. The father cat, King, was a solid black, short-hair cat with aqua-blue eyes. All of the tuxedo kittens' eyes were a bright gold color unless they were standing in the direct sunlight. The sun's bright light caused their eyes to sparkle and change into a translucent color of blue-green hazel.

The first few weeks after the hurricane was a strain on everyone, including the cats. People and cats tried to comfort and support each other by helping to find food, water, and shelter. Many people came from other nearby towns in Alabama and Georgia to help with cleaning up all of the brokenness.

Geneva arrived in town the first spring following hurricane Louise. She had lived all of her life in the north and was not used to the southern habits and style of living.

"What brought you down to Panama City Beach?" Big Joe asked her when she applied for a job in the kitchen at Smith's. He noticed she put her last place of employment at the Elks Club in Altoona, Pennsylvania.

"I read in the newspapers and heard on television about all the businesses down here needing people to come down to Panama City to work," she answered.

"So why did you leave your job at the Elks Club?" he asked. "You show here on your application that you worked there for six years in the kitchen as a prep cook and also at an establishment called Tom's Diner."

"They're getting ready to close down the kitchen at the Elks Club. Altoona is a dying city," Geneva answered, lowering her eyes to the floor to avoid looking directly into Big Joe's eyes. She wanted to be honest but didn't want to embarrass herself. She'd had another job besides the Elks Club.

Tom's Diner, a small counter-top service restaurant, was a block away from the Elks Club, and she walked past it daily. She begged the owners to give her a few hours when her hours were cut at the Elks Club. The kitchen at Tom's was too small for her to maneuver around in, and the owners told her that they liked her, but it wouldn't work out. She worked at Tom's Diner for only a couple of days.

She continued, proud to talk about her real kitchen experience working in the Elks Club. "The downtown area in Altoona has only a few stores left, and the Elks Club is in the middle of downtown. The club didn't have enough members to support the maintenance and upkeep of the building, so they started talking about shutting down the kitchen to save money. The bar made a lot of money, and the special parties were good, but not enough people came in to eat regularly to support the kitchen."

Geneva was struggling not to tell Big Joe more. The memories were still fresh. She could remember listening to the noise from the bowling alley in the basement drift up to where she worked in the kitchen all those years. The sound of bowling pins crashing was like the sound of money to her ears. People who bowled also ate in the club. The bowling alley was the first club amenity to close down soon after the Holiday Bowl was built in the nearby borough of Hollidaysburg. The Elks Club bowling alley was replaced by bowling leagues in the suburbs.

It was difficult for her to understand the dynamics. Why did Altoona, once a prosperous railroad town, home of the famous Horseshoe Curve in the mountains, decline? She lived there all her life and watched the demise of city landmarks steadily unfold when the importance of the railroad changed and factories closed.

"Oh, I see," Big Joe nodded his head. He took note of the change in her initial eagerness to talk. He sensed a hint of sadness in her voice when she spoke about the Elks Club and decided she was truthful about her work experience.

Big Joe hired Geneva on the spot. He liked her immediately. In the weeks following, she was quick to learn her way around the kitchen. She had an excellent attitude about working hard and doing everything that Big Joe asked her to do.

Occasionally, however, Geneva revealed another side of her personality. She was quick to show anger when she perceived injustice at work. It could be a server trying to play favorites with a line cook to get the food to the table faster. Or perhaps a dishwasher slipping behind a door to avoid the dishes piling up on the conveyor belt to the dish machine. Or even a busboy forgetting to replace the bag in a garbage can after emptying it.

"Hey you, why don't you get your butt out of your head," she'd proclaim under her breath but usually loud enough for at least one person to hear her.

Whenever an employee reported her nastiness to Big Joe, he'd have a short talk with her after work. She would apologize initially, but it always ended up with Geneva having the exact last words and advice afterward.

"When me and my little brother were young, we would get into fights about how we should feel about situations going on with our parents. My little brother had to call me Sista because that's who I was," she'd say to Big Joe. "My brother would tell me, *Sista, just because you're older than me doesn't mean that you're always right. Just like we don't live in a world of black and white, you being older than me don't give you the honor of being right about how we're supposed to feel about everything.*" Geneva would cap the story in a slightly sarcastic tone, "So here's what I think. Bottom line, Big Joe, you being the boss doesn't make you right about everything."

Big Joe, tired at the end of a busy night, would tell Geneva to go home and try not to let the bad work habits of other people get under her skin.

"If there's a problem, tell me first," he'd say. Then, to humor himself, he'd add, "Maybe that's why you don't like that cat you call DC so much because it's black and white. Good or bad, right or wrong, try to take it one day at a time and keep your feelings to yourself until you walk out the back door at the end of the shift."

Soon Geneva's nickname Sista became known to everyone working at Smith's after Big Joe let it slip out one night when he called out to her above the kitchen noise.

It didn't bother her when another employee at work occasionally called her Sista. It made her feel like she was being accepted at Smith's and fitting into her new hometown.

CHAPTER 3
SAND DUNES AND SEA OATS

Troubling thoughts were weighing heavy on her heart and disrupting her ability to function properly. An early morning walk on the beach was what Eleanore believed she needed to help ease her tensions and worry. The breeze from the Gulf of Mexico tempered the warmth of an Indian summer day in November. It was much more pleasant than the sweltering heat of the past summer.

The sound of the waves gently rushing in and out along the shoreline soothed her spirit. The aqua-marine-colored water sparkling bright between the two sand bars out in the distant Gulf of Mexico helped to clear her mind.

She talked aloud to herself while she strolled barefoot, pausing every so often to feel the soft, sugary sand slide between her toes.

"Indeed, this is the most beautiful time of year," she said to no one but herself.

It had been a year since what she now referred to as *That Wild October Ride*. So many questions and doubts about her current situation were running through her mind. She couldn't allow herself to think about what would have happened if she stayed in Pine Mountain and had never decided to drive to Panama City Beach. But lately, she'd found herself slipping into thinking about her crazy, impulsive decision to rescue Earl. She knew she needed to think about how much was learned about herself – strengths and weaknesses – during the one night when she didn't know if she would live or die. The hurricane named Louise changed her life forever.

"Maybe Casey is rubbing off on me. He's always saying if only he had done something different whenever he's unhappy about something that happened. He'll say, *what if I had done this instead of that*. I believe we come down too hard on ourselves. Once we make a decision, we own it.

They're just some things that we cannot control, like a hurricane, for example. There are times, and circumstances, when we can't wait to make a decision."

She laughed out loud. "Now maybe it's Darryl rubbing off on me. He's always talking out loud to himself. In fact, it's hard to get him to stop talking if ever he has an audience. At least he doesn't talk about himself all the time. He usually tries to make a conversation about something else that's interesting. Any day now, though, he'll have a lot more to talk about once I've made my decision."

Before she left to go on her solitary walk, she made a quick visit to see Darryl. He reminded Eleanore to keep her eyes open for miscellaneous, dangerous objects in the sand. "Keep your head down, and look ahead to avoid tripping over something sticking out of the sand," he said.

"I'm going to enjoy a solitary stroll on the beach to look at the sea oats and sand dunes," she laughed back.

"There's not many of them left," Darryl retorted, rolling his eyes. His first instinct was to ask her if she wanted company, but when she told him she wanted to be alone, his gut instinct warned him that something might be wrong.

"Where are you going to park?" Darryl asked.

"Treasure Island Marina," she answered.

"Good, you'll have a sidewalk to walk on all the way to the boardwalk of the second public beach access. Still, I want you to be on the lookout and be careful walking across Thomas Drive at the light," he said, waving goodbye before she walked away.

"There are enough sea oats left for me to enjoy, even if it's not the way it used to be," she proclaimed. "Just like you love the Gulf of Mexico's aqua green waters for fishing, I love walking on the beach. I'm also hoping I'll see a dolphin! Maybe it will be a pink one."

They shared a laugh together when she mentioned the pink dolphin. Eleanore enjoyed bringing up the pink dolphin story Darryl told her when she rode with him to the marina on the day they first met. She also loved the blue, glass dolphin he kept on the rear-view mirror of his truck.

    The debris that washed up on the beach after the hurricane was almost all gone. There were still a few large items embedded in the sand. Besides metal fence railings and wood pilings, people had located the concrete housing from an offshore buoy and the hull of a sailboat. It took time, money, and hours of people working with heavy equipment to remove all of the storm debris.

    "I'll never forget the first time I saw Darryl when he drove up to me in his truck at the gas station parking lot at the corner of Highway 390 and Highway 231," she continued thinking to herself as she slowly strolled barefoot in the sand. "He stopped to ask me if I needed help. I wasn't looking for someone to help me. I was thinking about whether there was a chance I could find Earl. When I got here, I realized how serious the situation was with the hurricane coming. I remember thinking I should go back home and give up on Earl. I became afraid after seeing all those people in their cars trying to evacuate. I felt that I let myself get in a bad situation on account of Earl. Then Darryl comes along, looking at me with those beautiful blue eyes, asking me if I needed help. I went back to thinking about Earl calling me and sounding so desperate. I knew I had to try and help Earl. Darryl telling me that he was driving to the marina was the intervention I needed to stay on my mission track.

    "Looking back on it, I firmly believe Darryl only said he was driving to Captain Anderson's Marina as a way to spend time with me. He told me he didn't want to go back to the hurricane shelter. Still, nothing will convince me that he was planning to drive all the way back to Captain Anderson's Marina.

    "That first day, riding together to the marina, he told me that the eyes are the window to the soul. He's never stopped telling me that since that day. I love the ways he looks at me, with his eyes reflecting happiness. Our relationship has grown over the past several months, but I'm not sure if it can be a forever thing.

"Today, I have the same feelings of uncertainty that I had when I drove down to find Earl. I'm pregnant with Darryl's baby, not married, and unsure if I want to stay here with Darryl. How, when, should I tell him? I know that I have to let him know real soon. And, I know he'll be so excited that he'll want to get married, jump right on into it, like when he asked me to get in his truck that day. I have a feeling that I'm about to go on a long, crazy ride with Darryl, and I'm not sure I'm ready for what could happen.

"One thing I'm sure about. Having a baby is a beautiful thing, even if I am a bit scared and nervous. It can't be as frightening as the night I spent with Casey on Earl's boat during the hurricane. Nothing will ever match that night, or at least I hope not."

Deep in her heart, Eleanor understood the root of her insecurity and fear. The last time she had similar feelings was the night she spent with Casey on *The Lucky Two*. It was the night when she came to the stark realization that she must make good decisions if she was going to make it on her own. Taking risks requires good judgment, but she also didn't want to hurt anyone else. Eleanore struggled with balancing her self-interests, what would be suitable for her, and what would be good for someone else.

During the night of the hurricane, and after discovering the next day that Earl was dead, Casey's compassionate handling of the situation gave her hope. It helped her understand that she needed to accept the help of honest people when it was offered.

Casey immediately offered to allow her and Darryl to stay in his house. Casey was aware Darryl lived on his charter boat, and when he saw the broken pieces of The *Star Chaser* floating in the lagoon waters at Captain Anderson's Marina, he knew he needed to offer help to Darryl,

It was Casey, too, who connected Eleanore with Big Joe and the job at Smith's.

It surprised Eleanore that Casey invited Darryl to stay at his house, as she sensed the tension between the two men when she first met Casey. She remembered seeing Casey standing in front of Earl's boat at Captain Anderson's Marina when she and Darryl arrived. Even more surprising was how Casey seemed to become a different person than the one she met on that day. He kept a low profile in his own house with his guests. In addition, he worked extra hours at his job.

Everyone becoming busy with responsibilities of the aftermath of the hurricane gave all three of them the space and time they needed to recover from their trauma.

However, it wasn't long before Darryl decided he was not comfortable staying at Casey's house.

"The house is a little small for the three of us, and I'm anxious to get back to work. I'm ready to go catch fish. I need to make some money. It will be safe for you to stay here at Casey's house," Darryl said to Eleanore. "He's not the same Casey I knew before the hurricane. He's changed," Darryl assured her.

"I'm not worried about staying with Casey. I'm concerned about you," Eleanore protested. "We've all probably changed a bit, but why would you sleep on the boat when you can sleep here, in a house, at night. I don't understand why you'd give up the roof over your head for floating on the boat every night."

When Eleanore protested, Darryl argued, "I lived on my boat, *The Star Chaser*, for years. I'm happy to do it again. Don't worry about my comfort. My comfort comes from looking up at the star-filled sky at night. I'll have the cats and, hopefully soon, some new neighbors to keep me company. I also still have my saxophone."

Darryl went to stay onboard *The Lucky Two* when March rolled around, and the weather warmed. The efficiency room he used to rent at the motel every winter no longer existed. Fortunately, the marina managers were forced to allow *The Lucky Two* to remain in the boat slip until the probate and legal matters of Earl Keith were resolved.

Life returned to a new normal the first spring after the hurricane.

Eleanore found it hard to ignore Darryl. She liked how he made her laugh when she was around him, and she enjoyed his carefree attitude. Darryl relentlessly pursued Eleanore to be with him whenever they both had free time. When the warmth of long summer days arrived, they shared their first kiss on the beach after watching a spectacular, flaming orange sun melt into the Gulf of Mexico. Then the relationship took the romantic turn Darryl wanted from the first time he set eyes on her.

Summer brought back beach tourists and more money to the restaurant employees. However, Eleanore knew that when summer ended, the money would not flow so freely.

"How am I going to have enough money to support myself and a child," she moaned. "I don't even know where to start."

Eleanore kicked at the sand and sucked in a deep breath, trying to enjoy the warm sea breeze blowing through her hair. She sighed in resignation. "I've already made the decision to have this baby. It's just when, and how, to break the news to Darryl and everyone else."

When Casey introduced Eleanore to Big Joe, she felt immediately comfortable and confident that she was in good hands. Big Joe showed his true character by offering to help her out before he even knew anything about her.

She had enough experience working as a waitress at the Kountry Kafe in Pine Mountain, Georgia, to handle the work at Smith's. She quickly learned that the kitchen staff and waitresses at Smith's were just like the people at the Kountry Kafe. She was coached and encouraged by mostly all of the employees. Eleanore was liked for her sincerity, honesty, and willingness to work hard. There were many tricks to serving multiple tables and learning a menu that covered various food choices.

"She's a breath of fresh air walking through the dining room," the owner often remarked to Big Joe when he watched her interact with customers. "She didn't leave her southern charm back in Georgia."

"Nor her good looks," Big Joe thought to himself, nodding his head in agreement with the owner.

Spring break started in late February and brought the first wave of tourists to Panama City Beach. That's when Big Joe hired a young, black woman named Geneva. For the first few weeks, Geneva kept to herself. The staff always tried to work together as a family. They welcomed the newcomer from up north, teaching her the kitchen layout and operations, just like they had done for Eleanore.

As spring season rolled into the thick of the summer season, Eleanore became aware that some of the kitchen staff resented Geneva. Mainly for acting as the kitchen watchdog, finding something, or someone, to criticize and correct, but Eleanore respected Geneva.

The first summer season after the hurricane introduced Eleanore to the fast-paced action of working in a busy restaurant in a tourist town.

Eleanore enjoyed the excitement of working at Smith's. The atmosphere was constantly changing with the different customers. It wasn't anything like serving the usual customers, people everyone in town knew, at the Kountry Kafe. She was meeting many new people from states all over the country. It was another side of the world compared to serving the regular customers at the Kountry Kafe who mostly asked for the blue-plate specials. There were famous people: politicians, businessmen, and athletes who came into the restaurant each year. Eleanore wasn't familiar with the well-heeled personalities. Still, she felt her heart flutter whenever an employee told another employee that someone important, with a well-known name, was dining in the restaurant.

The best part of working at Smith's was the amount of money she could make in one night.

On the flip side, all the employees worked quickly, frequently turning into exasperated, impatient human beings if any small thing went wrong. Over time, the easy-going, friendly-faced people she was introduced to on the first day turned into more hardened, serious people intent on making money.

"Maybe Geneva is someone I can talk to. She seems to have a good heart, even if she sometimes shows a bad temperament in the kitchen. She seems sensible about knowing the difference between right and wrong. Maybe I should ask her for advice. Ah, but she may not want to be bothered with my problems. I only know that I need to talk to someone else about my situation. I have to decide soon about whether I will stay in Panama City Beach or return to Pine Mountain."

Eleanore kicked at the sand and turned around to start the walk back to her car she left parked at the Treasure Island Marina on Thomas Drive, two blocks away.

"I know that I want to stay and continue working at Smith's. I know I can finish working through the rest of the fall. After that, I'm not sure what to do. I know that I can't live on *The Lucky Two* with Darryl, and I know I can't stay living at Casey's house," she sighed, near despair.

Her solitary stroll on the sand dunes, reflecting on her relationship with Darryl, didn't turn up answers.

CHAPTER 4
THE NEW NEIGHBORHOOD

Using his hind legs to propel his forward momentum, DC's rear leg claws scraped against the concrete each time he pushed off to gallop down the ledge of the seawall. He extended his front paw pads, exposing his translucent claws grasping at anything to gain traction. He continuously slipped and tottered from one side to the other of the concrete wall. Each time a front claw grabbed the concrete, a sheath of nail fell off, and each time a rear claw pushed off the concrete, a scraping noise echoed over the water.

DC reached the end of the wall, jumped onto the sidewalk, and clumsily skidded to a stop in front of the boat slip where *The Lucky Two* was tied to four, newly replaced, pilings. Relieved that he was back by the boat that he associated with comfort, DC flopped down on his side. Panting for breath, his tiny, pink, grainy tongue hung out of the front of his mouth, dripping saliva.

Although the head chef at Smith's, Big Joe, had talked to DC in a soothing tone of voice, DC didn't waste time socializing with him. Of all the times DC observed Big Joe sitting on the bench, DC never once saw Big Joe coax a cat over to him with a morsel of food.

On the other hand, the boat captain on *The Lucky Two*, Darryl Kay, fed DC and many kittens and cats scraps of fish every night, talking to them with comforting words. Darryl always ended his fellowship with the cats with a few words of hope.

"Have a peaceful night, my furry friends," Darryl would whisper loudly before going inside the cabin. Then turning his back to the smoky grey skies that would soon turn into light shades of purple and deep-dark blue before finally turning black, he'd step inside the cabin.

DC wanted, needed, some soothing words immediately. It was too early in the evening for him to be stressing about the mistake he'd made. He knew he had been too eager to bite into the bag. He should have sniffed, and investigated more, to find out the contents inside the bag. The unknown object he'd bitten into still left a discomforting, burning taste in his mouth.

When he'd seen the bag lying on the ground next to a car in the parking lot, he was curious, as all kittens are. The outside of the brown bag had a slight aroma of cooked food. He pawed at the bag and felt a round, soft-shaped object that was no bigger than his paw. As soon as he bit into the bag to rip it open, the soft object burst open, and a fluid leaked into his mouth, burning his tongue. He spent what seemed like an eternity trying to discharge the fluid and acidic taste of poison on his tongue.

Frothing and contorting his body and trying to gurgle up saliva from the back of his throat to wash out the taste, he made a mad dash across the parking lot, not stopping to look for cars or catch his breath. He couldn't calm down until he had all of the taste out of his mouth.

"That's a crazy kitten," Fat Cat mumbled, watching DC haphazardly leaping in the parking lot before rushing to the seawall. "I'm not surprised considering who the father is. I can't understand what Fluff, who we now have to call Princess, sees in him."

Fat Cat, the defunct and displaced leader of the gang of cats at Captain Anderson's Marina, crouched on his haunches in the new home he referred to as the cat condominium. It was a stack of discarded wood pallets at the marina's edge, where new boat slips were being constructed. Fat Cat stretched his neck out further to see around the corner edge of a pallet to get a better view of DC when he stretched out on the sidewalk in front of *The Lucky Two*.

The cat condominium where Fat Cat lived replaced his private residence where he lived before the hurricane. Fat Cat now had to occasionally share his residence with other cats that dropped by whenever they felt like it.

The marina storage facilities at the Lighthouse and Treasure Island Marinas', two other restaurants, and the gift shop at Captain Anderson's Marina had been heavily damaged by the hurricane. The deck where Fat Cat kept his home before the storm was gone entirely. The piles of debris had been moved to the parking lot perimeter at the Lighthouse Marina, waiting to be picked up and floated away on barges. What didn't float away, or sink to the bottom of the lagoon, was stacked into tall piles of twisted metal and building materials.

"What's gotten into him, I wonder?" Fat Cat said, watching the nearly-full grown kitten with interest. "He's behaving like he's in distress. He's not just acting crazy, like he usually does, bouncing around between cars. He looks like he might actually be sick. Maybe he's swallowed something bad. I wouldn't be surprised, as dumb as he is. He's not like Snaggle Tooth when he was a kitten and had his accident in the garbage dumpster. At least Snaggle Tooth had the good sense to run somewhere to lick his wounds and heal."

Snaggle Tooth, better known as ST, a loyal follower of Fat Cat, stayed close to Fat Cat at the condominium compound after the hurricane. Recently ST began to frequently expand his food hunting territory and wander away from the marina.

It had been difficult to account for everyone in the gang after the hurricane. Many cats dispersed to new locations. Not all cats could find food at the marina after so many deep-sea charter fishing boats were destroyed. The captains who moved their ships away from the slips were slowly returning. Some were still waiting for repairs. While other captains were waiting for the new pilings and docks to be rebuilt.

Although Fat Cat had a dislike for the clan of offspring produced by Princess and King, he still wanted to know the comings and goings of all the cats at the marina. Fat Cat never stopped thinking of himself as the leader, and decision maker, for the cat gang.

"I suppose I should alert King or Princess. Of course, they'd want to know if DC was in trouble," Fat Cat grumbled. "If I want to be the leader, I must remember that I have certain responsibilities for everyone here, including the cats I don't like."

Fat Cat jumped down from the plywood pallet. He made his observations and trotted a short distance across the parking lot, away from the sidewalk where DC lay. Fat Cat proceeded to trot down the sidewalk behind the wall of the fish cleaning house until he reached the corner between the seafood market and public toilets for people.

It was described as a minor miracle by the marina owners when they discovered that the back wall of the fish cleaning house survived the hurricane winds. The wall of the public toilet rooms used by humans and the interior rooms of the fish market was standing, but the roof of the multi-room complex was gone.

The interior room was quickly put back into use to clean fish coming in off the few charter boats, including *The Lucky Two*, that could operate out of the marina. A roof wasn't necessary for the workers to keep busy in the room, which still had running water, tables, and large basins for cleaning fish.

Few tourists strolled around the marina since the hurricane destroyed so much of its scenic appeal. People went to Smith's to eat, but that was the extent of their visit to the property.

King's former home, which he used to refer to as his castle, the storage shed filled with fishing gear and charter boat equipment was destroyed. He found a hole inside the wall between the public toilets and the fish cleaning house and decided it would make a good hiding place away from most humans. It was smellier than his previous home inside the shed, but he believed it would be safe for him, and Princess. There was just enough room in the cubby hole for them to jump between the building's walls and cuddle with their backs against each other.

"Marouw!" Fat cat opened his mouth wide, bellowing loudly when he reached the public toilet building.

"I think I hear Fat Cat," Princess whispered to King.

"You're right. That's exactly how you sounded sitting outside the cabin door of *The Lucky Two* when you wanted to get inside," King joked.

"You're exaggerating a bit," she mewed, slightly embarrassed, remembering the night like it happened yesterday. She never forgot how badly she wanted to get inside the cabin and out of the howling winds of the hurricane.

King laughed and changed the subject, not wanting to hurt Princess's feelings. "Fat Cat thinks if he can meow loud, it will make others respect him more. He likes to be the boss."

"Oh, don't I know it," Princess agreed, remembering the night before the hurricane when Fat Cat pressured her to leave the docks and go with him to find a safe place. She preferred jumping over the water onto *The Lucky Two* to find King over being with Fat Cat any day or night.

"I'll go out and find out why he's hanging around the fish cleaning house at this time of day. He usually doesn't come out until it's a bit darker," King said.

"I want to go with you," she said, and proceeded to follow King.

They crossed the bathroom floor beneath broken sinks and crouched down low when they reached the entrance without a door. After checking to see if it was safe, they scooted out the doorway where they faced Fat Cat sitting on the sidewalk, waiting for them.

"Well, hello, you two," Fat Cat said in a false tone of friendliness when they appeared. "I assume you're getting along well in the comfort of your new home?"

"Yes, we are. And you are doing well too?" King cordially responded.

"Of course," Fat Cat answered with a look of distaste in his eyes. "The way I'm looking at it, things could be better, but at least we've got somewhere to stay. I just thought I'd come down to let you know your youngest kitten, the runt of the litter, is lying on the sidewalk in front of *The Lucky Two*. He appears to be in a great deal of distress. He's been frothing at the mouth. Maybe you should go check on him."

"Seriously?" Princess immediately asked. Her eyes narrowed at Fat Cat. She wasn't sure if she wanted to trust Fat Cat's excuse for his unusual visit to them.

"I didn't come down here to socialize," Fat Cat answered. "I prefer to keep a close eye on what's happening at the marina from the top of my cat condo. If I see something that needs attention, I'm not the type to allow a fellow feline, in trouble, suffer."

"That's exactly what I was thinking, Fat Cat," King said anxiously. "Thanks for going out of your way to tell us. We appreciate it."

He and Princess bolted around Fat Cat and raced to the end of the sidewalk.

When Princess and King found DC, he had fully recovered from the toxic episode.

"Fat Cat came to tell us that you were in some kind of trouble. Are you hurt?" Princess anxiously asked DC.

"What kind of trouble did you get yourself into this time? Why aren't you staying with the group, with the other kittens, like we've told you to do?" King asked him in a concerned but stern tone.

DC turned his head, looked away from his parents, blinking his eyes several times before returning the stare of his parents. His eyelids drooped. The dash away from the parking lot took the air out of his lungs. His body was heaving up and down.

After catching his breath from the ordeal of racing around, DC finally answered his mother's question first. "I'm not hurt, but I feel awful." Turning his eyes to his father, he said, "The other cats don't want me hanging around with them."

King and Princess faced each other with quizzical eyes. It was a frustrating moment for both of them. How should they respond to their errant kitten, who was obviously distressed?

DC complained. "They call me names and make me feel like I don't belong with them."

"They're just making fun of you to see if they can get a reaction. They don't mean you any harm," Princess consoled. "It's not nice of them to hurt your feelings, but as long as you let them get away with it, they'll continue to do it. You don't have to listen to them, but you do have to learn how to stand up for yourself."

King added his thoughts. "They're not all bad kittens, your brothers and sisters. They will back you up if something bad happens. Don't your siblings say anything in your defense when someone else calls you names?" King asked.

When asked this question, DC pouted, and if kittens could cry, the tears would be rolling down through his whiskers, across his mustache, and to the bottom of his furry chin.

DC stood up and said to his parents, "Just leave me alone. I'm going to be fine."

DC turned away from his parents and leapt toward Smith's, back-tracking across the parking lot, running and kicking up sand in the bushes, when he reached the windows of Smith's restaurant.

DC was born into Princess and King's second litter of four kittens. DC, last to be born and the smallest, was the runt of the litter. At night he slept with his parents in the public restroom.

The other three kittens had grown large enough to get out on their own. They canvassed the docks, explored the piles of rubble, and rarely got into trouble. The new kittens were sheltered in the fish cleaning area near the public restroom, but still close to their parents.

The first litter of kittens born to Princess and King ended up preferring the new neighborhood, a cluster of homes in a subdivision across the road leading to Captain Anderson's Marina parking lot. Soon after the hurricane, word spread quickly amongst the marina gang of cats that the humans in the new neighborhood were feeding the stray cats.

Purr Baby, a young female cat from the new neighborhood, watched the scene between DC and his parents unfold. She was eager to hear DC's story.

Recently she had begun to secretly venture to the marina. She had heard rumors from the marina cats and clan of tuxedo cats infiltrating her neighborhood territory that the cats at the marina lived a different lifestyle. The culture at the marina was different. She had grown up with an overly protective father named Fernando. He repeatedly told her to stay away from the marina.

She, like DC, was teased by the cats in her neighborhood for the sole reason of purring too much. Everything that crossed her path delighted her senses, causing her to purr. She couldn't understand why other cats would have a problem with her loud purr box.

"That cat has so much swag," Purr Baby purred when she saw DC heading in her direction toward the bushes at Smith's restaurant. "When he gets a little bigger, he's going to be mine."

DC was happy to see Purr Baby. He flopped down on the soft, sandy ground. She was one of the few cats who treated him with respect. She was closer to being an adult, and liked to lick him like his mother, Princess, did when he was a tiny kitten.

"I saw you go after that paper bag and everything that happened afterward," Purr Baby gushed when DC parked his body beneath the bushes, close to her. "That scared me when I saw your mouth oozing bubbles. You were jumping and hopping around, like one of those crazy brown lizards we see in the bushes."

"I've got to be more careful about checking things out when I'm hungry. When I sniffed the bag, I could smell cooked meat. I thought the bag might have leftover food inside. The paper bag looked just like the kind humans throw into the garbage cans when they're done eating. Usually, I find food in the bag. I felt something soft when I touched it with my paw, and I thought I could just tear open the bag with my teeth. When I bit down on the soft piece, some awful, burning hot liquid burst into my mouth. I thought my tongue would never stop burning."

Purr Baby frowned. "It's not your fault that you get hungry, and it's not bad to be curious." Purr Baby wrapped her paw around DC's neck and started to lick his face. "You never know what's going to happen next, but we can never lose our sense of curiosity, because that's how we feed ourselves. We'd be in a heap of trouble if we only sit back in the bushes and watched the action of the world go by in front of our faces. We'll make mistakes, but we can't be quitters."

"Whatever, Purr Baby," DC said, resigning himself to put the traumatic event in his bucket of lessons learned.

Purr Baby held one paw over DC's back and continued licking his cheeks, nose, mouth, and ears while DC tried to explain to her how he felt about his situation.

"It's a hard world we live in, though, with some tough characters. That sneaky Fat Cat is one character I do not trust. He ratted on me, telling my parents I was in trouble. If Fat Cat acted differently, I might learn to trust him, but I always feel suspicious when I am around him. I get the feeling that he doesn't like me. I don't know why. It can only be for the simple reason, I know for a fact, that he doesn't like my dad."

Purr Baby agreed. "Yes, DC, I've also heard that Fat Cat is hard to like. I don't think it's just your dad that Fat Cat doesn't like. The rumor in my neighborhood is that there's another cat named Oscar that Fat Cat is jealous about. Something Oscar did during the hurricane that made Oscar the talk of the marina and in my neighborhood. I'm wondering if Fat Cat doesn't like to take the second seat to anyone."

"I've only seen Oscar a few times around here," DC said.

"I'm pretty sure that Oscar has permanently moved over to my neighborhood, where the humans live," she responded. "The neighborhood is just across the street. It used to be separated from the marina by trees. There were so many trees that you couldn't see the marina buildings behind them. The humans call all the trees *the woods*. Mostly all of the trees are gone as a result of the big hurricane. Now it's easy to get back and forth from the marina to the neighborhood. You can make a fast run to get over there, then get back here if you need to."

"When I get the courage, I'm going there to check it out," DC said.

"That's the spirit," Purr Baby said, purring louder, then adding, "I'll be happy to escort you! Let's plan to do it together one day."

CHAPTER 5
A NIGHT OF PROBLEMS

"Look at this trash lying in the parking lot," Big Joe complained to no one in particular, only himself. He recognized a ripped-up bag from one of the fast-food restaurants. Several packets of hot sauce were lying next to the bag. "I wish people would have a little more respect for other people's property. After all the work it took to clean up this area after hurricane Louise, we still get these special people who throw trash out of their cars. They're too darn lazy to take a few steps to throw their trash in the dumpster or find a nearby trash can."

Big Joe was leaving Smith's after another long night in a hot kitchen. He usually went directly to his car in the parking lot. Tonight, he decided to take a short walk to the docks to enjoy the peaceful sound of the lagoon water lapping against the sides of the charter boats. He'd thought about ending the night by taking a few extra moments to sit on his bench, but it was too close to the kitchen. It would remind him of his problems. He needed a quiet place to clear his thoughts. Usually he could think clearly, even when he was cooking in the noisy, sometimes chaotic, atmosphere in the kitchen he just left. Tonight, he couldn't clear the noise in his brain concerning the complicated personnel problems in the kitchen. The fires on the grills didn't bother him as much as the hot tempers of his employees.

How was he going to resolve the estrangements involving the staff at Smith's? The back of the house kitchen crew and the front of the house wait staff exchanged nasty remarks with each other again tonight. The arguments were happening more frequently and interfering with job performances. The differences needed to be aired out and cleaned up before the weekend started. The restaurant would fail customers if anyone decided to quit. He considered each employee a competent, hard worker who he couldn't afford to lose. Workers were hard to replace these days. Since the hurricane a year ago, it was an open market for people looking for jobs. If an employee became unhappy with their workplace, they could easily find a job somewhere else the next day. Help wanted signs were on every street corner.

"Heck, I even thought of finding another place to work," Big Joe thought. "I worked it out with the boss. He didn't want me to leave. So, he got me the bench, and I hired Geneva. I don't want any of the staff to leave."

The problems at the restaurant sometimes arose with Geneva, who thought she knew what everyone else should be doing. Big Joe found that he could talk to her, and she would eventually calm down when he pointed out that she had to take criticism if she was going to give it out.

On the other hand, working through problems with Sue, the salad girl, was more difficult. Sue broke down in tears tonight when Big Joe asked her to speed up her salad prep so she could help with expediting food plates in the kitchen. Sue was a perfectionist at producing beautiful salads, and that's all she wanted to do.

Sue also liked to talk all the time when anyone would listen. When Geneva was hired, Sue tried to find out more about Geneva, asking her questions about her background and family. Geneva told Sue a little of her family's background in Altoona, but kept it brief. That was all Sue needed to get started talking about her large family. She had an extended family, all of them living in the Florida panhandle.

Geneva was a good listener. She considered Sue to be an ally in the kitchen. She let Sue talk as much as she wanted. "Uh-huh," was all Geneva mostly said to Sue's one-sided conversation. Geneva kept her attention on her work at her prep table.

Big Joe tossed around the idea that perhaps Geneva and Sue were his significant problems. They occasionally had different opinions, but they were not disagreeable people. He concluded, very quickly, that they were not the source of the conflicts.

The biggest problem tonight was when Big Joe caught the line cook raising his voice at Dorinda. Instinctively Big Joe reprimanded the line cook on the spot.

"Get a better attitude," Big Joe walked over and told the line cook, who reacted by looking at Big Joe with resentment written all over his face.

"Why did the line cook lose his temper with Dorinda?" Big Joe wondered. "He's one guy who always keeps his cool even when he's working over the flames in the grill."

The last person he dreamed could ever be a problem was Dorinda, who had been a waitress at Smith's for more than a decade. Big Joe thought hard.

Geneva reported to Big Joe recently, during one of his *sit-downs and let's talk* meetings in the office, something concerning Dorinda. She overheard Dorinda from the window in her prep room, asking the line cooks to put her food orders ahead of Eleanore's.

Big Joe remembered Geneva's words. *"I'll try harder to ignore the small stuff, but I can tell it annoys the line cook when Dorinda tells him. It's written all over his face when she asks him to do that. Dorinda may have a good reason to do this. I don't know much about the waitress work out in the dining room. I just thought you should know."*

Big Joe found himself regretting that he never followed up on Geneva's report to find out if it was true. "I feel as though ignoring the problem seems to have created a bigger problem," he thought, shaking his head in disappointment with himself. "The trickle-down effect has started. Now the line cook is mad at me. The next thing I know, Sue will be upset if she finds out the line cook is unhappy, or anyone else in the kitchen for that matter. Sue keeps her allegiance to the staff who work in the kitchen."

Sue was super sensitive about the work that the kitchen crew did to create a good meal. If any part of the meal was unacceptable, the customers might forget about the beautiful salad she made.

Eve at Peace by Yvette Doolittle Herr

The last thing Big Joe needed was for Sue to start complaining about how the kitchen staff was not working together or how they were being treated by him. Not only would she cry, but if Big Joe didn't do anything to remedy the problem, it was possible that Sue would take a walk out the back door of the kitchen. Sue was devoted to making a good product, and that was what he wanted more than extra work from her. Big Joe needed Sue's salads.

"Sue doesn't have a reason to interact with waitresses, so I can't ask her to verify what Geneva told me," Big Joe thought. "She makes the salads in an assembly line on a table away from the prep room window, then carries trays filled with salad bowls to the window for the waitresses to pick up. As much as Sue likes to talk, she and the waitresses are too busy talking or listening to each other. Geneva is the one who is on stand-by if the line cooks need more vegetables for their sauté'. Geneva is more of an observer of what's happening until she is told to get something."

To Big Joe, the problem seemed like a connect the numbers dot puzzle in a child's coloring book, but a number was missing.

Big Joe began to reminiscence back to the day when he hired Eleanore to work at Smith's. "I remember after introducing Eleanore to the staff, Dorinda was the only server who seemed disinterested. She didn't welcome Eleanore with a hello or a handshake. Dorinda only lifted her hand in a short wave while everyone else welcomed her to the team. Some even hugged her and expressed condolences on her terrifying experience in the aftermath of hurricane Louise. Was that a sign that Dorinda disliked Eleanore?" Big Joe thought to himself. "Why would she hold a grudge against Eleanore?"

Big Joe considered Eleanore a prize employee on his crew, a new star. Not only did she possess a sweet personality, but she held no grudge against anyone. Plus, she was the most grateful employee in the restaurant just because she had a job. It would be just like Eleanore to not say anything about a problem with Dorinda.

Eleanore had become Big Joe's favorite waitress in the restaurant. She was shy but determined. When he heard the story of how she bounced back after the shocking news of the murder of her boyfriend, Earl Keith, Big Joe knew she was one tough woman. He never would have believed that a woman so young, pretty, and petite would be as tough as nails. And, making the difficult decision to allow Darryl to live on *The Lucky Two* was taking a leap of faith. She hardly knew Darryl. Big Joe had heard rumors floating around the kitchen that she and Darryl were having a romantic relationship or were forming a future business relationship.

"There was never a doubt in my mind that she couldn't handle the job as a waitress. After that wild experience with Casey on *The Lucky Two* and finding out she was a waitress in the small-town restaurant, I knew she could handle our customers. So many of our customers are tourists. They come from all over the southeast, and some are hard to please with their different tastes in food. Eleanore stepped into our restaurant like it was an old shoe she's worn for years.

"Dorinda, Dorinda, why are you setting me up for a showdown in the kitchen?" Big Joe hung his head down, held his hands together beneath his chin, and gently rocked his body forward and backward. "Right now, I'd like to see a cat, a kitten, or some innocent living creature that will lighten the worry in my mind. I can't stand people problems."

At the moment Big Joe wished for a living creature, besides a human, to distract his mind, his wish was granted. A two-inch-long, brown water bug scampered down the seawall, across the sidewalk, and stopped in front of him. It wasn't the innocent furry kitten that he hoped to see, but it was alive. Big Joe considered squashing it with his big, black kitchen shoes but gave the bug no second thought.

It was a common annoyance to find the water bugs in the kitchen garbage cans, but he didn't feel right killing it in its own habitat. If he'd found it in the kitchen, he wouldn't hesitate to kill it or ask someone else in the kitchen, like the dishwasher, to knock it off.

"I'm getting too soft in my old age," he grumbled. "However, I can't let Dorinda get away with what she's doing. I don't like her undercutting Eleanore or anyone else for that matter. Who will Dorinda want to target next for her own personal gain?"

Thinking about the daunting task of confronting Dorinda, of all people working in the restaurant, created a big dilemma.

"Dorinda's been a dependable employee for years. I don't even recall her ever causing trouble, and I haven't noticed a change in her. I do think she's always liked to put herself in the center of attention, with her good looks and an out-going personality. What would Dorinda's reason be to target Eleanore with a cut-throat attitude? I don't know how to approach this problem. My problem is her relation to the owners as a cousin. Who can I talk to?"

Big Joe took a deep breath and heaved a huge sigh. "How did I ever get myself stuck working in the restaurant business?" he rhetorically asked himself. "I like to cook. I like to eat. I like to please customers, but I don't know why I didn't stick with carpentry. It wouldn't be so bad if my only role was to just be a chef, grilling steaks and fish or simmering sauces, but I don't like dealing with a boiling pot of people's personalities."

Big Joe held his head up, sucked in a deep breath of salty air, and took in the view. He was making one last effort to cast his cares away for the night.

"Here they are, all lined up, what's left of the fleet that supplies our fish and puts food on my table too. I have to admire everything these boat captains do and have done to survive since the hurricane. They get up before sunrise for that early start and have to sleep in those small quarters. I don't know how they can sleep in such tight quarters," Big

Joe mused. "I shouldn't complain about how bad I think I've got it. My legs ache all the time, but that is because of my weight, and that's my own fault. I need to lose some of this weight. It's just so hard to be working in a kitchen and always be tasting the food. Those boat captains stay lean. They hardly have time to eat a full meal during the summer season."

Along with the few remaining charter boats at the marina, *The Lucky Two* was tied to pilings in a dock slip. It bobbed gently on the dark water in the lagoon. The fluorescent lights in the parking lot lit the surface of the glittering water. They illuminated the shiny, white fiberglass of the boats. The wood door to the cabin was closed, and no light shone through the cabin window.

"The last time I saw Darryl, he'd turned into one skinny guy, that's for sure. I'm not so sure he's feeling so well these days. Maybe he's just worried about the connection of this boat to Eleanore. He probably doesn't want to lose the opportunity to fish on this boat after losing his boat, *The Star Chaser.* He surely must appreciate everything Eleanore has done for him.

"The fact that Eleanore can persevere after carrying that load in her heart, the murder of her ex-boyfriend, and taking responsibility of the boat until the probate of the asset is finished up in Georgia makes her an amazing woman. It makes me want even more to rectify this situation with Dorinda. I'm going to sleep on it tonight. When I wake up in the morning if I haven't come up with an answer in my dreams, I'll meditate. There's got to be a reason why Dorinda has a thing against Eleanore. Right now, I need to get off my feet and head on home."

Big Joe turned his gaze away from *The Lucky Two* and headed back to his car. He was tempted to take a few more minutes to ponder the problem, sitting on his bench seat outside the back kitchen door of Smith's, but quickly dismissed that thought. He knew if he sat down, he'd have a hard time lifting his tired body back up.

"Wait a minute," Big Joe inwardly smiled and stopped dead in his tracks, pausing the echo of his heavy footsteps across the lagoon water. "Why didn't I think of this before?"

As if a light switch had been turned on in his brain, Big Joe suddenly recalled an afternoon earlier in the summer. Walking through the dining room, he remembered overhearing Dorinda talking with other waitresses during their break. She was reminiscing about the old days, long before the hurricane destroyed the beach clubs and when waitresses went out to dance after work.

"I used to love to go out and dance in the nightclubs on the beach after work," Big Joe overheard Dorinda tell the girls. *"This guy, Darryl Kay, played saxophone in a band called The Electrons. I was disappointed when the band broke up years ago."*

Big Joe remembered thinking at the time, "I don't know how those waitresses could work a six-hour shift on their feet in the restaurant and then go out dancing afterward. Maybe they liked the drinking, but I think they liked the music and dancing. They were younger back then, too."

Big Joe remembered dismissing the conversation he heard, his mind focused on his work.

Big Joe's brain was racing fast to connect dots.

"Dorinda actually mentioned Darryl's name!" Big Joe chuckled. "Ole' Darryl used to get yelled at by the other charter boat captains when he played his saxophone late at night on his charter boat. He loved his boat, *The Star Chaser.* I think I may have found an explanation for Dorinda holding a grudge against Eleanore."

Big Joe placed his forefinger beneath his nose and rubbed the beard stubble beneath his chin with his thumb. He laughed so hard that his big belly jiggled.

"I know where I can dig a little deeper to get the answer to this problem. Since Sista brought it up, the answer is going to come from Sista! I never see her talk too much to the waitresses. Sometimes she and Sue talk, but I'm pretty sure that Sista does more listening. I'm going to mention to Sista that we're all curious in the kitchen about Eleanore and Darryl. Are they a couple, or are they not? If Sista doesn't directly ask anyone questions, she'll mention it to Sue, who I'm pretty sure will do some talking." Big Joe was still chuckling as he was formulating his plan.

"I'll remind Sista that Eleanore's former boyfriend owned and operated that charter boat, *The Lucky Two*. I'll tell Sista that I used to buy fish from the boyfriend, and he gave me the best prices at the marina. That will make Sista raise her eyebrows. Usually, Sista's face is so blank. She really knows how to show very little emotion. But I bet she'll show some interest in understanding this bit of background news.

"I have no doubt that she'll be somewhat interested in knowing about Darryl and Eleanore. Not many women can resist a little bit of gossip involving romance. Employee's gossiping is a trademark in restaurant kitchens.

"I'll ask Sista to casually say something to Sue about it. Sue is more the type of person to be direct. Sue will come right out and ask Eleanore, without any introductory small talk, if she and Darryl are in a romantic relationship. If anyone would have the nerve to ask, Sue will be the one to ask Eleanore!"

Big Joe closed his eyes for a moment and gently shook his head as if to clear his mind. He decided the run-around plan he devised was totally illogical. "I just need to straight out ask Sue to find out. She's not one to hold back. Sista's not really the type to do the run-around. Neither Sista nor Sue have much interaction with the waitresses, but Sue makes their salads. Yeah, Sue will be the one to find out when she goes on break with them in the dining room."

Big Joe could have skipped all the way back to his car if he wasn't so tired. He couldn't wait until tomorrow. It was the first time he was more excited about going back to work the next day than going home after a long shift. Not only was he going to straighten out the problem with Dorinda, but there might be a little fun in it for everyone working in the restaurant. Through his many years of restaurant experience, Big Joe learned people loved to gossip about people who got into trouble after doing someone wrong.

CHAPTER 6
DESTINED FOR DOOM

Darryl felt confused and restless, which wasn't a normal state of mind for him. He usually found his peace fishing on the Gulf of Mexico or sitting on the charter boat deck at night, looking at the heavens. Instead, he felt unsettled and uncomfortable spending so much time alone.

It had been a couple of days since he last talked to Eleanore, which had happened from time to time in the peak of the summer season. On the days when he took *The Lucky Two* out fishing, he would miss her before her shift started. She often worked late into the night, and afterward, she went directly home.

The last time they talked, she had stopped by the marina to tell him that she was going for a walk on the beach. She hadn't come back to visit him since that day. The tourist activity was slowing down, which was expected after the summer season ended. He knew Eleanore still had to be working nights at Smith's, but she used to come by to visit him before her shift and also to feed the cats. She had done neither.

He watched the cats loitering on the docks, hoping and waiting for her to bring food, late one evening long after Smith's closed. He stood on the stern of *The Lucky Two* and threw fish scraps from his storage tank and left-over bait over the side of the boat onto the sidewalk.

"The cats are cool, but not enough to call real company. I can talk to cats, but you guys don't talk to me," he mumbled to himself after throwing the scraps and watching them hungrily lick them up. "Hey there, Princess and black cat," he called out to them after taking a seat outside on the deck. "Your momma hasn't been by here lately. I miss her."

After he decided to live on the boat, and with Eleanore's permission, Darryl began taking *The Lucky Two* out to fish. Since he didn't own the boat, he could not legally, officially, take charter customers. He had to fish by himself or invite someone to go with him as a guest. Darryl rarely found someone to tag along with him. Local people were too busy working to take a day off to go fishing with him, even if it was for a free ride.

The Lucky Two was an easy boat to handle for one person. "If Casey could do it during hurricane conditions, so can I," Darryl decided. Unfortunately, the equipment on the boat wasn't the most modern, so he took his chances and hoped for the best. For the time being, selling fish to Big Joe at Smith's gave him some spending money.

The first time he took it out alone, he thought it was as easy as taking a nap. After cutting off the engine, he cast out a couple of lines off the stern and watched the clear filament blow with the gentle breeze like the tail of a kite. He let the boat drift on the aqua blue waters that he loved so much. Nothing relaxed him more than being on the water, waiting for a fishing pole to bend or a bobber to sink. Without the company of any other fisherman to talk to, he allowed his mind to be hypnotized by the beauty, and quiet peacefulness of life while drifting on the Gulf of Mexico.

After returning to the marina from a day out on the gulf, there was nothing else to do but wait for the next chance to see Eleanore. There wasn't enough to do on a boat that he didn't yet own to keep his mind settled. Even his saxophone, usually another instrument of comfort to his soul, was not enough to calm his uneasiness. He wondered about Eleanore all of the time.

He also wondered about the man, Earl Keith, who used to own the boat, and the relationship he had with Eleanore.

After waiting a few more days and having not seen Eleanore, Darryl found himself wandering aimlessly one night in the parking lot, near the kitchen back door of Smith's. His heartbeat rapidly while he waited, hoping to see Eleanore come out the door at the end of her shift.

The benches for Smith's customers that had been there before the hurricane were gone. Most of the wood from the benches was in the same pile of rubble as the wood from broken docks. He eye-balled the junk and noticed the neck of a discarded banjo sticking out of the pile.

"I remember seeing that banjo floating in the water when I got back here the day after the hurricane," he thought, surprised to see it again. "I wonder who played it? A banjo and a saxophone would make an interesting sound together. I wonder how those guys from the hurricane shelter are doing? Mr. Pete on his guitar and that young kid playing with his drumsticks. Can't remember his name. He named us the PADs. Alan. Yeah, Alan was his name. That was some night to remember, sitting in the Mosley high school gymnasium. I still have that little song I wrote on the cash register receipt. It's tucked away in my wallet."

The creaking sound of Smith's screened back door of the kitchen opening jolted his memory to the present time.

A dark-haired woman, slight in built and wearing the navy blue, sailor-themed uniform, stepped out the doorway. She let the door slam behind her and, flinging her purse over her shoulder, started to walk toward the parking lot. Before she could get very far, she heard the voice of a man. He did not shout, but the sound of his voice surprised her and caused her to jump backward.

"Hey, you!" Darryl called out.

Dorinda stopped and turned her head toward the man's voice. She saw the shadowy figure of a man with both hands in his pockets standing on the sidewalk, near the boat slips. He took a few steps forward and stood under the cone of orange light cast by the sodium light in the parking lot. She was immediately concerned about why a man was loitering in the parking lot so late.

Darryl removed his hands from his pants pockets and held one arm up to wave at Dorinda, and began to approach her at a fast pace.

"I wonder if I could talk to you for a few minutes? I have a friend who works at Smith's," Darryl spoke loudly. "I'm trying to check on her. Her name is Eleanore. Do you know her?"

Dorinda frowned, squinting her eyes to focus on the man walking toward her in the dark. Then she recognized Darryl.

"Can you do me a favor and let her know that I'm waiting to see her?" he asked Dorinda.

"Don't I know you from somewhere?" Dorinda asked, ignoring Darryl's question.

"Can't say that I remember if we've ever met," Darryl answered, caught off-guard by her question. He immediately began quizzing his brain for clues. Finally, he focused on the woman's eyes, which appeared in the evening light to be sending evil signals.

"Don't you play the saxophone?" she asked, remembering Darryl from her days dancing in the nightclubs after work.

"Well, yes I do," he reluctantly answered, less than enthusiastic about the direction the conversation was going.

Feeling nervous now, Darryl wondered if he should have remembered the woman whom he thought attractive, except for a large nose. There had been many women who had crossed his path during his nightclubbing days years ago.

He asked, "How do you know that?"

"I'm pretty sure I remember you playing in a band. The band called *The Electrons,*" pausing momentarily before adding, "The band played in a nightclub on the beach years ago."

"Yes, thanks. That's right." Darryl suddenly got a bad feeling in his gut, like he just tripped and stumbled onto something sharp and dangerous.

He cautiously added, "I mean, that's right about the name of the band. It's amazing you remember me from way back then. That was quite a few years ago."

"Yes, it has. Your hair was a lot longer back then," she smirked. "But, you're still cute. I'll never forget all the nights I went dancing and had fun," Dorinda pursed her lips, smiled, tilted her head to one side, and gave Darryl an admiring look. "These days recently haven't been fun. Can't find a place to go out, listen to live music, dance, and have fun. What say you?"

Slightly embarrassed by her forwardness and unflattering remark about his hair, Darryl self-consciously shuffled his feet and began to rub his bald head, an old habit he was trying to stop. He did it whenever he felt uncertain of what to say next. The vibes he felt, his internal radar, sent signals that this woman was sketchy, possibly dangerous.

"Those were the days, weren't they?" Darryl mustered an answer. The memories of working in the beach nightclubs were actually not great memories for him anymore. "Yes, these days recently have been tough on all of us," he offered.

"Ever since the hurricane, we have to get used to living a new normal way of life, is what I hear from everyone I talk to," Dorinda said.

His earlier mood of restlessness momentarily took a turn for the worse.

Always the optimist, Darryl quickly changed the subject and asked Dorinda, "Is Eleanore still working right now?"

"I believe she left about an hour ago," Dorinda answered, not taking any time to think about her response.

"I need to see her. I want to talk to her about something," Darryl said, sounding a little too desperate. "Are you working tomorrow night too?"

"Yes, I am," Dorinda answered. The gears in her brain shifted into a fast speed, and she began thinking about an opportunity presenting itself in the flesh. The one person at the restaurant she despised, Eleanore, was obviously the object of this man's love.

"If Eleanore's working tomorrow, can you let her know that I'll be waiting inside the cabin on *The Lucky Two* for her after her shift? I'm living on the boat and taking it out during the day to fish. I don't do anything at night. Tell her I'll wait as late as she needs me to wait, even if it's after the restaurant closes."

Ever since Darryl went to live on *The Lucky Two*, it felt much too awkward for him to go back to Casey's house to visit Eleanore. He'd gotten used to having privacy with her when she visited him on *The Lucky Two*.

"Sure, that's not a problem," Dorinda said, then raised her arm to point toward *The Lucky Two*. "That's the boat over there, right?"

Darryl vigorously nodded his head yes, and said, "Yes, that's it. Hey, thanks a bunch, and have a good night."

Darryl and Dorinda turned and walked away in different directions, just like the agendas they were each thinking about.

Dorinda slid into her car, smiled, and said out loud before she started the engine, "Now I've got an ace in my hand. This is going to be so easy. Little miss Eleanore; little miss goody-two-shoes who everyone adores; little miss sweetness is going to get her heart broken."

The next night Dorinda arrived at work thirty minutes early. She wanted to avoid being seen by any of the other waitresses talking to Big Joe.

She found Big Joe in his office, looking at a pile of papers. She lightly tapped on the open door.

Big Joe looked up and saw the subject of his upcoming investigation into personnel problems standing in the open doorway. "Hey there, Dorinda," Big Joe said. "Something you need to talk to me about?"

His hope was that Dorinda was coming to see him to tell him something that would clear up the more frequent, nasty outbursts happening between the kitchen crew and the waitress.

"I came in early to ask you if it's possible to change the schedule tonight. I'd like to be the last waitress to be cut off the floor. I know that sometimes you shift the schedule to accommodate other waitresses," Dorinda looked at Big Joe with her big, brown, begging eyes. "I need a little extra money to pay my bills. My tips haven't been so great lately, and with my seniority, I'm hoping you'll agree." Dorinda focused on Big Joe's eyes, reading his reaction to her request. Not seeing a favorable face, she decided to add, "I've been working here a long time, longer than some of the other waitresses."

Disappointed that Dorinda's request to talk was not related to the staff problems in the kitchen, Big Joe said in a gruff, sarcastic voice, "Don't we all need a little more money these days? I'll do it tonight, Dorinda. Now I'll have to figure out who to cut early tonight."

Big Joe jerked his head back to the paperwork on his desk. Not hearing a *thank you*, he loudly added, before she got far out of the office doorway, "Maybe you should try to show these customers your sweet side if you want to make some better tips."

Dorinda huffed, took one step backward, and popped her head in the office doorway. She said sarcastically, "I bet Eleanore won't mind going home early tonight."

Big Joe turned his head back to look at Dorinda's face in the doorway. Holding back his anger, he said in a steady voice, "Truthfully, you might be right about that, Dorinda." Big Joe pushed his bushy eyebrows together and gave Dorinda a look of severe distrust. "I don't think that she's been feeling all that well lately. It's so nice of you to think about her," Big Joe said, returning his own words with heavy sarcasm.

At the end of her shift, Dorinda left the restaurant to see Darryl with only one thing on her mind. She boarded *The Lucky Two*. Turning her head slightly, putting her ear close to the door, she listened for any noise coming from inside the cabin before knocking on the door.

"I hope that I can get out of here quickly," she thought. "I'm beat up after working that long shift. I'm ready to get home."

"Well, this is a surprise," Darryl said, hoping it to be Eleanore and opening the cabin door before Dorinda had a chance to knock. "I felt the motion when you stepped onto the deck. Come in, please." He rushed her inside the cabin and quickly shut the door.

Dorinda asked Darryl if she could sit down.

"Yes, please sit down," Darryl said, pointing to a chair by the table. "Did you see Eleanore? Tell me what you know?" he eagerly asked, settling down on the chair opposite hers.

Lying, she said, "Eleanore doesn't want to see you anymore," covering her lie with her lips drawn into a thin, tight frown. "I'm sorry."

"What? Why?" Darryl stuttered the two words several times. His mouth hung open. His gaze dropped down to the floor. His face, and body language, revealed a sadness that anyone with a heart could feel.

Dorinda's face expressed concern, but the feelings in her heart burst with victory.

"She didn't give a reason," Dorinda said, struggling to conceal her happiness. She continued with her lie, speaking slowly and persuasively. "I'm thinking it might be that man she's living with now. You know, the marine patrol officer who rescued her through the hurricane. Everyone at the restaurant knows that she lives with him, you know. Isn't his name Casey Howard?"

Darryl lifted his head, closed his mouth, and locked his eyes onto Dorinda's eyes, searching for truth. This was the last answer Darryl wanted his ears to hear. It made the hair on his arms rise as if a big blast of cold air just blew into the cabin through an open window.

"I can't agree with that, Dorinda. What should I do? Do you have any suggestions?" Darryl was desperate for advice from anyone, even a stranger like Dorinda. "You women know about girl feelings better than men do," he lamented. "They're always telling their girlfriends things that they wouldn't think to say to a guy."

Dorinda wasn't expecting the watershed of emotions that Darryl displayed. The men in her life had never expressed those kinds of sentiments for her. Darryl was genuinely desperate to repair whatever had broken in his relationship with Eleanore.

Shamelessly, Dorinda stuck to her lie and her plan to rip through the hearts of Eleanore and Darryl.

"Do you have a place to use the bathroom here on the boat?" Dorinda suddenly asked.

"I suspect you'd be a lot more comfortable using the one back at the restaurant," Darryl replied flatly. "This one on the boat is not one for the faint of heart. No comfort zone, so to speak."

"I don't like going back into that building once I've left," Dorinda frowned. "I've seen enough of those people for one night. Besides, they are cleaning up the floors in the kitchen now. I think my heart can take the beating if I use the bathroom on the boat. Do you mind?"

Distracted by the change of subject, Darryl pointed his finger to a small door at the boat's bow. "Be my guest," he said dejectedly and slumped in his chair to wait for her.

After what seemed a longer time than average, Dorinda finally stepped out of the tiny space.

Darryl asked, "Things go okay in the head?"

"Head?" Dorinda asked, with a puzzled look on her face, not knowing what he meant.

"Yeah, that's what we call the bathroom on a boat. I didn't hear the typical noises going on in there, like when I take people out on a charter. All I heard was banging up against the wall," Darryl tried to joke about the private matter, "and we're not even fighting waves in the lagoon."

"Oh, I was trying to be discreet," Dorinda said, trying to control the red flush spreading across her cheeks after Darryl questioned her activities in the head. Using a boat head wasn't in her repertoire. She wasn't experienced in taking off her pants in such a small space, and on top of that, she lost her balance when her big toe got caught in her panties as she was pulling them completely off. She said a four-letter word in her mind before she delicately slipped the panties behind the small trash bucket beneath the sink.

"I guess I better be going now," Dorinda said, hurriedly making her way past Darryl, still sitting in his chair.

"Will you at least try to find out more information for me?" Darryl asked when she opened the door. "I'm here every night. You can knock on my door if the lights are still on. Just any news would helpful," he pleaded. "I need to know where my destiny in life is heading."

"I'll try my best," Dorinda answered, glancing back at him briefly before she walked out and closed the cabin door.

CHAPTER 7
HIDDEN SECRETS

The excitement Ricky felt while he waited, alone, in the room was difficult to contain. He'd been brought to the windowless room at one o'clock, immediately after his lunch. The young woman was supposed to be there soon. His lifelong habit of fidgeting took over every movable part of his body. The fingers on both of his hands were drumming on the pad of paper secured to a clipboard he brought with him. He remembered the last time she was there. She asked him to write down answers, but he didn't know if she would bring the paper.

He couldn't remember having a feeling of pleasant anticipation like this before. Since the day she first visited him, he couldn't get her off his mind, so eager he was to have her visit again. Having the beautiful, gentle woman talk to him was a respite from his daily contact with the other prisoners and the prison guards, who rarely spoke to him.

This pleasant feeling was nothing like the relief he felt when the patrolman found him walking down the side of the road on Highway 20 after the hurricane. Although he was thrilled to see the patrol car pull over, thinking he was being rescued from his troubles, he soon felt a dark wave of doom creep into his life. The Walton County officer turned him over to the Bay County sheriff's department, after which he was booked into jail for the murder of Earl Keith.

Ricky quickly realized his problems were more significant than the hurricane he survived.

At first, he was overwhelmed with the worry of making decisions without the guidance of his best friend, Vince. But, adjusting to the prison environment became easy for Ricky. His life was not much different than before, when Vince told him everything to do. Except for the boundaries of the prison walls, his structured life in prison made Ricky realize he had broken through a barrier. He was convinced that he could be a survivor through anything.

The fear he felt spending the night alone during the night of the hurricane and the terror of watching the rattlesnake crawl away from his best friend Vince were temporary feelings. Vince, his only friend from childhood who had always guided him, was out of his life. Peace in his soul did not come from the security inside the prison walls. His life had been forever changed the night he spent alone in Vince's truck. The dark clouds in his life cleared when the brilliant rays of sunlight stretched across the sky the morning after the hurricane.

Furthermore, he knew his soul was saved from any more despair. He asked for a bible the first night he spent in prison, but it was weeks before one was delivered to his room by a prison guard. No note came with the bible, and Ricky never asked who provided it. He was just relieved when he received it, and could finally read it. The words he read daily brought him comfort and strength to endure the harshness of his environment. He no longer lived in dread.

It had been over twenty-five years since he sat facing the judge and jury for the death of Earl Keith. Too many unanswered questions, too few clues, and no witnesses except Ricky painted a picture of guilt.

The court-appointed defense lawyer pleaded with the jury, trying to convince them that they could not find Ricky guilty of murder based on circumstantial evidence.

The prosecuting state attorney told the jury that the oversized silver snake ring that Ricky was wearing when he was found by the Walton County Sheriff's deputy was convincing evidence. It was the only telling evidence. The bloodstain in the eye of the snake on the ring matched Earl Keith's. The money the police found wrapped up in a bloody t-shirt Ricky was carrying, providing a possible motive, was another piece of evidence.

The description of events, what actually happened that day, in Ricky's words, was not enough to help find him innocent. When his defense lawyer read Ricky's written explanation verbatim, the words Ricky wrote himself, some of the jurors snickered and had to be admonished by the judge. Ricky turned his reddened, freckled face to his lawyer and quickly scribbled the words, *it ain't very nice for people to be laughing at me* on the attorney's yellow legal pad. Writing down his thoughts was the only way Ricky could communicate with his lawyer. Ricky's lawyer whispered in Ricky's ear, *"Son if you had taken more time in school to learn to write better, you might not be sitting here right now. I'm only doing my best with the information you've given me."*

Ricky knew he had committed no crime. His conscience was clear. Without the tools and resources to fight the courts, he had accepted the lawyer's recommendation for a plea deal, admitting guilt to murder.

Today Ricky was bracing himself to communicate with the nice beautiful young lady through his written words. His instincts told him she wasn't the type of person to laugh at him or admonish him for the answers he wrote down on the paper.

Occasionally, new prisoners would ask Ricky to write down gossip about the prison guards or other inmates. Ricky always had three answers: *At night, I cover my ears with my hands, I always cover my eyes with my pillow, and I can't talk.* The gossip amongst the prisoners was that Ricky was maybe a little crazy, and for sure, he was deaf, dumb, and blind.

"I wonder what she's going to ask me. I hope that her questions are easy to answer. I'll have to try to find the best words when I put the pencil to the paper. I try to block out details of that last day of freedom outside of these prison walls. Then, again, they're not easy to block from my memory. I hope she won't ask me about the hurricane. I hope she'll ask me about Vince. I can honestly tell her that Vince was responsible for the murder, but it seemed more like an accident to me. I just don't know how to write it all down in words. I just don't know how to explain it.

"I don't remember anything about the man Vince murdered. I couldn't tell her the first thing about him. That was the biggest problem when Vince and I went back to the marina to get back the money we paid the charter boat captain to go deep-sea fishing. We didn't know his name, and we couldn't even describe what he looked like. All we could remember was the name of the boat, *The Lucky Two*. I'll never forget that other boat captain, though. He looked busy on his fishing boat, trying to get ready for the hurricane that was coming. The crazy nonsense he talked about made Vince really angry. That boat captain looked at us like we were foolish idiots. I hope she doesn't bring him up."

Ricky's anxiety level increased when he heard the clicking of footsteps out in the hallway, getting louder.

"That's her," he nervously thought. "The prison guards wear rubber-soled shoes. It's a girl taking shorter steps and wearing heeled shoes that click when they hit the floor."

The footsteps echoing against the concrete walls of the hallway stopped outside the closed door of the room.

Ricky's jittery nerves sped into high gear. When the door opened, his lips were twitching, and his mouth was dry. He was having trouble keeping his mouth closed.

"Hello there, Ricky," Eve said in an upbeat, cheerful voice before taking a seat at the table across from him. "How are you today? You look a little nervous. Don't be."

The prison guard following Eve shut the door, moved to a corner of the room, and sat in a chair exactly like Ricky's and Eve's. Usually, a guard would stand by the door during the visit. Still, the guard knew that Ricky wasn't a hostile, threatening type of prisoner. It was institutional policy for the guard to be in the room at all times. The safety of the visitor could never be compromised.

Ricky wasn't sure of himself despite his first impression of the young woman as a warm, friendly, sincere visitor. He never considered the guards as warm and friendly. Guards were usually shouting orders to the inmates. Ricky prayed he didn't do anything that would upset the guard. He'd never been in trouble. He always made it a point to react quickly if they commanded him to do something. It was a behavior he learned from his friend Vince. He didn't want to upset the woman or the guard.

Ricky tipped his head to the left, trying his best to smile at Eve and stop fidgeting.

"I've only got an hour to spend with you. I hope you're feeling good."

Ricky, feeling a little more relaxed after she said these simple words, was able to slightly nod his head, affirming her hopes.

"That's good news," she said, still smiling. "I hope you are ready to get started because there's a lot I want to cover. If you are uncomfortable at any time, I want you to let me know. I'm ready to get started, are you?"

Ricky stopped tapping his fingers on the paper pad attached to the clipboard. The warmth in her voice calmed his nerves, and her eyes expressed a sincere, tender heart.

Eve continued, seeing that Ricky had calmed down. "Do you remember that the last time I was here, I asked you if you would agree to answer some questions? Are you still comfortable with writing down short answers for me? I see that you've brought some paper."

Ricky blinked, smiled, and through tightly pursed lips, vigorously jerked his head up and down. Her questions were simple so far. He was worried about writing down his answers. He was hoping her questions would not be more complicated than the ones she'd already asked.

"Well," she continued. "I've had time this past week to think a little more about my visit with you. I decided that today I want you to know a bit of me and my background before I start asking you questions. Eventually, I want to know more about you, too, of course.

"First of all, I am a lawyer. I've been working since I finished college. I grew up in Georgia. After high school, I went to the University of Georgia in Athens. Go Dawgs!" Eve laughed when she said Go Dawgs. "I've learned that you were originally from Opp, Alabama. Mostly everyone from Alabama says Roll Tide. Do you follow college football?"

Eve at Peace by Yvette Doolittle Herr

The corners of Ricky's mouth turned upward into a faint smile. He gently shook his head no. Football games were sometimes allowed on the TV in the prison commons room, but football was a sport he never followed.

"It's unusual for me to meet someone from Alabama who doesn't watch football!" Eve laughed again. "Were you actually raised all your life in Opp?"

Ricky nodded his head yes.

"Well, like l said, I was raised in Georgia, and that's where I work. I came here, to Florida, for a short hiatus. I wanted to return to Panama City Beach. We used to visit when I was a very young child. I used to love coming to the beach. Did you come to the beach often when you were a child?"

Ricky turned his head side-to-side several times, like a person watching a tennis match. He wanted to say *no, never, not once did we ever go to the beach. When I was a child, growing up, all we ever did was play in the woods. I only heard of the beach, and I've regretted going to the beach ever since that one time I went with Vince.*

"That's a shame. As a small child, I remember the beach being a great place. We had so much fun playing in the sand and water," she said. "As I got older, we didn't get the chance to go. My parents were busy, so we spent more time on the rivers and lakes in Georgia. We didn't have much time to travel."

It didn't seem possible but, Ricky felt like his body had lost all gravity, and he was floating above the chair he sat on. He'd never felt so at ease and comfortable with a woman in his life. She was telling him about herself, wanting him to get to know her. He'd not met many women, but the encounters in his past, those that he could remember, had left him feeling insecure and uneasy. He'd always felt rejected by the female population.

He'd even add his mother to the category of female rejection. His mother had always been angry at him for chumming around with Vince. Vince was the only person who'd given him more than a lecture about how to survive in life. Vince had protected him from the bullies at school. The guards at the prison protected him now.

Eve kept talking, all the while keeping direct eye contact with Ricky. "I've been doing research about your criminal case. I have tracked down some of the family history of your friend Vince. I'm hoping to find some connections possibly relevant to your defense. I found out that your friend Vince originally was from Augusta, Georgia, and moved to Opp after a family crisis. Do you know if he had any other relatives in Georgia?"

Ricky's fingers and toes start to twitch. A nervous edge returned. He was in a Florida prison being visited by this gentle, young woman, a lawyer from Georgia. Still, she had not yet spoken of her purpose in seeing him. Her mention of Alabama and Georgia didn't bring any good memories to the forefront of his thoughts.

Ricky remembered Vince telling him he moved from Georgia to Alabama after his parent's marriage ended because his father originally was from Alabama. Vince also mentioned that he had siblings, at least one older sister, but Ricky didn't know where they lived. Vince's mother was from Georgia. Ricky reminisced about Vince talking like a crazy man in the truck after leaving the murder scene. Vince was talking to his mother, Sissy, telling her that he could be proud of her Georgia boy. Is that why this young woman was here, visiting him? Did she only want to find Vince's family in Georgia?

Suddenly Ricky's legs jumped beneath the table and began to fan back and forth. His bottom lip quivered.

Eve immediately recognized that she had upset Ricky. Quickly she tried to calm him. "It's not essential for me to know Vince's relatives. I was mainly curious. I thought you might be interested in sharing some of your personal memories about your friend. I've read the court records and your plea bargain. I gather that he was your best friend.

"I've researched the vital records on where he was born, as well as his parents. I haven't been able to piece together what happened to everyone in his family, except for a sister.

Forget, for now, that I asked you that question. I can see how much it has upset you. I want to tell you that it's not the most important thing that I want to know."

Eve's next words were spoken with a hint of hopefulness in the tone of her voice.

"What I'd really like to know is if you remember the man, the boat captain, who talked to you that day you went back to the marina to find Earl Keith. I learned from sources, I cannot tell you who they are, that he was helpful in directing you how to find Earl Keith. Can you remember the boat captain who helped you? Can you write down what he looked like"?

Ricky found himself feeling totally confused about the woman's line of questioning. But still trusting her motives, he gently tilted his head upward to indicate that everything was okay with her asking questions. After all, she apologized to him for making him feel uncomfortable, and she also had a pretty smile.

Ricky sat still in thought for five minutes, staring directly at the young woman who sat erect and very still, across from him at the table, patiently waiting for his response. Her question troubled him because he had a vague sense of knowing that she was taking him down a path he didn't feel ready to walk on.

Remembering the one person who had little involvement with their misadventure gave Ricky an odd feeling that expressed itself in his stomach. It felt like it was tied up in knots.

The chatty boat captain and the clerk in the convenience store were the last two people, besides Vince, that he spoke to before he lost his tongue. Ricky still remembered all of those conversations.

How could he forget going back to Captain Andersons's Marina or talking to the boat captain, who gave Vince a tip on finding Earl Keith's truck? Particularly the information on which direction to leave town? Ricky remembered the boat captain talking about some strange things, which seemed unrelated to Vince's questions. It angered Vince, who was in a hurry to leave. The captain couldn't clearly describe Earl's truck but did tell Vince to look for a blue dolphin hanging from the truck's rearview mirror. Vince was ready to roll.

Ricky's eyes grew big, and he smiled sheepishly at Eve. He gently bobbed his head up and down as if in agreement with the young woman's need to know. His confusion disappeared.

Ricky grabbed both sides of the clipboard with the yellow legal pad of paper attached to it. He was only allowed to carry it under the direct supervision of a prison guard since it could be considered a weapon in open areas of the prison. He grabbed the pencil tied to the metal hinge of the clipboard with a string, wiggled his backside, sat up straighter in the wood chair, and proceeded to write down his memory of talking with the boat captain.

CHAPTER 8
BIRDIES, BUGS, AND BUTTERFLIES

Princess and King were not the only cats to start a family after the hurricane. Feline overpopulation created new challenges for the hungry cats and kittens living at the marina. New kittens appeared everywhere from seemingly nowhere.

Oscar, whose reputation elevated to a superhero amongst the female felines, fathered many new kittens after he was discovered roaming around in the new neighborhood across from the marina. His confidence skyrocketed after surviving the ordeals of the hurricane, and he was eager to show off his masculinity to the neighborhood cats.

Oscar often returned to the marina to visit his cousin Dog Ear.

"How can anyone like Fat Cat," Oscar thought as he was making his way to the marina one day, not long after DC's encounter with a packet of hot taco sauce. "I have to give him credit for helping my cousin Dog Ear survive the hurricane, but he has become so hard-hearted. He's lost weight, too. His skinny body only makes his big round head look bigger and meaner. He acts so fat-headed most of the time. He doesn't need that big head to remind us of who he is, a has-been leader who still wants to be the boss of everyone. But it looks like the only way I'm going to see my cousin, for now, is by coming over here."

Fat Cat noticed Oscar in the distance from his perch on the cat condominium, slinking across the road and into the marina parking lot.

"I can appreciate why Dog Ear respects him," Oscar thought, unaware that he was being watched by Fat Cat. "However, I don't understand why anyone else would stay at the marina. There's King and Princess, and their kittens, along with ST. ST has been loyal like Dog Ear to Fat Cat, but I've also noticed him sneakily visiting the new neighborhood a time or two. I think ST's discovered that finding food in the new neighborhood is a little bit easier than finding it here at the docks."

Oscar scooted across the hot pavement of the parking lot. Then began trotting back and forth on the sidewalk in front of the boat slips, holding his tail straight up, high in the air, waiting to be noticed.

"Oscar's having another one of his single, one-man parades," Fat Cat growled to Snaggle Tooth, who was watching Oscar with Fat Cat. "Let's go," Fat Cat suddenly barked.

"Go where?" Snaggle Tooth asked.

"I haven't decided yet," Fat Cat grumbled. "Oscar's probably over here to check on his brother, Dog Ear. If he's not looking for Dog Ear, or a new girlfriend, then he's looking for me. He'll puff out his tail and brag about how he's got it so good over there in the new neighborhood. Then he'll have the nerve to ask if there have been any good scraps from the fishing boats. These days, Oscar talks out of both sides of his mouth."

ST wasn't sure precisely what Fat Cat meant by talking out of both sides of your mouth. It made no sense to him. ST only had half an upper lip left on his mouth. If he had a full upper lip, did it mean he could talk out of both sides of his mouth if he wanted to? Would he want to? ST restrained himself from asking Fat Cat what he meant.

Ever since the hurricane, Fat Cat's temperament ran on a short fuse. Fat Cat had become prone to sudden outbursts of anger over small matters. Whenever ST sensed that Fat Cat was in a foul mood, he avoided asking Fat Cat any questions. It was clear to ST that it was not the right time to ask Fat Cat any questions.

The two cats jumped from the highest point of the woodpile, where they usually spent most of the day, down to the sidewalk. They avoided the bushes next to the restaurant windows during the day now that the shrubbery leaves were gone and had not fully grown back. The bushes were not the protective camouflage/hiding place they used to be.

"Let's run down to the Light House Marina and check out the rubble," Fat Cat said. Maybe some tiny critters are roaming around in there that we can catch."

ST reluctantly followed Fat Cat. The piles of metal debris left lying on the ground at the Lighthouse Marina had the potential for an accident about to happen. To venture inside reminded him of the time he sliced his upper lip on a broken bottle jumping inside the dumpster behind Smith's. He was an inexperienced young kitten when that accident happened. Even if he was cautious today, he might accidentally slice off the other side of his mouth on a sharp piece of metal. Missing one upper lip was enough for him.

He'd rather not go, but he understood the possibility of finding food was important, too. "Maybe there will be new, interesting things to see," he thought.

Always conscious of his scarred lip, ST learned to be proud of his nickname, ST. The exposed fang on his mouth became his signature, the basis of his reputation as a brave cat, overcoming adversity. He displayed his fang like a trophy. It attracted attention from the fishermen, restaurant employees, and the diners who came to eat at Smith's.

The injury had cost him pain and pride at first, but it taught ST to be cautious. Despite being careful to a fault, he never lost his curiosity.

As they trotted down the sidewalk, making sure that they would not be seen by Oscar, ST thought about how many things had changed for the gang of cats at the marina. The docks at Captain Anderson's Marina were not the same. There were not as many charter boats or people. Most of the old hiding places were missing. New hiding places that could be considered safe were hard to find. More kittens and an open border to the new neighborhood across the street from the marina created a new set of issues. The rules for territory, and hierarchy, were not clear. One thing was clear to ST, however. The loss of the restaurants that shared marina space with Smith's, and the loss of charter boats, made it much harder to find food.

However, a good change was that the boat captain of *The Lucky Two* was not the same irritable man who originally lived on it and yelled at the cats. The charter boat captain of *The Star Chaser*, Darryl Kay, was now living on *The Lucky Two*.

Darryl was as friendly to the cats as he was before the hurricane. Whenever Darryl sat outside on the deck of *The Lucky Two*, he'd throw bits of food, calling out to them in a joking voice, "Come on over here, all you pussycats."

The quick reopening of Smith's restaurant, provided a relatively reliable food source in the dumpster. But with that and even with Darryl's occasional fish scraps, the cats often struggled to find food to eat during the week.

A young woman began to regularly come to the docks early in the evening and leave two small bowls of dry cat food on the sidewalk. A small crowd of cats watched and waited in the bushes by the windows of Smith's. After she poured the food from the bag into the bowls, she would stand on the sidewalk calling out the name *Princess*. Soon Princess and King would appear. The woman remained while both cats ate. When King and Princess left, the woman did too. After the woman left, it was a free-for-all on who could race faster to the bowls left on the sidewalk to eat the remainder of the food.

"It's confusing," ST thought. "Why is Darryl living on *The Lucky Two*? And, where did this woman who leaves bowls of food come from? I know where all these new cats came from, though. I thought we had enough cats in our gang before the hurricane. Now there, we have multiplied into an unmanageable number."

Even more confusing to ST was the disappearance of the Florida Marine Patrol officer, Casey Howard, who used to be a daily fixture at the docks before the hurricane. He could always be found standing at the docks when a charter boat returned from a deep-sea fishing trip. Casey was the man on board *The Lucky Two* when it returned to the marina with Princess, King, and Oscar.

More confounding to ST was the difficulty of dealing with the changes in Fat Cat's personality.

"On top of all the changes in our lives, I have to deal with Fat Cat, who is bossier now than he was during the days before the hurricane. I remember hoping that King would take over the responsibilities and become the leader of our gang of cats. All King seems to care about is taking care of Princess and their kittens. He doesn't socialize much at all with the gang anymore. I don't have any other options except to stick with Fat Cat. He's always been my leader, and I'll be his loyal follower for helping me survive the hurricane."

Fat Cat had joined all the other cats in welcoming back King, Princess, and Oscar when they arrived back safe at the marina after disappearing the night of the hurricane and returning the next day on *The Lucky Two*. However, Fat Cat's primary interest was Princess. When she snubbed him completely for King, Fat Cat's hatred for King grew stronger.

"Can you at least try to keep up?" Fat Cat turned his large head slightly backward and fixed the shiny, black slits of his eyes on ST, who was following several steps behind. "The last thing I want is for Oscar to see us," Fat Cat grunted.

Fat Cat began to trot faster, and ST followed close by his side. Neither cat wanted to be seen in the open, deserted expanse of the marina parking lot during the middle of the day. When they got close to the pile of twisted, metal debris lying near the Lighthouse Marina, they crouched on four paws, close to their bellies, until they reached the edge of the seawall.

The metal debris was piled up near the sidewalk, close to the water's edge. Until another new barge arrived to pick it up and reduce the size of the pile, it was home to various small creatures. Since many of the trees were without leaves and limbs, small chick-a-dee-sized sparrows stuffed bits of paper and wood inside the hallows of the twisted metal. The scratching noise of tiny claws scurrying around inside the pile of metal did not even tempt ST.

"I'd like to feast my eyes on a rat, bug, lizard, frog, or small birdie. I am not at all interested in exploring the source of the noise inside that pile of rubble," ST announced to Fat Cat.

"Umm," Fat Cat replied and flopped flat on his side, panting after the quick dash he'd finished.

ST tilted his head back and sniffed the air, hoping to catch fish scents or any other food scents. His old habit of finding shapes in the clouds grabbed his attention.

An early morning downpour of slanting rain left the lagoon water smooth. White, billowy clouds, pushed by a gentle breeze, lingered above in the vast expanse of deep blue.

"Look up there," ST said to Fat Cat. ST watched the clouds taking shape. He saw a rabbit with bent, floppy ears; a crab with pinchers reaching high; a lion with pointy ears; a duck with outstretched wings and two tiny webbed feet; and finally, a school of fish.

"What?" Fat Cat panted, raised his forepaw, extended his claws, and swiped at ST to show irritation. He had not yet fully recovered from the jog and was still trying to catch his breath.

"I think I saw butterflies," ST laughed, more at himself than at Fat Cat, missing him altogether with his bony paw.

ST didn't want to admit to Fat Cat the images he saw in the clouds. It was easier to tell Fat Cat a small lie. ST knew that it was possible that a real butterfly, or bird, or bee could fly past them at any moment, even though he had not seen many this year. The migrating Monarchs usually made a stop in the Florida panhandle every year. Last year's hurricane had blown away most of the butterfly gardens.

"Are you trying to be funny? I don't think you're so hilarious, ST," Fat Cat hissed, bored by ST's distractions. "I know that you're trying to sidetrack me from thinking about Oscar. That's exactly what you are doing. It's not going to work. All you do is dream and fantasize. Put your imagination to better work, and start getting serious about your situation. We're half-starving all the time. We have no good place to call home. Stop being ridiculous, and think about finding a meal."

ST trotted a few feet further down the seawall, putting some distance between himself and Fat Cat. It was the easiest way to ignore Fat Cat's negativity. His feelings weren't wounded by Fat Cat's harsh remarks. He'd gotten somewhat used to them, but not entirely. It hurt him more to know that Fat Cat was so unhappy and angry.

"And don't forget that nickname of yours. ST works just as well with being a *sidetracked* cat as much as being a *snaggletooth* cat. Which one gives you more pride? You have a reputation to protect, just like me." Fat Cat meowed loudly to reach the perky ears of ST.

Fat Cat stood up and inched closer to ST.

Ignoring Fat Cat, ST let his thoughts get lost in the clouds again. "I'm imagining fish up in the clouds. But, the thought of fish only makes me feel hungry. I'll have to look for something else and get my mind off food."

ST gazed down upon the clear, glassy water, smooth after the stormy morning. An occasional tiny raindrop from a stray cloud fell to the surface, touching the surface like a pinprick on a piece of paper. ST watched as larger circles appeared, created by the suction from the mouth of a fish. The various-sized circles spread out across the water's surface.

As usual, when the fish rose to the surface of the water, pelicans and seagulls swooped down, gliding close above the lagoon, looking for a fish to catch. Once one was spotted, they crash-dived into the water, making a loud splash.

"Fish are down there, swimming in the water looking up for food, just like birds are flying in the sky looking down into the water for food. On land, we have to listen for noise or spot a movement and wait. If I wasn't afraid of water, I'd hang my paw in there and see if I could scoop up a fish, like those birds," ST commented to Fat Cat.

"Those pelicans and seagulls have always annoyed me," Fat Cat responded. "I've seen the pelicans come dangerously close to stealing our food that the boat captain throws. The seagulls are even worse, and they are far too noisy for my ears. I have to admit, though, that those pelicans are interesting to watch when they dive into the water. It's fascinating to see such a big bird, with a big neck and beak, fling its head into the water, wings spread out wide, and bounce back up out of the water like a life preserver thrown off a boat. Next thing you know, it's gulping down a fish."

Fat Cat's uncharacteristic complimentary remarks about the pelicans surprised ST. ST turned his attention back to the sky. He lifted his chin and nose upward and blinked his eyes against the wind. All of the clouds had disappeared, but his eyes followed a group of pelicans, wings spread wide, gliding together in a straight line, high above the lagoon.

ST smiled inwardly with a conviction in his heart that everything would work out just fine between Oscar, King, and Fat Cat. "It's going to work out fine," ST thought, "as soon as Fat Cat begins to see that he has to stop all this squabbling about who is in charge. If Fat Cat will pay more attention to the example of the pelicans flying together, he'll be able to bounce back too."

CHAPTER 9
SISTA'S NEW CHALLENGE

"Sista, Sista!" Geneva heard Sue's voice eagerly, loudly, trying to whisper above the noise of loud music drifting out of the restaurant kitchen. Sue was walking toward the table where Geneva was sitting. Sue's small feet were taking quick, short steps across the carpeted dining room, like a duck waddling across the grass.

At the start of the summer season, Geneva resigned to Sue's repeated use of the name used by her brother, and allowed Sue to call her Sista. "It's not a problem for me when you call me Sista," Geneva finally told Sue, appeasing the woman she needed to stay on good terms with while they worked closely together. "Just don't call me that name in front of the other employees who work here."

"I'd like to call you Sista," Sue admitted to Geneva once she learned about the nickname. "It's an honor to have a nickname. My first name is not Sue. Sue is what I chose to be my middle name. No one can pronounce my Korean name, but everyone can pronounce Sue. Many Korean women take the middle name of Sue. It's like my nickname, too."

Geneva, finished with her prep work, was sitting at a table by herself in the dining room corner. She had a brief window of time to sit down and rest before the kitchen turned into a crazy beehive of buzzing employees feeding customers. Now was the time when she wanted to close her eyes and enjoy a few moments of silence, thankful for the good fortune that she still had her job at Smith's. She didn't want Sue's gossip interrupting her moments of peace and quiet. She would hear enough of Sue's jabber during the work shift.

The restaurant doors would soon be open to customers in less than thirty minutes. The employees sitting inside the dining room, where the air conditioning worked better than in the kitchen, took one last break before the hustle of a busy night began.

Sue grabbed a table chair and dragged it across the carpeted floor to sit close to Geneva.

"What," Geneva said with a heavy sigh when Sue sat down next to her at the dining room table. "Don't you remember me telling you not to call me Sista in front of the other employees?"

"I got some news," Sue chirped, ignoring the reprimand. "Big Joe. He asked me to find out information about Eleanore," Sue said gleefully. She sounded like a child who had just found the presents under the tree on Christmas morning and needed to tell her siblings.

When Big Joe pulled Sue aside to ask her to find out the status of Eleanore's and Darryl's relationship, he started by telling Sue he selected her for an important task. He cautioned Sue about not telling anyone else in the kitchen, fully knowing it would be impossible for Sue not to share the news with Geneva. Big Joe had no doubt Sue would have to tell someone, and of all the people working in the kitchen, Geneva was the safest person to let in on the secret. Sue didn't ask Big Joe why he wanted the information. Sue's heart swelled with pride, knowing she had Big Joe's trust.

"What are you talking about?" Geneva asked, piqued by the mention of Big Joe's name. He was her boss, and Geneva paid careful attention to any news about her boss.

"He wants to know if Eleanore and Darryl are a couple. You know, going together, like boyfriend and girlfriend. He asked me to find out. That Eleanore girl is friendly, but she doesn't talk much to anybody here at the restaurant. I don't think she's ever said more than two words to me. If she has, it's been about asking if I can add an extra tomato to the salad," Sue said. "I like to talk, but I'm not sure I can get her to open up to me, you know, tell me about herself. It's kinda like you, Sista. You don't talk too much about yourself."

Geneva narrowed her eyes, cut a glance over at the table where Eleanore was sitting, then said bluntly, "I won't take any offense by what you just said about me, Sue. I think it's good to keep some stories about yourself secret and not tell the whole world about it."

Sue's gleeful face changed to a pout. She stared at Geneva several minutes, not saying a word, elbows on the table, her hands cupping her chin.

"What do you mean?" Sue finally asked Geneva.

"Just what I said," said Geneva. "I don't want everybody in the world to know my personal business. Furthermore, I have a hard time talking about other people's personal business. On the other hand, you said Big Joe is interested in knowing this information. Did he tell you why he wants to know?" Geneva asked, a little more curious by Big Joe's interest in Eleanore's personal business.

Sue removed her hands from her face and immediately became animated again. "I'm not sure, but he hinted that Eleanore doesn't seem to be very happy. Maybe he's worried about her leaving. Actually, he really didn't tell me why he wanted to know. I'm just guessing. All I know is he stopped by my counter and asked me if I knew anything about Eleanore's personal situation, her boyfriend, for example. I told him no. Then Big Joe says to me, then why don't you ask around. See if you can find out some information for me."

Geneva's face turned serious. She pulled her eyebrows together and tilted her head closer to Sue. Squinting at Sue, Geneva said, "There's got to be a reason Big Joe wants to know," Geneva said more intensely. "It seems like a straightforward question to ask someone, but sometimes, for some people, it's too personal. It can be a delicate situation. You can't be going up to her and just asking straight out, you know, *Hey Eleanore, is Darryl, your boyfriend?*"

Sue aggressively nodded her head, agreeing. Happier that she had Geneva engaged in the situation as a conspiratorial partner, Sue said, "Sista, I've seen you get straight to the point with some of the kitchen staff. You're known around the kitchen as Sista." Sue paused a moment, wondering if she made a mistake using the word *Sista* again. Reading Geneva's facial expressions was difficult most of the time. Wasting no more time, Sue continued, "Sista, everyone at work respects you. You work hard, and you know right from wrong. I've heard you tell a line cook to watch what they say in front of the waitress and use better language. There was the time you walked over to the dish sink and told the dishwasher to stop hiding around the corner. I bet you can find out about Eleanore easier than I can. I'll let Big Joe know, or even you can let him know."

Geneva took a deep breath and exhaled tiredness. She said to Sue, "I'll give it a try. I don't know how soon I can find out."

After she agreed to try to find out the information for Big Joe, Geneva pushed her chair away from the table, slowly stood up, and said to Sue, "Let's get this work shift over."

The question in Geneva's mind was how was she going to find time alone with Eleanore? She was a prep person and rarely interacted with wait staff getting their salads. The front of the house, including bartenders and busboys, had their cliques, and the back of the house had theirs.

Sue and Geneva made their way back to their stations in the kitchen.

Geneva played out different scenarios in her mind. What strategy could she use to get the information? The questions simmered in her mind until the craziness of a busy night overtook her thoughts.

After work, walking to her car, she thought, "I'm going to figure out a way. I might get under the skin of that Dorinda girl. She seems to have a thing against Eleanore. I've heard the line cook snap at Dorinda for asking him to put her ticket order in front of Eleanore's ticket. I'll ask Dorinda why she doesn't like Eleanore. That will get Dorinda's mouth started. If Dorinda doesn't like me asking questions, what can she do to me? I can't see Dorinda picking on me. She needs me to do a good job if she wants to make her money. Food has to turn out good for the customer. I could fix it, so her plates don't come out off the line so nice."

Geneva smiled at the thought of standing up to Dorinda if she tried to give her any trouble for nosing around in her business. Geneva said to herself, "What could be the reason for Dorinda to be hateful against Eleanore? Eleanore seemed to be the sweetest waitress in the building."

"Maybe that old Dorinda is just jealous of another girl being prettier than her. Unfortunately, I have seen this happen in my lifetime," she thought, reflecting on the days, and the people, when she worked at the Elks Club back home in Altoona.

Geneva heaved her tired body inside her car. Before turning the keys to start the engine, she glanced at the charter boats floating in the marina.

"There's *The Lucky Two*," she said to herself. The light is shining through a window, so I know that boat captain Darryl is in there, but I doubt Eleanore is in there with him. Who would want to live in that small cabin in the first place? I'm going to place my bets on believing that Eleanore and Darryl are just friends."

She started up the car's engine and placed one hand on the gear shift. At the sound of the rumbling motor, three cats zipped out from beneath her car. Geneva caught the motion out of the corner of her eye.

"Those cats are always hanging around Smith's garbage dumpster at night," she said out loud, "and when they find something to pick at, they grab it and run under these cars in the parking lot to eat it. It's as if they don't want to be seen, but then they're putting themselves in more danger hanging out beneath a car."

She took a few minutes to watch the cats scamper safely away from the car before she backed out. The last thing she wanted was to hear a cat screaming after it was run over by her own car.

While waiting a sufficient amount of time for the cats to disperse, another movement caught her eye. A shadowy human figure appeared on the sidewalk, walking away from Smith's and toward the lagoon where the charter boats bobbed in the slips.

"Who would that be? Geneva wondered. "It looks like one of the waitresses. Is that Eleanore? They all come out the back door of the kitchen, like me, but she's heading in the wrong direction. She should be heading this way, to the employee side of the parking lot, and getting in her car to go home."

The waitress turned her head to look over her shoulder, to see if anyone was watching.

"No! That isn't Eleanore! It's that Dorinda girl!" Geneva whispered to herself, half in disbelief and half in anger. "Now, what's that girl up to?"

The waitress walked at a fast pace until stopping at *The Lucky Two*. She stepped onto the stern of the boat, walked across the deck, and raised her hand to knock at the cabin door. When the door opened, she stepped inside.

"Uh, oh," Geneva mumbled under her breath while she watched the cabin door shut. "I'm not liking what I saw. The answer for Big Joe is definitely not Eleanore and Darryl."

CHAPTER 10
LISTEN TO SISTA

Geneva's younger brother, Charles, born five years after her, grew up under the wing of his older sister.

When they were young, Charles' sister was assigned to watch Charles after school, making sure he was inside the house while their mother and father worked.

Charles' mother never missed a chance to hug and tell her children when they were young how much she loved them. Still, coming home after working long hours at a job in the laundromat, she was too busy taking care of the household duties to give them much attention.

Geneva gave Charles unconditional love because she knew he needed it, like she needed it too. When trouble found him, she always backed Charles with encouragement.

"Stand strong," she'd tell him. "I'll always have your back."

Charles' father was less than a model father. His influence on Charles' life could not be considered as good, positive, or supportive by anyone's stretch of the imagination. Charles didn't recall ever having a conversation with his father about what Charles would do in life. Charles carried only the memory of his father as the man being asleep on the sofa when Charles sometimes woke up in the middle of the night to use the bathroom. When Charles left for school in the morning, his father would already be gone to work at the railroad yard. He had a job as a gandy dancer, a slang term used for the men who laid down sections of railroad tracks. Charles couldn't remember the last time when his father came home for dinner to eat with the family. When his father came home late, after everyone was in bed, he was never sober. The man banged pots and pans in the kitchen of the small apartment the family rented in Altoona, ate alone, then fell asleep on the sofa.

Charles's father was named Maximilian by Charles's grandfather. The grandfather hoped that by giving his son such a strong name, he would become somebody noteworthy in Altoona. Much like the great European emperor in the fifteenth century who spawned other world leaders. Charles' grandfather wanted more than anything for his son to rise above the slavery and poverty of their forefathers. Charles' great-great-grandfather had escaped through the underground railroad, eventually finding his way to a western Pennsylvania town called Altoona after first swimming across the Ohio river and taking his first step of freedom in the town of Ripley, Ohio.

The irony of what he had achieved, or more so not reached, in life never escaped Maximilian. His own great-grandfather was so brave to risk his life and find his way to Altoona, where the railroad business was preeminent. The symbolism of working for a railroad company lured Maximilian into taking the first job he was offered at the railroad. After all, his ancestors benefited from the underground railroad.

Soon the job of 'dancing' for the railroad, which he ended up doing for the rest of his life, felt like a return to slavery. All of the trains with a destination going further west traveled on the tracks through Altoona, and the tracks needed constant maintenance.

In the early days, after both of his children were born, Maximilian tried to be a good husband and father. Maximilian came home after his day at work. He loved the babies and his wife. He wanted to give his family the best things life could offer. The children were small, and the demands for supporting them with the little things that entertain children were not so great. It was easy to sit on the floor and play with them or watch the television. As they got older, their needs became more challenging. His job demanded so much of his energy that he couldn't find the physical and emotional power that his family needed from him at home.

Eve at Peace by Yvette Doolittle Herr

After so many years of trying, Maximilian developed bad habits. He took up drinking alcohol at the local watering hole, called The King's Table, to escape the daily drudgery of manual labor and responsibilities at home. When he showed up at the bar, his cheerful friends greeted him with the same old joke. "*Hey, there's Max! I bet he's made his first million working at the railroad. Max! Good to see you! We've been waiting on you to buy us all a round of drinks.*" Settling down to a few hours with friends was more comforting to Maximilian than staying at home. He enjoyed the nickname Max, used only by his friends. His father, being proud of the name Maximilian, never called him by the nickname, Max.

Maximilian's downward spiral into the pit of alcoholism started when Geneva became a teenager. In the early days, he always came home, ate dinner with his family, and left to go to the bar after dinner.

"This is going to change, by God," Charles and Geneva could hear their mother say to herself when the apartment door closed behind their father.

Geneva and her mother schemed to the extreme to keep his father home after they finished supper. They stuffed his overcoat under the covers in Geneva's bed. They took his wallet off the table by the door and stuffed it beneath a sofa cushion. They hid his shoes in the refrigerator. None of these tricks worked. As the children got older, the family quit trying to keep him home. It didn't matter that they stopped trying because eventually Maximilian went to the bar as soon as he got off work. He came home late at night, banging pots and pans in the kitchen, to reheat his dinner.

Geneva never stopped feeling lucky after the day she saw the *Help Wanted* sign in the window at the Elks Club in Altoona. She was happy to have the opportunity to learn how to cook in a kitchen where they served more than baked or boiled potatoes with a slice of plain bread. Meats, vegetables, desserts were all on the menu, and fried fish on Fridays was one of her favorites. She became skilled at preparing different kinds of food. More so, Geneva felt pride when people expressed an appreciation for her cooking.

Eve at Peace by Yvette Doolittle Herr

After being hired to work in the kitchen at the Elks Club in Altoona, Geneva soon realized that cooking was not a bad line of work. Even if she came home tired every night after standing on her feet for hours, she enjoyed cooking. She loved to eat, for one thing, and she knew she would be able to taste food that she'd never get at home. Creativity in the kitchen became her passion and key to her happiness. The praise for the meals she prepared gave her a sense of accomplishment and satisfaction.

When Geneva told her father about her new job, Maximilian was less than pleased. He knew that many of the upper management team working in the railroad company were members of the Elks Club.

Geneva and her father met in the kitchen one night after she came home from work, and he was reheating food cooked hours earlier by her mother.

"Nice. Haven't we come full circle? Me still laying railroad tracks; your mother doing laundry at the laundromat, and you working as a cook in a kitchen," her father Maximilian said with intentional, vicious sarcasm powered with the fuel of a night of drinking at the bar. "You're going to work for those rich white men at the Elks Club. They're the ones who run the railroad and decide who gets the best jobs in town. It sure isn't us, now, is it? We're people of color. Ha, ha, the joke is still on us."

"Well, I know that I won't ever go hungry working in a kitchen," Geneva immediately replied in a cutting voice, sharper than Maximilian's. "Around here, I never know if there's going to be food in the refrigerator. Used to be that sometimes I might find a pair of shoes hid in the refrigerator, but I don't even find them in there anymore. And speaking of shoes, one of those so-called rich white members at the Elks Club came back in the kitchen one night and noticed the old shoes I was wearing. He gave me some money to buy a decent pair of shoes, which is something you've never offered to do for me."

Geneva never was afraid to speak her mind to her father. She especially loved an opportunity when he said something that opened the door for a response that could silence him.

"Of one thing I can be sure," Geneva continued, "there's always going to be the scent of whiskey in the kitchen when you get home late at night after we've all gone to bed. That odor lingers on the sofa and everywhere in the house all the time."

Maximilian snarled at her, raising his upper lip to show his disgust with her last comment. He turned his head back to the stove to look away from Geneva, trying to end the conversation.

Geneva didn't stop digging into her father's soul, knowing that a window had been opened. "Maybe it's time for you to swallow your pride. Don't you think your pride is going down with every swallow of that whiskey you drink?"

Geneva walked out and left Maximilian alone in the apartment kitchen. She couldn't look at his face and watch the tears well up in his eyes. It happened all the time. His emotional pain was no more significant than hers, but she had learned to stop crying over his years of neglect a long time ago. She was discovering, and was earning, her own path to happiness.

Upon graduation from high school, Maximilian refused to allow Charles to go to work at the railroad. "He's never going to work on those tracks," he shouted at Charles' mother one night. "I'd rather see him move somewhere else to find a job. Working on the train tracks is like working on a chain gang."

Charles's mother was tired and had enough trouble trying to keep the family clothed and fed. Afraid of what Maximilian might do if she argued with her husband, Charles' mother waited and watched in silence as Charles picked up the habit of idleness, lying on the sofa during the day. Charles walked the streets at night to turn the couch over to Maximilian, when his father finally came home.

Unwittingly, and unfortunately, Maximilian passed the heavy burden of life's sad disappointments on to his own son, Charles. Through no fault of his own, Charles became a follower, not a thinker.

It wasn't the weight of the family responsibilities that drove Maximilian to drink. It was the weight of his own father's expectation. Maximilian was expected to become somebody great in Altoona. In his own mind, he'd become a complete failure. It was more than Maximilian's heart could handle.

Every morning, before she left the apartment to go to her job at the laundromat, Charles' mother kissed him goodbye. She said, "*Listen to whatever Sista tells you to do, stay out of trouble today, and don't ever forget my advice."*

Charles' mother understood that changing Charles' father's drinking problem was hopeless unless he wanted to stop. She tried to coax him, trick him, and convince him it was wrong but couldn't stop him from drinking.

This was her advice to Charles: *"You never, never, need the kind of problem your father has. Stay away from drinking at the bars. Don't let alcohol become your best friend because if you do, it will become your worst enemy."*

CHAPTER 11
NOT GONNA BE A SLAVE

The call for laborers in every field of work to help rebuild Panama City after hurricane Louise went out all across the country.

When the news reached the newspapers in Altoona, the timing couldn't have been better. The Elks Club was losing membership. With fewer members supporting the club's activities, the hours' Geneva was given to work in the kitchen became less and less. She had the feeling she would be let go from her job soon, if not any day. In December and New Year's Eve, the holiday parties had kept things alive in the kitchen. A slow start was leading to a bad finish.

One night Geneva's mother brought home a newspaper left lying on a table in the laundromat.

"Look at this," her mother pointed to the newspaper and tapped her finger at the story. "Here's an opportunity for you to have long-term employment, maybe cook in a busy restaurant. I hear the climate in Florida is good this time of year. No snowstorms in January, like the one we have here in Altoona right now!" she laughed.

Geneva read the first few paragraphs of the story, nodded her head, and vocalized her opinion, "Hmmm, sounds interesting."

Instead of allowing Geneva the chance to set roots somewhere else, and come back for Charles, her mother added, "You've got to take Charles with you, too. It will give Charles a chance to change his life. I can't do anything with him. You're the only person he looks up to. He's never looked up to me. He needs to set his sails on a new course in life."

A few nights after their conversation, Geneva came home from the Elks Club and was surprised by her mother.

"Here's some money for you and Charles to go down to Panama City," her mother said to her, stuffing an envelope filled with a couple of hundred dollars into Geneva's hand. "There's opportunity there for you. With your work experience in the kitchen, I know you'll be able to get a good job. Charles is a young man with energy. He can work as a laborer. Between the two of you, I know you'll make it together. It's an opportunity for him, too, to get away from the sour grapes he's experienced here. His dad hasn't been any help, forbidding him to work at the rail yards. Truth is, the railroad is slowing down too. Men are getting laid off work there."

"What about you, momma?" Geneva asked. She loved her mother and was reluctant to leave her alone with Maximilian. Her mother would be the only person he would take his anger out on if the children were not there. "I don't want to leave you. I want you to come with us, too."

"Oh, no dear," Geneva's mom said. "I'm old. I would be a burden. I'm not ready to make that kind of move in my life right now. I still have my job. I will be fine here. I got my friends if things don't work out. When you get settled, who knows? Maybe I'll move down south too. I doubt that your father will go, but if I'm gone, he'll have no one else. There's no other family here for him. He'll have to change his mind about living in the south."

Geneva, always expected by her mother to look after her brother, Charles, and keep him out of trouble, committed to taking him with her on the journey to wherever she could find the next job. Work opportunities, and the ability to advance in a career, was little to none in the dying town. Charles willingly followed his sister to Panama City.

Geneva packed up her mother's old car with only the minimum belongings she thought she might need to set up the house. Both she and Charles took clothes suitable for warmer weather.

They drove all day and straight through the night, stopping once to sleep a few hours in the early morning, before dawn, at a rest stop in Florida near the border of Alabama. Charles and Geneva's mother cautioned them with her concerns. She heard rumors of evil white people still living in the south who would be ready to harass black people traveling in a car. Maximilian's comments to Charles about working on a chain gang on the railroad tracks fueled their fears. They decided to keep driving through all southern states until they crossed the state line into Florida.

When they arrived in Panama City, they stopped at a convenience store to make a quick phone call to their mother to let her know they were safe.

Geneva continued driving south on Highway 231 until it intersected with Highway 98. Then she turned to head west. Neither Geneva nor Charles had traveled outside of the state of Pennsylvania before. They had spent twenty-four hours mostly riding in silent anticipation of what they might expect when they arrived in Panama City.

Charles, looking out his window at the scenery, spoke first when they arrived.

"Man, Sista. This landscape looks so different than the mountains in Pennsylvania. It's so flat, and the trees - they're so different."

"Those are pine trees, Charles," Geneva said.

"Well, I see some trees, but mostly tall tree-trunks with no leaves, twisted trees, and trees broke in half," Charles said. "I think they used to be tall pine trees. And what about all these buildings missing roofs? If there is a roof on a building, it's covered with blue plastic."

The visible effects of the damage caused by hurricane Louise were evident. Charles had been looking at it for nearly twenty miles while they drove down Highway 231.

"Charles, now that we're here, just keep your eyes looking out for a motel that looks like it might be inexpensive. We can't afford anything fancy. I have a feeling that we can find something in Panama City cheaper than looking for somewhere to stay on the beach. Most likely, the motels on the beach cost more. We're going to have to stay in a motel for a night or two until we can find a room, or apartment, to rent on a long-term basis," Geneva said nervously. "I'm going to take a ride to the beach first. That's where all the restaurants will be. I hope there will be a place that has a help wanted sign in the window. Remember? That's how I found the job at the Elks Club. Somewhere there's got to be a place where we can find a phone book. There will be an address for an employment office that posts jobs for laborers."

"Sista," Charles said impatiently. "Why don't you find a motel room first? If you think the rooms will be cheaper, we can go ahead and check into a room. All motel rooms have phones and telephone books. I don't think I can sleep in the car again tonight. I'd like to get some sleep before I go looking for work somewhere. Your brain is running on gas fumes, just like the gas tank in this car. We're going to need some gas, too."

"I'm going to give you credit for thinking, Charles," Geneva said. "We should stop at a gas station first. They always have a phone booth. Possibly with a phone book hanging on a chain, too. Back in Altoona, people stole the phone books from the booth, and all you'd see left is the chain dangling from the counter. Hopefully, the people here don't do that too."

Geneva and Charles laughed together. When they left Pennsylvania, the January cold weather had settled in. The warmer weather made them feel carefree. Florida was feeling good to them already.

They pulled into a gas station and noticed a sign that said welcome to St. Andrews. Behind the station was a grocery store.

"Over there might be a place to pick up some provisions," Charles said to Geneva, pointing his finger toward a grocery store. "It doesn't look like some fancy, expensive grocery store. The sign says Discount Groceries. That's a name I like."

"Uh, huh," Geneva said. "We'll check that out. First, let me check out this gas station."

Geneva went inside the gas station to ask about a phone book. She came back to the car within minutes.

"We're in the right vicinity, brother. The man in there said there's a couple of cheap motels down this road here,"

Geneva said. "He called this area old St. Andrews. There's a marina and a couple of motels. I also asked him about the best place to look for a job. I told him I was looking for kitchen work, and I had a brother looking for work as a laborer. He told me that all of the restaurants on the beach are looking for cooks, and he said there's a place down this road where we can stop to look for a job for you. It's a building at the corner of the marina. Maybe somebody at the marina will be looking for someone to work on their fishing boat," Geneva added.

Charles said, "I want to be working outside in this nice sunshine doing construction, or maybe some kind of maintenance. I don't know anything about fishing, and I don't know how to swim, so working on a boat doesn't sound like something for me. I know one thing for sure. I don't want to be slaving in a hot restaurant kitchen washing dishes. You can be in the kitchen, but it's not the kind of work I want to do."

Geneva frowned when she heard Charles. "Let me tell you something, Mr. Big Shot. You're reminding me of daddy. The dishwashers in a restaurant get paid money to do a job. They are just as important as everyone else, except for the cook. If the dishes don't get washed, then customers don't eat. If people don't get to eat, there's no business. No business, no money. Now shut your mouth on that subject."

Geneva and Charles were turned away from the only two motels in St. Andrews. The first one, called the Casa Amore, was an avocado-green, two-story, cinder-block building with an empty parking lot. Geneva left Charles in the car and knocked on a room door on the first floor. An aged wood, painted sign, nailed to the door indicated it was the office. She then turned the door handle. The door easily opened. Inside a small room sat two men and a disheveled looking woman staring back at her with a surprised look.

"I was told at the gas station down the street that this would be a good place to rent for a night or two," Geneva said, somewhat unnerved by the unwelcome looks of the men.

After being told the motel didn't have a vacancy, she asked the man at the desk about the weekly rental cottages a block away. The man told Geneva the Casa Amore managed the cottage rentals, and all the cottages were also already rented.

"I think they were a little bit on the pricey side anyway," Geneva lied to Charles when she got back in the car. "The man was nice enough to give me directions to another motel called the Denise Motel. He wrote down the address. He said to drive back east on Highway 98 until we get to Harrison Avenue. Then take a right-hand turn and go south on Harrison Avenue, which will take us into downtown Panama City."

Driving south on Harrison Avenue, all the way to where the road ended at the marina, she and Charles got their first peek at St. Andrews Bay. They got out of the car and stood in the marina parking lot for a few minutes to look at the water.

"Boy, I like the looks of that water and all those boats," Geneva said to Charles "but, it looks like I must have passed the motel. I don't see a motel here on the waterfront. I'm turning around and going back."

They found the motel thirty minutes later. It also was a two-story, cinder-block building, but the white paint barely covered the spray-painted graffiti. A torn screen covering a window displayed the office sign for the Denise Motel.

When Charles saw the sign, he commented, "I see that the name of this place is a girl's name. I think I'll call it De-Nice motel."

Geneva chuckled at his joke. After checking into the sparsely furnished room, it wasn't long before they both were sound asleep. They forgot about their plans to drive to the beach where Geneva could find work and where they could finally eat a meal.

Geneva's mother was right. The next day she was hired, on the spot, at Smith's, a prominent, well-established restaurant on the beach. When asked about her cooking skills, Geneva rambled on about all the specialty dishes she cooked at the Elks Club.

"I can make almost any kind of pie. You name it, and I can find a way to make it. I made shoo-fly pie, lemon meringue pie, chocolate pie, but the club members used to really like my custard pies. And, I make my pie crusts from scratch. For dinner, I used to make braised beef tips with gravy over rice. I didn't do much frying, but people did like fried fish on Friday nights. Then I have this recipe for pork chops and potatoes that people loved. I baked it with a lot of onions. I also made chicken and dumplings with a lot of paprika in them. I've made some Italian dishes, like veal parmesan. I think the one item I cooked that people liked the best was my au gratin potatoes. I put a generous helping of cheese and real cream in my au gratin potatoes. Guests would ask for second helpings, and we would run out."

Geneva was only a little disappointed when she was told she would be hired to help prep seasoned vegetables for the line cooks. Maybe one day, she thought, Smith's might like to try out her au gratin potatoes. On the other hand, she was excited and grateful to be hired for the job.

"This restaurant is big and so busy that they need to hire a person to do only one thing? Just chop vegetables?" Geneva thought, surprised by her luck. "I'm confident that when they see my kitchen skills, they'll allow me to get my hands into other foods."

She was relieved that she had experience frying fish on Fridays at the Elks Club. The menu at Smith's consisted of mostly fish dishes. "I plan to surprise that man with my creativity in the kitchen," she said to herself. She was proud of the accomplishment of being hired to work at a big restaurant with a clientele and reputation more significant than the Elks Club in Altoona.

Charles was hired the same day by a small construction company doing repair work on apartment buildings damaged by hurricane Louise. When asked about his labor skills, Charles didn't know what to say at first. After a few minutes of silence, knowing he needed to say something, he told the interviewer that he liked working with his hands and enjoyed being outside in the sunshine.

"I've never done any kind of real job," he told the interviewer with raw honesty. "I can empty trash, pick up trash, sweep floors, and rake yards. I know I don't want to wash dishes. I'm eager to work, though. I thought I would be working at the railroad yards when I graduated from high school, but my dad wouldn't let me do that."

The job manager was somewhat surprised at Charles' unusual answers, then asked if he knew how to use power tools or other equipment. Charles sadly shook his head no. "I'd like to learn how to operate some equipment," Charles quickly said, adding, "I can probably use a hammer and a regular saw. I'd like to learn how to operate some power tools if someone would be willing to teach me. I'm a pretty fast learner."

Charles was asked if he didn't mind using a broom or a shovel now and then.

"I'll do anything you ask me to do," Charles told the interviewer.

Charles was thrilled when he was hired on the spot for general maintenance work.

Charles soon learned he probably should have taken a job working in the kitchen with his Sista. Maximilian's pride was part of his genetic code. Charles' enthusiasm changed when he watched other employees using fancy tools. At the same time, he was primarily assigned to sweep floors and dig holes.

Amongst themselves, the construction workers referred to Charles as Mr. Gofer. When he first heard it, he was confused by why they would call him Mr. Gofer, but learned very quickly why. The construction crew needed Charles to go get things for him.

"Hey, Charles, I need you to go back to the shed and bring me back another box of nails. Hey, Charles, I need you to walk to the truck and go get my drill. Hey, Charles, I need you to go over to the yard and bring back a panel of sheetrock.

Hey Charles, would you go pick up those wood two-by-fours and set them down here?"

Charles definitely did not like the job. He thought he was doing work for the glory of others and found himself stuck in a rut, and he didn't know how to dig himself out of it.

It wasn't as if he had expected the work to be glamorous. He told the man who interviewed him for the job that he didn't mind using a shovel, or a broom, or a rake. He was assigned to do those tasks; however, he didn't expect to have that many bosses telling him to go get things for them.

"I'd be better off washing dishes in the kitchen," he grumbled, still doing what he was told. "It's easier to do something without somebody telling you what to do all the time. I could have just been running a dishwashing machine. It couldn't be hard pulling a handle on a machine, but Geneva tells me the dishwasher is always hiding. I'd go ask for a job at her restaurant, but she got mad at me when I told her I didn't want to be no slave working as a dishwasher. She would laugh in my face and tell me I told you so if I went to her right now and asked for help."

When the summer months arrived, the unfamiliar heat of Florida made Charles feel worse.

"I know one thing. It couldn't be as hot working over a steaming dishwasher as it is outside in this steamy heat. I'm sure that there's got to be some air conditioning in restaurant kitchens," he thought.

Charles' attitude grew worse with each passing week. His reputation for being a likable person deteriorated with the construction crew.

His days living as a free man were numbered, in part, because of the reputation he earned at his job. No one spoke favorably of Charles when the police came to the job site to question all employees about their whereabouts on Halloween night. Something about a woman found murdered left everyone pointing the finger at Charles.

Charles never dreamed that his life could be worse than the one he left in Altoona.

He never dreamed the day would come when he thought about the times his father, Maximilian, would compare working on the railroad tracks to working in a chain gang or the day he would be asking his Sista to help get him out of jail.

CHAPTER 12
THE BIG QUESTION

Geneva's opportunity to talk to Eleanore about her relationship with Darryl happened the day after Sue told Geneva that Big Joe asked for information.

Geneva didn't have to figure out a way to corner Eleanore into the conversation. She saw Eleanore sitting by herself, as she often did, at a table in the dining room of Smith's. Eleanore's eyes were staring out the same window, which was the prized view of customers who wanted to watch the sunset while they ate dinner.

"There she is," Sue whispered to Geneva. "Now's your chance."

Together, Geneva and Sue left the kitchen prep room to take their break before the restaurant opened. Geneva and Sue were usually the last to finish up their prep work before the night began but left earlier than the waitresses. On the contrary, the waitresses completed their prep work early but were the last to leave the restaurant. There was little time to waste.

"Mind if I join you?" Geneva asked Eleanore and pulled out a chair before Eleanore had a chance to answer the question.

Eleanore was sitting slumped over, with her elbows on the table and both hands cupping her chin. She slowly turned her head and looked at Geneva with vacant eyes as if suddenly removed from a daydream.

"Of course, Geneva," Eleanore said respectfully, removing her hands away from her chin and placing them on the table.

"Why are you sitting here, off by yourself and not talking to anyone?" Geneva asked and scooted her chair up close to the table, purposely putting her back to Sue, who was sitting at a table with another kitchen employee. "You look like you don't feel well. Maybe you had a bad day? And, by the way, thank you for calling me Geneva. It feels good to have someone show a little respect and call me by my real name. I know everyone at work likes to refer to me as Sista when they're working, so I'm okay if you want to use the name Sista, too, every now and then. Sue likes to call me Sista. You call me either Geneva or Sista, whichever you want."

"I think Geneva is such a pretty name," Eleanore replied. "I'm just feeling a little worn out today for some reason. I've got lots of things on my mind."

"You thinking about your boyfriend?" Geneva asked, point-blank, forgetting what she told Sue about it being wrong to come right out and ask such a personal question.

Caught off guard by Geneva's question, Eleanore didn't hesitate, and quickly answered, "Yes."

Eleanore briefly considered the fact that everyone in the restaurant must know she was living with Casey. "Is this what's in Geneva's mind?" Eleanore thought to herself.

Surprised by Eleanore's direct answer to her question, Geneva asked, "Is it the boyfriend you lost? The man who owned *The Lucky Two*? I know the story about you coming down here and surviving the night of the hurricane. I hear you are living at the marine patrol officer's house," Geneva said cautiously, then asked, "How's that going?"

"Living with Casey, you mean?" Eleanore stated flatly. "Oh, Casey is a very nice man, but he's not someone I could call my boyfriend," Eleanore answered, then quickly added, "Casey's been a good friend this past year, letting me stay at his house. I've been able to save money this summer, which is good. But, Casey's not someone who I'd be interested in having a relationship with."

An awkward moment of silence passed between the two women. The pause in the conversation gave Eleanore time to dismiss the nervous fluttering in her stomach and Geneva time to think about what to say next.

"No, I'm not thinking about Earl," Eleanore spoke first. "He was my boyfriend a long time ago. Even when I came down here to check on him, I wasn't sure if I would get back together with him. Things in my life have sort of exploded since then."

"Tell me about it," Geneva asked, hoping what Eleanore meant by *exploded* would provide the information she knew Big Joe wanted. Her work shift in the kitchen started in a few minutes, and she didn't have much time for long details.

"I thought that I might die during the night of the hurricane. At first, I was afraid of Casey and what he might be thinking of doing to me. At one point, Casey really frightened me. After we got the boat to a safe location, tied up and secured, he stepped up close to my body and tried to kiss me. All I said to him was, *please don't*, and he stopped. After that, he became a very gentle, compassionate man. He made me talk to him, I think, to help me overcome my fears, but he was nervous about the hurricane too. Something about that night changed him, or maybe it was after we got back to the marina."

Inwardly Geneva smiled, as she listened to Eleanore talk, because she thought she was getting close to figuring out what was going on. It was coming together. Dorinda was targeting Eleanore because she didn't want Eleanore interfering with Darryl. She saw Dorinda go on the boat, didn't she? Maybe Casey, the marine patrol officer, had become the man who Eleanore was turning to for comfort, and Eleanore didn't want to admit that he was her new love interest. Casey was the man who Eleanore was talking about now. Yet, something was not making sense. Geneva thought she might be making progress, and yet something was wrong because Eleanore looked so sad. All Geneva needed was to hear Eleonore say it. Darryl was who she loved and had been her boyfriend, but now Casey was becoming her love interest.

Eleanore stopped talking, and her face turned red and somber. The memory of Earl had darkened her mood. She remembered the night at the bar called *Stumpy's* back in Pine Mountain. She had been decisive in telling Earl that he could go to Panama City Beach, buy a boat, and become a charter boat captain without her. She remembered her resolution to be always thankful after Casey had safely brought her back to the marina. Now she felt weaker than she had ever before felt in her life.

"What is it, honey?" Geneva asked.

Eleanore's thoughts rebounded back into the present moment.

"Geneva, I'm pregnant with Darryl's baby," she whispered the words in her soft, southern voice. Water welled up into her clear brown eyes, and a line of tears rolled down both of her cheeks.

Geneva's big brown eyes opened wide. She sucked in a deep breath and swallowed hard. Trying to suppress her emotions after Eleanore's shocking announcement felt impossible. The news was not what she was expecting, and putting her further away from figuring out the Dorinda, Darryl and Eleanore triangle.

"Uh, huh," Geneva managed to say, as if Eleanore had told her some tidbit of everyday casual conversation, like the weather. Geneva felt her nerves tingling on her skin.

Eleanore began talking faster, blinking hard to try and stop the tears, shaking her head from side to side while the words kept flowing out of lips moistened by tears.

Geneva gently shook her head up and down in short, quick nods, to let Eleanore know she was listening to every word. She was thankful that Eleanore kept talking. It allowed Geneva time to absorb the shocking news.

"I'm not afraid of having this baby," Eleanore stated matter-of-factly. "I'm more afraid of my feelings for Darryl. I can trust him, I know. What I don't know is whether he is a good fit, the right personality for me. Could I spend the rest of my life raising a child with a man who is such a free spirit? He's not overly ambitious nor very serious unless you want to hear him play his saxophone. He's happy doing only the minimum to survive."

Geneva angled her shoulders and turned her head away from Eleanore. She saw Sue sitting at another table with other kitchen staff. She could see Sue's big smile and eyes glued on her and Eleanore from across the room.

"Honey," Geneva said, turning back to face Eleanore, "you need someone to talk to about this. You can trust me. Right now, it's time for us to get back to work. I've got to get into the kitchen, but I'm willing to meet you after work tonight and let you talk more about it."

"Please don't tell anyone," Eleanore pleaded.

"That's not me to do something like that, spread a rumor, you know. How about we sit outside on Big Joe's bench tonight after work and talk for a bit?" Geneva asked.

Eleanore nodded her head slightly, agreeing with Geneva, and said, "That's probably not a bad idea. Are you sure? You are usually finished with your work and leave before we do. I've got my station to clean up after my last table. That will mean you may have to wait thirty minutes, or more, after you're finished for the night."

"That's okay, honey," Geneva answered. "If I can sit and rest my tired legs, I'm glad to wait. It's not that hot outside in the evening this time of year, and the breezes on the water will blow away some of my worries, too. We got to find an answer to that big question in your life."

The rest of the night, Geneva caught herself being short-tempered with Sue, who kept nudging Geneva in the side of her rib cage with her elbow.

"I can't talk about it tonight, Sue," Geneva repeatedly said in a brusque voice. "I've got some things to think about first. You'll get all the updates when I know more. You've got to be patient and understand."

While she worked, Geneva kept thinking about the problems that she was facing. She knew she had to force herself to stay calm, but it was difficult.

"As if worrying about my brother being accused of murder and in jail, waiting for a trial, isn't enough. And I have to figure a way to tell my poor mother back in Altoona that everything will work out fine. First, I need the courage to call her. By some strange chance, I've let myself get involved in Eleanore's life. She is such a sweet young lady who may have more significant problems than mine. She told me she could trust Darryl, but I seriously doubt that after I saw Darryl open the door for Dorinda when she boarded the boat. Whoa, I feel bad for that girl. I hope I can find the right words to say to her later tonight.

"I also wish Sue would stop stabbing me in the ribs, grinning at me like all of this is some kind of joke. The last thing I need to do is to lose my temper with Sue. I hate it when she pouts. I need her working with me."

CHAPTER 13
KINGS AND KITTENS

On Panama City Beach, the scarred and wounded landscape of the neighborhood close to the marina was masterfully rebounding from hurricane Louise. The first spring season brought new growth on the few old oak trees that were left standing. Like palm and crepe myrtles, trunks of any other fibrous trees that could bend with the fierce, hurricane-force winds and survive being uprooted were left standing bare of their old-growth leaves. Still, new shoots of leaves were emerging at the top of their tall trunks. Though all of the tall pine trees were gone, the low-lying ground cover of tropical plants and foliage created a sense of return to normalcy.

However, for the gang of cats, normalcy was returning slower and taking a different look. There was competition for dominance and power. New kittens brought more competition to find places to live and find food. Who would be the cat to control and make the decisions about the coming and going of all the cats? The possibilities at the marina seemed limited. The opportunities in the new neighborhood seemed unlimited.

Oscar split his time between the marina and the new neighborhood across the road from the marina parking lot. Oscar preferred the new setting, but going to the marina was the only way he could spend time with his cousin, Dog Ear. The family bond between them could not be weakened or forgotten.

Like ST, Dog Ear was permanently disfigured. He considered the event that caused his disfigurement as one where he narrowly escaped death. He nearly suffocated when his head got stuck inside a tin can. The consequence of his foolish action was getting his ear ripped off when the can was pulled off his head by a young girl working at the marina gift shop who was a witness to his struggles.

Dog Ear never heard very well after he lost his furry ear. Not being able to hear clearly made him a nervous wreck and caused him to repeat himself. He was always hoping other cats might repeat what they said. This habit caused other cats, especially Fat Cat, to become annoyed and lose patience with him.

Dog Ear spent his days and nights at Fat Cat's condo. Dog Ear followed and listened to everything Fat Cat said. He felt immense gratitude to Fat Cat for getting him through the hurricane. As much as he hated being in the stinky dumpster all night, getting wet, and listening to ST complain, he knew that was the only place he could have survived. His cousin Oscar had disappeared, and he had no one to turn to for guidance. Thus, his gratitude to Fat Cat was paid in unconditional loyalty.

At first, ST wanted nothing to do with the new neighborhood. Most of the big oak trees were gone. The remaining ones, stripped of leaves, were a reminder of the time he spent isolating himself in those woods with the squirrels' nests, waiting for his torn lip and his pride to heal. Gradually curiosity about the new neighborhood took hold of ST. Oscar visited Dog Ear often, bragging about the food and felines. The changes in the woods and the wisdom ST learned from his own experience, convinced ST that checking the new neighborhood out couldn't hurt him. When ST visited the first time, he was pleasantly surprised by the opportunities to play, eat and socialize.

Oscar liked to brag that he was the one who had the most dangerous and frightening experience of survival. Even though he didn't suffer any bodily injury except for a bloodied nose that healed and left no scars, most cats would agree that his story topped the list.

Bragging about surviving the road trip under the hood of Earl's truck to Pine Log Forest State Park was his favorite thing to do.

"I just thought I was going to take a little nap out of the sun under the hood of that charter boat captain's truck. The next thing I know, he's cranked up the engine and is driving away, leaving the marina. I wrapped my body around a plastic box and clung tightly to the hoses connected to it, digging deeper with my claws as the wheels bounced the body of the truck from side to side. It wasn't easy to ignore the roar of the engine or the loud whirring of the wheels on the road below," Oscar repeated the story to kittens and cats in the new neighborhood.

"It was no time for me to be a fraidy cat, I can tell you that! The first time the truck stopped at a gas station, I couldn't decide if I should get off or stay inside. After all, I thought that the man might be going back to the marina, and I didn't want to be left at a gas station. When the truck finally came to a stop in the gravel parking lot near some trees, I was relieved and grateful." At this point in the story, Oscar would stop to lick his forepaws a few times before resuming the narrative. He wanted to be sure he had the attention of all the female felines.

"As soon as the truck stopped the second time, I thought it was time for me to jump out from underneath the truck's hood and make a getaway. I didn't know where I was, but I knew that I didn't want to ride inside the truck anymore! I bolted to the first bush, which was a good thing because I could have been run over by another truck that pulled into the parking lot right next to the charter boat captain's truck. The other truck, with two men in it, stopped briefly and left in a hurry. I never saw the boat captain get out of his truck. A man from the other truck threw an object into the bush where I ran, and it almost hit me.

"At first, it wasn't so bad being in the woods. I watched, from a distance, all of the cars speeding on the highway. I knew it was dangerous to be out in the open, near the road. Finally, it got dark, and that's when the winds got really bad, blowing rain and sand against me, burning my eyes. I burrowed my body beneath a palmetto bush, which I soon realized was a big mistake because the needles on the tips of the leaves of the bush kept stabbing me in the nose!"

At this point in the story, Oscar would stop his narrative to walk through the crowd of listeners, holding his tail straight up, high in the air, looking each one in the eye to see if they were impressed. If he sensed he'd lost anyone's attention, he spoke in a bolder voice, "And that's not all. Wait until you hear about the boat ride on the rolling seas with two other cats from the marina!"

The mention of other cats being involved in the adventure always seemed to draw the listeners back into his story. If it happened to other cats besides Oscar, they would think, it could also happen to them. After all, it was a lesson to learn, and the adult cats believed it was a good reason not to venture over to the marina.

Oscar told the story about the strange young woman finding him burrowed in the bushes. She held him on her lap, holding on to him tight, while they rode on a four-wheeler on a dirt path, darting around trees. When the four-wheeler reached the edge of the woods, they were at the water's edge. She dropped him on the floor inside the cabin of the charter boat named *The Lucky Two*, where he joined two other cats, who he knew were members of the gang at the marina.

"We, me and the other two cats, tried to comfort each other, but it seemed impossible. We were sliding around on the floor each time the waves rolled beneath the boat and rocked it," Oscar said. "I never felt so brave since that day, and I was so grateful when we got back to Captain Anderson's Marina. I have to admit, though, that whenever I go visit my cousin Dog Ear at the marina, and see *The Lucky Two,* I never want to go near that boat again." Oscar didn't disclose one part of the story. He was paralyzed with fear when he had to jump off the boat across the debris-filled water and onto the sidewalk.

Oscar never ceased to be amazed that he survived the day, and night, of hurricane Louise. After coming too close to ending all of his nine lives in one single day, he realized he wanted to forever live his life to the fullest.

The reputation he earned for being a courageous cat fueled his fun. There were multiple opportunities for him to socialize with female cats and become a father to their kittens. Soon he earned another reputation. The adult cats in the new neighborhood called him Play Boy.

Oscar's favorite female cat in the new neighborhood was Fresca. Still, he found himself becoming keenly interested in a cat named Purr Baby. Oscar noticed that the other cats seemed annoyed by Purr Baby and avoided her, but Oscar didn't know why. Oscar saw her as a beautiful cat, always energetic, happy, and purring.

He'd seen Purr Baby leave the neighborhood and venture over to the marina a time or two, but never followed her there. Oscar was unaware that Purr Baby had a love crush on DC.

Purr Baby's parents, Fernando and Baby Cakes were born and raised in the neighborhood. They were owned by separate families, but since they were outdoor, roaming cats, they created a breed of kittens with traits of Bengal and Calico. The colorations of the kittens varied. Some sported soft, tan fur on their bellies dotted with brown spots, and coarse fur of dark stripes covered their back. Other kittens had blended patches of orange and black fur all over their body. All the kittens, adopted by various families in the neighborhood, had large paws to carry their husky bodies. Fernando and Baby Cakes were proud of their offspring. They regularly marched them from home to home, searching for playmates and attention.

One day, after noticing his beautiful daughter Purr Baby running across the yard that borders the road to the marina, Fernando decided it was time to give advice. "The rumor is that there's a mongrel cat named Fat Cat over at the marina who hates any mixed breed cats," Fernando said.

"I bet I know who spread the rumor," Purr Baby retorted. "It's Oscar, who thinks he is tougher than the rest of us. Everyone calls him by the nickname Play Boy."

"I think it's best that you stay away from that marina," Fernando said, ignoring Purr Baby's assessment of Oscar. "If you'd listen to Oscar's story, bad things can happen to cats at the marina. There's plenty of fun here in our neighborhood. Oscar has contributed to bringing more kittens to the neighborhood for you to play with, and the squirrels are returning to the neighborhood, too. Squirrel kittens will give you plenty to do, chasing them around the yards. It's a playground of fun here. You'll find nothing but trouble at the marina. The gang of cats at the marina have a reputation for being reckless and tough."

"I don't care much for Oscar, daddy," Purr Baby replied. "Oscar already has enough girlfriends. There's a sweet young cat at the marina that everyone calls DC. I like him a lot. His parents are King and Princess."

"DC, hmmmm," Fernando said. "What's that stand for, I wonder?"

Fernando knew about DC's parents, King and Princess. DC had many siblings already roaming around the new neighborhood.

"The humans think he's a dumb cat," she answered. "Oscar probably thinks he is dumb, too, but I don't. DC is curious, playful, and he likes me."

"Like I said, those are tough cats at the marina," Fernando said, becoming concerned when he heard the name of the cat as his daughter's choice for a companion.

"Maybe there's a wise, adult cat here in the neighborhood, a cat psychic, who could explain to us why DC has the name," Purr Baby insisted. "There's got to be a reason for his behavior. It can't be all his fault."

"If the cat isn't crazy, then DC could also stand for demon cat. He's got a bunch of siblings here, in our neighborhood, who won't have anything to do with him," Fernando argued.

"I think DC wants to stay close to his mom and dad. DC has parents with good names to give him the love he needs. His siblings are here for only one reason. They get to eat food without even putting any effort into finding it," Purr Baby argued back. "DC knows how to be a real survivor, like his mother and father. He's not a dumb cat! He's not a demon cat! He may act a little crazy because he is full of energy. That's not the same thing as being dumb or a demon. One day, maybe, he could become the leader of the gang of cats at the marina. His mother's name is Princess, and his father's name is King. DC could become a king, too."

With those last words, Purr Baby darted away from her father and sped across a yard, stopping briefly at the road to turn her head to look for cars. She was on her way to the marina despite what her father said.

Fernando sat down on his haunches. His two front paws, locked straight and stiff, were tucked close to his belly. He swatted his tail back and forth on the ground and grumbled while he watched Purr Baby run, "Where did she come up with the idea to find a pet psychic? Whoever heard of such a thing? What's going on with this new generation of cats? Talking to that girl is like talking to the dirt I'm sitting on. She won't listen to a word I say."

In confusion, Fernando could only stare ahead until he lost sight of Purr Baby. Mentally exhausted, he laid down, stretching his front paws straight out in front of his body and his rear paws straight back. He rested his head on top of his front paws. He closed his eyes and tried to imagine ways he could keep the marina cats out of his neighborhood.

CHAPTER 14
COMPLICATED CONVERSATION

"I had a short chat with Eleanore just a few minutes ago out in the dining room," Geneva mumbled to Big Joe, who was shuffling his shoes through the prep areas of the kitchen on his way to check the grills and ovens. Big Joe stopped dead in his tracks, raised his bushy eyebrows, and looked at Geneva with a surprised look on his face.

With no time to waste to get ready for a busy night ahead in the kitchen, Geneva was quick to the point. "Sue mentioned to me you wanted her to find out if Darryl is Eleanore's boyfriend."

Big Joe moved his bulky body closer to Geneva. "Yeah, that's right," he said, lowering his voice. "I'm curious because I'm trying to get down to the bottom of something going on between the kitchen crew and the dining room crew." Big Joe stood over Geneva's shoulder and moved his face closer to hers. He spoke in a whisper. "How's it you're doing the talking with Eleanore? Sue's usually the one to find out, and spread, the gossip around here."

"Sue just happened to mention to me your interest in knowing whether there is a relationship going on between Eleanore and Darryl. I suggested to Sue that it might be better for me to find out that information from Eleanore. I told Sue that Eleanore seems to be a private kind of person, and she might trust me. When I saw Eleanore sitting alone in the dining room during the break before the shift started, I asked if I could join her at the table. We had a brief conversation, but it wasn't enough time to go over all the details. Eleanore told me that she needs to do more talking about Darryl, so I invited her to join me after work, on your bench, if that's all right with you."

"Of course," he replied, trying to act nonchalant. "Sit out there as long as you like, but be careful. Don't be out there too late. You never know what kind of trouble might be lurking out there in the parking lot. It could be something more dangerous than those cats."

Geneva detected eager anticipation in Big Joe's voice and appreciated his thoughtfulness for her safety. Looking directly into Big Joe's eyes, she nodded. "Yes Sir, I know. We'll sit as long as it takes to get to the bottom of the story, and we'll keep our eyes out for two-legged and other four-legged creatures."

Big Joe looked back at Geneva with inquiring eyes. Something in her face reflected a hint of trouble, but he would wait for the complete story later.

"Let me get on to work. Maybe if you can get here a little earlier tomorrow, you can fill me in with details in my office," Big Joe smiled at Geneva. "I really like you, Sista!" he said before turning away to leave.

Geneva waited for Eleanore after the dinner shift, as she promised she would. Sitting in solitude with her eyes closed, she soaked up the cool breezes blowing against her skin.

"This feels so good, being outside. I think it's calming me down a bit," she thought. "I needed a break from worrying about Charles. If I went directly back to the apartment after work, that's all I'd be doing."

Geneva stared at the clear dark November sky filled with stars, relaxing in the quiet time, until Eleanore arrived.

At first, it felt odd to be sitting side-by-side with Eleanore on the bench that Big Joe usually occupied. The two women were not close friends, but the setting felt very intimate.

To ease the awkwardness, Eleanore began the conversation. "Like I said earlier at the table, in the dining room, I don't believe doing the minimum to survive is enough."

"I believe that doing the minimum to survive is one of the worst qualities for anyone to have," Geneva interjected. "That's been the problem for too many of the people in my family. My father's name is Maximilian. He told us he was given that grandiose name by his own father so he would become, one day, a great success. My father turned into a complete failure. He became a drunk before I was a teenager. He couldn't handle the pressure of providing for a family. He gave up when he thought he had to work too many hours to get ahead in life. He didn't like to read either. If he had read a little more history, he would have found out that there was an emperor in Austria in the sixteenth century named Maximilian. Austria is in Europe. The emperor's family eventually fell into hard times too. There was murder, and bad marriages, and crazy sisters and brothers. Whoa, they had it bad because the common people, who were supposed to be loyal and pay taxes, were not happy with the extravagances of the royalty. They rebelled and overthrew the family. Maximilian, the emperor, had a huge set of problems taking care of his family. He had to marry some of his children off to royalty in other countries. Then a couple hundred years later, one of those families named one of their children Maximilian. He was an archduke, got sent to Mexico, and ended up getting murdered. It happened right after our civil war in the United States ended. Regular people distrust royalty is all I can think. But I think ordinary people, like us, have the opportunity to live a much happier life. I don't believe that the name Maximilian comes with bad luck. I think my father was just as much lazy as he was bitter about life in general. That's why he drank.

"Here we are, living in the only country in the world, I believe, where you can get ahead if you work hard, and my father chose to drink and do as little as possible. He didn't think he had an opportunity to advance himself. He didn't think taking care of his family would be one of the greatest jobs a person can do."

Eleanore was befuddled and taken aback by the historical details Geneva revealed about her father's name. For a few minutes, Eleanore felt like she was listening to Darryl, who also loved to talk about history.

"I know what you're saying," Eleanore said, looking at Geneva with a blank face because she didn't quite understand the entire connection between the emperor Maximilian, Geneva's father, and Darryl.

Eleanore didn't like the idea of putting down Darryl so completely. "Darryl actually does have good qualities too. I know for a fact that he doesn't like to drink. He told me about all the drunks he had to deal with in the bars when he played in his band, *The Electrons*. Anyway, I think Darryl's best quality is he's always happy about life."

"Isn't that the most important thing?" Geneva asked. "Lots of people have a big family and plenty of money, and they're still miserable. I don't know if you have family, or he has family, but I suspect neither of you has much money. So, let's talk about the important things. Does anything ever make him angry?"

"I can't recall anything that has made him angry, except for maybe the first day we met," Eleanore replied. "When Casey was leaving the marina with *The Lucky Two,* and me on board, Darryl acted very serious, almost angry. He hollered at Casey about making sure that nothing happened to me."

"So, what is it that makes him happy?" Geneva asked, ignoring the incident Eleanore just described.

"He likes fishing and gazing at the stars," Eleanore answered without hesitation, then added, "and playing his saxophone, of course."

"Does he gaze into your eyes?" Geneva asked.

"Gaze? What do you mean?" Eleanore asked, confused by the question.

"I suppose it's like when you're talking, and you look over at him, he can't stop staring at you, directly into your eyes," Geneva stated flatly.

"Not as much as the first day I met him. At least I don't notice it as much anymore." Eleanore's voice drifted off. The breezes of the lagoon carried other sounds to Geneva's ears. Geneva waited, knowing that Eleanore would eventually pick up where she left off.

Soon Eleanore spoke again. "I think I began to feel our differences, kind of like what happened with my first boyfriend."

"How so?" Geneva asked, wondering if Eleanore had unresolved feelings about her past boyfriend.

Eleanore's mention of her deceased boyfriend piqued Geneva's interest. She felt like she was going in the right direction if she found out more about Earl Keith, the man who had been murdered. What was it about Darryl that reminded her of Earl Keith?

Geneva would also be interested in learning more details about the murdered boat captain. The rumors were still floating around the marina about the man put in prison for the murder. There were many questions in everyone's mind about the murder.

"The first clue was when Darryl told me he didn't want to change the name of *The Lucky Two* to what I wanted to name the boat. When I survived the night on the boat through the hurricane, I declared on my safe arrival back at the marina that I wanted to rename the boat *Two Lucky*. Once Darryl started living on *The Lucky Two,* he dreams up a new name. The boat he owned before the hurricane was called *The Star Chaser.* He told me he believes in celestial guidance and announced that once he becomes the legitimate owner of *The Lucky Two,* he would like to register the boat in a new name. It's taken a year, but he's collected the insurance money from *The Star Chaser.* He's waiting for the probate court back in Pine Mountain to finish changing the name on the title work on *The Lucky Two.* It has to be changed out of Earl's name. Guess what Darryl wants to name the boat?"

Eleanore sucked in a deep breath through her nose, briefly stopping the flow of her words. Her mouth was working faster than her brain. She inhaled deeply several more times to catch her breath, as if she'd just finished carrying a big tray of plates across the dining room floor. She waited for Geneva to answer her question.

Geneva waited for thirty seconds and, in exasperation, finally said, "I have no idea. "Plainly, dear, I don't. Do you really want me to guess?"

Ignoring Geneva's question, Eleanore said, "*Faithful Fisher Man.* Faithful is one word, but not fisherman. He distinctly told me it was two words – one for fisher and one for man."

Geneva parted her luscious lips, which quickly spread into a huge cheek-to-cheek grin, showing her white teeth across her brown, shiny face. Her smile turned into laughter. When she stopped laughing, she said, "My word, that is a slightly odd name, but I do like it."

Eleanore's eyes glistened with a hint of moisture. She squinted at Geneva and said, "This is the first sign of his selfishness. He's putting his own desires and self-interest in front of mine. I am not sure he is capable of putting the needs of me, or a child, before his own." She spoke the words *a child* with added emphasis.

Geneva quickly became serious again. Different thoughts, like flashes of lightning, charged her mind.

"Yeah, that man might be selfish after all," Geneva thought to herself. "He's allowing a woman named Dorinda to see him on the boat that Eleanore wanted to rename *Two Lucky*. Little does this poor girl Eleanore know that he's been seeing Dorinda. This is what all the acrimony is about. Dorinda's been visiting Darryl on a boat named *The Lucky Two*, probably thinking she's going to be too lucky with him. It puts things in a whole new perspective. Maybe that's why he didn't want to go along with the idea of renaming the boat *Two Lucky*. Maybe he's having a guilt complex knowing all along he's been cheating on Eleanore."

Geneva dug deep for self-control and said to Eleanore in a respectful tone of voice, "Maybe I need to take some time to think about this situation. For now, this is the only advice I can give you. Don't hurt him if you think he really loves you. Give him a chance. And, just remember this. Everyone is important. No baby, no one, is illegitimate."

Geneva said this to Eleanore, buying time and not wanting to upset her. She was going to need someone else's guidance about what to tell Eleanore. Someone like Big Joe.

"Here's the last of what I want to say tonight," Eleanore said. "I don't want to be just a pretty woman for a lonely man. I know a man needs a woman, but a woman needs a man she trusts. A man who will always make decisions that are in the best interest of the relationship."

Geneva's nostrils flared, and her chest heaved. She formed a circle with her plump lips and blew the air out of her lungs like she was blowing up a balloon. She sat silent, gazing out over the lagoon. She didn't know what else to say after hearing Eleanore's final words. Geneva only knew that Darryl was not the lonely man Eleanore thought he was. Geneva doubted Eleanore could trust Darryl right now.

The two women sat on the bench for another five minutes, listening to the quiet of the night and breathing in the salty air.

"Geneva," Eleanore spoke softly, "you said something earlier tonight about your father. I suspect you have worries yourself. We've only been talking about my problems. Do you have anything you want to tell me?"

"Eleanore, I told you a short version of my family, but my problems go deeper than that. My mother would become so desperate with her situation. She'd occasionally bring out a deck of Tarot cards and start reading them. She believed that the future in those cards would bring her some relief. She wanted so badly for her situation, and the future for her children, to be better. Those cards didn't help us out one bit. Yet, she never gave up reading and hoping."

"I think my mother owned a deck of Tarot cards too," Eleanore said to Geneva.

"Is that right?" Geneva asked, slightly intrigued, although she wasn't really asking a question. "Somehow, I am not surprised, even though I don't know anything about your mother."

"You said your mother had children, so you're not an only child?" Eleanore innocently asked.

"No, dear. I'm not. I have a younger brother named Charles," Geneva answered solemnly. "I had to watch after him a lot when we were growing up. I can't really talk about him much right now. They're things that have happened that are not good. He's was always in some kind of small trouble all his life. It had to do with the kids in the neighborhood. I used to fix it by telling him to walk away from the kids who were giving him a hard time. Now, he's gotten himself into big trouble. I'm learning that there's not much I can do to get him out of trouble this time."

"I'm so sorry to hear that, Geneva," Eleanore said.

"It's probably time for us to pack up our troubles, go home and sleep on them. We can think about them tomorrow," Geneva said.

Both women walked together to the parking lot where their cars were waiting.

Eleanore opened up her heart to Geneva when they sat together on Big Joe's bench outside the restaurant kitchen after closing. She didn't know how long they talked, but her throat was parched from talking so much.

After arriving at Casey's house, Eleanore was too tired to do anything but flop down on the bed. She slept more soundly than she had slept in days since discovering she was pregnant. It was like a burden had been removed, even though she knew it wasn't.

"Geneva didn't give me any firm answers or tell me what to decide. Geneva only sympathized with me and asked all the questions I need to answer for myself," Eleanore thought before falling asleep.

"What can I do to help this poor, young pregnant girl," Geneva worried as she drove back to her apartment. "She's got to make a decision about a baby, and whether she wants to stay with the baby's father. I did encourage her to give Darryl a chance. But I'm wondering if he isn't the right man for her. I know many women stay with a man for the wrong reasons. Just because it's their child doesn't make it a perfect match made in heaven. Once there are problems with the relationship, the children suffer. And boy, don't I know all about that. My parents are a perfect example!"

Geneva arrived home with more than one more worry on her mind.

"Where do I start?" Geneva asked herself, slumping down onto the thread-worn sofa in her one-room efficiency apartment. She stared at the soft glow of the yellow light from the floor lamp.

"Ever since that downtown Halloween party, all I can think about is my brother, Charles. I've not been able to tell anyone at work about what's happened to him. I've never talked to anyone at Smith's about my family, not even Sue. What's worse is I can't pick up the telephone and call my mother to tell her. She'll have a heart attack from worrying if she knows that Charles is in prison for the murder of a woman.

"It's taking every bit of discipline I've got to not tell Big Joe about my brother. I want to ask someone for some advice, but I don't want my name connected to a murder that's been in the news all over town the last few weeks. It could ruin my reputation.

"I haven't been in Panama City even a year yet. Things were going well. Charles and I both had jobs, and we were paying our bills. I can't go back to Pennsylvania and leave Charles down here. There's nothing back in Altoona for me, except mom."

Tears formed in Geneva's tired eyes.

"Now, this situation with Eleanore is making me feel worse. How, what, am I going to tell Big Joe? He'll be asking me for an explanation after meeting with Eleanore after work tonight. I can't be the one to tell him about Eleanore's predicament.

"As God is my witness, I've done my best. I'm just going to have to have a talk with God before I go to sleep tonight. Lord knows I need some rest!"

CHAPTER 15
DEMON CAT AT THE HALLOWEEN PARTY

At the tender age of six, Charles became known as DC by the children in his Altoona neighborhood. Someone came up with the idea because Charles always wore ragged, torn clothes. From the perspective of young eyes, tattered clothes were seen as unclean. It didn't take long before all the children called him DC. Knowing the meaning of the nickname, the young boy from a poor family hated the nickname, which stood for Dirty Charles.

Because they made fun of him, Charles made a pastime of surprising the kids on the playground by sneaking upon them, and scaring them when they were least expecting it. Sometimes he would extend his leg to trip an unsuspecting person who happened to walk past him. Children considered Charles' behavior worse than annoying. Children liked him less for his antics that occasionally caused minor harm. Few children were willing to play with him.

He continued to refine his childish habits when he became a teenager and into his adult life. It was his way to get attention when he was a child, but the adults liked it less. People called Charles DC for another reason. People considered him to be acting like a demon.

For most of his life, Charles was avoided or totally ignored. The consequence of his dirty deeds was loneliness, which compounded into laziness by staying at home most of the time.

He arrived in Panama City with his sister after the hurricane and quickly found a job in a construction yard. He told his co-workers in Panama City that instead of Charles, they should call him DC because that's what people called him back home in Altoona. He didn't tell them DC stood for dirty Charles or demon Charles.

"I used to run around with a lot of cool cats back home, in my hometown up north in Pennsylvania," he bragged to his co-workers. "I was known as the demon cat amongst the gang of cool cats I hung around. I had a reputation of taking on anyone if they tried to mess with me. No one messed with me."

The persona of a demon cat felt much more masculine, and a shield of protection from the strangers he did not know. The new men didn't know about his actual reputation back in Altoona. For the first time in his life, Charles felt he might earn a little bit of respect, instead of scorn.

Even though Charles was labeled as the gofer, it didn't take many days before the other men began to call on Charles by the nickname DC. The impression Charles made on his co-workers was generally that of a braggart possessing a snarky attitude. In their minds, those qualities translate into an untrustworthy type of person. The nickname he was called in Altoona became his nickname in Panama City, producing the same results. Rather than welcoming him into a circle of camaraderie, Charles realized he was being avoided by people again.

Charles didn't know, wasn't taught, many social skills by his mother or father. Geneva was his sister, not his parent, and he didn't consider her the boss. "*You are not the boss of me,*" whenever Geneva was telling him what to do or what not to do. Although he was happier than he could ever recall in his life, because he was working and making money, he didn't know what he should do to make amends with his co-workers. He wanted to ask for his Sista's guidance, but was wary of how she might react. Charles decided to settle in his job, taking the bad days with the good, and not complain.

Although she came home later, after the long drive from the beach, his sister seemed comfortable in her job working nights at the restaurant at Captain Anderson's Marina.

By late March, Charles and his Sista were settled into their new living arrangements. They'd left behind the worries of late winter snow in Altoona and a father coming home drunk. They both had regular employment, an apartment they could afford, and shared the hope for the opportunity to create a new future toward a better life in Panama City.

On the last night of Charles' freedom in Panama City, he attended a community Halloween party.

By the end of October, almost exactly one year after the hurricane, the people in Panama City were eager to celebrate their hard-working recovery efforts, and eager to enjoy a good time. A Halloween party, arranged by the city leaders, was held outside at the Panama City downtown marina. Live bands playing a variety of music, candy for children, food booths, and thousands of people dressed in costumes drew families, young and older people alike, excited about the party.

During the year after the hurricane, Charles became slightly better acquainted with a few of his co-workers. When he heard about the party, he asked a few men if they were going, and would they like to go together with him. Not one was interested in wearing a costume or joining Charles.

Halloween night, when reality fades into fantasy, people dress like a character to pretend to be someone they want to be, or only to disguise who they really are. Everyone is playing a game of deception. Murder is not generally on the mind of the fun-seekers; however, murder can be on the mind of an evil person who thinks they can get away with a crime. It might be easier to get away with murder by taking the opportunity to wear a costume and hide behind a mask.

Charles went to the community Halloween party, alone, as Count Dracula from Pennsylvania. He wore a tattered, loosely-fitting, black suit he picked up at the second-hand clothing store, a black mask covering his eyes, and a pair of removable, plastic Dracula fangs covered with fake blood.

A girl dressed in black, fishnet-style tights, a lacy black gown, black-feathered wings hooked on her arms, and a black-feathered hat soon caught Charles's attention. She wore no mask, but heavy black make-up covered her eyes.

"She sort of seems like maybe she's my type," Charles thought, mustering up the courage to take a chance to meet a girl and maybe be able to dance with her.

Charles involuntarily assumed the personality he had tried to avoid. He was the young teenage boy known as DC with grandiose thoughts of achieving attention through mischievous acts. He was planning to be the man who would be with the girl wearing the black wings and black feathered hat. He plastered a sly, smirky smile on his face and hurried through the crowd, toward the girl, ready to catch her off guard with a tricky line.

"Who are you supposed to be in that costume?" he asked when he walked up to her and intentionally bumped his shoulder against her body. He desperately wanted to meet someone different. Since arriving in Panama City, he'd only interacted with the people he worked with at his job and his Sista.

"I'm a fallen angel," she answered. "Man, you look spooky," she nervously said, putting one hand on her cheek as if she had lost her own mask.

"Maybe I should have asked you your name instead," he said, trying to be friendly and pushing his body closer against hers.

"No sir, I don't tell my name to anyone I don't know," she replied in an icy tone.

"Would you like to dance?" Charles asked. Being used to rejection, he became even more encouraged by the girl's standoffish attitude and nudged his body a little closer.

Without saying another word, the fallen angel drew up her hands and shoved Charles hard, away from her. She turned her back to Charles and swiftly walked away into the large crowd of people. Charles stumbled backward, then regained his balance. Angered by the girl's actions, he yelled at her, "Hey girl! Why'd you do that?"

His voice didn't fall on deaf ears. The girl, and others, heard Charles yelling at her.

The following day the fallen angel was found by a woman walking her dog along the St. Andrew marina shoreline. The fallen angel was lying in the sand, face-up, with her black feathered hat pulled down over her face. Her costume was left undisturbed, and her neck was covered in dried blood.

Eve at Peace by Yvette Doolittle Herr

She had been brutally murdered. A deep knife wound, from one ear to the other, punctured her throat.

Later that day, the television news posted a police file photo of the woman and asked for the public's help solving the crime. Several attendees at the Halloween party reported to the police that a man dressed in a Dracula costume was seen talking to the girl. Charles's co-workers identified Charles as the Dracula at the Halloween party. He was known as the Demon Cat in their work yard, and just the type of person who could have done such a thing.

In Charles' mind, the heinous crime was either a targeted tragedy, or a random act of violence, of which he had no part. He had no one to speak on his behalf for an alibi, not even his Sista.

Charles was booked into jail. His defense was weak. With no tangible evidence, and only the testimony of other people who knew Charles, a quick jury trial convicted him of murder. He was transported to the prison in Greenhead.

When Charles arrived in prison, the last thing he wanted to do was attract attention from the other prisoners. The men looked at him like they could give him a lot of grief if he so much as looked at them cross-eyed. He didn't want any more trouble. For the first time in his life, he didn't have the help of his Sista.

After a few weeks of keeping a low profile and staying under the radar with the other prisoners, Charles singled out one particular inmate as someone he might have a conversation with. The man didn't strike Charles as a loner, avoiding others, but he never spoke when he interacted with other prisoners. The man often carried around a clipboard with a pad of paper. Charles decided to sit next to him at mealtime when the opportunity presented itself.

"Are you writing a story or writing letters to people on that pad of paper?" Charles asked him one morning in the cafeteria after sliding next to him at the breakfast table.

Ricky nodded his head no. He quickly scribbled on the yellow pad, writing the words, *Sorry, I can't talk.*

"Man, I had no idea. Why can't you talk? You can hear me, right?" Charles asked.

Ricky nodded his head to answer yes and then opened his mouth wide to reveal what was left of his deformed tongue.

Repulsed by the sight of a small piece of flesh dangling inside a mouth of crooked and missing teeth, Charles' eyes bugged out of the sockets. He quickly squeezed them shut.

Charles sucked in a quick deep breath through his nose and opened his eyes again after counting to ten. Avoiding direct eye contact at first, he started a one-sided conversation with Ricky.

"I always thought that I was the captain of my own ship. I could navigate myself through any situation. My mom said to stay out of trouble and avoid bars. That's the advice she gave me, and I believe she was right. I admit I've been a pain to some people, true, but I've never really tried to hurt anyone. I'm not the type of person who has malicious intentions.

"I got set up by somebody. I know it," Charles told Ricky, letting his face fall into the palms of his hands for a moment before holding his head up high again. "I got led down the wrong path going to that Halloween party. I thought it would be fun. I wonder if it could have been the color of my skin that got me in trouble."

Charles redirected his eyes back to Ricky's face. The influence of his father Maximillian's bitterness was settling inside his soul, and he wanted it gone. Looking at Ricky made Charles think of a different place and time.

Ricky, after listening to Charles' story, struggled with his own feelings. He felt sorry for Charles. Ricky understood how it felt to be wrongly accused, and blamed for committing a murder.

"Something about your eyes, the way you look at me, tells me you were not the one to be blamed for the crime that put you in this prison. Is that how you got in here too?" Charles asked. "Did someone set you up to go somewhere you shouldn't go? Someone led you down the wrong path?"

Eve at Peace by Yvette Doolittle Herr

Ricky squinted at Charles with a serious intensity that momentarily surprised Charles. Then Ricky gently nodded his head yes.

"Well, then. How come you act like you're so happy in this place?" Charles asked.

Ricky shrugged his shoulders, tilted his head to the left side, raised his eyebrows, and pressed his lips to form a smile. He waited for Charles to say something.

A few minutes of silence passed.

Ricky tapped Charles on the shoulder. Then Ricky grabbed his own chin with the thumb and forefinger of his right hand and pulled his eyebrows close together, as if to show he was in deep thought. Suddenly Ricky was loudly clapped his hands together. When he stopped clapping, he pointed one finger up toward the ceiling.

"Man, you are one frustrating dude," Charles groaned.

Charles let his head drop downward, shook it back and forth in disbelief, and sighed. "I have no idea what to think of you."

That night, in his cell, Ricky wrote down words that he thought might bring comfort to Charles. It took him nearly an hour to think through exactly what to write down, but he had all the time he needed before lights went out. He wanted to find a way to give Charles, the new inmate, a path to finding comfort.

Ricky thought, "I believe this new man, Charles. He found himself in the same situation as me. He was in the wrong place at the wrong time. I'm going to lead him to the book that will bring him comfort. It's been my comfort ever since I got here a year ago."

The next day Ricky handed the note, with the words he wrote, to Charles.

I understand how you are feeling. I ended up in a situation where, I now know, I allowed myself to be put in the wrong place at the wrong time. It was by my best friend, Vince. He was my friend since childhood. I couldn't go against him, because he protected me from the other kids who liked to bully me on the playground. Those were the kids who wanted to call me poor white trash. Vince had a terrible temper. I never tried to make him mad at me, so I went along with everything he said, even though I knew he was sometimes wrong.

Before I got in prison, I thought I was going to die in a hurricane. I prayed to God if he saved me, I would never forget Him. I lived. I'm thankful, even though life isn't always a fun experience. I was trying to express a hallelujah when I clapped my hands together. I think I frightened you.

I don't believe the color of your skin is the reason why you are here. Believe me when I say that it's not the color of your skin that I see. That is a heavy burden if you continue to believe it. Don't hold that anger in your heart. Anger is poisonous.

There is always forgiveness. We must give it, as it has been given to us. All we can do – the best we can do -- is love one another. Your burdens can be lifted by reading the bible. I have one.

CHAPTER 16
CASEY'S REBOUND

Positive changes occurred in Casey Howard's life after the hurricane devastated so many other people's lives. Thousands of people who were left homeless in the vicinity of Panama City needed assistance. With their possessions destroyed, and no place to live, many decided to stay with relatives in another state. Those people who lived in Florida as a transplant from another state chose to go back home to get a new job, stay with family, or start over. They never wanted to experience another hurricane in their life.

Casey was amazed that the damage that occurred to his home was minimal, and he felt gratitude for the positive direction that his life was moving. He couldn't remember a time in his adult life being happier than he was now.

Casey's knowledge of the bays, creeks, and bayous learned in boyhood became valued by the Florida Marine Patrol district office. He was reassigned to patrol duties, and he no longer had the job of counting fish that came in on the charter boats. The responsibilities in his new position with the Florida Marine Patrol made him feel worthy and more respected. Instead of getting into trouble for taking *The Lucky Two* out of Captain Anderson's Marina on the day of the hurricane, he was lauded with praise for protecting humans and property. His friend Sharkey, who offered to help him store the boat in his storage facility at Treasure Island Marina, came to Casey's defense when the question was raised about taking the boat out into North Bay during the hurricane.

He took more interest in the upkeep of his home since becoming responsible for Eleanore's comfort and safety while she lived with him.

He found a new respect for the marina cats after observing their resiliency and survival abilities first-hand.

The only thing that had not changed in Casey Howard was the distrust he felt for Darryl. In March, Darryl moved out of the house to stay on *The Lucky Two* and took the boat out occasionally to fish. Casey had a feeling that Darryl and Eleanore were seeing each other after Darryl left his house, but realized it was their business and none of his. Counting the fish Darryl caught was none of his business either.

"I'm getting to know this wonderful woman at work," Eleanore announced to Casey at his house on her first night off since pouring out her heart to Geneva on Big Joe's bench. Geneva was the only person who knew of her dilemma. "We had a long talk after work the other night."

Eleanore, hoping to start up a conversation with the man who always had very few words to say, knew that she needed more than one person's advice before she made a decision. She believed she could trust Casey.

She had experienced some morning sickness in the first few weeks but could hide it from Casey. Casey left for work early in the morning, so he didn't notice her sluggishness, and it was customary for anyone to feel tired when they came home after working a night shift at Smith's. Although Eleanore was beginning to feel better physically, she needed relief from her mental dilemma.

Eleanore needed to make a decision about telling Darryl about her pregnancy. She needed to decide whether she wanted to stay in Panama City or return to Pine Mountain, Georgia. She didn't want to make a foolish decision. The last impulsive decision she made, to leave Pine Mountain, had brought mixed results in her life.

Like Casey, Eleanore was grateful for many things, too. For one, she was happy that she survived the night on *The Lucky Two* through the hurricane. She was very grateful to Casey for letting her stay at his house. And, most of all, she was thankful for the waitress job at Smith's. She never envisioned that a person could make so much money serving food in a restaurant.

On the other hand, her relationship with Darryl, the man who led her to Captain Anderson's Marina and *The Lucky*

Two to find Earl, didn't feel right. Something was missing, and she wasn't sure what it was. So much was at stake in her decision: the future of a child's life.

Eleanore and Casey were sitting in the small living room of Casey's concrete block home, watching a program on the television. It was a weeknight, one of the few nights Eleanore didn't have to go to work at Smith's.

Without taking his eyes off the television to look at her, Casey said, "Is that so? You haven't talked about making any new friends at work before. Is it somebody from around here who's a local, or is it someone who came down to work after the hurricane?"

"She came down here with her brother after the hurricane. She told me that they heard about the many jobs and the need for workers," Eleanore answered.

"Where did they come from?" Casey asked.

"She's from Altoona, Pennsylvania. She worked as a cook in the Elks Club up there."

"That's pretty far away. So, what does her brother do? Is he working at Smith's too?" Casey asked, curious to know a little more about the people who were obviously not of a southern origin.

"No, her brother is not working at Smith's. I got the impression he might be in jail. All she told me was that he got into some trouble. I don't know what kind of work he does. She doesn't want to talk about her brother. Mostly she talked about her father. His name is Maximilian, and he drinks a lot."

"That's not good news. We don't need troublemakers coming down here," Casey cleared his throat and decided to change the subject. "By the way, have you checked on your cat, Princess, lately?" he asked, knowing that might be a more straightforward subject for him and Eleanore to talk about.

"Yes," Eleanore answered in a shaky voice that caused Casey to turn his head to look at her.

"Why the glum face?" he asked with concern. Casey could feel the sadness in her eyes.

A long silence followed Casey's question. He turned his face, but not his attention, back to the television show.

In truth, Eleanore had not fed the cats at the marina in the last few days. For one reason, she didn't feel like Princess was her cat anymore. Princess never came up to her when she approached *The Lucky Two*. It was as if Princess had found a new family, and Eleanore didn't matter anymore.

There was another reason why Eleanore didn't go to the marina to feed the cats. Eleanore wanted to avoid the obvious. If she saw Darryl, she would have to be honest and tell him the news about her pregnancy. But didn't want to let him know until a decision was made about staying or going back to Pine Mountain. No one at Smith's, not even Geneva, knew that she was seriously considering going back to Pine Mountain.

The busy summer season was over, and the slower winter season was fast approaching. Somehow, Eleanore thought, she could pull her life back together in Pine Mountain better than keeping her life together in Panama City. Maybe she could reconnect with her co-workers at the Kountry Kafe. Her old boss, Johnny, would give her a job.

Another idea she had was to move to Atlanta. After all, that had been her dream when Earl was alive. She always wondered what it would be like to live in Atlanta. She only knew she wanted to make the right choice for herself and the baby. She needed to resist the temptation of someone else's emotions getting in the way of her making a good decision for herself.

Eleanore finally broke the silence, causing Casey to turn his head to look at her.

"Oh, I'm still thinking about the lady at Smith's. Her name is Geneva, but a lot of the employees call her Sista. They do that because Big Joe found out she had a brother who called her Sista, and sometimes Big Joe calls her that. He uses an affectionate tone of voice when he says it. The other employees refer to her as Sista when they're upset with her. They think she doesn't mind her own business. So, there's this one waitress, named Dorinda...."

"Wait a minute," Casey interrupted Eleanore. "Does this Dorinda have jet black hair and a nose that looks like a hook, like the beak of a bird?"

Eleanore crinkled her nose and giggled. "That's a short description. I think she's in good shape for an older woman. She does seem to like to flaunt her assets, I guess you could say. She wears a lot of make-up and walks in a certain way that makes you look at her. In short, she attracts attention."

"Well, that's nice to know," Casey chuckled. "I bet it's the same Dorinda who is related to the owners. I noticed her around the docks when I first started counting fish. She was always flirting around the charter boat captains before she went into the restaurant to start her shift. She'd have on her waitress uniform. Years ago, the girls used to have to wear white shirts with pointy collars and a red tie; tight black skirts; and a wide, red, elastic belt. The belt was the worst. It cut so deep into their waist it looked like they were strapped into a harness, like a horse wearing its saddle."

Casey and Eleanore laughed together.

"Those were the days!" he said. "Man, I cannot believe she's still working as a waitress at Smith's. I thought she would have put out a pole and hooked some guy by now."

"Oh, my! The uniform sounds horrid," Eleanore said, still giggling about Casey's description of Dorinda. "Well, picking back up where we left off. Dorinda caused some trouble for one of the cooks last week, and that made Big Joe snap at the line cook and made Geneva unhappy. I heard she went and talked to Big Joe about it. I hope she doesn't get herself into some deep trouble, because, after all, you said Dorinda is some kind of kin to the owner. Family usually means other employees should keep their distance."

"Yeah, well, those family situations are delicate matters to handle. I have a feeling Big Joe is more important to the owners. He's been their chef, and a good one, for a long time. They won't let him go. He's the man who manages the kitchen. He's the one who gets the food out to the customer, and that's the most important thing to the owners. They want a good product for their customers. If the product's no good, Smith's reputation slides, and they don't make money. I can see by the look on your face that you might be worried about your friend Geneva."

Eleanore sighed and slid deeper into her chair. It wasn't just Geneva's problems. It was really her own problem, but talking with Casey about Geneva's situation was more manageable.

Even though she'd asked Geneva about her brother, Eleanore didn't dig deeper. She felt guilty for being so wrapped up in her own problems. Geneva probably had worse problems.

"Hey, you look down in the dumps," Casey said, closely eyeing her face for any new clues about her emotions. It reminded him of the night they spent together on *The Lucky Two*. He couldn't help but feel affection for her, but knew the boundaries had been set for him that night.

"Did I say something to upset you?" Casey asked, trying to break the long pause in their conversation.

Eleanore didn't say a word. She didn't know what to say.

She thought, "I am not in control of myself right now. With some careless abandon, I let my emotions get me into this situation. Although I've made mostly good decisions after surviving the hurricane, I fear that future events will further challenge my ability to control my decisions. Somehow, in some way, I have to be strong and use good judgment. I have to make the best possible decision for this child."

Casey decided sitting at the house, watching the television, wasn't going to improve Eleanore's mood, which would eventually rub off on him. Her mood reminded him of the darker, final days of his marriage. His ex-wife's unhappiness was rooted in money problems. Money was the last thing he wanted to talk about with anyone. Casey sensed, however, that Eleanore's mood could not be about money problems. She wasn't paying rent to him, and he never saw her spend money or bring home anything more than groceries. He knew she had to be saving money. She had experienced the slower winter season last year, and he knew she was smart enough to understand how to budget.

Suddenly Casey stood up from his chair, stretched his arms out in front of his body, clasped hands together, and said, "I think maybe it would be a good idea for us to get out of the house. Let's go for a ride in the truck. It's not good to always be staying at home on your night off from work. There's still some daylight left. We could drive to the county pier and watch the sunset. After that, we could drive to the marina and check out the cats. They start roaming around down by the boats once it gets dark. You could bring some food and leave it out for them. Maybe you'll see Princess and those other two cats we had on *The Lucky Two*."

Casey, eager to see Eleanore in a better mood, thought his suggestion would put a smile on Eleanore's face. He'd not visited the marina ever since he was reassigned to other job duties. He was happier now that he didn't have to be down at the docks counting fish. He admitted to himself that there were some things about working at the marina that he missed. Still, he also appreciated the fact that he could avoid seeing Darryl.

"Heck, maybe we can even catch up with Darryl and see what he's been up to lately," Casey joked. "I haven't seen Darryl in a long time."

Casey believed his comments about seeing the cats, and seeing Darryl, might bring a smile to Eleanore's face, but it didn't.

Eleanore thought a few minutes about seeing Darryl, then quickly rationalized the situation. If she was with Casey, she wouldn't feel forced to talk to Darryl about serious matters. It would be just a visit between the three of them.

Eleanore remained quiet for what seemed like forever to Casey. Reluctantly, she said, "It's probably a good idea to get out of the house. I know I'd like to watch the sunset, and I probably should check on the cats." She sniffed and said, "Yes, that all sounds like a very nice idea."

On this late November evening, when the temperatures were turning cooler and the days were getting shorter, the palette of colors in the fall sky was magnificent, unblocked by a filter of humidity. Swirling shades of pink, lavender, blue, and gold-laced through the wispy evening clouds.

Casey pulled his truck into the parking lot of the county pier and parked.

"Do you want to walk out on the sand?" Casey asked.

Eleanore said, "No. I think we can watch the sunset from here."

They sat in the truck, quietly watching the final slanting rays of the sunset filter through a single cloud before breaking below the cloud. The bright, orange, fiery ball was slipping into the gentle waves in the Gulf of Mexico. Twinkling light danced on the surface of the water, like stars sparkling in the sky at night, reminding Eleanore of the nights she walked on the beach with Earl a few summers ago.

"Ready to head on over to see those kitties at the marina?" Casey asked when the glow of an orange sky was all that was left to look at.

"I suppose it's time," Eleanore said flatly. "I'd like to see my cat, Princess."

"Something bad is going on," Casey thought. "I've got this bad feeling in my gut."

He cranked up the truck's engine, backed out, and said, "Let's get going."

Despite the beautiful sunset that they shared a few minutes ago, the weight of a gloomy mood settled on both of them. They shared silence in the dark cabin of the truck during the ride to Captain Anderson's Marina.

CHAPTER 17
CHARLES' CONFESSION

Ricky and Charles were walking tandem in the prison yard outside. Small groups were allowed to go out for exercise an hour each day. The guards selected the time of day and which prisoners could walk together. Each day the men who were paired together were different. Ricky's personality seemed to be a good match with the new prisoner Charles.

The past year in prison, Ricky had earned a good reputation with the guards. He caused no trouble for the guards. He didn't talk or misbehave.

Even though he was a good listener, Ricky was not well-liked by other men simply because he did not speak. The other prisoners didn't trust the man who never spoke.

Ricky seemed to be comfortable interacting with Charles soon after Charles first arrived. The guards noticed Charles hook up with Ricky within his first week.

It surprised the guards when the new black inmate gravitated to the one white man who didn't have another close friend in prison. Most new prisoners, black or white, took a few days to scout out the population before they began to affiliate with anyone.

The cool morning sunrise began with a smoky grey sky. The sun-kissed the curve of the land, casting yellow rays of light through the barbed wire of the prison fences. Sunlight, filtered by a grey groundcover of fog, slowly spread out across the prison yard. Starting with a bright orange glow, the sky gradually changed to a bronzed red and then finally to a sunny, powdery blue, signaling another glorious day ahead.

Ricky frequently glanced up toward the sky. His eyes caught the spectral image of a misty, grayish-lavender funnel forming in the sky. The funnel descended, touching the ground in the center of the prison yard. He elbowed

Charles and pointed to the vision. Fifteen minutes later, the direct, bright light of the sun took out the image.

Ricky lamented that he couldn't explain the transcendent experience to his walking buddy. Thinking to himself, "It's November, and I'm positive those are the souls of people who have been forgiven, ascending into heaven. Someone has been praying for them. I remember reading it somewhere that after Halloween, people who've been dead a long time have a chance to rise up to heaven. Then they become the angels that watch over us. Was it a Sunday school story? I don't remember. I think it was an old Irish folk story. That sounds right. It's about the light overcoming the darkness."

Since his incarceration a year ago, Ricky tried to forget the trauma he experienced during the hurricane, waiting for the night to end and the daylight to appear. Ricky spent most of his free time in the prison library, reading as much as possible about saints and angels. He always read the bible at night. It was the one presented to him by one of the prison officials after asking for it on his first night. Ricky always wondered if the bible was provided by his court-appointed lawyer, whom he never saw again.

Charles was still in shock and confused over the quick verdict on his murder conviction. He was surprised when the justice system operated so swiftly. He didn't have any idea on how to take his present situation day by day.

Despite the glorious day outside, Charles was disheartened and worried on this crisp weather morning. Charles viewed the morning walk with Ricky as an opportunity to vent his feelings to a captive audience that didn't complain or give advice. He sensed that Ricky was listening.

"I appreciate the note you wrote to me. Man, I love this weather, but I am still locked up inside these prison walls. I used to run all the time. I used to run freely on the streets of my hometown, back in Altoona," Charles talked while he walked, looking at the ground, not expecting any reaction from Ricky. "I'd run past the playgrounds. I hear the laughter of those children on the playground in my head. I miss it; the sound of their laughter."

Ricky heard the sadness in Charles' voice, and though he wanted to, he couldn't say anything to make him feel any better.

"My momma is going to be so upset, so sad when she finds where I am. My Sista worked in the Elks Club back in Altoona. I expect now that I'm here, and Sista has no one to help her pay rent, she might go back home to Altoona. She will be the one to tell my momma all the details of what's happened to me." Charles felt comfortable talking to Ricky, knowing he could trust a man who wrote him a note about forgiveness and wouldn't say bad things back.

Ricky listened, understanding that Charles has a lot to get off his chest. Ricky didn't mind. He was enjoying the memory of the beautiful vision he just witnessed.

Listening, and enjoying a moment of inspiration, had been precisely how his friendship with Vince worked. Ricky mostly listened to Vince, too. It was easier for Ricky to stay quiet, that is until Vince asked him to answer a question. Ricky had lived in fear of Vince's anger, knowing that if the answer didn't please Vince, his ranting and raging would begin, escalating into some unexpected catastrophe. Ricky especially feared Vince's eye with the white, crescent-shaped spot. When he occasionally thought about Vince and his anger, Ricky remembered how he imagined flames of lightning and white smoke pouring out of Vince's eye.

In the few days he spent with Charles in prison, Ricky already learned similarities between Charles and Vince. One thing Ricky didn't know for sure about Charles was whether he had a short fuse like Vince, who was easily angered. Ricky didn't see any anger in Charles' eyes. What Ricky observed in Charles' eyes was a mixture of sadness, anger and innocence. Ricky contrasted Charles' eyes with Vince's eyes and remembered that Vince's dark, glaring eyes signaled danger whenever he was awake.

Both Charles and Vince grew up in homes where they had limited parenting, and fewer resources. The tooth fairy of life didn't sprinkle any favors on their pillows at night.

Charles didn't have a visible marking on his body, none that Ricky could see. There were no scars on his face or arm, revealing whippings from a parent. He learned that Charles had a loving mother. Unlike Vince's mother, Sissy, who didn't stay home with her children whenever she was not working.

The most obvious difference between Charles and Vince was the color of Charles's skin.

When Ricky was growing up in Alabama in the 1960s, Ricky was aware that many white people viewed people of color differently back then. By the 1980's Ricky saw people in Alabama treat people of color much better than they used to. Ricky didn't see the color of Charles's skin. He only saw a broken man accused of a crime that Ricky started to believe the man was not capable of committing.

"I had no expectations," Charles confessed. "That way, I wouldn't ever be disappointed. I learned that from my dad. My grandfather, his father, gave him the name of a famous person. That name gave my dad a sad and heavy heart because he couldn't live up to the greatness that person achieved. My dad's name was Maximilian. He told us he didn't like being called Max. He wanted people to say the complete name. *You call me Maximilian*, I heard him say once when we were at the store or somewhere, which was rare for us to be together out of the apartment as a family. I may have even heard him say it when we went to the funeral of a family member. I don't know. It struck me as odd that he wanted to be so high and mighty, yet he lived his life in such a low place. It was like he wanted to be someone important around his own people. Everyone knew he wasn't any better than them. I never understood why he let himself go down the drain. He spent more time at the bar than at home.

"I always thought I would work in the railroad, but my dad wouldn't let me. He told me he didn't want me to be a gandy dancer, laying down railroad tracks. I always thought it would be fun to work for the railroad. I wanted to ride on the caboose. Most people think the engine is the most important car. The caboose is equally important and not second to the engine. All the cars in the middle of the train are just traveling. The caboose is the car where the conductor makes decisions. Men on the caboose looked out for other train railcars to see if the axles were overheating. They're looking out for the safety of other people.

"I've heard people when they feel like they're getting whipped around by decisions of others, like they're riding on the caboose of a train. Without the caboose, people in the other cars don't have the insight of where they've been or where they're going."

Ricky momentarily stopped their walk together and tapped Charles lightly on the forearm. Ricky nodded his head and blinked his eyes fast to express his keen interest in everything Charles was saying.

The walking resumed, along with Charles' confession of feelings.

"My momma would often tell me I should keep my eyes to the sky, but my Sista sometimes told me I had my head in the clouds.

"Man, I'd never kill a woman. My mother, and my Sista, were the best people I knew. I never met any man who could be as kind as a woman is. My dad wasn't really unkind. He was a bitter drunk, but he never harmed me, my Sista, or my momma. My momma told me not to let alcohol be my best friend because it would be my worst enemy. I wanted to make friends in Panama City. I've never had a real friend.

"I got framed by those men I worked with at the construction yard. They saw me talking to her at the Halloween party. They think I did that girl; I have a hard time saying murdered her. Witnesses? Witnesses to what? I didn't even touch her. They got no DNA from me on her body.

"All I really wanted to do was ask her to dance. I tried to be polite by asking her name, and she walked away from me.

I thought it would be good to sort of introduce ourselves before we start dancing together.

"I got so tired of being alone at night, holed up in that efficiency apartment. My Sista was always at work at night. Now that I was working, had a job, and had some money, I wanted to spend it. I wanted to find a girl to go eat dinner with and have a conversation with, someone besides my Sista.

"I remember her eyes, though. She looked right through me as if I wasn't there. Then she told me she didn't tell strangers her name. Her behavior gave me a kind of chill in my bones. That woman, all dressed up for a Halloween party in a black costume, telling me she was dressed up to be a fallen angel, was evil!

"My biggest problem was I couldn't account for my whereabouts after I went home. My Sista was at work when I was at the party, so I wasn't there when she got home from work. Then Sista falls asleep after working a hard shift at Smith's, and she never hears me come back home, mostly because I didn't want to wake her up.

"None of this Fallen Angel's other friends could be tied to her disappearance. The only idea the police can think of is that some stranger at a Halloween party met up with her, and it turned into a botched attempted acquaintance rape. The police found nothing! They never found the murder weapon. Everyone she knew had an alibi of who they were with and where they were that night. I believe that a bunch of her friends were at that Halloween party. They had to be! Somebody's lying!

"The police claimed it had to be a random act of violence done by a stranger, some newcomer who came into town to work after the hurricane. I admit my reputation at work wasn't the best. When I got there, I told the men to call me DC for Demon Cat because I hung around with a lot of cool cats back home in Altoona. Turns out that the workers didn't like me much, either. They told the police that I had a snarky attitude.

"I don't drink, and I don't smoke, but I will admit I might have a bad attitude about some things if I think they're not right.

"Heck, all those guys ever did was tell me to go get this and go get that. I worked and did what I was told. Not one of them ever asked me how I was doing or told me I was doing a good job. I admit I could pull an attitude, but it was the first job I ever had, and I was happy to be earning some money. I never had any money of my own in Altoona.

"When I was a kid, I got the nickname DC for always having dirty clothes. Do you know how much that hurt? Mean kids, yeah, calling me *dirty Charles* and then just DC. I couldn't help it that my clothes were dirty. Here was my mother, working at a laundromat, and those owners didn't even give her the chance to wash her own kids' clothes. They said she had to pay for detergent and had to do it on her own time and carry it home by herself. My father told me that they didn't want white people to know that their clothes were washed in the same machines as a black family's clothes. I don't know if that's true. I tend to believe my mother didn't have enough money to put into those machines at the laundromat.

"For the life of me, how did I end up going from just being an innocent kid with a nickname pertaining to my dirty clothes to becoming known as a demon who would commit murder? I admit that when I got older, I kind of liked the nickname DC. I used to be a character, doing things to annoy people to get some attention. I didn't have any friends to speak of, really. I'd run around with a few other guys, playing chase in the streets at night to see who could run the fastest. When your family is poor, there's not a whole lot of things to do. My momma told me to stay out of trouble, and I did. Other kids were stealing and causing damage to people's property, but I never did any of that stuff.

"I can't spend the rest of my life in this Florida prison, but how the heck can I get out? Is there a way I can get someone to send me back to Pennsylvania?

"How am I going to let my momma know where I am?" Charles hung his head in sadness and shook it as if he couldn't find the answer to his own questions. "I'm going to have to let her know, and she's going to have to tell my father. This might be my father's breaking point. It might set him over the edge, and he'll do something crazy. Gawd."

Ricky thought Charles may start crying at any minute. Ricky wasn't allowed to carry his clipboard and yellow pad when they were exercising in the yard. He fast-footed to the guard standing by the door and gave him the hand signal to use his yellow pad. It was a signal that the lawyer asked by the state to represent Ricky devised. It was the most straightforward way for the lawyer to get information from Ricky during the trial, and he recommended it to the prison officials when Ricky arrived at the prison. "*Press your thumb to your mouth if you want to write down something you want to communicate to me,*" the lawyer advised Ricky.

"You need to tell me something?" the guard asked.

Ricky shook his head side-to-side, then pointed his finger at Charles.

The guard allowed Ricky to go to the shelf by the security doors, where the clipboard was kept during yard walks.

"Your one hour is about up," the guard said to Ricky. "Go get your clipboard. You two go inside, sit at a table, and wait," the guard grunted and pointed his forefinger at Charles, who was standing alone in the center of the yard watching.

Ricky shook his head up and down. The guard's cold indifference didn't bother Ricky. It was the same way everyone else was treated.

Carrying the clipboard close to the side of his leg, Ricky rushed to the nearest table, sat down on the metal seat, and waited for Charles, who received a verbal command from the guard that his exercise time was over.

In a few minutes, Charles came inside and sat down at the closest seat next to Ricky at a hexagonal metal table in the center of the room.

Ricky carefully wrote on his yellow pad, printing the words in large block letters so that Charles could read his writing. When he was finished, he gently slid the metal clipboard, turning it sideways, to face Charles.

Charles read the words, "*Maybe a letter to your momma, to let her know how much you love her, would help you feel better right now. I know it would make your momma smile.*"

After reading Ricky's words, Charles looked up at Ricky. His big, brown eyes didn't reveal any emotions, and then one of his eyes welled up with water. A big tear rolled down Charles' cheek.

Ricky began to write fast, feeling rushed to get the words down before Charles completely lost all of his composure. "*Didn't your momma ever tell you to never trust anyone wearing a mask?*" Ricky wrote. "*People who wear masks are trying to hide something. That girl might have talked to you, and things might have worked out differently if you hadn't been wearing a mask.*"

Charles sobered up after reading Ricky's words. With penitential fervor, Charles said, "There's a lot of things I should have thought about before walking up to that girl," Charles' voice cracked with emotion. "I remember hoping that I was going to meet somebody new. Maybe somebody who wouldn't judge me for wearing dirty clothes. Instead, I was judged for wearing a Dracula costume. I didn't have any idea that wearing a mask would matter. Most people wear a mask on Halloween. Maybe I should have taken my mask off. I should have figured that a girl dressed in a costume representing a Fallen Angel might mean she was the Angel of Darkness or something like that."

Charles stopped to take a breath. "You're right. I want to write my mother and tell her I'm going to be okay. Can I borrow a piece of your paper? Is that allowed? I don't know-how, or when, I can repay you, though."

Ricky nodded his head, yes, and for a moment thought about his mother.

Ricky never wrote to his mother, knowing she would have been mad and would have said *I always told you not to hang out with that boy, Vince.* Ricky wished his momma had felt differently. Otherwise, he might have written her, too. After he was informed that she died, it was too late.

    Ricky smiled at Charles, knowing it was the right thing for Charles to do.

CHAPTER 18
SHOWTIME

Casey made a slow right turn off Thomas Drive and let the truck coast into the marina parking lot. He wished he had more time to figure out what was going on with Eleanore. Watching the sunset didn't improve her mood. Casey had a sinking feeling that feeding the cats or seeing Darryl would not do it either. The atmosphere in the truck's cabin felt familiar, and he wanted to figure out how to improve the strain on their companionship.

"This silence reminds me too much like the ride back to the marina on *The Lucky Two* after we left Pine Log Forest State Park," Casey thought. "That was easy to figure out. She just found out that Earl died. She didn't talk, and that was understandable because it was something so tangible. I can't even dream up what the problem could be right now. I only know she hasn't been acting like the same old Eleanore lately. She's always been so cheerful. If I have to take her back to the house in this kind of mood, it's going to rub off on me. I don't need that. I've finally gotten my head back to a good place."

Casey tried to put an end to the gloom that was darker than the evening sky.

"Here we are at the marina," he said in a cheerful, booming voice over the rumble of the engine. "I bet you're glad you're not working tonight."

"Hmmm, I don't know," Elenore responded, folding her arms across her chest as if getting ready to protect herself.

Casey parked the truck alongside the docks, away from Smith's, and turned off the engine.

"Is there something wrong?" Casey asked, point-blank. "Do you mind if I ask what's bothering you? Is it something that I've done? I mean, you're not usually so down in the dumps." Asking, Casey still doubted he would find out the reasons for Eleanore's moodiness.

Instead, Eleanore surprised him with an answer.

"I've got a feeling that Darryl will come out of *The Lucky Two*, and when he sees us here, together, he may get the wrong impression," she said. "He's never seen us together outside of the time all three of us stayed at your house after hurricane Louise."

She didn't like to lie, but this was more like a little white lie. Darryl wouldn't be very eager to have contact with Casey again, given their history back in the days when they interacted professionally at the marina. She knew, however, that Darryl would be happy to see her.

"Hey, all we're going to do here is feed the cats," Casey said. "If Darryl sees us, it's no big deal to me. I haven't been down to the marina since my duties have changed. Since being reassigned to patrol, and more office work, I've been kind of wondering about how things are going. I'm feeling a little at home, again. Funny how I hated coming here and counting fish catches, and now I feel a little nostalgic, like I miss it a little bit."

Giving Eleanore a big smile, Casey said, "Darryl and I will get along just fine. He's going to be happy to see you, and so are the cats."

Casey reached behind Eleanore's seat, grabbed a six-pound bag of dry cat food, and lifted it to the front seat. Eleanore picked up the metal bowls she bought explicitly to feed the cats. They both stepped out of the truck simultaneously. They walked toward the sidewalk, stopping directly in front of *The Lucky Two.* Eleanore noticed the yellow light beaming out the starboard window of the cabin, casting a dim light on the lagoon water. She nervously placed both bowls down on the sidewalk and took the cat food bag from Casey. Taking a metal cup out of the bag, she proceeded to fill one of the bowls. She hesitated for a few moments, then kneeled down and began clanging the metal cup against the metal bowl. The noise brought Princess and King and the other cats interested in being fed, out of their hiding places.

The clanging noise also reached Darryl's ears. He was flipping pages, trying to read a book while lying down on the roll-out bench he used for a bed inside the small cabin.

Less than thirty seconds later, Darryl's face appeared peering out of the cabin's open door.

"Hey, you two, Darryl gingerly stepped out of the doorway and onto the deck of *The Lucky Two*, grinning, genuinely happy to see Eleanore. It was natural for him to smile when he saw her. He intentionally avoided making eye contact with Casey. If he did, he might say something sarcastic. The suspicious rumor Dorinda told him still hurt.

"Eleanore, I haven't seen you in a few days. Where have you been?" Darryl never stopped smiling at Eleanore.

Casey knew Darryl's question wasn't his to answer. Casey kneeled down on one knee to make an attempt to pretend to pet Princess, who had shown up with King. Princess jumped away from Casey's hand, having no interest in being friendly to Casey.

Eleanore didn't immediately answer Darryl's question.

"I'm here to feed the cats," she finally said, without looking at Darryl. She was struggling with her emotions.

"Well, I can see that. And, it's good to see you too." Darryl jumped off the deck of the boat and onto the sidewalk. "I've been trying to feed these kitties every night," he laughed. "I know how important they are to you."

Darryl walked up to stand beside Eleanore and Casey.

"Hello, Darryl. How have you been doing?" Casey politely asked, adding, "I have to say it's sad to see so many of the charter boats missing."

"I've been doing pretty good. Fishing has been good, but it's not the same. I don't like going out by myself," Darryl forced himself to look at Casey when he answered. "I'd really like to take out a few guys on a charter, but I know I have to wait until everything with the boat is legal. I'm playing by the rules."

Eleanore noticed an icy edge in Darryl's voice. Eleanore looked up from pouring dry food into the second bowl and focused her eyes on Darryl. "Maybe my absence has pushed his limits," she thought. "When we were staying together at Casey's house, he was usually more laid back whenever he talked with Casey."

"That's good," Casey said, trying his best to be friendly to Darryl after sensing the coldness in his voice. "I mean, it's good that the fishing is good. I think it's also good to decide that you're not taking any charters on the boat until everything is resolved. It's crazy how long it has taken the insurance companies to resolve claims after the hurricane. A lot of homeowners are having trouble. It's good that you got your payout for *The Star Chaser*, and hopefully, you'll be able to get a clear title on *The Lucky Two* to purchase it real soon. Then you'll be able to operate the boat as a business."

Darryl quickly diverted his attention from Casey back to Eleanore. "I still want to take you out on the boat with me sometime, Eleanore," Darryl said, tilting his head and grinning big at her, knowing that he'd asked her that question before. "Remember how I promised you I would take you out fishing on the Gulf of Mexico one day?" The shine in Darryl's smile flashed brighter than the shine on his bald head.

"Yes, I remember," she said. "Maybe we could do that one day," she replied, barely audible.

Darryl's suggestion brought back memories of riding with Darryl in his truck the day before hurricane Louise, going to Captain Anderson's Marina to find Earl. She was looking for Earl because Earl had called her to tell her that he had made a mistake.

She suddenly remembered her mother's warning to her so many years ago when she was still in high school, head over heels in love with Earl. Her mother's words were, *"Being married to any man is hard. If you decide to marry a poor man, I can guarantee you that life will be hard. If you marry a rich man, life will be much easier. If you ask me, you'll be better off marrying someone like Earl. He'll be a rich man one of these days."*

Eleanore never wanted to be with Earl for his money. The money he inherited from his grandmother to buy *The Lucky*

Two was to chase his dream, not theirs together. Eleanore never got the chance to ask Earl the real reason for why he called her. Did he realize he was wrong to leave her because he genuinely missed her or was it because he was failing at his business?

Eleanore suddenly realized that Darryl's feelings for her would never change. His expressions showed that he was always thinking about her feelings. She wished she wasn't so conflicted about her own feelings for him.

While Eleanore's thoughts ran wildly through her mind, Casey avoided looking at Darryl by turning around. He stood at the edge of the seawall and distracted himself by looking down into the water. Darryl stared at Eleanore. Both men could feel Eleanore's tension. For Casey, it had been ongoing since the evening began.

Finally, Eleanore broke the silence. "Casey, would you mind waiting for me out here for about ten minutes? I'd like to have a private conversation with Darryl."

"No, no. I don't mind. I'll stay out here and walk around a bit. Maybe a few more cats might show up, and I'll have a chance to chat with a few cats," Casey chuckled, trying to lighten the mood. "You two go right ahead and have some time together. If you don't see me walking around, you can find me sitting over there." Casey pointed toward the concrete table and bench that survived hurricane Louise in front of the fish cleaning house. "I'll be doing some reminiscing about all the fish I used to count."

"Darryl, let's go inside *The Lucky Two* and talk for a little bit," she said.

"That's a grand idea," Darryl said and grabbed both her hands.

"Wait a minute," Eleanore said. "Will you take the bag of cat food?" she asked. "I don't know if any other cats will show up with us around. Is there enough room inside the boat for you to store it? That way, you can feed the cats if I can't get over here."

"Yeah, sure there is," Darryl said enthusiastically and grabbed the bag sitting on the sidewalk. "You need any help getting on the boat?"

"No, I'm fine," Eleanore said, extending her leg over the gap between the sidewalk and the edge of *The Lucky Two,* then stepping onto the fiberglass deck. "I've done this before, remember?"

"Oh, yes, I remember," Darryl nervously laughed and passed the bag of cat food to Eleanore standing on the deck. He gingerly stepped onto the boat and took the bag of cat food back from Eleanore. He walked to the cabin door, opening it with his free hand.

"Here," Eleanore said. "Let me take the bag of cat food and find a place to store it."

Darryl handed it back to her and said, "I think the best place to store it will be in the head. There's a little bit of room in there beneath the sink. I think the bag would be in the way inside the cabin. There's not really a good shelf to store it on. I might trip over it if it's sitting on the floor."

Eleanore opened the door to the head. Reaching down to move the garbage can toward the wall to make room for the bag of cat food, she suddenly found herself gasping for air. On the floor beneath the sink, lying there was a pair of lacy, pink ladies panties.

Eleanore's mind froze. Without giving it a second thought, she held on to the bag of cat food and kicked the panties with her foot until they were lying on the floor in the middle of the cabin.

Darryl's jaw dropped when he saw the garment lying on the floor. He tried to form words with his lips, but couldn't find the right ones to say. It was just as much a surprise to him as it was for Eleanore to see the panties.

"I can only imagine what's been going on here, but I don't want to," Eleanore said, her nostrils flared in anger. "I won't be asking any questions, either. Just consider this as a good reason for us to part ways." She spit on the floor where the panties lie and briskly walked past Darryl, avoiding any physical contact with him.

"You're leaving me now?" Darryl's asked in a squeaky voice.

Eleanore knew he wasn't asking a question. She knew he was making a statement. She swallowed hard, too, to choke back her tears, and answered resolutely, firmly, "Yes."

Eleanore stormed out of the cabin door and hopped off the boat onto the sidewalk, clutching the bag of cat food with both arms tightly wrapped around it. She immediately started to cry uncontrollably. Within minutes her sobs became loud wails, echoing despair across the water of the lagoon.

Darryl jumped off the boat and ran after her.

Holding the bag of cat food with one arm wrapped around it close to her side, Eleanore jerked her other arm straight out and held the palm of her free hand in front of her to make sure Darryl didn't come any closer to her.

"What's going on here?" Casey shouted.

Casey, who had not had enough time to get very far away on his walk, ran up and skidded to a stop in front of Eleanore.

Eleanore was shaking, sobbing, and choking with each gasp of air between sobs. She couldn't answer Casey's question.

"Did you do something to her?" Casey spun around to face Darryl. Casey knew he had to try and control the anger building inside his gut.

"There's been some huge misunderstanding," Darryl stuttered. "I'm not sure how or know where to start to try and explain it."

"Get started quick," Casey barked, "because we're leaving here in about ten seconds."

"It starts with that waitress, Dorinda," Darryl blurted out the words.

"Her name sounds familiar to me," Casey said, with some control in his voice, cautious and still suspicious. He didn't want to mention that Dorinda's name came up earlier in the evening in the conversation he and Eleanore had at his house.

At the sound of Dorinda's name, Eleanore sobbed louder. Of all the waitresses at Smith's, Dorinda was the waitress who treated her the worst. Now Dorinda is connected with Darryl.

"Talk faster, Darryl," Casey nearly shouted again.

"So, I asked her to check on Eleanore because I had not seen her in days. Dorinda came over here to tell me some crock of a story that Eleanore was not interested in seeing me anymore. After she told me that story, she asked me if she could use the bathroom. I told her it wasn't the best place, and she should go back to Smith's. Now I know why she was banging around in there so much." Darryl's words came fast and furious, along with some spit. He knew he couldn't waste any time to salvage the situation.

Eleanore listened, conflicted about believing Darryl's answers. She didn't want to think he would hurt her like this, and there was mounting evidence against Dorinda.

Darryl stepped forward and tried to place both hands on Eleanore's face, wanting to hold her face as if it were her heart. He put his hands on both of her shoulders instead.

"Back off, buddy," Casey said loudly. "Eleanore's upset and doesn't need you trying to touch her. Now I think I understand why she's seemed so sad. I brought her here tonight to try to cheer her up. Watched the sunset, come over here to feed the cats, and to come to see you. Then all this stuff explodes in her face. You're a jerk, Darryl."

"I'm okay," Eleanore said to Casey in a shaky voice.

Eleanore lifted Darryl's hands away from her shoulders. What she really wished for, more than anything, was to feel his arms wrapping around her, holding her tight, like he did on those nights the past few months when she visited with him on *The Lucky Two*. Under these circumstances, it wasn't hard to fight off those feelings.

Darryl let his arms drop down like stiff rods and let his hands slap his thighs. Eleanore took two steps back, away from him.

Despite the distinct feeling that he was losing the battle, Darryl pressed on.

"I know Dorinda has been cruising around this beach for a long time. She told me she used to follow my band, *The Electrons*, when I played in the nightclubs on the beach. Do you know how many years ago that was? I gave all that up. She told me she worked with Eleanore at Smith's. Why would I allow myself to get hooked up by an evil woman who was only setting me up to cause me pain? I asked her to check on Eleanore, and she came to see me one night. It was nothing more than that. You have to believe me."

"That doesn't explain how you got hooked up with Dorinda in the first place, does it?" Casey shot back.

Darryl wasted no time answering. "I was wandering around Smith's parking lot, hoping I'd see Eleanore leaving after her work shift ended. Instead, I ran into Dorinda," Darryl said.

Looking directly at Eleanore, Darryl said, "I know what you're thinking. It's all about Dorinda. She means nothing to me. Dorinda's greatest delight is taking pleasure in seeing other people get hurt. She only thinks about herself. Believe me, Eleanore," Darryl implored.

Eleanore, after hearing the explanation, felt somewhat relieved. Up to now, she never had a reason to distrust Darryl, and putting Dorinda in the story helped to make the explanation seem plausible.

"I want to believe you, Darryl," she reluctantly said, averting her eyes away from Darryl. "I can't right now. I'll need to find out more, possibly from Dorinda."

Casey snorted and said, "Don't believe that story. If it's the Dorinda who I remember, she's probably gotten her hooks into Darryl. She's always been a fisher of men."

Nearing tears again, Elenore blurted, "It's all too much for me to think about. I need to be alone. Can we leave now, Casey?"

Eleanore and Casey exchanged a quick glance, turned their backs to Darryl, and quickly walked back to Casey's truck.

Darryl felt his body slowly go numb while he stood alone on the sidewalk in front of *The Lucky Two*. He shoved his hands in his pockets, letting his arms go limp, and watched the red tail lights of Casey's truck make the turn out of the parking lot of Captain Anderson's Marina. Within seconds after losing sight of the truck, Darryl turned around and leapt onto the deck of *The Lucky Two*. He was inside the cabin within another second, grabbing the keys to his truck.

Darryl sped out of the marina and turned off the lights of his truck when he arrived an entire block away from Casey's house. He put his truck into park, left the engine running, and squinted to see in the dark. When he believed it was clear, Darryl drove his truck closer, stopping on the opposite side of the street, two houses away. He sat in his parked truck, hoping that he might see Eleanore walk back out of the house. If only he could talk to her, he thought. The only thing Darryl could think to do was follow the object of his love.

"I wonder if she suspects that I'm out here," he thought. "All the lights are on in the house. They're awake. She's probably still too upset to go to sleep."

Darryl fought with himself. He badly wanted to honk his horn or walk up to the front door and knock on it. Casey would be the person to confront him if he did either. Darryl was aware that there was a strong possibility of getting himself in trouble with Casey if he tried to push the situation too far. Casey was the person protecting Eleanore right now.

After an hour of waiting, the lights in Casey's house went dark.

It tore at Darryl's heart, knowing Eleanore was so upset and that she might leave him forever. Darryl felt at a complete loss when he drove away from Casey's house.

When he pulled into the parking lot at Captain Anderson's Marina and passed the neon lights of Smith's, an idea flashed into Darryl's mind.

"And to think that I trusted that strange woman because she remembered me from the days when I played in the band. Crap, how can I be so gullible sometimes?" he asked himself. Disgusted, he added, "I need someone to give me a good slap on the behind."

Darryl parked his truck in front and marched down the sidewalk to Smith's. He stomped inside the front lobby, planning to give Dorinda a piece of his mind for the trouble she caused. He suspected that confronting Dorinda might be a hopeless cause. Still, it didn't help the situation if he said nothing at all. He needed to get something straight with her. He was going to tell Dorinda to never come near him again, and if she ever made trouble for Eleanore, he would see to it that she would regret it.

"I want to speak to the waitress named Dorinda," Darryl said as calmly as possible to the hostess, who looked terrified by the disheveled man with wild eyes and an angry voice.

"Just a minute, sir," she nervously said, and promptly left to go back into the kitchen to find Big Joe.

"What's up?" Big Joe said in a half-friendly tone when he came out to the lobby and saw Darryl pacing back and forth.

"That tartlet, Dorinda, set me up. She's trying to ruin my relationship with Eleanore. I want to warn her that she needs to stay away from Eleanore and me, forever!" The words spewed from Darryl's mouth with his spit.

Big Joe's instincts immediately recognized the potential of a fiery collision between two combustible personalities. Standing taller than Darryl, Big Joe said with authority, "You must leave now, Darryl, or there might be other problems for you. Your problems with Dorinda will have to be resolved outside of the restaurant."

Deciding not to argue with Big Joe, Darryl left the restaurant lobby and stomped back to *The Lucky Two*. He never noticed the cats in the bushes following his every step back to the boat.

CHAPTER 19
ROMANCE AND REVENGE

It was past dusk when Fat Cat left the pile of wood that had become his living quarters. He cautiously jumped down to the sidewalk and was planning to make a trip to the dumpster outside Smith's kitchen when the familiar sound of someone banging on a metal bowl and the voices of people stopped him in his tracks. He knew the familiar sound meant cat food was being poured into the bowls. He raced toward the bushes beneath the windows at Smith's to wait for the humans to leave. Afterward he'd check to see if there was any food left in the bowls.

"I can't stand it anymore," Fat Cat snarled while listening and watching the humans engage in loud angry voices in front of *The Lucky Two*.

"I remember that bald-headed man. He's Darryl, the boat captain who used to throw fish at us from his boat, *The Star Chaser*. And I recognize the taller man. He's the one who used to wear sunglasses and always be at the docks around the time the charter boats returned at the end of the day. He'd watch the fish being thrown onto the sidewalk and always carried around a clipboard. The young woman is the one who always calls for Princess whenever she comes to fill up food bowls." Fat Cat summed up his observation of the three people ending their heated conversation on the sidewalk.

"What I can't figure out is why the boat captain who took off in his truck the day before the hurricane with Oscar riding inside the engine, never came back. Darryl now hangs out on *The Lucky Two*. It's better that we have Darryl here. That other charter boat captain was always in a bad mood and hollered at us cats," Fat Cat thought while he waited.

Fat Cat watched the young woman get inside the truck with the taller man and leave. Then he saw Darryl run onto

The Lucky Two, race back out of the boat, get into his truck, and also drive away.

With the humans now gone, Fat Cat ventured out of the bushes and trotted down the sidewalk toward *The Lucky Two*.

Fat Cat stopped at the bowls and greedily ate a large portion of the dry cat food. When he felt satisfied, he stopped for a few minutes to lick his forepaw and slide it behind his large head, over his ears, with a final pass across his face. The luscious taste of cat food triggered the saliva on his tongue. In the past year, his fur had become dry, mottled, and unattractive.

When he finished washing, he walked down the sidewalk, frequently stopping to turn his head and look around to check the surroundings.

"I don't have to have eyes in the back of my head to see who might be following me," he reminded himself. "I'm wondering if ST might just show up tonight. I would prefer to have some company. I hate to admit it, but I miss him not being my regular companion every night."

He began to ruminate on the difficult circumstances created by the hurricane. Lately, he couldn't find ST when it was time to venture out at night. His suspicion was ST was wandering over to the new neighborhood to visit with his old friend, Oscar. If, and when, ST returned to the condo, it was much later in the evening, and after Smith's closed. " I have Dog Ear around almost every night, but he doesn't have a clue about anything."

Fat Cat struggled to understand why he lost his power of influence. He used to be the leader of the gang of cats. He was the one who alerted the cats to take shelter when it was apparent that a hurricane was coming. His leadership helped ST and Dog Ear survive the storm.

He looked past the boats tied to the docks. Fat Cat noticed the customers inside Smith's gazing out the windows above the bushes. He knew that people sat by those windows to eat dinner to look at the last colors of the evening sunset. Now that it was dark outside, the customers' attention turned to the food on their plates.

Now that his belly was full from eating food in the bowls, Fat Cat cancelled his plans to visit the dumpster. He decided to go lay down, alone, in the bushes near the westside wall of Smith's. He would be closer to feeling the breezes blowing over the lagoon water, and further away from the lights shining out the restaurant windows.

Fat Cat crouched on four paws in the soft sand beneath the bushes. Feeling comfortable and believing that he was safe from any humans, he laid down on his side. His tail curled up around his body, and his front paws tucked beneath his breast bone. The dark evening sky covered him like a blanket.

Comfortable in his solitude, his eyes were closed tight in a deep sleep until he heard the footsteps of two customers from Smith's, hurrying down the sidewalk. Knowing that he was further away and well hid beneath the bushes, he didn't budge a muscle. His eyes opened to reveal narrow black slits, and he twitched his ears to follow the sounds until he was sure that the humans were gone.

Fat Cat's resting period was short. The sound of leaves rustling caused him to lift up his head and open his eyes up wide. The black slits grew, filling up the space of his eyes. He turned his head toward the direction of the noise and saw Princess and King shuffling through the bushes, creeping low on their four paws, inching closer to him.

"There's Fat Cat," King mewed softly to Princess when he saw that Fat Cat noticed them.

"What are you two up to tonight?" Fat Cat asked, genuinely surprised to see that they were coming to visit him.

It was still no secret that Fat Cat had never lost interest in Princess and that he detested all her kittens with King. Their two litters of kittens bruised Fat Cat's ego. Why would they be visiting him in the more secluded spot where he chose to be alone?

"Coming over here to see what you think about all the fireworks that just happened out there," King said.

"Fireworks?" Fat Cat asked, pretending not to know what they were talking about. "What do you mean? Is there some kind of celebration that I don't know about? I didn't hear fireworks. I can't stand the noise of loud bangs. I remember back in the old days; we'd occasionally hear the sound of a gun fired off by a boat captain. That was an unpleasant noise, to say the least."

"Maybe it would be better to call the event fire words," Princess said. "You heard the argument, I expect, with the woman who used to be my owner. She's been feeding us since the hurricane. I saw you go over and eat some of the food that she left in the bowl, Fat Cat."

"I always go and eat some of the food she leaves. It's always in a bowl right in front of my cat condo, as I like to call it. I usually see you two out there eating first. I go out after you guys are finished. I didn't see you guys around, so I helped myself," Fat Cat answered. He was not embarrassed or overly concerned about his lack of etiquette. "I'm not the only cat here at the marina that eats the food she leaves. Most of the time, DC is there, along with you two, helping himself too. Where is DC, anyway?"

Princess and King were surprised to hear Fat Cat ask about the one kitten who didn't join his siblings in the new neighborhood. They knew DC was hanging out at the marina.

"You haven't seen DC today?" Princess asked.

"Normally, I see him every day. I just didn't notice he was around," Fat Cat answered sarcastically. "Not like a few days ago when he was having convulsions, and I had to find you guys to let you know to check on him."

"We appreciate that you did let us know about DC being in trouble," King said. "Mind if we join you?" King asked.

King didn't wait for an answer. He positioned his sleek, black body beneath the bushes, plopping down in the soft sand a foot away from Fat Cat. Princess followed. DC's parents were going to stake out their territory beneath the bushes, whether Fat Cat liked it or not. It might take some time, but the parents knew DC would eventually make his appearance. They would also keep their eyes half-open for other cats venturing out, looking for food near the docks and Smith's. Later in the evening, when the humans cleared out of the restaurant and parking lot, they would all run freely on the marina property. It was prime time to investigate the food scraps thrown into the dumpster behind Smiths and the other trash cans used by the charter boat captains.

An hour later, all three cats were startled by the loud noise of a door slamming. It was the back door of Smith's kitchen.

Fat Cat's whiskers, double the width of his head, curled down, below his chin, like the handlebar mustache of a man. His mind became alert, preparing for the possibility of needing to make a quick getaway. After dropping his whiskers, he returned to a crouching position, wiggled his hindquarters, and swished his tail in readiness for a great dash away if it became necessary.

The eyes of all three cats were glowing like crystal balls shining in a dark, candle-lit room.

The sharp voices of two people, a woman, and a man, drifted through the air into the bushes like thick, rolling fog. Their argument grew louder and louder with each word.

"I'm going to get to the bottom of this," yelled Big Joe. "I don't have any space left in my patience pocket to deal with unnecessary problems. The hostess comes running back to the kitchen to tell me that Darryl Kay is in the lobby looking for you. She says he's hopping mad. I'm suspicious, and I don't want trouble, so I go out to see him instead of allowing his anger to fester in our restaurant lobby. The man is beyond belief upset about some stunt you pulled. I don't need to know the details, do I?"

"I don't have a clue what you're talking about," Dorinda answered, glaring back at Big Joe with her dark eyes narrowed to a sly-eyed stare.

"You don't? Really?" Big Joe asked, incredulous by Dorinda's audacity. "I have had another kitchen employee tell me this week that you're causing trouble and that you got into a disagreement with the line cook about expediting plates. Something about you getting your food out faster and getting your orders ahead of Eleanore's order. I actually heard the line cook snap at you the other night, and I had to tell the line cook to cool it. Tonight, I'm being told by the hostess that Darryl Kay is out in the lobby and wants to talk to you. Like I just said, I'm going to get to the bottom of a problem that involves you and Eleanore Mungo."

"Okay, I went to see Darryl," Dorinda said. Dorinda's admission was straightforward, without the slightest bit of humbleness. "And I went because he invited me to come see him. That's all."

"Okay, maybe I get it," Big Joe conceded, but he really didn't have a clue what was going on. "Maybe, I'm beginning to think, you're playing a high card to flush out Eleanore."

Dorinda quickly changed the subject. "It's that black bitch that's causing all the trouble in the kitchen, Joe."

"Wait a minute," Big Joe blurted each word with added emphasis, sidelined by Dorinda's characterization of Geneva. "Those are harsh words, Dorinda," he said with controlled anger, though his face clearly expressed it. "You should be ashamed of yourself. I never, ever, want to hear you, or anyone, say anything like that about Geneva. She's worked harder than some employees who have been working here a lot longer than her. Furthermore, she's good at what she does."

"Are you speaking of me when you say some employees don't work hard?" Dorinda asked in a tone of fake innocence. Dorinda sensed Big Joe was alluding to her connection as a relative of the owner. She never admitted to it, but she sometimes liked to slack in her duties if she could get away with it. "I don't' think you have the right to say that to me."

"Attention, and being in the spotlight, is all that greases your wheels, Dorinda," Big Joe raised his voice. "That's all you ever want. Here's what I think. Eleanore comes along and gets more attention than you, makes more money than you, so you're going to throw a wrench at her."

Dorinda's brain worked fast to find a new angle to turn the conversation in her favor.

"You've got this all wrong, Joe," Dorinda smirked and placed her hand on her hip to accentuate her control over the argument. "If it helps matters, I'll have a conversation with Eleanore about this thing with Darryl. I'll set things straight with her myself. Right now, I have a table waiting on their food, and you probably should get back inside too. Aren't you supposed to be working on the grill?"

Dorinda quickly turned her back on Big Joe and stomped up the concrete step and through the kitchen door.

"What's going to be our lead story tomorrow?" Big Joe wondered. "The one person who should feel guilty is trying to cover up her guilt."

Big Joe threw up both his arms, let them slap back down on his apron sides, and mumbled, "I'm so fed up and frustrated."

Big Joe dropped his head, shook it side to side, and followed Dorinda through the kitchen door on the path back to work. He needed to check on the cook he left covering for him at the grill station.

"What was that last thing he just said?" Princess whispered to King.

"I couldn't hear it, and you don't have to whisper now. They both have gone back inside the restaurant kitchen," King answered.

"I have a bad feeling about everything that's happened tonight," Princess mournfully mewed to King. "First, Eleanore comes running out of *The Lucky Two* sobbing, followed by Darryl. Next, we hear Casey yelling at Darryl. Then we hear the kitchen staff arguing outside, and bringing up Eleanore's name."

"Which is what brought you two over this way, right?" Fat Cat sarcastically asked. "You really didn't come over here to visit me. You wanted to be closer to the kitchen."

The hair on King's back rose. He could find no reason for Fat Cat to get involved in the conversation he and Princess were having. King sat down on his haunches and placed his two front paws tightly together, like a soldier standing at attention. He intentionally avoided making a comment to Fat Cat, and addressed Princess.

"I think everything is going to be fine, Princess," King said, attempting to reassure Princess. "I'm sure Eleanore will come back to see Darryl. Did you watch her eyes and the way she kept looking up at him? She wanted to believe him. You heard her say that."

"Yes, but she left in a hurry. After she left, Darryl ran to his truck. When he drove away, the wheels were squealing. He left here driving like a maniac."

Princess blinked away the tears forming in her eyes. "It all makes me very nervous. I don't know what to make of it all. What if Eleanore never comes back? Indeed, I haven't shown her much attention since I've decided to live at the marina, but I can't stand the thought of her never coming back to the docks to visit us."

"That's right," Fat Cat interjected himself back into the conversation. "What if Eleanore never comes back? Who's going to feed you? Darryl? We don't get much from him. Maybe a new girl will come out here every night to feed you."

"You're talking nonsense, Fat Cat," Princess hissed, clearly annoyed by Fat Cat's sarcasm. "It was evident in the last argument we just heard that other girl has a cold heart. I'm worried, and you should be too. Eleanore might leave the marina for good. It might be you, Fat Cat, that misses her feeding ritual."

King relaxed his stance. He turned his head over the side of his shoulder and began to lick his back. King enjoyed hearing Princess stand up against Fat Cat.

"Do you really think you can depend on your big boy, King, to take care of you and feed you? I suspect he loves to eat out of the garbage dumpster behind Smith's," Fat Cat laughed. "I hope you enjoy leftovers from the dumpster. Good thing the restaurant is open; otherwise, you two might have to journey over to the new neighborhood for food handouts like the rest of your kittens do."

In one swift move King swung his head around and lowered it, zeroing in on Fat Cat's eyes. King's body stiffened. All four of his legs turned into rigid muscles, poised to attack. The fur on his back rose high. He first growled, then hissed at Fat Cat before leaping forward.

Princess leaped out from the bushes and ran in the opposite direction. When she reached the seawall, where the boats were docked, she stopped and turned to see King chasing after Fat Cat across the parking lot.

Fat Cat ran fast, but King caught up. Both cats ran circles around each other. Princess could hear their claws scratching against the pavement.

Like a bird circling above, swooping down to snatch its prey, King suddenly jumped onto Fat Cat's back. Both cats were howling and alternating between rolling around the pavement as one giant ball of fur and then separating. They were like two boxers in a boxing ring, putting some distance between their bodies before making the next punch. The animalistic screeches of the fighting cats traveled across the water and amplified beneath the lagoon bridge.

Princess quickly forgot about Eleanore. Her distress increased five-fold as she watched the fight between Fat Cat and King.

"I've been waiting too long to get my claws into your hide," she heard Fat Cat scream at King.

"We're going to have this out once and for all," King screamed back at Fat Cat.

There was nothing Princess could do except watch the drama.

When they stopped fighting, they were suffering from wounds. Blood trickled from patches of bloodied fur. Neither cat admitted defeat when they both retreated, licking the blood off their injuries.

"You haven't seen the last of me," Fat Cat hollered, bolting toward his condo.

Chapter 20
DREAMERS

Big Joe's huge body lumbered through the kitchen door. The door slammed hard behind him, making a loud noise that caught the attention of the kitchen crew, who kept working, pretending that they didn't notice him. Standing for a few moments to observe the activity before him, he wasn't sure if his brain was more tired than his legs. Still, he was acutely aware that he suffered from fatigue that was beginning to overpower his physical and psychological powers.

He brushed past the dishwasher, who was standing not far from the doorway. Instead of heading directly to the grill, Big Joe headed to the salad room where Sue and Geneva were standing side-by-side at their workstation.

Big Joe leaned over Geneva's shoulder. In a confidential whisper loud enough to be heard over the kitchen noise, he said, "Geneva, I'm going to need to talk to you after work tonight."

Geneva turned her head upward and looked at Big Joe with questioning eyes.

Big Joe knew he sounded tired, but he was talking to Geneva. She was not one of the employees who needed to hear him speak in his usual, authoritative manner.

"You want me to meet you in your office, sir?" Geneva asked, uncertain if it was about something she did wrong, or if it was the problem they'd been working on with Dorinda, Eleanore, and Darryl.

"No, I want to sit outside, on the bench," Big Joe said. "If that's not a problem for you. I'm ready to get out of this stuffy kitchen tonight. I'd like to sit by the water where there should be peace and quiet, and a fresh cool breeze."

Initially, to Sue's ears, the words sounded like Big Joe mumbled something about talking while they worked. Then, her brain quickly processed everything he was saying.

Sue's eyes popped open wide while she listened. She bent her head down lower to tend to the tomatoes she was slicing on the stainless-steel table, trying to pretend she wasn't eavesdropping. Her fingers were fumbling with the salad ingredients. Her whole attention was on hearing every word of the conversation.

"That's fine with me, sir," Geneva answered. "If I get out of the kitchen before you, I'll just wait for you outside. I'll be sitting on the bench."

"I'll lock up after everyone has left," he said. "It won't take me too long. Maybe ten minutes."

Big Joe's shoes made a heavy, clomping noise as he walked across the salad room floor and went back to the fire over the kitchen grills.

Once Big Joe was gone, out of sight, Geneva jerked her head back to look at Sue.

"Don't you be talking to anyone about me meeting with Big Joe after work tonight. I know you were listening to every word he said," Geneva hissed at Sue, clearly warning her to mind her own business. "If you do, I'm not going to be at all happy with you. I have a bad feeling about all of this stuff with Eleanore. Big Joe's upset about something, and I think I know what that something is all about. We all know he walked out the back door with Dorinda a little bit ago. That's all we know right now."

"The kitchen heat is finding a way into the salad room," Sue said with the giddiness of an eight-year-old girl about to celebrate at her birthday party. "I can't wait until tomorrow to find out what's going on. I know what he wants to talk to you about. He wants to know about Eleanore. You still haven't told me anything about what she said to you at the table in the dining room the other day. I want to know too! I think something exciting is about to happen."

"We shouldn't talk about other people's business anymore," Geneva snapped back, wishing that Sue would stop asking about Eleanore. Geneva was well aware that Sue could carry on a one-sided conversation if there was a good topic for discussion. Sue might continue talking about Eleanore all night.

Like Big Joe, Geneva felt her body and spirit growing tired. Dorinda's role in Eleanore's situation frustrated her; her brother Charles' situation worried her; working side-by-side with Sue was draining her energy.

Mustering up patience, Geneva grumbled what she thought would be a natural explanation Sue could find easy to believe. "It might take a couple of days, or even a week, for the matter with Eleanore to get settled. I know Big Joe wants any conflicts resolved. He just needs a little more time to get to the bottom of things. Let's not talk about it again until we know all of the answers. It may not even be a story that needs to be shared. Big Joe will take care of whatever needs to be done. Right now, you and I need to focus on our jobs."

Geneva's attitude and reluctance to talk surprised Sue. Most of the time, Geneva exercised an opinion when someone was doing something wrong at work.

Slightly disheartened by Geneva's standoffishness Sue simply said, "We need to wait for more answers. That sounds like a good plan."

Sue had come to respect Geneva during the past year, and she liked working with Geneva. She took a deep breath, smiled at Geneva, and added, "Patience, right? All good things come to those who wait."

Geneva, relieved to hear Sue's reaction, and acceptance of her suggestion, said, "Sue, I think you're a lovely person. I'm so glad I get to work with someone as nice as you."

Geneva genuinely liked working with Sue. Sue was dependable, consistently in a good mood, conscientious about her work, easy to talk to, and genuinely friendly to everyone. Her only downfall was that she was super sensitive, overreacting to other people's problems. Sue wasn't the type of person Geneva could depend on to talk to about her worries over Charles. Geneva left her problems at home.

Throughout the night, Geneva struggled with anxiety over what Big Joe had in mind to talk to her about. When food orders began to slow down, Geneva occupied herself with rearranging kitchen tools. Nervous restlessness was not a familiar feeling she ever dealt with before. What would Big Joe say when they met later that evening? Would he be angry? Would Big Joe ask her questions she couldn't answer?

Geneva decided she would not convey the news to Big Joe about Eleanore's pregnancy. The situation was too personal. She knew she could tell Big Joe that Darryl and Eleanore had relations, but nothing more. It was Eleanore's responsibility to tell Big Joe, when she was ready, what her plans were.

Big Joe, precisely as he promised, arrived at the bench ten minutes after Geneva sat down.

"Give your legs a rest," Geneva said in a soft, gentle voice.

Big Joe heaved a big sigh, plopped down, and stretched his long, thick, heavy legs out in front. He dug the heels of his heavy work shoes into the sand.

"Pretty nice to sit out here when it's quiet, nothing stirring, and look at the sky full of stars. It's nice, isn't it, Geneva?" he said.

"Yes, sir," Geneva answered.

"Do me a favor, Geneva. Don't call me *sir* when we're not on the job." Big Joe's said in a strained voice. "I understand why you say it, but here, outside the kitchen, I need to relax and feel comfortable. I'm not the boss out here."

"Okay," she answered, feeling less worried about what Big Joe was planning to talk to her about.

Big Joe took a very deep breath. The words spewed out like water draining down the kitchen sink, fast and smooth. He began by telling Geneva about the argument he had with Dorinda and what started it. When he finished, he asked, "What have you found out about the relationship between Darryl and Eleanore? Something tells me the answer is more complicated than what we expected when all this started."

"Yes, sir," Geneva timidly answered. "Oops, I didn't mean to say *sir*. I'm sorry."

Big Joe and Geneva chuckled, trying hard to lift the heavy, emotional burdens of their night at work. They sat in silence for a few minutes before Geneva spoke again.

"All I can tell you is that Eleanore told me Darryl has been interested in her. He's been wanting their relationship to take a new direction. She's not so sure, but she's trying to be open-minded about becoming serious as a couple. Something has happened between them, and I can't tell you more than that. Eleanore needs to tell you herself. I have felt so bad for this young girl. She's confused about Darryl, and she should be," Geneva paused to look at Big Joe's reaction to her words.

Big Joe stared back at Geneva with a blank face, obviously finding himself nowhere nearer to the bottom line. He still had no answer to the simple question of whether Eleanore and Darryl were a couple.

Geneva understood Big Joe's confused reaction and continued without disclosing any more information regarding Eleanore's personal predicament.

"The fact that Dorinda is involved makes this whole situation much more of a problem," Geneva said, thinking that now would be the right time to tell Big Joe about seeing Dorinda boarding *The Lucky Two*. "I really don't know what's going on in Dorinda's life that would explain why she would hold a grudge against Eleanore. But I can tell you that I saw Dorinda walk onboard *The Lucky Two* one night when I was sitting in my car getting ready to drive away after work. It's as confusing to me as it is for you."

Geneva stared up at the night sky, avoiding the reaction on Big Joe's face to the new information. She talked faster.

"I've got my own personal problems. I've known some people who think that they have problems, but we never know how bad our problems are until we walk in the shoes of another person. There's not much you and I can do to intervene, except to tell that nasty girl Dorinda to stop harassing our sweet Eleanore when we're at work. Suppose Dorinda continues to do her harassing in subtle ways, like trying to get her food orders before Eleanore? In that case, it will make the atmosphere terrible for all of us. The bottom line is, whatever is happening between Darryl and Eleanore will have to be left up to them to figure out."

Big Joe's lowered his head, gently shaking it in agreement, while listening and processing every word.

"I guess I've said enough for now," Geneva sighed and turned her head away to look at the water. She waited for Big Joe to respond.

"Sista, I like the way you tell it like it is. You tell it like it should be. I appreciate an honest employee, and more importantly, you're a person who I can trust." Big Joe patted Geneva on the back.

"So, I should go home now and get some rest," she said, rising from the bench, still avoiding his eyes.

Big Joe stood up and groaned, "Man, my legs hurt. I think you have the right idea. I'm going home to sleep. I think I know what I need to say to Dorinda tomorrow. You've been very helpful, Sista."

A gentle but sad smile formed on Geneva's face. She loved hearing Big Joe use the name her brother used to call her. It was a grim reminder that she had to go home with the hope that her dreams would bring some new ideas on how to deal with the problem of Charles being in jail.

"Sweet dreams tonight, Geneva. I know all of this has been hard on you. I'd apologize for some of the things Dorinda said to me outside of the kitchen. Some people probably heard the whole argument. But I think you know how I feel about her. What she's doing is wrong. I know I want to ask her to apologize tomorrow. I hope she'll cooperate. I'm certainly going to need a good dream to help me figure out what to do about her and how she's been treating Eleanore."

They lifted their tired bodies off the bench and walked side-by-side through the parking lot until they each reached their cars. Smiling, Geneva looked directly at Big Joe and said, "Sweet dreams, Joe."

CHAPTER 21
LIVING ON ANOTHER PLANET

Staring at the dark walls inside *The Lucky Two* would do his soul no good. Darryl needed to get out, talk to someone besides himself.

Still dressed, he got back into his truck and aimlessly drove around the neighborhoods south of Thomas Drive. Eventually, he decided to pay a visit to Sharkey, the Treasure Island Marina manager and someone he had not seen in a long time. Sharkey, who he knew to have a sympathetic ear and a warm heart, was intimately aware of the history of *The Lucky Two* and how Casey got involved in the bizarre, if not crazy, mess from the beginning.

Sharkey lived only a few blocks from the Treasure Island Marina in a cement block house similar to Casey's house. The cement blockhouses were a staple style of construction used for the first homes built on the beach. Most of them were survivors of past hurricanes, unlike the stick houses built in modern times.

Sharkey greeted Darryl at his front door with a hearty, one-armed hug and handshake. He didn't think to ask Darryl why he was unexpectedly visiting so late.

"Man, it's good to see you. What a surprise. I haven't kept up-to-date with many people since the hurricane," Sharkey said. "Come on inside. Sit down and tell me what's going on," Sharkey smiled and with a swoop of his arm waved at Darryl to sit in a worn but sturdy-looking, brown wicker chair. "I've been super busy trying to clean up the at the marina boat storage facility and start back business," Sharkey said when he shut the front door. "All I've been doing is going to work and afterward coming home to read my history books, like I always did, only I fall asleep a lot quicker these days. You been reading any good history?"

Darryl didn't wait to sit down before starting to talk.

"I guess you remember the drama over *The Lucky Two*?" Darryl said, flopping down into the chair.

"How could I forget that one?" Sharkey chuckled and took a seat on his sofa. "Speaking of history, that became quite a famous story around here. Especially the way it all ended with the captain of the charter boat getting murdered and the girlfriend ending up living with Casey, who originally wanted to store the boat at Treasure Island." Sharkey laughed a little harder and added, "The story might become a legend one day. There's a lot of hurricane stories people can tell, but that one is a doozie." Sharkey stopped laughing. He saw the serious look on Darryl's face.

"Well, it's been a continuing saga, as you might imagine," Darryl said. He hung his head, staring at the floor, and began to rub the top of his bald head. "I came over here because I need to talk to someone about the girlfriend of the man who was murdered. The girl who was rescued from the hurricane by Casey. That's if you have the time. I'm sorry to barge in on you like this."

Sharkey squinted his eyes and took a sharper look at Darryl. There were lines of fatigue buried in Darryl's face and forehead. Dark circles beneath his eyes reflected worry and possibly depression. Sharkey knew Darryl's easy-going personality, and this was not normal.

"Sure, shoot, brother. We can talk about the charter boat, fishing business some other time," Sharkey said sympathetically. "I'll call it an early night on the history book I'm reading."

Darryl slumped down deeper into the chair and began.

"So, after the hurricane, I accepted Casey's offer to stay at his house, only because that's where the girl decided to stay too," Darryl paused. He sighed, rolled his eyes upward, and shook his head as though denying the reality of all that had happened.

"It quickly became too awkward after a few months with the three of us together in the same house," he continued. "When March rolled around, and it stopped being so cold, she suggested that I stay on *The Lucky Two*. She thought maybe I could make some money fishing until the probate issues were finalized. I plan to use my insurance settlement money for *The Star Chaser* to buy *The Lucky Two*. Her name is Eleanore, by the way."

"I forgot her name," Sharkey said. "It's been a year since the hurricane. Actually, I don't think I've ever seen her."

"She's a beautiful girl," Darryl rushed to say. "I fell in love with her the moment I saw her. It had something to do with her eyes. The way she looked at me when I offered to drive her to Captain Anderson's Marina. It was kind of like the old love story of Cupid's arrow going right through my heart."

A sheepish look came over Darryl. "I don't know. It just happened," he said.

"So, what's the problem?" Sharkey asked. "Has she become interested in Casey now?"

"Oh, no. It's not that at all," Darryl said. "At least I don't think she is."

Darryl dove into his love story with Eleanore, using words like sweetness, kindness, honesty, determination, and soulfulness. He ended by telling Sharkey the last time he saw Eleanore, she was going for a walk on the beach, and it had been a couple of days since he'd seen her until tonight.

"Eleanore and I have seen or talked to each other almost every day since I've been staying on *The Lucky Two*. She always comes to the boat, feeds the cats, and stopped in to see me. I can't understand why she would give me the cold shoulder. I never go to see her at work, or Casey's house, so I approached a waitress in the parking lot of Smith's. I asked if she would do me a favor and check on Eleanore. The waitress's name is Dorinda."

At that point in the story, a red flag was raised and waved in the face of Sharkey. He had been sitting comfortably on his sofa, patiently listening, nodding his head, and smiling at some of the details Darryl provided. At the mention of Dorinda's name, Sharkey scooted to the edge of the sofa cushion and held up both his hands like he was trying to stop a car in the middle of the road.

"Wait a minute," Sharkey said. "Stop right there. Did you say the girl is named Dorinda?"

Surprised by Sharkey's sudden reaction, Darryl nodded and waited for Sharkey to speak.

"That girl, Dorinda, is a *schmo*," Sharkey said, and sniffed like a bad smell suddenly drifted into the room.

"What do you mean?" Darryl asked.

"I can't think of a better word for her. She's stupid," Sharkey said. "I went out with her, I think twice, many, many years ago. Dorinda may be beautiful on the outside, but she has scars on the inside. She lifts her skirt for anyone. With each new man she dates, she reopens the wounds and makes her scars wider. She hasn't figured out life yet. She acts up when she doesn't get what she wants. Who wants to be around a person like that? Certainly not you."

Darryl rubbed his bald head again, an old, nervous habit as if he was searching for a solution from a crystal ball. He didn't want to tell Sharkey the rest of the story, but knew that he had to.

"I had no idea," Darryl said, when he finished the rest of the story, ending with a desperate plea for help. "What can I do now?"

"I'd say that leaving those panties on the boat was like her leaving a calling card, only she knew you weren't interested in her. I can't say I'm full of advice about what to tell you to do next to make things better with Eleanore. Still, I think having a beer together at Estelle's Escape might help," Sharkey said, standing up. "A worrying mind is not good. If you worry that it's not going to work out, it probably won't. We have to come up with a plan and make things work."

"Sounds a little dangerous to me," Darryl replied, relieved that Sharkey was on his side. "Just keep Estelle's mouth out of my business. She's been around a long time, and she knows everything about anybody. I don't need her talking about me."

Sharkey laughed, "Yes, Estelle knows the personal business about many people in this town, but she also knows when it's the right time to talk about someone. I doubt that she's going to ask you about your business."

The two men walked to the bar on Thomas Drive called Estelle's Escape, only two streets away from Sharkey's house. The bar was across the street from the beach and close enough to make it a popular hang-out for the many locals who worked in the seasonal industry of restaurants and entertainment. Anyone interested in going for a walk on the beach after work could get a beer at Estelle's Escape to put their minds in a better mood and then walk across the road to set their toes in the sand.

"I don't think I've seen either of you two guys since before the hurricane," Estelle greeted them when the two men bellied up to the bar. "Y'all been doing okay?"

Both men nodded their heads and provided Estelle with toothy smiles. It was good to see Estelle, who was someone who didn't take any punches from customers and always preferred the regulars, the locals. The tourists didn't know the unwritten rules of the bar: *keep your hands to yourself, take your arguments outside, and make it to the toilet if you feel the urgent need to be sick.*

"You're looking a little glum, Darryl. What will you have?" Estelle wiped the counter with a wet bar rag, crossed her arms, and leaned over the counter. "Let me get a closer look at you two," she said, grinning ear-to-ear, adding, "tell me the latest news."

"Not much on my end of the marina that's different from anywhere else. But Darryl, here, has gotten himself into trouble by falling in love," Sharkey said.

Darryl looked at Sharkey with his blue eyes expressing horror. "What did I tell you before we got here?" Darryl whispered loudly enough for Estelle to hear what he said.

Estelle looked at both men with keen interest and a twinkle in her eyes. "Two draft beers for you guys going to be good?"

In unison, Darryl and Sharkey said yes, and watched Estelle turn around to pour the drafts.

"Don't you worry, my friend. I ain't naming any names. I'm going to use some hypotheticals," Sharkey said, offering Darryl an impish, thin-lipped grin and a wink.

"I don't know if I like that look on your face," Darryl said, rolling his eyes.

Estelle returned to the counter with two mugs of beer and said, "Give me the short story on the trouble. Name the who, when, how, and what. I already know about why people fall in love."

"Imagine Darryl's gone to live on another planet," Sharkey began.

A unified loud groan from Estelle and Darryl stopped Sharkey momentarily.

Sharkey laughed when he saw their eyeballs roll to the ceiling, then took a long pull from his glass of beer, ignoring their reaction.

Sharkey continued with his hypothetical version of Darryl's problem.

"All right, let's pretend it's not Darryl. It's somebody else. This person has taken a companion with him so he wouldn't be alone. The companion becomes distant, doesn't want to have anything to do with him, and he doesn't know why, so he goes and asks an alien for help. The alien turns out to be a schemer and, for unknown reasons, and tries to sabotage him."

Darryl busted out laughing, as did Estelle.

Sharkey, pleased with himself, went on. "The companion returns to visit Darryl and discovers the *sabatogery*."

Darryl and Estelle's devoted attention momentarily halted. They both groaned again.

"I made up that word," Sharkey laughed, pleased with himself. "I may use it again."

The beer made Sharkey forget that he was not supposed to use Darryl's name.

"Anyway, the companion becomes intensely upset with Darryl and abruptly leaves before Darryl can fully prove his explanation. What should Darryl do next?"

Estelle loved a good story, but needed to serve beer to another customer. "Let me think on it for a minute or two," she said. "I'll be right back."

"I like the way you didn't name any names," Darryl said with solid sarcasm. "Very clever." Darryl took several swallows of his beer.

Sharkey resumed his rhetoric. "I was thinking on the way over here that living on that boat, *The Lucky Two* is bad karma for you and the girl. Eleanore is her name, right? Y'all need to put that in the past if you want to start a new history together. I don't think you need to be buying that boat. It will always be a reminder to her. Maybe that's what was bothering her so much. Now you've got the problem that Dorinda created, but I think you can get past that. It's the boat, man."

"I was going to give the boat another name," Darryl said in defense of himself.

"That won't change anything," Sharkey said. "Living on that boat is always going to be like living on another planet for you. It's not *The Star Chaser*. It will always be her ex-boyfriend's boat, and she won't ever forget it. She won't want to live with you on the boat even if the name isn't *The Lucky Two*."

Darryl realized what Sharkey was telling him was true.

Solemnly Darryl nodded in agreement. "Rootin' Tootin' truth," he mumbled, looking into his nearly empty glass of beer.

When Estelle returned, she noticed Darryl's mood had changed.

"I like the way you frame things, Sharkey," she said. "I didn't want to know any names. I've got to listen to enough people's problems with their friends, family, and spouses. They come in here to drink their beer. After a beer, or two, they get loose lips. I should charge a listening fee."

Estelle gave Darryl a stern look and said, "Straighten up, Darryl. Wipe that frown off your face. Life's not all that bad. Here's what I think. Take action. Go after that companion. Whatever it takes, go get her. Find out what's bothering her. As far as the alien goes, put as much social distancing as possible between you and the alien. Revenge is not as sweet as you may think. It brings bad karma."

Sharkey arched his eyebrows and gave Darryl a look with eyes that said, *what did I just tell you about karma*?

Darryl sat silent for a few minutes. He picked up the mug, tilted it upward, and drank the remainder of his beer to the bottom of the glass.

Darryl perked up after finishing the beer and sat taller in his seat. "I'm ready to go," he said.

Looking first at Sharkey and then at Estelle, he said, "I've been living on another planet and forgot about all the stars in my own universe. The celestial sky is for all of us dreamers, but it's time for me to stop running in circles chasing dreams. Before the hurricane, I considered how many more years I could work operating a charter boat. I felt like I was getting too old to be doing it much longer, even though I love fishing. I need to find my purpose and home. Hopefully, I can convince the girl I love that I need her to be with me. Whatever it takes, I'll do it."

"Remember, Darryl," Estelle said as the men slipped off their barstools and before they turned to leave. "Love your enemies as you love the ones who love you. Wish them no harm."

"That sounds like something that came right out of the bible," Darryl remarked to Estelle. "Is that the same as do unto others as you would have done to you?"

Estelle shrugged her shoulders and said, "Doesn't sound like you went to church very much, Darryl."

"Well, no," Darryl said, dragging out the words, "I'm not embarrassed to say that I haven't. But it doesn't mean I don't believe in the power of God, greater than my own."

"Then maybe you could use a few lessons. Go sit in a church pew some Sunday," Sharkey said. "C'mon, we need to leave. I have to get up early, and you don't need to drink any more beer."

Darryl and Sharkey left money on the counter, saluted Estelle, and said together, "See you next time."

Estelle smiled to herself as she watched both men walk out the door. "If they only knew," Estelle thought. "So much heartache in life could be avoided if people would only follow some simple principles."

When Darryl returned to the marina, the restaurant lights were off, and all humans were gone.

Darryl turned off the engine to his truck and stared at the blue dolphin hanging from the rear-view mirror of his truck. The glass dolphin glinted in the lights from the parking lot. The shining dolphin reminded him of the conversation he and Eleanore had about dolphins on the first day he met her.

Darryl's old habit of talking out loud to himself kicked back into gear, fueled by the beer. He needed to reassure himself before going back inside for the night.

"A symbol of protection for the sailors and fishermen. I suppose there's a glimmer of hope that I convinced Eleanore tonight that Dorinda means nothing to me. In that case, that will be the start I need to get our relationship back on track. I can't lose Eleanore for a stupid stunt pulled off by a woman who thinks I might have noticed her dancing when I was playing my saxophone in the band years ago. I can't, for the life of me, understand why this woman wants to act so aggressively, but I do know that I need Eleanore. "

From his high perch in the woodpile of the cat condo, Fat Cat eyed Darryl sitting in his truck and could hear Darryl talking out loud to himself. He, too, noticed the dolphin through the windshield.

He watched Darryl uncharacteristically slam the door of his truck, causing the blue glass dolphin to sway slightly.

"How coincidental that Darryl and I share the same bad luck," Fat Cat mused. "He's trying to get his girlfriend back, and I'm still trying to make an inside track on Princess."

CHAPTER 22
RICKY'S REQUEST

In a steady, soothing, voice Eve spoke to Ricky.

"Ricky, I want you to write something, anything, you can remember about the day you and Vince were trailing Earl in his truck. Were you trying to evacuate from the hurricane? What you and Vince wanted was to get your money back, right? Am I right?"

Ricky was listening. He knew he shouldn't be surprised that this visit would include questions about that day, but thinking about it always made him feel uncomfortable, even though it happened such a long time ago.

Eve continued, "A small detail that may not seem significant to you may be important to helping me find freedom for you. When you left Captain Anderson's Marina, try to remember what you and Vince were talking about and what you planned to do. I've written down four short questions. I'll read them first. Look at them, then write down your answers."

Eve read slowly from a piece of paper while Ricky listened.

"Who got out of the truck after you stopped at Pine Log Forest State Park? If you got out of the truck, what did you do? If you stayed in Vince's truck, what did you do? What did you see Vince do?"

When Eve finished reading the questions, she said, "Write down the answers to the questions I've written down. Then I want you to think about what you, and Vince, were doing after you stopped in the parking lot. I have an hour, so don't rush. I am hoping the questions will jar your memory of some other details of what happened that day. Any small detail might be very significant."

Eve's questions were easy, but thinking about what happened in the parking lot at Pine Log Forest State Park made Ricky's head throb. Ricky's eyes rolled to the ceiling, searching for answers, then let his head drop, propped his elbow on the table, and cupped his chin into the palm of one hand. He rubbed his forehead and drummed his fingers near his hairline. Her questions were the same questions he was asked to answer by his court-appointed defense attorney, but he struggled writing out the answers back then.

He never liked to think about the day of Earl Keith's murder, but he felt forced to do it since she asked him.

Ricky clearly remembered Vince driving the truck like a madman on Highway 79 and ordering him to count the money he took from Earl's truck. Ricky remembered how Vince's mood changed after he heard how much money there was. Vince kept talking about how his mother would be proud of him. Ricky remembered Vince singing the words *We're gonna be Jammin'* over and over. Vince's plan was to go to a hotel in Biloxi named the Windjammer. They were going to gamble in a casino.

Ricky thought. "She wants me to remember everything that happened when we were in the parking lot at Pine Log Forest State Park. She didn't ask me to remember what happened after leaving the parking lot or the night I spent alone during the hurricane. All I need to write down is what happened in that parking lot."

Ricky thought a moment about where to start. He began to write.

First, I didn't get out of the truck. Vince got out of the truck, walked over to Earl's truck, and threw a punch at Earl through the window. Earl's head and shoulders slumped over his steering wheel. I saw Vince run around to the passenger side of Earl's truck. Vince threw something in the bushes. I saw the bushes move. Then Vince ran back and got into his truck. When we got back on the road, Vince threw the money on my lap and asked me to count it. Vince was happy when I told him how much we had.

When he finished writing, Ricky re-read his sentences. Everything seemed right, even his spelling, but he couldn't stop staring at the paper for several minutes.

"I do remember seeing Vince throw something into the woods before he got back into the truck, but I have no idea what it was. I wish I knew," Ricky thought. "I wonder if I should erase that part. I don't remember if I mentioned it before. She'll notice that I'm erasing and probably tell me to stop. I'll just leave it, but I hope she doesn't ask me what Vince threw into the bushes. I only remember thinking that I wish Vince would hurry up 'cuz we needed to get out of that parking lot fast. I remember thinking that there was a good chance that the charter boat captain might lift up his head off the steering wheel, shake off the punch, and start chasing us in his truck to get the money back. I had no idea what Vince stopped to throw. I never asked him, either."

"Okay," Eve said, after reading what Ricky wrote. "This helps a bit. You don't know what Vince threw away?" she immediately asked.

Ricky, embarrassed, slightly shook his head no.

"I'm going to say that you've given me some good information. Once again, I commend you on remembering and telling me the details. Since our time is nearly finished, I will cut my visit a few minutes short today. Thank you for answering my questions and writing out the details as you remembered them. I know it's not easy for you." Eve said. "I'm going to read the deposition you gave to your attorney and check it against this information. I'll be back again in a week, maybe two. I think I'll need some more time to do a little more research before I can come back to visit. I hope that's okay for you, too?"

Ricky gently nodded his head to agree. He felt somewhat disappointed in himself, thinking that the answers he wrote down might be inadequate, and that was why she might not come back to visit as soon. He was also disappointed that the visit was cut short. He liked sitting in the same room with Eve. She was the nicest woman he'd ever met.

Eve returned to the beach house she was renting and spent hours going over Ricky's answers and the deadly encounter in the parking lot at Pine Log Forest State Park.

Eve at Peace by Yvette Doolittle Herr

In the transcripts Eve read from Ricky's court case, nothing was mentioned about the detail of Vince throwing an object. She wondered what kind of questions the defense lawyer asked Ricky? Had Ricky's lawyer asked him any questions, or dug any deeper for more information? Ricky's communication problems, and the immediate shock of living through a hurricane, may have been too much stress for the court-appointed lawyer.

She curbed her feelings of anger about Ricky's inadequate defense at his trial and, instead, focused on the new information.

Eve rubbed the yellow piece of paper between her forefinger and thumb several times, staring at the words. *Vince threw something into the bushes. I saw the bushes move.*

"Bushes. Bushes. What kind of bush was it? What object could be small enough, or big enough, to make the bush move? Ricky noticed the movement," Eve kept asking herself, re-reading Ricky's scrawl on the piece of yellow legal paper one last time before laying it down on the desk.

"Florida has many native plants. What grows in north Florida?" Eve picked up the piece of paper again and waved it in front of her face, back and forth like a fan.

"I know weeds grow tall in an open field, but all of those pine trees in Pine Log Forest would most likely limit the height of the weeds. Ricky wrote the word bush. Spanish Bayonets are a type of bush, has some size, but the leaves are thick and solid. They have those pointed tips, like daggers. They probably wouldn't budge an inch if someone threw something at them. Any object would just bounce off the Spanish Bayonet bush.

"Wait a minute," Eve opened her eyes wide and held out the piece of paper she'd been using to fan her face. She stared hard at the words and said, with a huge smile, "This is such an easy answer. It had to be a Palmetto bush. Palm plants are common in the State of Florida. Even the State of Florida flag has a Palmetto Palm on it. Palm branches, like the ones the ancient Egyptians used for fans. Palm branches, a symbol of goodness, greatness, and victory. Palm branches like the ones used to line the path for Jesus' entry into Jerusalem. I have this feeling, deep in my gut, that a Palmetto will break this case open for me. I feel a victory. If I hadn't been born on the eve of an Easter Sunday and grown up knowing about the Easter story, I might not have made a connection to the palm leaves."

Eve began pushing her brain to come up with an object that Vince would throw. "It was something that Vince could hold in his hand, so it couldn't be huge but heavy enough to make the bush move. Keys to the truck? No, the keys were found in the ignition. Besides, he ran around to the passenger door. Vince picked up something out of Earl's truck. It was obviously something on the front seat. His wallet! It had to be Earl's wallet because the police found no identification in the truck and needed someone to identify him."

Ecstatic about the conclusion, which she believed was more than just a hunch, Eve jumped up from her chair. She stretched her arms up above her head and ran in place, just like a child who had just won first place in a school contest.

"That's it. It was Earl's wallet," she shouted and eased back down in her chair.

"I can go back to the park and search. If they had searched the area after finding Earl, they probably would have found it. Still, the authorities were too busy trying to resolve hurricane problems to conduct a search. They probably concluded the wallet was stolen and thrown away later along the road. Any good leather wallet could last twenty years lying beneath a bush in Florida weather. I'll need to decide what area to start looking for it. I know that the truck was parked facing north, but that wouldn't tell me which direction Vince threw the wallet. I need to get started on this as soon as possible."

So excited about her revelation, she contacted the Florida Department of Natural Resources the next day. She sent them a copy of the note Ricky had written and requested permission to scour the area. She wanted the expertise of a park ranger to accompany her when she conducted her search of the site.

She returned to Pine Log Forest State Park and met with the ranger waiting for her to roam the grounds near the area where both trucks pulled in on that day. The park was nearly in the same condition as it was all those years ago. No improvements had been made. The gravel stones in the parking lot, the painted sign at the entrance, the logwood fence, and the expanse of broadleaf pines standing tall above everything else were postcard perfect.

After they introduced themselves, Eve asked, "Has there been regular slash burnings in this park?" She was hoping he would say no. Slash burning, a method used to mitigate out-of-control forest fires, would destroy anything she was looking for except metal. Eve wasn't looking for metal.

"No, ma'am," he answered. "These acres of pine tree growth are easy to manage compared to some of the other forested areas we have in Florida. This area is closer to the Gulf of Mexico, so the soil is sandier. Deep woods forests have more mulch from other natural vegetation. Mostly what grows here are the palm, nettle weeds, and sand weeds. They don't get very tall, so we don't need to do control burns. The weeds die back in the winter. I can't remember the last time we had a natural fire in this area. Lightening sometimes causes a fire in the forest, but most fires get started by people. If they pull off to the side of the road, their hot car engines may set off dry grass to start burning. Once started, it can easily get out of control. Sometimes a cigarette butt thrown out the window sets off a fire in the dry grass. We don't get many cars stopping here, though, since there are no facilities. This is more of a parking lot for people who want to hike in the woods. The trailhead is over there," he finished and pointed to a marker several yards away.

Eve stood in the middle of the gravel parking lot, waiting for the park ranger to begin to lead her in the search.

Eve's interest in the murder case that happened years ago intrigued the park ranger. He'd heard about it, but knew little about the details of the people involved. It was one of the most unusual events in the history of the park. He wanted to talk a bit about the case's background.

"The last thing anyone would expect to find after a hurricane is for someone to be found murdered," he said. "They had to take four-wheelers through the woods to get to the person who could identify the man. Some woman was riding out the hurricane on the man's charter boat with one of the marine patrol officers. That fact, in itself, was another strange piece of the puzzle. The marine patrol officer who heard the announcement on the boat radio of the discovery of a man's body in the truck at the park called us. He asked us to come to pick them up at Dismal Creek, where they were waiting in the bay. A pretty famous case in our history book of the park. I can't imagine someone being so upset to commit murder over the loss of a little bit of money. I think I heard that it was about seven hundred dollars. How all those people came to be connected is something we never could figure out."

"Yes, it seems unusual to me, too," Eve agreed, trying to conceal her amusement over the park ranger's interest in the salacious story.

Eve and the park ranger began their walk into the wild brush bordering the gravel parking lot.

Eve and the park employee each used a long, slender metal rod to poke into the ground. There was a straight edge of metal on one side of the rod they used to dig and scrape the dirt. On the other side, there was a twelve-inch, sharp metal point to poke into the palmetto, weeds, and the ubiquitous Spanish bayonets. Eve tried not to be scared when she saw the tail of a swamp snake slither away, but couldn't control the spontaneous, high-pitched gasp that emerged from her mouth.

"Sorry about that," she groaned, embarrassed by her reaction to the snake. To herself, she thought, "Why would I be so surprised to see a snake?"

"It's okay, ma'am. Don't worry too much. They don't like you either, unless you surprise one by stepping on it," the park ranger said. "Once a snake feels the vibrations from our footsteps on the ground, it's unlikely we'll see any more snakes. About this time of year is when they're starting to look for a permanent winter home. Just be sure to stop dead still if you hear a sound like a baby rattle. Rattlesnakes are around here too. You don't want to get bit by a rattlesnake.'"

The park ranger and Eve spent three hours stomping on the ground, trampling their feet in short circles that grew wider and wider. By the late afternoon, the heat, coupled with humidity fueled by brilliant sunshine, caused Eve to sweat profusely. Her clothing clung to her body. She persisted in the search until Earl's wallet was found short of thirty feet from the stone gravel parking lot. The leather wallet was surprisingly intact, covered by layers of dried pine needles, weeds, and palm fronds.

The discovery of the wallet and the potential that there was new evidence to help Ricky get out of prison thrilled Eve. There would be DNA on the inside of the wallet. Would there be a match to the DNA found on the snake ring? There was almost no other evidence connected to the crime except for the blood found in the snake's eye on the silver ring. The blood matched Earl's blood. Ricky was wearing the ring when he was picked up by the sheriff's deputy on Highway 20. Yet, Eve firmly believed that Ricky took the snake ring off Vince's finger. For one, the snake ring didn't fit Ricky's personality, plus he was found wearing the oversized ring on the middle finger of his left hand. She knew Ricky was right-handed from watching him write. If Ricky threw a punch at Earl, he would have done it with his right hand. She also knew there was a slim possibility that Vince's DNA could be found on the snake ring and could match any of Vince's DNA found on the wallet.

Ricky was better prepared when he was notified about Eve's next scheduled visit. He wrote a short note to give her.

I have a friend named Charles. He arrived here almost exactly a year after I did. He was also convicted of a murder that he didn't do. He's innocent, just like me. Can you help him too? He can explain everything.

CHAPTER 23
EVE MEETS CHARLES

So distracted by her excitement to tell Ricky the excellent news, it was the first time Eve didn't notice the depressing entrance to the prison compound after turning into it. A sprawling complex of one-story, cinder block buildings painted white, surrounded by razored barbed wire fencing layers, covered more than three hundred acres of flat, mostly barren ground. A dozen prison buses, windows painted white and reinforced with horizontal metal bars, were parked in the perimeter of the prison parking lot. She often wondered who traveled in these buses and where they went.

Eve started the meeting by telling Ricky that she found Earl's wallet and explaining how finding Earl's wallet was compelling new evidence in the case.

"You gave me a valuable clue the last time we met," she told Ricky.

Eve knew that there were new techniques in lifting fingerprints off objects and processing DNA. In the recent world of forensic science, latent fingerprints can survive up to forty years on a non-porous surface. A good lab would match the DNA on the ring and any plastic inside the leather wallet.

"The wallet's been sent to state labs for testing for DNA. Even though the wallet was outside, in the elements, there's still a chance they may find Vince's DNA on the inside of the wallet. If so, there's a strong possibility it could clear your conviction in the murder," Eve said. "You said you never got out of the truck. If that's the truth, I know you didn't touch Earl's wallet."

Ricky shyly smiled and calmly nodded his head in his typical style to show that he was listening and somewhat understood what she was telling him. Nothing she said alarmed or excited him and sent his nervous system into twitches.

Perplexed by Ricky's subtle reaction, Eve said, "It will most likely take a few months for the results to come back," she added, trying to curb her enthusiasm. She thought to herself, "Why is it that Ricky didn't appear that interested in the news."

Then Ricky slid his clipboard across the table and pointed to the note he'd written on behalf of Charles.

Ricky watched Eve as she read the note, studying her face. He watched her eyebrows arch up higher and higher, setting wrinkled lines across her forehead.

Eve read the note several times before looking up at Ricky. She nodded her head up and down and spoke.

"Yes, I am willing to meet with your friend Charles, but it will take permission of the prison superintendent. I'll have to do some research on the case first, which will take me some time. I cannot ask the superintendent to see a prisoner without the background information to justify the meeting. That's what I had to do to get permission to meet with you."

Ricky's lips parted into a rare, spontaneous smile. This was the first time that Eve noticed a few of his teeth were missing, like half of his tongue. Years of neglecting his oral hygiene caused the problem. In prison, there were few occasions, or reasons, for him to smile at someone. This was such an occasion. Ricky was not overly conscious about his appearance and didn't think about being embarrassed. The most important thing for him at the moment was the warm, good feeling in his heart. He felt a small measure of success, believing that he might have found a way to help his friend, Charles. Ricky knew this was only the first step; there was a long way to go.

Scenes of his future, trying to live as a free man outside of prison, muddled Ricky's brain. After Eve's last visit, when she asked him to write down answers to her questions about Pine Log Forest, he thought, "What if she gets my conviction overturned? I don't even know if I want to leave prison. I'm comfortable here. I don't have anywhere else to go," Ricky thought many times at night, alone on his cot. "I'm happy reading my bible. The food isn't too bad. Some of the other prisoners aren't nice people, but all of the prisoners leave me alone. They don't bother me at all. Occasionally someone will say a few words to me to acknowledge I exist. Typically, nobody here, except for Charles, talks to me at all. Charles doesn't talk to me as much as he did the first weeks after he arrived. We understand and appreciate each other, though. We know that we've been sentenced to live our life here based on unfair convictions. Neither of us committed the crime. I know Charles still wants to get out of here. He has a sister and maybe other family. I often hear him muttering about wishing he stayed back home in Pennsylvania. Charles thinks he should have taken a job working with his sister at the restaurant where she works since it turned out he's become a dishwasher in the prison kitchen anyway. I bet Charles would like to meet this woman Eve and tell her his story. He can talk, and it's not as much effort for him to tell his story. I feel this young woman can find the facts and get to the truth in Charles' case. I'm pretty sure that Charles would live a clean life if given a chance to get out of this prison."

Ricky was anxious to communicate his ideas to Charles. Writing them all down on paper was tedious, but he was determined. He didn't want to get out of prison and be on his own. He would need a friend outside of prison, and he knew that friends would be hard to find for him. Charles had already been his friend for a long time.

He wrote about them getting out of prison together. In conclusion, Ricky wrote, "She'll want to help you if you're innocent, and I believe that you are innocent. If you tell her the story that you told me about the Halloween party, I bet she'll believe you too. She's always asking me to remember small details that help her figure out how she can get to the truth. She's like a bloodhound, sniffing around for facts."

Charles was skeptical when he read Ricky's ideas.

"I've been in this prison a long time, as have you, and for me, it feels like time has stood still. Nothing changes. The uniforms are the same, the walls are the same, and the food is the same. It's only you and me getting older. Why should I even bother talking to that woman?" Charles asked Ricky, stunned by Ricky's idea.

Ricky felt deflated and rejected when he heard Charles' reaction to Ricky's proposal to meet Eve.

As soon as he saw the disappointment on Ricky's face, guilt consumed Charles. This poor, skinny, white man had been a trusted prison friend to him for more than twenty years. He, Charles, had just treated his best friend, Ricky, very poorly.

Charles immediately corrected his response. "Man, you're an amazing friend, you know that? I can't believe you're thinking of me when you have a lawyer trying to help you get out of this place. She can probably dig up dirt on your case a lot easier than mine," Charles said to Ricky. "Yeah, I'd like the chance to talk to someone different. I like it when my Sista comes to see me, but she doesn't come like she used to. There's not a whole lot of stuff we can talk about. Sista can tell me all about the things going on in her life, but there's nothing for me to talk about my life in here. Life truly stands still while I'm in here. Maybe you're right. My life can be more than this kind of daily existence. There is more of the world out there that I never had a chance to see or discover."

Charles agreed to meet with Eve to satisfy Ricky's wishes. His initial instincts told him not to trust a young, white woman. However, he couldn't find reasons to justify why he had these feelings about her. "Is it my father, Maximillian, who gave me this instinct not to trust the white woman?" Charles wondered.

Charles said to Ricky, "I'm going against my better judgment to meet with this woman at least one time. I'm doing it for you, Ricky. If I think she is truthful about having my best interest in her mind, then I'll give her a chance. I only have to meet with her once to get a good feeling about the whole thing."

His court-appointed attorney quit the case after his sentencing. His Sista, in the beginning, had talked about finding another attorney, but that never materialized. This was the first time that another attorney wanted to visit him.

Like she promised Ricky, Eve requested background information on Charles's case from the Department of Corrections, State Attorney's Office, and Panama City police department to research the murder case. The file was filled with more paperwork than Ricky's, but, unlike Ricky's case, Charles was convicted on no concrete evidence. The evidence in Charles' case, the testimony of witnesses, was even more circumstantial. While she knew Charles had a sister, she knew his sister could provide very little information. It was better, for now, to leave the sister alone. A better time to open up the old wounds with his sister would have to wait until she knew more information from Charles.

Charles was not prepared for Eve's methods of getting to know her client. As she did with Ricky on the first day she met with him, her usual tactic, as with any other client she had, was to first establish a rapport. Asking personal questions, and telling a bit of herself, was a way to feel if the *vibes,* as her father used to call it, between two people were working. It was her way to build and establish trust. It was also her way to trust her instinct about the client. Was the person lying or telling the truth? Body language, eye contact, and the tones in a person's voice were good hints.

"My name is Eve," she started after she sat down at the same table, in the same room where she met with Ricky. "Some people might think that evil in the world all started with Eve, but that's not what I think," she said. "In fact, my name originated with the hope of man. My father wanted to call me Easter, but my mother won the battle of the name game. *No way I'm going to give my child a name like that!* she told my father. My mother let me know that parents like to give their child a name that had a special significance of something important in their life. It could be how, or where they met, or a favorite drink, where the child was conceived, or after a famous relative. It gives the child a memory, as if we need more, to live with the rest of our life."

Beginning to feeling like he tripped into a ditch and was struggling to find a way out, Charles created an opening to interrupt Eve. "So, you were born on Easter?"

"No, I was born in-between Good Friday and Easter Sunday. I was born on a Saturday, the eve of Easter Sunday. That's how my mother thought of the name of Eve. It meant nothing more than that to her, but for me, I felt it always had something to do with the fall of man. Think of Adam and Eve in the Garden of Eden. For a long time, particularly as a child, I always associated my name with the fall of man. I found comfort in the name when I realized why I was given the name. My parents were validating a special event in history, which has meaning for all the world's people. If Jesus came to forgive our sins, then it included Eve's too."

Eve tried to read Charles' face for clues. He showed no reaction, puzzlement, disgust, or dismay to her story about herself. He decided he looked bored.

"Now, tell me a little bit about yourself," Eve stated, ready to learn more about Charles.

Charles slid into the theme of the conversation she started.

"Since you've been talking about names, I'll tell you about my name. My father was named Maximillian. He liked the name, and he hated the name, too. Supposedly, there was a great emperor in Europe named Maximillian. My father never lived up to the dream of becoming a great man. I was named Charles, after the emperor Maximillian's son. The kids in my neighborhood nicknamed me DC, which stood for Dirty Charles. My clothes weren't always clean."

Charles's eyes glared at Eve, looking for her reaction to the story he told of how he got his name. He wanted her to know how he had suffered for his name.

"Well," Eve cleared her throat. "That establishes something about our names," she said and quickly changed the subject. "Tell me about your goals and what jobs you had after graduating from high school."

Eve at Peace by Yvette Doolittle Herr

Charles wanted to meet with the lawyer to tell her about the night he met the Fallen Angel at a Halloween party. He wanted to explain that he had nothing to do with the murder when the woman was found dead the next day. Charles heard Eve say something about the fall of man, but how could he bring up the Fallen Angel when she asked him about what jobs he did after high school? Where was the lawyer going with this line of questions? Why did she need to know about his background? Was he wasting his time?

He was locked in the room with her and a prison guard for at least an hour, so he saw no other choice but to answer her question.

"When I was a young boy, I always thought that I wanted to work for the railroad. I wanted to work on the caboose," Charles spoke deliberately. It was an honest answer, and Eve detected the pride in his voice.

"On the other hand, once my father heard about my intentions, he was adamantly opposed to me going to work for the railroad," Charles continued in a voice laden with disappointment. "My father said all I'd do at the railroad is lay down rail tracks or load supplies onto the caboose. So, I spent time, once I finished high school, doing odd jobs. Things like yard work and shoveling snow off sidewalks. I even briefly considered working at the Boyer candy factory, but I didn't like the idea of hanging around inside a building that smelled like chocolate." Charles smiled slyly when he uttered the last example to Eve.

Charles never considered the candy factory. It wouldn't have made him feel very masculine making chocolate candy all day or coming home smelling like a chocolate bar. After lying about being interested in working at the Boyer candy factory to Eve, he thought to himself, "It might have been a better place to meet a girl than at a Halloween party."

"Actually, the caboose on a train is one of the most important rail cars," Eve casually commented, ignoring the other jobs Charles mentioned. She was sitting straight, shoulders lifted, with her arms folded across her chest, her lips pursed, and an intense squint in her eyes. The intensity of her body language belied her feelings of insecurity. Something about Charles was not clicking or making sense to her. Ricky indicated to her that Charles wanted to get out of the prison. "*He's innocent, like me,*" Ricky wrote on the note he gave her. The word innocent was written in capital letters.

Eve changed her line of questioning. Charles' facial expressions, and his last answer about the candy company, made it evident that he did not take her seriously and he was shutting her out. "So, what brought you to Panama City?" she asked, already knowing his background.

Charles began telling Eve the story about coming to Panama City with his sister to find jobs and how he quickly found work at a construction yard. He then began to explain why he went to the Halloween party and then suddenly found himself in prison.

As much as she hated admitting it to herself, Eve found it challenging to listen to Charles. She was taught in law school to put all other cases aside when she met with a new client. Still, the potential of new evidence to help Ricky get out of prison was taking priority when she sensed Charles' dismissive distrust.

Suddenly Charles said something that snapped Eve out of her momentary lapse of attention.

"There are no significant events while I'm alive in this place to measure the passage of time. I would greatly appreciate it if you could help me get out of prison," Charles said. "Ricky and I both would appreciate it."

The intensity of his words, and the abrupt way he said them, caused Eve to decide to tell Charles what she had learned from the investigation in his records.

"The Fallen Angel, the one you met at the Halloween party, was known around town for selling vices. From some of the court records, I've learned that she was very popular for certain kinds of things at a motel called the Casa Amore in St. Andrews. Her popularity was widespread and well known," Eve said. "Sex was a pricey item she sold to support her drug habit, which was even more expensive. Her real name was Rose. My initial assessment of the findings in her file is that she might have been involved in a group organized for the sole purpose of engaging in criminal activity."

Charles, stunned and speechless by the information about the woman he found attractive at the Halloween party, rolled his eyes in disbelief at his error in judgment, his stupidity.

"You didn't know her, but I'm discovering that a lot of other local people knew her," Eve continued. "Small town secrets that have been buried for years have a way of bubbling back to the surface. Given a little more time, I think I might be able to dig deeper. I read witness statements saying she pushed you away at the party, and people heard you yelling back at her. That action alone, Rose pushing you away, put you in the picture of being a suspect. I, too, would like to find out who really murdered Rose."

Eve studied Charles' face, looking for a reaction to the information she shared about the Fallen Angel. She saw a pair of dark brown eyes, vacant of any emotion, looking back at her.

Too many years of confinement had dulled his sense of hope.

CHAPTER 24
DEMON DREAMS

Like the murder at Pine Log Forest State Park, the murder of Fallen Angel also became a story of urban legend in the community of Panama City.

Each year, when Halloween came around, people talked about the outsider who committed a heinous act against a local woman during a party that should have been a celebration. It was a party much needed by everyone in Panama City, weary from a year of hard work, recovering, and rebuilding after the prior year's devastating hurricane. An outsider coming to the community to supposedly help in the recovery, then committing the murder made the people feel betrayed.

The murder of Fallen Angel haunted John, a black man with a day-time job and a night-time business on the side. After the night of the murder and from that day forward, John began to lose his mind.

By the anniversary of the third Halloween following Fallen Angel's death, the murder haunted him so much that John lost all control of his sensibilities. He was taken, against his own will, into the dark despairs of insanity. The memory of the evil crime destroyed his inner peace.

Before the murder, John's confidence never wavered. He loved women, and there wasn't a woman in the social circle he'd known for years who didn't love him. John kept his body in shape by working for a construction company as a carpenter. He was tall, lean, and muscular. His hair was long, wrapped up into braids that fell over his shoulders and down his back when they weren't tied together while he was working. High cheekbones accented his dark-colored, smooth skin. A strong jaw showcased his perfectly set of bright, white teeth.

After Hurricane Louise, the construction company where John worked hired more people to help rebuild the damaged structures in the city. That's when a teenage boy named Charles was hired by the company.

John, and his co-workers, considered Charles to be an out-of-towner wannabe with a slightly cocky attitude. They couldn't find a reason to engage Charles in any genuine personal friendship. Charles was a decent, reliable worker at the job site, but the men already had a social network, and they weren't interested in expanding it by adding the young man from Altoona, Pennsylvania. The mindset of the men already working at the construction company was that the influx of hurricane workers were temporary residents who would go back to their hometowns after all of the repair work was finished.

On the Halloween party night, John noticed Charles amongst the crowded party in downtown Panama City. When he saw Charles approach, and talk, to the girl dressed in the Fallen Angel costume, jealousy exploded in John's brain.

"That's one of my girls," John said to himself. "I'm not letting that out-of-towner go hunting around in my territory. Even wearing that ugly costume and mask, I can still recognize him. It's Charles. He thinks he's some kind of cool cat on the job, but I'll show him who he is. He'll be sorry for wandering up to one of my women. I'll catch up with him later.

"Right now, I need to work fast. I'll remind her that she's one of my girls, and that she doesn't talk to any other men unless she has my permission."

By the time he found Fallen Angel circulating amongst the crowd of partygoers, John was agitated, as much as jealous. Being around so many new strangers, people he didn't know, left John feeling anxious and ready to leave the celebration. John was used to being in charge of the party, and at this one, he was not.

John was ready to be alone with a girl for the night. He was tired after a long week of work, and he needed someone to hold and comfort him. There were plenty of other girls John could have picked, but Fallen Angel was the one he chose to be with that night, more so because he thought she might be violating his terms.

"Hey, Rose," John said in a gruff voice when he found the girl in the Fallen Angel costume. "I'm ready to blow this pop concert." His manner belied the intensity of his irritation.

"I want my picture taken first," the girl in the Fallen Angel costume said to John. "Your girl Lucille has brought a new girlfriend to the party tonight. I can't remember Lucille's friend's name right now, but I know she wants to meet you and find out more about the business. You'll want to get to know her. Lucille's friend also brought a camera to take pictures of all the people in costumes. I don't get a chance to dress up like this very often. I want to get a photo of myself dressed up so pretty. If I have the photo, it will make a nice memory of this night."

John looked at Lucille's friend, a younger girl. He wanted to ask her name but dismissed it as a distraction that he didn't need at the moment.

"If someone is going to take a photograph of you, I'd better be in it, too," John insisted, looking past the young girl with eyes full of hate. "I'm the better-looking one," he said before he wrapped one arm around the Fallen Angel's shoulder.

After the photograph was taken, Fallen Angel told John she wanted to dance. "The band is good, John-boy," she said as she hooked her arm onto his arm. "Let's dance awhile before we slip off somewhere. It'll do you some good. You seem a little uptight tonight."

John, unconvinced this was a good idea, conceded to Fallen Angel anyway.

"One dance, then we're going. You know I'm the boss," he said with an authority she was used to hearing in his voice. He tightly gripped her arm above the wrist and pulled her close to him. They danced together to a song with a fast beat, but John gripped her tighter and tighter at the waist.

"Okay, so you're hurting me," Fallen Angel whimpered when they finished dancing to the song. "I want to go. Let's get this night over with. Where we going?"

Eve at Peace by Yvette Doolittle Herr

"I ain't going anywhere just yet," John growled at Fallen Angel, "but you're going to head on down to the Casa Amore right now. I'll be there at midnight. If you're not there when I get there, you'll be sorry. This whole costume party is over for you."

John walked away from Fallen Angel and wandered back into the crowd to look for Charles. He found some of the crew from the construction job instead. "Any of you seen that new guy, Charles?" he asked.

"Oh, you're talking about the guy who likes to think of himself as a cool cat," one man said.

The group of friends from work laughed.

"DC, for demon cat, right?" another said.

The friends laughed again.

"Yeah," John answered. "He's dressed up in a costume trying to look like Dracula. I believe that's what he thinks he's supposed to be. He's wearing a mask. I saw him hitting on one of my girls, Rose, just a little while ago."

"Yeah, we saw that too," one man said. "I saw him get really close to her, then she pushed him away."

"I want to find Charles and tell him to stay away from her," John angrily responded.

"Good luck finding anyone in this crowd," another man remarked. "It's getting thicker and thicker with people. The costumes they're wearing are crazy, scary, and wild-looking. I'm about ready to leave."

"I'm not going to stay here any longer, either," John told the group of huddled men who were being pushed and shoved by a steadily growing crowd. "This isn't my type of party anyway. I'll settle things with Charles at work," John said. "I'm going home. Momma always has some leftovers in the refrigerator. I'm hungry."

John made his way through the crowd, walking away from the marina and in the direction of his mother's home on the east side of Panama City.

Under the cover of darkness, John slipped into the densely wooded neighborhood through the back yards of small, wood-framed houses until he reached a street.

Stopping to check and see if any person was nearby watching, he switched course and headed in the opposite direction of his mother's home.

He back-tracked several blocks past Harrison Avenue until he located an alleyway behind a strip of houses fronting Beach Drive. Walking as fast as possible, he reached a small park with a historical marker commemorating a civil war salt works. Not wanting to be seen out in the open, John cut across the road to walk in the sand, along the beach fronting St. Andrews Bay.

When he arrived at the Casa Amore, John kicked at the door of Rose's room. Rose opened it within seconds.

"I've been sitting here on the bed, waiting for you, just like you told me, John," Rose said.

"Get up," John said to her in a hoarse voice, fueled by jealousy. "Let's go take a walk down to the water."

"You sound angry, John," Rose spoke softly. "Let's just stay here. I can fix whatever it is that made you angry with me."

"No," he answered, a hard edge in his tone of voice. "I need fresh air. Come on now, and shut the door."

John started to walk, and Rose obediently did as she was told, following behind him.

He found himself angry at Rose for talking to the new worker at the construction yard, the man who called himself Demon Cat, the man named Charles. No other man was supposed to have a desire for Rose except him and whomever else he chose for her.

John walked to a short stretch of beach across the street from the Casa Amore. Once reaching the water's edge, he forcibly pushed Rose to the ground. He was kissing her face but holding her neck, choking her at the same time. When she stopped breathing, he didn't know why, but he only wanted her to never breathe again. He pulled a switchblade knife out of his front pocket and in one quick motion, slit her neck from ear to ear. It felt like an accident, but John was very intentional in his action. He looked at the switchblade he was holding in his right hand and immediately knew he would have to dispose of the weapon.

He ran back toward his mother's house, taking unlit side streets and dark alleyways different from how he ran to the Casa Amore. He arbitrarily selected a home in a neighborhood far away from the beach in St. Andrews. He lifted the lid of a garbage can sitting in the driveway and slipped the switchblade beneath a stuffed bag.

Later that same night, hours after he left Fallen Angel to lie alone, bleeding in the sand, he woke from a restless sleep. He took a deep breath and suddenly felt the presence of something in the room with him. He forced his eyes open and, without moving his head, directed his eyes toward the door of the room, then the floor. When he looked upward, he saw, floating above him, near the ceiling, an object that seemed to look like a cloud.

John opened his eyes wider to see better.

"Damn, what's that?" he whispered out loud, startled and not yet fully awake.

He found himself staring hard into the darkness at the translucent, filmy, grey cloud. It reformed into the same shape each time it dispersed to a new spot above his bed.

The materialization of a discernable shape caused John's legs to jerk on the mattress.

Becoming fearful, John pulled the covers of the bed up close to his lips and stuffed a sizable portion of the bed linens into his mouth. He hoped to quiet any sounds he might make while keeping his eyes focused on the thing that floated about the four corners of the ceiling.

Eventually, the translucent cloud floated within inches above John's bed and formed into an egg-shaped body, the size of an adult human being. John saw a wing, shaped like a butterfly's, flap on each side of the body as if a wing was needed to keep itself in motion. While hovering over John's bed, a large human-sized head formed, then round lips, and finally, a bulbous nose. A single eye, the size of a marble, materialized above the nose. Suddenly John saw bright, gold, and red sparks flash out of the eye. Two small hands with long fingernails reached out in the front of the body and began waving at John.

John was sure he heard a voice whispering to him.

"C'mon John, dance with me."

"That woman's spirit has put a spell on me," his mind screamed while his body convulsed uncontrollably after hearing the words.

Fearing the vision, John pulled the covers of the bed over his head until the morning light shone through the window of his room a few hours later.

After the murder of the Fallen Angel was discovered and reported the next day, word spread quickly in the inner circles of the locals.

John returned to work at the construction company, making it a point to tell everyone he blamed himself for not protecting the girl. Witnesses at the Halloween party, including John, claimed Charles was harassing the Fallen Angel at the Halloween party. All the finger-pointing at an out-of-town worker, who had no friends, made Charles the likely suspect to commit a random act of violence on a well-known, local woman who didn't seem to have any enemies.

For John, the visions and voices continued, becoming so frequent and frightening that John struggled to separate them from reality. Loss of sleep eventually caused him to perform poorly at work. His co-workers complained. When the company boss asked John to explain what was causing the problems at work, John confessed to his boss, "There's a demon in my house. It haunts me every night. I can't get no sleep while this demon is hovering over my bed," John told his boss. "It wakes me up. I'm afraid that thing will attack me in the dark and invade my body if I close my eyes."

John's boss told John that he was imagining things. He let John know that if he didn't shape up, he would have to find another job.

"I'm going to suggest that you go to a clinic and talk to a counselor. I think it would help you," the boss told John. "You've become a stranger and not the John we all used to know."

Soon, John was seen in the work yard talking loudly to no one. While some thought that he was talking to himself, John talked to the demon haunting him day and night.

The change in John surprised and puzzled his co-workers, family, and friends. What caused the man to go crazy, they wondered? He wasn't known to drink to excess or take drugs. If he had a fault, it was liking too many women. Even the women who had worked at Casa Amore were puzzled when they were abandoned by him.

Most people blamed the changes in John on the death of one of his favorite girls, Rose, pinpointing it as the start of his decline. John couldn't accept that she was gone, they thought. He didn't want to let her go.

After he was relieved from his duties at the construction company, John never found another job. He spent most of his hours thinking of a way to lose the demon that followed him, like a shadow on a sunny day.

A year after he lost his job, John was kicked out of his mother's house, leading him to become indigent and homeless. John became unfamiliar to those who knew him. His conduct and appearance had changed dramatically from the man they used to know only a few years ago.

People who knew him as he used to be, and those who didn't, talked about him, saying that he had crossed over a line, to a point of no return. No one could rescue him from the darkness in his inner soul. From being a man with confidence, who made all the women swoon over him, he had become a complete lunatic. His family, and all the woman who loved him, couldn't help John. They became afraid of his behavior and avoided having any contact with him.

It was common to see John wearing clothes covered in dirt, shuffling down the sidewalks of downtown Panama City, waving his arms, talking loudly, and frequently turning his head to look behind him as if he were being followed. His long wild hair, blending into his wild beard, swung like a horse's tail with each turn of his head.

Rarely sleeping anymore, he loitered in vacant buildings and alleyways. Whenever he saw an opportunity, he slipped into the corner drug store to steal gauze and cotton balls. He taped the gauze over his eyes when he wasn't walking and over his mouth when he wasn't talking. He often stuffed the cotton balls inside his nose and ears.

"No demon is ever going to find a way to enter my body," John told himself. "I'm protecting myself against the evil spirits of that woman."

One day John became desperate. Using a toy gun he found on the city park playground, he tried to coerce the drugstore clerk to give him medical supplies to cover the holes in his body.

After being arrested for attempted armed theft, John was evaluated in the county jail by a psycho-therapist who diagnosed him with late-onset schizophrenia.

Deemed as a chronic threat to himself and the public, John was sent to the Florida State Hospital in Chattahoochee, a prison hospital for the criminally insane.

Once he was locked up, John was forgotten. His friends preferred to think of him as the man he used to be, not the man he had become.

CHAPTER 25
DORINDA'S DEPARTURE

Geneva left Smith's to go home to the small efficiency apartment at the Denice motel in downtown Panama City. It was a long enough drive to give her time to think about what had happened at work that night, and the conversation she had with Big Joe on the bench.

"How in the world will Big Joe resolve the problems with the restaurant staff," she wondered. "That Dorinda acts like a spoiled, selfish girl. I think she might have the upper hand on Big Joe. Most of all, I hope that sweet girl, Eleanore, makes a decision soon. The longer she waits to tell Darryl, the more stress she'll put on the baby."

As soon as Geneva stepped inside her apartment, she could feel the reality of her own problems.

"It's only been a few weeks since that girl was found murdered. I cannot believe that Charles is not here with me. I can't stay in this apartment without him. There's no way I can afford to pay rent, alone, for just me to stay here," Geneva thought. "I'd better come up with some idea to get out of here, because I don't see Charles getting out of jail any time soon. Even if they can't find the evidence against him, the authorities will keep him in that jail for months, until they find the evidence. And, I cannot go back to Altoona and leave Charles down here to fend for himself alone."

Charles had given Geneva his share of the rent money before he went to the Halloween party. He wanted to be sure that there was enough money to pay rent if he went out and spent more than he should at the Halloween party. He told Geneva he planned to buy something to eat for himself at the party, and maybe he might find a girl to buy something to eat. Geneva remembered his last words to her, "*I don't like eating alone all the time."*

Eve at Peace by Yvette Doolittle Herr

Even though the rent was paid for November, Geneva knew she wouldn't make enough money to pay rent for December. Smith's hosted some Christmas parties for large groups, but the regular customers and tourists would dwindle. There would be fewer nights that Big Joe would add her to the schedule. She knew what was coming. The employees who worked at Smith's the greatest number of years, like Dorinda, would get the most hours to work during the slower winter months. Geneva was low on the seniority list. A couple of nights a week in the kitchen would not give Geneva enough money to cover rent by herself.

Geneva laid down and stared into the darkness of the room. The pillow beneath her head was soft and comforting, but not comforting enough to take the edge off the worry in her mind.

"I don't know too much about Sue's personal life outside of work. I think she might live alone too," Geneva thought. "I'm going to ask Sue tomorrow if she lives alone. I think I overheard someone once talk about Sue being a widow and living in a house trailer on the beach. Maybe Sue would be willing to let me pay rent to her if she has an extra room in the trailer. I'll ask, suggesting that some extra money in the slow months might help her and help me save money to find a cheaper place closer to work. I pretty sure that Sue likes me, and I like her."

Geneva knew she was going out on a limb, asking Sue if she could live with her. "Desperate people resort to desperate measures," Geneva thought. "Sue's not a hard person to get along with even though she talks all the time. I think I could work on her to slow down her mouth. I was able to do that tonight. It wasn't something I intended to do, but it was necessary and turned out to be pretty easy. She didn't act like her feelings were hurt, like she gets when Big Joe looks at her the wrong way. It's going to be Sue or living in the car for a while, I'm afraid."

The brain cells were working hard. Geneva tried imagining herself becoming good friends with the diminutive,

Asian woman who had a knack with a knife. "Yes, we are a team, aren't we, in the salad room?"

The more she thought about it, the more Geneva found the thought of becoming better friends with Sue a pleasant idea. For the second time that night, Geneva smiled.

"Sue and Big Joe. They're pretty good people. I believe I'm heading in a good direction. It might even be easier to live with Sue than with Charles. Oh my, Charles," Geneva moaned. "I can't even imagine him killing anyone! Well, there's nothing I can do about his problem tonight. I need to get some sleep. At least I might rest easier knowing I might have an option to resolve my problem of finding another place to live. It's not only that I cannot afford this place without Charles, but I don't like being here alone anyway.

"How Big Joe finds out about Eleanore is an entirely different matter, but there's time. A few more days, and that will be resolved by Eleanore. I only need to resolve the problem of finding a place to live somewhere I can afford. If not with Sue, then hopefully someone, or somewhere else. Once I find a new place to live, I'll focus on what to do about Charles. Dear God, help me stop worrying about my brother."

Geneva rolled over to her side. Her single bed barely accommodated her body.

She ended the night by saying, "Thank you, Lord. I'm glad we had this talk tonight."

She closed her eyes and fell into a deep, dreamless sleep. She slept better knowing that Big Joe was going to take care of the problem with Dorinda. She slept better, knowing she might have a solution to her living arrangements.

The following day Geneva woke up refreshed, ready for a new night of work in Smith's kitchen. She preferred being busy. It took her mind off worrying.

She arrived at Smith's early, hoping to avoid any direct contact with other employees. The first thing on her agenda was to find the right words to use when she asked Sue about her living arrangements. Geneva put her purse away in a drawer and began to pull out knives and cutting boards.

Suddenly she got a distinct feeling that someone was watching her.

Geneva wasn't expecting the showdown, but once it all started, she showed her fighting skills.

Dorinda slid quietly, like a snake, into the salad room.

"Hey, there, big woman. I thought I needed to talk with you before we start busting our buns out on the floor tonight. I had to have a talk with Big Joe last night. Did he mention anything to you about it?" Dorinda asked. "I have the feeling that you and Eleanore are good friends. I noticed you talking to her at the table on break the other day. Apparently, Darryl came to the restaurant last night looking for me. I can't imagine why Darryl would be looking for me."

Dorinda didn't attempt to mask the insincerity of her words. Every word dripped with sarcasm.

Geneva groaned, sucked in a deep breath, and pulled herself together. She wasn't about to let Dorinda get the best of her with an insulting characterization. She twirled her heavy body on the heels of her shoes to square off face-to-face with Dorinda. She took one step forward, away from the table where she worked and stood straight and tall.

"Dorinda, yes, I'm a big woman and proud of it. Furthermore, it's none of your business what Big Joe and I talk about," Geneva said in a steady, strong voice.

"I'm going to make it my business, you black bitch. You're the one who's been causing problems with all the staff around here," Dorinda said, letting a snide smile spread across her face. Her painted red lips slightly parted, then opened wide to let out a laugh that sounded like the cackle of a hen inside a chicken coop.

Geneva momentarily reeled backward but kept her balance on her feet, quickly recovering from the assault. Stunned by the name she had just been called, she shot back hard at Dorinda.

"So, what was your business when I saw you boarding *The Lucky Two* after work the other night?" Geneva innocently asked, recomposed. "You think that fisherman, Darryl, might have any interest in a woman like you?"

"That's my business, and it's none of yours," Dorinda snarled. "You're such a spy around here," she added, followed by another shrill spew of crackling laughs.

"Dorinda, do you have ice running with the blood flowing through your veins?" Geneva asked, controlling her anger by holding on to the table behind her. Her hands and knees were shaking. "You look like you're a few years too old and a few sizes too big to be wearing that uniform. Shouldn't you be doing something else with your life besides waitressing? Don't you have some other talents other than chasing another woman's boyfriend?"

Dorinda stopped laughing and glared at Geneva with coal-black, icy eyes and lips shut tight.

Geneva stared back at Dorinda and continued. "You might think you're some kind of honey, but sweetness doesn't flow from you at all. I think Eleanore took away all the attention you thought you deserved when she became a better waitress than you."

"You're the big *B*, only a white one," a woman's voice screamed over Dorinda's shoulder.

Geneva's eyes, and mouth, popped wide open when she saw Eleanore standing behind Dorinda in the doorway of the salad room.

Eleanore, too, was visibly shaking. She shoved past Dorinda into the salad room and stood by Geneva. Both women faced off with Dorinda.

"Well, well, well. Here's the little darling of the restaurant, and she's acting like a sneaky rat, hiding behind walls," Dorinda shouted back at Eleanore.

"I'd be careful of who you're calling a rat, Dorinda," Eleanore said loudly. In a more controlled voice, she added, "Dorinda, you're just a dreamer with a cruel imagination. What made you think that little pink panty trick would work?"

"It's not going to end here," Dorinda growled and hammered her fist against the wall before storming out of the salad room.

Dorinda bumped into Sue, who was walking through the kitchen, on her way into the salad room.

"I heard a commotion. You ladies yelling in here could be heard all the way to the back door of the kitchen," Sue said when she arrived in the salad room. "It's a good thing I got here early. I can find out what's going on. Everyone around here is acting crazy lately."

Eleanore grabbed both of Geneva's trembling hands. "Are you alright?" Eleanore asked. "I am so sorry! I hate what just happened. I don't know how all of this has become so complicated, getting you involved with my problem."

"I'm fine," Geneva said.

Geneva let go of Eleanore's hands and gave her a hug. "We need to get ourselves together. Big Joe's going to probably hear about this. If Sue heard us arguing from the kitchen door, other people probably heard us too."

For a few minutes, all three women stood quietly, alternating looking at the floor to each other, not sure what to do next.

Geneva spoke first. "Sue, let's get our salad preparations finished," she said. "If we hurry, we can have a little more time out in the dining room at the break table before the shift starts. We'll catch up then."

In a deep, authoritative voice, she said to Eleanore, "You come right back in here to us if Dorinda gives you any trouble. She's got a foul mouth, and you don't need to give her any more lip to fuel her fire. She'll be ready to pounce on you. The best thing for you to do is turn your back on her. I'll meet you in thirty minutes at our break table in the dining room, okay?"

Eleanore nodded her head and, giving Sue and Geneva a smile of confidence, left to tend to her side work in the main dining room.

Geneva's idea to approach Sue about living together had to be postponed. This would not be the night to start a conversation with Sue about something personal. The subject of the evening would be all about what just happened between Dorinda and Eleanore. If Geneva even thought of starting a conversation with Sue, it couldn't be about living arrangements. Sue was in a foul mood, expressing annoyance after being nearly knocked down by Dorinda rushing out of the salad room.

"Working here is beginning to feel like participating in a three-ring circus," Sue nervously said. "There's action in every part of this kitchen and not very nice action tonight." Sue picked a knife up off the table and waved it in the direction of Dorinda's departure. "That woman is not nice. Little pink panty trick, is that what I heard?!?"

Dorinda found Big Joe blocking her path on her way through the kitchen to her waitress beverage station.

"Not so fast, young lady," Big Joe said as politely as his nerves would allow. "I heard that argument in the salad room, just like everyone else in the kitchen. If I remember correctly, I told you last night to never use those words again when talking about Geneva," Big Joe paused. Seeing the aloof look in Dorinda's eyes made him angrier.

Big Joe raised his voice. "You see, in case you've never noticed, other people are working here who have the same skin color as Geneva. I know they don't like it one bit, either, hearing what you said to Geneva. You need to take off that apron and leave. Now! You're fired!"

"I don't think my cousin is going to like it one bit either, when he hears about you telling me I'm fired," Dorinda mimicked Big Joe's tone of voice.

Big Joe stood square in the center of the hallway with his arms crossed firmly against his chest, both fists tucked beneath his armpits. His eyes glared red beneath his furrowed, bushy eyebrows. In a confident, controlled, voice he said to Dorinda, "I'll explain things to the boss later. I think he'll understand my side of the story better than yours."

Dorinda spun around and walked away from Big Joe.

Minutes later, Dorinda was standing behind the bar in the restaurant's lounge. The loud sound of breaking glass could be heard throughout the entire restaurant and kitchen.

Everyone in the restaurant suddenly stopped what they were doing and watched Big Joe move quickly out of the kitchen. They waited in silence to hear what might happen next.

Dorinda was reaching for another bottle to throw against the wall when Big Joe arrived at the bar. Broken bottles, glassware, and alcohol covered the floor. Dorinda stopped throwing her fit when she saw Big Joe.

Big Joe stopped, observed the damage, half-closed his eyes, and tightened his lips. He shook his head from side to side as if doing so would awaken his senses to a new scene other than the one he faced. He took in a deep breath, expanding his chest, and took a minute to think. His face bore a thoughtful expression of disdain and discomfort.

Dorinda glared back at Big Joe, posturing her body in a stance of defiance.

The expression on Big Joe's face changed to one of a person who had seen enough nonsense for the night. Yielding to the obligations of his job, Big Joe began to speak slowly, controlling the anger he felt.

"I don't understand the necessity of your actions, Dorinda. I'll let you explain them yourself to your cousin. You must leave now. If you don't, I will call the police."

CHAPTER 26
SPIRITUAL ADVISOR

After the explosive argument with Dorinda at Smith's, Eleanore could hardly wait to finish her shift at work. She had been a nervous wreck all night, spilling a drink and mixing up food orders when she delivered them to customers.

Eleanore felt deeply hurt and confused by the way Dorinda talked to Geneva. Why would Dorinda be so nasty to Geneva, she wondered.

Eleanore had lived on Panama City Beach just over a year but had met very few people outside of her job at Smith's. Geneva was one of the nicest people she had met so far, and it troubled Eleanore to see the nice woman trammeled.

The experience gave Eleanore more reason to believe Darryl's explanation about Dorinda.

As he did every night, Casey was sitting on the sofa watching television. After she came home, they usually shared a few words about their workday, then went directly to their rooms.

Tonight, Casey thought he heard Eleanore slam her car door a little too hard after he listened to the car engine shut off. He watched Eleanore storm into the house, toss her purse down on the kitchen table, and flop down hard on a chair next to the sofa.

"Looks like you had a hard night. Something happen?" Casey asked, trying hard to sound casual but, sensing from her actions, she was emotional about something. In the past year, he had never seen her be so dramatic. After the incident at the marina with Darryl, there was no telling what might have happened tonight.

Eleanore wasted no time relating to Casey what had happened at Smith's, carefully watching his face for his reaction to each detail. She noticed his eyes roll several times. Casey repeatedly shook his head in disbelief while Eleanore told him the story.

When she finished telling him all that happened, Eleanore waited a few minutes before asking him, "What do you think about all that?"

Casey was dumbstruck by the audacity of Dorinda's behavior. "Well," he slowly said, not knowing where to start. "My goodness. I don't know what to say after hearing all of this. Sounds like a really wild night at Smith's," was the best answer he could come up with.

"That woman really does have a cruel heart. How could she blame Geneva for Big Joe's anger?" Eleanore pouted, becoming more angered after having to repeat the event in her mind. "Tonight's experience was worse than the night before."

"True," Casey agreed, wondering to himself how far Dorinda would go next time.

Eleanore continued venting on Casey's open ears. "Big Joe only wanted to protect Dorinda from a confrontation with Darryl last night. Instead of showing any appreciation for Big Joe's intervention, Dorinda gave Big Joe a hard time. Then Dorinda takes it out on Geneva, blaming her for the problems in the kitchen when we all know it's Dorinda who is causing all of the problems."

Lastly, Eleanore added, "And, the only reason Darryl would march over to the restaurant after we left would be to give Dorinda a piece of his mind for her stupid trick. She only wanted to hurt me. Why? I don't know. I've never said or done anything to hurt Dorinda," Eleanore lamented to Casey. "It makes me sick to my stomach."

Eleanore sighed and slinked down deeper in the chair. She stuffed her hands beneath the soft bottom cushion and pulled it up, snuggling it close to her body.

When it appeared to Casey that Eleanore was calming down, he thought it was time to try and shed some sane reflections on the incident.

"We know that Dorinda's just a selfish woman, Eleanore." Casey started. "I think I mentioned to you before that she was hanging out at the marina years ago. In my opinion, a lot of women are selfish for many different reasons. Many times, the reason is about money," Casey paused, thinking about what he was trying to say.

Casey remembered the arguments about money he had with his ex-wife. It was the main reason why things didn't work out in his own failed marriage. Darryl didn't have any money, so it made no sense to approach the problem as a money issue.

Maybe, Casey thought, Dorinda really was jealous of Eleanore. "But, for what reason would she be jealous?" he asked himself.

Eleanore sat up straighter in the soft cushion, waiting impatiently for Casey to continue. She crossed one leg over the other, swinging one foot as if she was kicking some imaginary pest out of the way.

Eleanore's mind was racing through scenarios to explain how money could be the motive of Dorinda's behavior and how unfair it was if money was the reason. She became angrier to think that Dorinda might have schemed to get herself, Eleanore, out of the picture at Smith's, only for the opportunity to make more money. Why would Dorinda drag Darryl, who was innocent, into the picture to make her plan work?

Starting with a snort of disgust, Eleanore vigorously shook her head no and said, "No, No. If Dorinda wanted more money, it doesn't make sense to drag Darryl into the picture. And, if that was her idea, her plan backfired. Big Joe fired Dorinda."

Eleanore's irritation with the idea of money being the cause of Dorinda's evil actions made Casey try another angle.

"I don't know why Dorinda, and people like her, have to be so hateful," he said. "She's probably been hateful all of her life. Especially when she can't have what she wants. Maybe she had an obsession with Darryl when he played in the nightclubs back in the old days. Darryl was in a band before he bought his boat, *The Star Chaser*. Maybe that's where Dorinda got the idea to go after Darryl. Maybe Dorinda thought Darryl had money." Casey was trying hard to understand the complicated, messy situation.

Casey continued, "She's still a pretty woman, even though she has a few more years on her than you. Most pretty women like to be adored. Maybe she used to have a big crush on Darryl years ago. Maybe you came along and upset her apple cart, like an invasive species of fish that destroys the balance of the habitat for the native fish species. When he asked her about you, she might have gotten a little bit jealous."

Casey's new message didn't help.

"Stop," Eleanore said, pulling one hand out from beneath the seat cushion and holding it up in front of her face. "I've had enough for the past two nights. I can't drive myself crazy trying to understand why all of this is happening. My circumstances, family history, and coming here to help Earl were not completely in my control or even exactly my choosing. Remember the night we spent together riding out hurricane Louise? We talked all night and learned intimately about each other's lives. I think you know me. I'm going to figure this out," Eleanore spoke with renewed strength and determination. "I'm going to get some sleep tonight, which shouldn't be a problem since the last few nights of sleep have been bad. Then starting tomorrow, I'm going to move forward with my life."

Casey was relieved to hear Eleanore sound more like the old Eleanore he knew. She was showing her grit and would use logic to work through her feelings.

The next day Eleanore reported to work, as usual, hoping for a calmer evening, hoping for the best, and not expecting that things could get worse.

Eleanore walked through Smith's kitchen, which was usually abuzz with active workers talking gossip while they did their food prep. There was plenty of gossip to talk about after last night. What she saw were people working silently with their heads lowered to avoid looking at anyone.

Eleanore headed straight to the small salad prep room to find Geneva.

She saw Geneva standing with her back to the door, bent over, working at the stainless-steel table, with Sue by her side. Sue looked up first and saw Eleanore. Sue's face spoke trouble.

Geneva felt the presence of another person standing nearby and turned to see who it was. Tears welled up in her eyes when she saw Eleanore.

"My sweet girl, Eleanore," Geneva said, struggling to control blubbering the words. "The big boss is in the office having a talk with Big Joe. They've been in there together for over an hour. I'm afraid that the worst might happen. I sure do hope Big Joe doesn't lose his job because of what happened last night. It wasn't Big Joe's fault that Dorinda came unglued."

"Let's not talk about it now," Eleanore said. "Let's all pray that everything will work out, and we'll talk later."

When Smith's opened its doors for customers, Big Joe was back at his grill. He didn't talk to anyone like he usually did during work. When he came out of his office, he sent the dishwasher to tell everyone from every work station to gather in the kitchen after Smith's closed and the last customer had left.

Some employees had to wait to clock out, but everyone gathered in the kitchen, as requested when the restaurant closed. The employees from the front desk, bar, dining room and kitchen were all packed together, standing in separate groups, waiting to hear what Big Joe had to say.

"I'm going to say this plain and simple," Big Joe started. It was the quietest the kitchen had ever been with all the employees standing together in it. No knives were chopping, no exhaust fans were blowing, no dishwashers were running, and nobody said a word. Big Joe continued. "I had a good talk with the boss. He wants me to tell all of you that he appreciates all the good work everyone does to make this restaurant a success. He regrets the unfortunate incident of last night, but he wants to give Dorinda another chance. The boss told me Dorinda is extremely sorry for what she did and apologizes to anyone and everyone, she upset. She will be taking a week off and then reporting back to work next week to work the hostess station. I'm asking everyone to treat her with respect."

A collective groan and shaking heads didn't surprise Big Joe. He knew employees would be dismayed by the news. The announcement wasn't easy for him to accept, or deliver, either.

"We have put this behind us. All y'all go home now. Get a good night's rest," he said.

Big Joe wearily turned, opened the kitchen door, and stepped outside. His large, hairy hand held the door open until all of the employees, filed in a line, passed through it. Big Joe said good night to each one, struggling to maintain his composure when Geneva departed.

Eleanore rushed up to Geneva's side once she made it out the door.

"I need to talk to you, please," Eleanore said.

"Not tonight," Geneva staunchly replied.

"I can't believe what just happened," Eleanore said breathless, trying to keep up with Geneva's quick pace.

"If you're going to talk to me while I'm trying to get to my car, talk about something else," Geneva said.

"Okay, then. Remember the night we talked outside after work that night on the bench?" Eleanore's words came as fast as their footsteps. "We talked about how both our mothers had a deck of Tarot cards."

The mention of the cards brought Geneva to a dead halt in her stride. She gave Eleanore a quizzical look. "So?"

"So, I want to go see a spiritual advisor," Eleanore said, managing a smile.

Geneva let out a genuine laugh that came from deep inside the belly. Eleanore's unexpected announcement, revealing that she was pregnant with Darryl's baby, she knew, was the reason why Eleanore wanted to go see a spiritual advisor.

Geneva put one hand on her hip and held on to her purse with the other. "If that doesn't beat all. All this mess of seriousness these last two days, and you come up with this idea. I know you still haven't decided what you're going to do yet. But you know what? I need some alternative answers in my life too. You and I both have problems, and I think a diversion from work would do us, two girls, some good. You and I can't go dancing together, that's for sure. Are you feeling good enough to go after work tomorrow night?"

Eleanore impishly grinned like an elf. "Yes," she answered emphatically. "I've told Casey, my roommate, about you. He always waits up for me to get home from work at night. He wants to be sure that I'm safely home. I'll tell him I'm going to be out with you tomorrow night, and I will be a little bit late."

"I take it you know where there's a spiritual advisor?" Geneva asked.

"On my way to the grocery store, I pass by a small grey house on Thomas Drive. There are flashing purple lights in the front window and a huge plywood sign painted white stuck in the ground next to the front door. A human palm painted red with a blue eye in the middle is on the sign, along with a phone number below the palm.

"The house is not far from that bar called Estelle's Escape. It's about a ten-minute drive from Smith's," Eleanore explained. "I'll drive by and get the telephone number before I go home tonight. It's not out of my way. If the lights are blinking someone will be there. I'll call tonight to find out if we can get an appointment for tomorrow night."

The next night, after work, Geneva and Eleanore rode together in Geneva's car to the spiritual advisor's house. Geneva was slightly worried about agreeing to go with Eleanore. She knew Eleanore possessed an innocent, but not a naïve heart. Still, she hoped Eleanore wouldn't make a serious decision about Darryl solely on the woman's words.

"You said the name of this woman is what?" Geneva asked.

"She said her real name is Evelyn, but she goes by Madame Star," Eleanore laughed. "That's how she answered the telephone, but with a very deep, low-pitched, sweet voice. I was quite surprised when she told me how much it would cost for a palm reading. I thought it would be much more than five dollars. Of course, the Tarot card reading is more expensive because of the time she needs to interpret the cards. I think ten dollars is not too bad, though. I was surprised that she would take both of us so late in the evening, but she told me that's when she sees most of her clients."

"No, no, it's not expensive," Geneva agreed. She felt anxious and a little nervous. She kept reminding herself that the experience was to humor Eleanore, more than to take any advice the spiritual advisor would give her. "It's been a long time since I've done anything besides work, eat, and sleep. I have a feeling this may be entertaining. Just remember, Eleanore, I don't want you to put too much emphasis on the meaning of the cards. What she tells you is not the truth. Go with your heart and good sense, young lady."

Geneva slowly pulled into a narrow, dirt driveway on the side of the house. "I'll stay in the car until she opens the door. You get a good look at her face, first. If you feel like it's safe, turn around and wave your hand at me. Then I'll get out of the car."

Eleanore stepped up to the front door on her tiptoes, as if she needed to be quiet. She fisted her hand and tapped on the wooden door lightly with her knuckle. When the door opened, and Geneva could see that it really was a woman, she took a quick breath and blew a short sigh of relief through her nose.

Madame Star was wearing an ankle-length, loose-fitting blue dress, covered in a pattern of yellow stars of all different sizes. She wore a pair of blue, satin ballerina slippers that matched the background color of the dress fabric. A yellow, fringed shawl was draped over her shoulders and accentuated her shoulder-length black hair, which was highlighted with a streak of gray down the left side of her face.

The woman opened the door, smiled at Eleanore, and asked, "Are you, Eleanore?"

Eleanore nodded her head without speaking.

"When you called, you said there would be two people. Is your friend going to come inside?" Madame Star asked, directing her eyes and motioning her head toward Geneva sitting behind the steering wheel of her car.

Eleanore turned around and waved her hand at Geneva to indicate it was safe to come up to the house. Geneva reluctantly opened her car door.

"Come in, come in, and have a seat," Madame Star said to them once Geneva climbed up the steps and onto the porch.

They stepped over the threshold of the door and into a room with walls painted a dark shade of grey. The room was illuminated by the flashing purple lights, taped to the front window, and a small, round lamp covered by a yellow, satin-fringed lampshade. The lamp sat on a round, three-legged table. A cone of incense was burning atop a star-shaped, yellow ceramic plate on the table, near the lamp. A thin line of smoke spiraled up from the cone, spreading the scent of herbal flowers throughout the room.

Inside the dimly lit room filled with a smokey purple haze, Geneva found herself squinting to see the facial expressions of Eleanore and Madame Star.

Madame Star closed the door and turned the deadbolt lock. She motioned to a captain's chair next to the table with the lamp. "One of you will need to sit there and wait when I read the cards for the other person in a separate room," she said in a deep, silky voice that seemed incongruous with her slight body frame. "When I read Tarot cards, I only take one person at a time," she said.

"The time I'll be giving each of you is fifteen minutes, maximum," Madame Star explained. "I have a timer, which helps me stay on track," she said, followed by a throaty giggle. "Sometimes, even I can get too caught up in the meanings of the cards. First, I'll ask each of you to tell me a few things about yourself and then tell me something about someone important to you. It may be more than one person influencing your life right now. I will assume that these are the people who are going to affect your future. Once the cards are picked, it doesn't take me long to interpret the results of the ones I turn over. I will allow a few minutes for you to ask me some questions. My experience with people is that someone may ask me to repeat something I said. Still, usually, they do not have questions once I have finished explaining the meaning of the cards."

Geneva and Eleanore nodded and turned their heads to face each other, trying to read the expression on the other person's face through the smoke.

"Do we pay you first?" Eleanore asked.

"Yes, please," Madame Star answered.

Eleanore dug into her purse and paid for herself and Geneva. "My idea, so I'm paying for you too, Geneva," she quickly said.

Geneva didn't feel that it was the right time, or place, to protest, so she nodded her head in agreement.

"Who wants to go first?" Madame Star asked, holding her head straight and shifting her eyes back and forth from Geneva to Eleanore. Beneath the thin-lined eyebrows, Geneva imagined she saw the eyes of a woman who had just finished burying a body in her backyard.

"I'll go," Eleanore eagerly answered, then hesitated and looked at Geneva. "You don't mind, do you, Geneva?" she asked, feeling somewhat greedy and embarrassed by her sudden response.

"No, you go first," Geneva answered, hoping that she didn't sound too nervous. She was glad that Eleanore volunteered to go first and wished she could calm down her nervousness before it became her turn to go inside the room with Madame Star.

Geneva stepped over to the chair and cautiously eased her bottom onto the hard, wooden chair. She laid her purse on her lap and held it tight, keeping her eyes glued on

Madame Star, who remained standing in the middle of the room with Eleanore.

Madame Star glanced at Geneva and said, "I hope you're not uncomfortable waiting out here alone. There's no one else in the house to bother us. If, however, you feel nervous, please knock on the door. It's not a problem. I understand some people may get anxious if they feel like they are waiting alone in this room for too long."

With those last words Madame Star turned the handle on the private room door and pushed it open. She lifted up her arm, motioning Eleanore to enter. The dimly lit room cast a pale light on Madam Star. Geneva watched Eleanore walk into the room. She saw smoke from the burning incense filtering through the fringe of Madam Star's shawl.

"I hope I'm not seeing a ghost following them into the room," Geneva thought and groaned after Madame Star shut the door. "I don't like the idea of waiting in a room where there could be other ghosts. If it was just me, here by myself, I would take my tired legs and march them back out the front door!"

CHAPTER 27
NO APOLOGIES

Eleanore watched Geneva clumsily stumble across the floor in the front room, and rush to the front door without saying a word. Eleanore had been waiting, excited to tell Geneva what Madam Star had told her, but now she couldn't wait to hear what Geneva had to say. Geneva was obviously anxious to leave the spiritual advisor's house.

"I can see that you are upset," Eleanore said to Geneva when they were safe inside the car with the doors closed. "Don't you remember warning me not to take seriously anything that the spiritual advisor told me?" Eleanore asked.

Geneva stared ahead for several quiet minutes, through the car windshield, reminded by the flashing purple lights of the fear she felt when Madam Star read her cards.

"It's all my fault," Eleanore apologized, speaking softly and looking at Geneva with intense concern. Geneva was shaking profusely and gripping the steering wheel of her car like she was holding on for dear life to the edge of a sinking boat.

Geneva's beautiful, full lips quivered. "I'm the one who agreed to go with you," Geneva croaked. She believed if she held the steering wheel tightly, it could control the shaking she felt throughout her entire body, not just her hands.

Eleanore's strongest desire at that moment was to say, or do something, to help Geneva. She couldn't find the words to say, so she waited for Geneva to speak first about her experience at Madam Star's.

"Give me a few minutes to catch my breath," Geneva finally stammered, then took one hand off the steering wheel to find the car keys in her purse. She struggled with her shaking hand to insert the key into the ignition. She opened her mouth, took in a deep breath through her nose, and noisily blew the air back out through slightly parted lips.

"Are you okay? Do you think that you can drive?" Eleanore nervously asked. She wasn't sure if it was safe to be riding with a person who was driving and so visibly upset.

"I'll be okay. Talk to me, Eleanore. Talk to me so I can drive," Geneva repeated, and turned the key to start the car's engine. "I'll calm down, I promise."

Geneva slung her right arm behind Eleanore, turned her head, and looked over her shoulder. She pressed her foot lightly down on the gas pedal and began backing the car out of the driveway. When it was ready to put the car into drive and steer forward on Thomas Drive, the shaking was more under control. She turned her head slightly to cut a glance at Eleanore. "Wow," she said to Eleanore in a calmer voice. "That place spooked me more than the ride in the haunted house at Lakemont amusement park back home in Altoona."

Eleanore smiled. "You can't be serious, Geneva. What was it that spooked you? I didn't feel uncomfortable at all. When I was alone with Madame Star or waiting for you to finish, it all seemed like a game to me. I'm sorry, though, if that's how you feel. I don't mean to laugh. I just think it's funny what you said about a haunted house."

"Tell me everything that woman, Madame Star, told you," Geneva said. "You came out of the room with a big smile on your face, like you heard something good. I want, need, to hear you talking to me. It will help me to think about something other than the things she told me. Mind you, I won't forget what she told me, and I'll share it with you after I've had time to process it. Tonight, I'm not ready to share with you the predictions she told me about my future."

For Geneva, waiting for her turn to hear Madame Star felt like the longest fifteen minutes she had ever waited for anything. The smoky room, the flashing purple lights, and the apparition she imagined floating in the yellow fringed shawl set off Geneva's mind to wandering down a slippery slope of fear and ambiguity.

Geneva's session with Madame Star did not go well. The first thing that Madame Star did was ask Geneva to shuffle the cards. Geneva was not prepared to touch the Tarot cards. Just holding the cards in her hands gave Geneva a peculiar feeling, but she couldn't find her voice to protest Madame Star's request.

After Geneva finished shuffling the cards, she placed the deck in front of Madame Star, who picked up six cards and put them face-up, pointing in the same direction. The artwork on the cards and how Madame Star chose to arrange them intrigued Geneva at first, until she studied the drawings on the cards. She let her eyes lock onto three particular cards.

One card depicted a man with a dark face riding a horse and holding a sword. Another card had the image of a woman in a sitting position holding a sword in one hand and a set of scales in another hand. The third card showed the image of a skeleton walking through a dark, muddy bog.

Geneva didn't want to hear any interpretation of the card that was the skeleton. In her mind, she already knew it meant death and didn't want to know who was going to die. She wanted to hold her hands to her ears to block out the words that Madame Star would say, but it was impossible.

Madame Star bent her head down, tightly pressed together her lips, and arched the lines of her eyebrows. Madam Star sat straight, with her shoulders squared to the back of the chair. She held her forefinger above the cards for a moment, then lightly touched each card with intention, lastly returning to the card with the woman holding a sword and set of scales. Touching it a second time, then she spoke slowly, in her deep, silky voice, interpreting the meaning of each card.

"First of all, I see a contradiction in the cards," Madame Star started. "Everything depends on the knight with the sword, who represents bravery, or sometimes ill will. The card of death can mean anything from someone close to you dying, to something smaller, like a permanent scar on the mind. But the lady with the scales represents justice or proper balance. Someone in your life has good intentions. The outcome will be pending until the events of the past, and present, come into harmony in the future."

Geneva's nerves tingled. All the recent events in her life, from Dorinda's deceit to Charles' incarceration in jail for murder, seemed to be present in those cards lying on the table in the dim-lit room.

Geneva didn't want to know any more about her future. She let her mind wander off to her memories of working at the Elks Club in Altoona. At the same time, Madame Star continued to intertwine the significance of the other three cards, which had less visionary influence than the first three.

Her thoughts rambled in different directions. "I can still picture the front of that building in Altoona, even though I went straight to the back door of the building and into the kitchen. If you were a member, you would look up at the four-story building, walk inside, sit in the parlor in front of the marble fireplace with burning logs, or go to the main bar. Go downstairs and go bowling or go up a flite of stairs and order drinks and food. Go up another flite of stairs to a grand meeting room, sometimes used as a ballroom for fancy dances, but mostly where the business of doing good deeds was discussed and decided. I was very happy being in that kitchen in the Elks Club, stirring up my own ingredients for a good life. I got a good job at Smith's. I need to hang on to my job and work my way through these problems."

Madame Star finished talking about the cards and looked up. Her eyes met Geneva's eyes, which were opened wide, exposing the white cornea surrounding her pupils' dark, pigmented color. Madame Star's eyes, also dark, bored into Geneva's face. Geneva thought she saw a crescent flashing like lightning in Madam Starr's left eye. However, Geneva detected a softening in Madame Star's body language.

"Clearly, those are worried eyes looking at me," Geneva thought to herself. "She must find the information disturbing, too."

"Do you have any questions?" Madame Star asked, sensing that Geneva's mind had wandered away from the reading.

Eve at Peace by Yvette Doolittle Herr

Geneva shifted her eyes to take one more look down at the cards lying on the table, and vigorously shook her head no.

Geneva pushed her chair away from the table to stand up. Both of her legs wobbled backward and sideways, like they were made from rubber. Geneva placed both hands on the back of the chair where she'd been sitting and waited for Madame Star's next move.

Madame Star stood up from her chair and walked to the door. She held the doorknob for a few seconds, then turned to look at Geneva, still holding on to her chair.

"I always regret it when I have to tell someone disappointing information," Madam Star said sympathetically. "If you'd like to return for another session, I'll be eager, just like you, to hear a better report about your future. Please come back again, soon. I'd like to reread your cards."

"Not in your lifetime," Geneva thought to herself, shuffling her feet on the wood floor, following Madame Star out of the room. "I will never be coming back to this place for any more mind-punishing, trash talk."

As Geneva had asked her to do, Eleanore began talking, telling Geneva about her time with Madam Star.

Geneva drove slower than usual down Thomas Drive.

"First of all, Geneva, don't you remember warning me not to take anything the spiritual advisor said seriously?" Eleanore asked. "Well, the stuff she was telling me was so ridiculous. How could I take any of that seriously? I can tell you one thing, though. I am so happy now."

"Well then, tell me what she told you," Geneva said, hoping to get her mind off the details of what Madame Star told her.

Eleanore continued, "I can't remember all the pictures on all of the cards, but I kept thinking that the interpretations made no sense. There was one card, though, with the word *judgment* on it. I couldn't stop focusing on that picture, nor did Madam Star, as she seemed fixed on the card and became quite tense, as though it was interpreting her future or life. She excused herself for the lapse and continued. The picture was of a man and a woman. Between them was a sitting child, facing them. The woman was holding the hand of the child. Above them was what appeared to be an angel blowing a trumpet. She told me that this card represented many things. When she said the words determination, decision, forgiveness, and opportunity, my mind trailed off into another dimension. All I could think of was me, the baby, Darryl, and his saxophone."

"Whoa," Geneva said more than once while listening to Eleanore recant her experience.

Geneva, curious about whether Madame Star wanted Eleanore's repeat business, asked Eleanore when she finished, "Did Madame Star invite you back for another session?"

"Yes, Geneva, she did. I told her thank you, and that I may call her for another appointment one day," Eleanore answered, then broke into loud laughter. "Those cards represent a lot of hocus pockus, Geneva. I can't believe you became so upset. I made a decision while I was waiting for you to come out of the room. I didn't consider anything the spiritual advisor said to be significant. That's why I'm laughing, and I feel so happy now. It was a better experience than going out dancing!"

Listening to Eleanore and realizing she had not taken her own advice, made Geneva feel silly

Geneva said, "You're absolutely right about reminding me that I warned you. To think that I fell for those silly stories. Did the smoke rings from the incense burner in the front room seem to swirl around you like ghosts, while you were waiting on me? I think waiting in the front room unsettled me more than the cards I picked. That's what started it for me. I'm sure Madame Star likes to impart good information to her customers and see happy results. I understand that she can only tell us the meaning of the cards we picked, it's all chance, but she could sure use some advice on creating a calmer atmosphere inside her house. It sure would have helped my mood before I went in to listen to her tell me about my cards."

"Geneva," Eleanore sighed, "I'm so glad that you've calmed down. You've been driving like an old lady, twenty-five miles an hour in a forty-five mile per hour speed zone. The police might think that you're drunk and stop us. Hurry up. I'm eager to get back to the marina. I'm going straight to *The Lucky Two* when we get back and knock on the cabin door. I've made my decision, and it has nothing to do with what Madame Star told me."

"Are you going to tell me your decision, sweet girl?" Geneva asked, although she felt like she already knew.

"I'm not confused, nor am I uncertain. Before coming down to Panama City Beach to find Earl, I prayed. Praying is what I've been doing before the day I told you I was having Darryl's baby. As I told you, I didn't know if Darryl will always consider my feelings about decisions that affect both of us. I may have made choices in my past that, I know now, were based on incomplete information. I've concluded that we're never going to have all the facts when we need to make a quick decision. One thing I do know, though. I know that Darryl loves me. I saw him sitting in his truck parked out on the street in front of Casey's house, waiting for me, that night I found Dorinda's panties on *The Lucky Two*. I've been trying to decide if I love him. I realized tonight that I do love him. I could pick him apart, but why? He's not perfect, and neither am I. He doesn't know about the baby. If I told him about the baby, he would go crazy if I didn't stay with him," Eleanore paused.

Geneva spoke, quickly taking the opportunity to give good advice to Eleanore. "We are, each and every one of us, responsible for our feelings. Some people feel real hate in their hearts. I believe hate starts with not being in control, or getting what you want. You want Darryl to think exactly the way you think. No two people are ever going to think the same way about everything. You don't hate that man. I believe that you love him. Release the love you hold in your heart, and block out any hate, although I don't believe you're the kind of person who is capable of truly hating anyone."

Eleanore nodded her head. "I know that he has some faults, but he loves me. I see it in his eyes. Thank you for those kind words and for helping me think through this decision."

"There you go, young lady," Geneva jumped at the opportunity again to encourage Eleanore to pursue love. "You're on the right track now."

"I must choose the option that will not harm me or anyone else," Eleanore continued. "I'm going to give this baby a name. I have to choose to love someone, and who better to choose than someone who truly loves me? I am not in trouble, as some people might say. This baby is a blessing. God is responsible for the universe, the planets, the stars, and all living things. I'm going to leave it in God's hands to take care of the outcomes. He only asked us to love his creations. You're right about hate, Geneva. Hate in the heart is the creation of the devil. In other words, evil with the letter D in front of it."

With her eyes focused square and solid on Geneva, Eleanore said, "I cannot predict what happens. These Tarot cards meant nothing. They didn't provide answers. I have made a difficult decision, but the one that I believe is the right one. It's time for me to act on what I want, and where I want to go. No child is illegitimate."

"Amen to that!" Geneva passionately agreed. "No creation, no child, is illegitimate."

After hearing Geneva's measured words, Eleanore decided she must go see Darryl tonight.

"Would you stay at the marina for a few minutes after we get there?" she asked Geneva. "I need to tell Darryl tonight. I'm too excited to go directly home."

"Of course," Geneva patted her on the shoulder. "It would be my pleasure to be there when you tell him the good news."

Eleanore vigorously nodded her head up and down. "It's the right time. I can't waste any more time," she said, breathless with euphoria.

All the way back to Smith's, the two women talked and giggled, like teenage schoolgirls in excited anticipation of Darryl's happy reaction to the good news. Before long, they reached the lagoon bridge. Geneva, glad to see the parking lot lights of Smith's come into view, smiled and said, "I wish I could see Darryl's face when you tell him. I'll just wait in my car until you come back out of the boat and signal to me that it's all good. You can wave at me, like you did at Madame Star's house. I can't imagine anything would be wrong once you tell him the good news, but there may be a chance he's not there on the boat."

It had been a long time since Darryl lost all control of his emotions. Tears welled up in his eyes when he answered the knock at the cabin door and saw Eleanore. Eleanore was coming back to him, and with the greatest gift, a man could want. She was going to have their baby.

"You've made me the happiest man living on the planet. I'm going to make you a promise to love you forever, and I will do anything to make sure that I never make you cry," Darryl choked on the words as a stream of tears rolled down his cheeks.

"Let's go. I want to follow you back home to Casey's house," Darryl's voice squeaked with excitement. "I hope Casey is still up. I want to see his face when we tell him the good news."

"Yes," Eleanore said. "That sounds like a good idea. I already told Casey that I would be later than usual tonight because I was going out with Geneva. I'm sure he'll be up waiting for me, though. He always has waited up for me. He might not stay up long since he has to get up early for work, but I'm sure he'll stay up for a little while when he hears the news."

Geneva, still waiting in her car, watched Darryl and Eleanore walk out of the boat cabin wearing broad smiles on their faces. She waved to Eleanore out of her open car window and tooted her horn.

Geneva had a warm feeling throughout her body when she backed out her car and drove away from Smith's.

"I'm so happy for those two lovebirds," Geneva kept thinking the entire drive home. "Maybe, one day, love will find me, too."

CHAPTER 28
CURIOSITY KILLS THE CAT

Fat Cat, feeling depressed about the unrealized hopes and dreams of making Princess his girlfriend, was at his wits end. The brawl with King left him physically weak and weaker in spirit. After their fight, King went back to the public restroom with Princess, and Fat Cat retreated to the bushes.

Fat Cat's confidence was fading.

"I don't like the idea of being alone so much and not being the leader," he grumbled. "Life was much more enjoyable when more cats were hanging around the marina. Dog Ear can't hear a word I say, and ST is not the companion he used to be.

"I used to be the leader for the gang of cats. I tried to keep them safe. I was the one who warned them about the hurricane coming. I told them where to find shelter. ST and Dog Ear stayed together, safe with me until the hurricane was over. Now, look where I am. I'm living on a pile of discarded wood pallets and hunting alone for my food while the other cats go to the new neighborhood for food. The only permanent resident cats at the marina now are King and Princess. I believe that's only because they have to keep an eye on their crazy, dumb kitten who has little common sense. DC, dumb cat. Harumph!" Fat Cat snorted, fiercely shook his head, and rubbed his forepaw several times across his face as though he were rubbing away a bad smell.

The toot of Geneva's car horn caught the attention of Fat Cat.

Fat Cat flipped over from lying on his side and rose to a crouch, keeping his front paws bent close together beneath his breastbone. A few minutes later, he watched Eleanore and Darryl step off *The Lucky Two*. He wasn't entirely beneath the bushes, but he knew he couldn't be seen by the humans.

He watched Darryl escort Eleanore to her car, holding her hand, then kiss her before he opened the car door for her.

"Odd scenario happening this late at night," Fat Cat thought, slightly amused. "Just a couple of nights ago, they were fighting like cats, and now they are holding hands and kissing. I wonder what happened to change their feelings about each other? Maybe I should give more credit to that crazy fisherman. After all, he always talked to the cats."

Fat Cat watched Darryl lean inside the open window of Eleanore's car, say a few words, kiss her again, then walk to his truck. Darryl started up the engine, rolled down both the driver's and passenger windows, then suddenly threw open the driver's side door and stepped back out of the truck. He slammed the door hard enough to make the truck rock.

"That's odd," Fat Cat thought while watching Eleanore drive away in her car and Darryl jump back on *The Lucky Two*. "The truck's engine is still running. He must have forgotten something, and he's coming back."

The light from the parking lot lamps shone through the front windshield of Darryl's truck, and the steady breezes of the lagoon water blew through the open windows. The blue glass dolphin swayed and glinted, catching the attention of Fat Cat.

The dolphin had been in Darryl's truck for as long as Fat Cat could remember.

"That blue glass dolphin only adds more insult to my misery," Fat Cat fumed.

A nasty rumor running rampant in the new neighborhood had finally reached the ears of Fat Cat. Dog Ear heard it from Oscar on one of his visits to the marina, then reported it to Fat Cat. The rumor had something to do with kissing a dolphin.

"*Oscar told me that the day that you kiss a dolphin,*" Dog Ear said to Fat Cat, without repeating himself, "*is supposed to be how you can earn enough respect to become the leader of the gang of cats at the marina again.*"

"What does kissing a dolphin have to do with bragging rights?" Fat Cat wondered. "It has nothing to do with being brave. It has everything to do with humiliation. Why in the world would a cat kiss a fish?"

The rumor about kissing a dolphin. The humiliation of rejection. Oscar's rising reputation in the new neighborhood. ST's loyalty shifting to the new neighborhood. Even though Fat Cat had protected ST and Oscar's cousin Dog Ear during the hurricane, Oscar never gave Fat Cat any sign of appreciation. It all seemed so unfair to Fat Cat.

Fat Cat boasted to himself, "I'm going to regain respect around this marina. It's not going to be Oscar, or King, or King's kids who will be the big shots of the marina. I'm going to take that title back, and I'm going to do it by taking a ride with Darryl the next time he leaves the marina. When I get back, I'll be carrying that blue dolphin in my mouth. It will glint like it's doing now. I will show everyone what I can do. Then they'll know who is the boss cat at this marina."

The sound of Geneva's car horn had woken up King and Princess, too.

"You wait here," King said to Princess. "I'm going to take a run outside and see what's going on in the parking lot. It's unusual to hear a car horn at this time at night."

"Be careful," Princess cautioned him. "You never know what other kinds of animals are hanging around the marina. There've been reports from our kittens that coyotes have been seen by cats in the new neighborhood. A coyote might get an idea to roam over here to check out the food smells in the trash dumpster behind Smith's. A hungry coyote could rip you apart."

"You're right, and I will be careful," King stopped and turned his head back to tell Princess before trotting through the public restroom door.

King sped away across the parking lot, belly slinking low, close to the pavement. Arriving at the first boat slip, he huddled beside the piling, where a large party boat, gently rocking in the water, was tied. He stopped, sat on his haunches, raised one forepaw, and began to lick it, keeping his head raised, alert, and ready for any motion. In a few seconds, the black pupils of his eyes, fully opened, spotted the iridescent glow of another set of eyes. King dropped down and crouched. He postured his back haunches to be ready for an attack and in preparation to defend himself. He beat his long, slim, black tail against the concrete sidewalk and reacted to the potential threat with a growl. His whiskers twitched.

King waited for the movement of a body that matched the glowing eyeballs. Then he recognized the large, round head of Fat Cat.

The sound of human footsteps diverted King's attention. King watched the movements of Darryl and Eleanore, too.

Both cats, King and Fat Cat, still wary of each other, stayed in a guarded position, alternating their attention to the humans. Fat Cat suddenly jumped up and began to gallop across the parking lot. He ended his run with a high jump into Darryl's truck through the open passenger window.

Surprised, King thought, "That's unbelievable. Why would Fat Cat do something so crazy?"

King shared with Princess what he'd witnessed when he returned to their living quarters. "It's almost as if Fat Cat was in the bushes spying on Darryl."

"There's more to it than just that," Princess said. "I think I know the reason why Fat Cat jumped into Darryl's truck."

Princess had heard from her kittens, who often came to visit her at the marina, that the rumor of Fat Cat kissing a dolphin was spreading around the new neighborhood.

"Remember how we talked about Oscar's bragging rights once we were all back, safe at the marina, after the hurricane?" she asked King. "You said the day Fat Cat kisses a dolphin would be the day he surpasses Oscar's bragging rights."

"Yes, I do remember saying that," King answered.

Princess continued. "Our kittens told me about Oscar having the reputation of being a playboy in the new neighborhood and how Oscar's always bragging. I told them that Oscar better be careful. Fat Cat used to brag about being the boss at the marina. It's easy to lose bragging rights, I told the kittens. I said the day Fat Cat kisses a dolphin is when Oscar will lose his bragging rights. I think that I'm responsible for Fat Cat's actions. I hope Fat Cat is careful. He's not young like Oscar was when he survived his adventure."

"I've also heard from our kittens that Oscar's been all over the new neighborhood talking about his truck ride," King commented. "I'll bet Fat Cat has the idea in his head that he needs to prove himself by taking a ride in Darryl's truck. It's only a coincidence that a dolphin is hanging in Darryl's truck. If Fat Cat does want to kiss a dolphin, I will give him credit for being humble and brave. Let's think about other things before we go to sleep."

King and Princess revisited the memories of a year ago, riding together on *The Lucky Two*. With that, they shared a snuggle of contentment before curling up against each other to sleep for the night.

In his rush to follow Eleanore back to Casey's house, Darryl forgot his wallet. He didn't want to risk being caught driving without his driver's license. After retrieving the wallet off *The Lucky Two,* he jumped back into the front seat of his truck and screeched out of the parking lot, hurrying to catch up with Eleanore.

Darryl's mind was so focused on the surprise visit from Eleanore that he never heard the growling noises made by Fat Cat. Four claws on each of Fat Cat's two back legs scrambled for traction on the floorboard of Darryl's truck.

As soon as Darryl stopped at the traffic light to make his turn onto Thomas Drive, he realized a cat was inside the truck. Fat Cat opened his mouth wide, barring his fangs. He screeched and hissed at Darryl, who tried to reach over to grab him. Fat Cat scrambled up to the front seat with his claws extended, barely missing Darryl's out-reached hand. Before Darryl could say a word, Fat Cat was leaping out of the passenger side window.

"I'll be dog-gone," Darryl paused his frenetic haste to catch up with Eleanore and laughed in shock. "What the heck is that ugly, old, orange cat doing in my truck? I recognize him. I've seen him around the marina for years. What made him want to climb inside my truck tonight?"

Fat Cat's heart was pumping hard, fueled by the adrenaline produced by his fear. He raced down the road, taking bold leaps until he reached the entrance to the Captain Anderson's Marina parking lot. He ran off the road into a weed-filled ditch and kicked up dirt, climbing up to the other side. A large sign for Smith's restaurant, built up from the ground, was lit up by ground lights placed between shrubbery and flowering plants.

"This looks like a safe place to stop and take a break," Fat Cat thought and slowly trotted further up the slope to the landscaped sign sitting at the top of a berm. He flopped down on his side to the ground, panting hard to catch his breath, trying to slow down the fast beating of his heart. "That was quite a scare," Fat Cat thought. "I'll have to admit that Oscar has a valid reason to brag."

"What was I thinking?" Fat Cat asked himself after he'd calmed down. "The truck smelled like burning oil, and the loud noise was worse than the engines of the double-hulled head boats at the marina when the captains start them up. I can't stand the smell of engine fuel, and the jerky movements inside the truck were more than I could take!"

Fat Cat ruminated on the risky adventure. He realized his own stupidity, fueled by his own discontent, nearly cost him another one of his nine lives.

It was the same feeling Fat Cat had the day after surviving the night of hurricane Louise.

"Yep, that experience was worse than the night of hurricane Louise. I'm getting too old for this kind of living. I can't keep expecting myself to be in charge of everyone and everything. I'm not happy at the cat condo, nor do I want to move myself to the new neighborhood that everyone else speaks so highly about. It's not that I wouldn't mind a change of scenery, but I don't know if the other cats would welcome me there. How could I fit into that new environment? Do I start with Oscar? He seems to have taken the leadership role in the new neighborhood. Maybe this is the right time of the day, or better to say night, to take a quick stroll over there to check it out. First, I'm going to need to catch up and get some rest. The truck ride really took a lot out of me. This old body is tired. These bushes seem like a safe place for a short, quick cat nap. I can't imagine any dangers are lurking near here. It's well lit, and so far, seems to be quiet."

Fat Cat lifted his head to take one last look around. His head didn't reach far above the plants. He felt secure that he was safe in his surroundings. He lowered his head, wrapped his front paws over his ears, tucked his back legs up into his belly, and let his slightly curled tail drape across his back paws. Because he was in unfamiliar surroundings, his ears stayed perked, on alert for any noise.

CHAPTER 29
TIME FOR A CHANGE

In the few minutes before Darryl arrived at the house, Eleanore blurted out in two sentences what was going to happen. She was overjoyed with relief after her decision.

"Darryl's on his way over here. I'm having his baby!"

Casey, who was expecting to hear a report about her visit with the spiritual advisor, dropped his jaw.

Casey didn't have time to process the information before he heard Darryl's truck pull into the driveway behind Eleanore's car. Casey rushed to the open door and watched with Eleanore to see Darryl make a grand entrance, tripping his way across the yard to get to the doorway.

Once inside the house, Darryl grabbed and hugged Eleanore.

Casey stood dumbfounded and eventually patted them both on the back, repeating the word congratulations several times.

Then the three friends sat down.

"Before we even get started on anything else, I have to tell you, the strangest thing just happened to me on my way over here. I promise this won't take long," Darryl said, his heart pumping fast with enthusiastic joy over the news, and events, of the evening.

"Sure, we believe you, Darryl," Casey laughed. "I remember how you used to talk to the guys at the marina. You always knew how to make a short story long."

"So quickly," Darryl started, ignoring Casey's comment, "I realized after I got in the truck that I picked up my keys but forgot my wallet. I ran back to the boat to get my wallet and went racing out of the marina to catch up with Eleanore. I didn't hear a thing until I get to the stoplight at Thomas Drive. I see that ugly, orange cat from the marina hissing and screeching at me from the floorboard of my truck. I reached out to grab him, but he went flying out the window, paws stretched out in front and back, like a super cat wearing a cape. I saw him running in leaps down the road in my rear-view mirror," Darryl laughed. "I'm sure if I got a hold of him, he would have torn into me with his claws and teeth."

Eleanore and Casey laughed, along with Darryl, at the freakish story.

"You did tell that story in record time, Darryl. Listen, I am so very happy for both of you," Casey said. "What I heard tonight is all good news to my ears. The past week has been rather unsettling, especially seeing Eleanore upset."

"Not more for you than for me!" Darryl said. "A weight has been lifted off our minds."

"I know you two need some time to talk alone. Since I have to get up early to go to work, I'm going to head on to bed. I'll catch up with you guys later, Casey announced, standing up from his chair.

Casey walked over to Darryl and held out his hand. The two men shook hands for the very first time.

Casey said, "I sure hope you'll let me help if you need some. If you want to consider it, I can connect ya'll with a wedding planner who performs weddings at Eden gardens in Point Washington. It's out in the middle of nowhere. A sawmill was there in the 1800s. The creek by the property was used to float pine trees into the sawmill from the Choctawhatchee Bay.

"It really is a beautiful place to have a wedding. There's a big, two-story, old plantation-style mansion, sprawling oak trees, and gardens filled with flowers most any time of the year. If you think you can wait that long, January is when the camellias are in full bloom. The original owner's wife probably kept herself occupied with gardening."

"I remember you telling me about the sawmill and the creeks the night of the hurricane," Eleanore said, respecting her friend's expertise. "I hope it's not Dismal creek."

Surprised that Eleanore remembered the name of the creek on the Intracoastal where he anchored *The Lucky Two* during the night of hurricane Louise, Casey laughed and said, "No, no. The name of this creek is called Peach creek. Perfect name for a girl from Georgia, like you, about to plan a wedding."

"I might be interested. Thanks for everything, Casey," Eleanore said. "Have a good night's rest. You're way past your bedtime. I'll talk to you tomorrow."

The conversation between Darryl and Eleanore turned serious after Casey went to bed. They began to talk about their plans for the future. Uncertain about whether they should stay in Panama City Beach, Eleanore decided it was a good time to tell Darryl about the things that happened at work at Smith's. When Darryl heard about the incident involving Dorinda, his disbelief and frustration with Dorinda turned into anger.

"How can they allow that woman to come back to work at Smith's after what she did?" he raised his voice. "That woman is far too volatile. What she did at Smith's is very disturbing. She may do something to you, Eleanore. She's dangerous, I'm telling you. Women never stop having their grudges. You and I need to get out of this town. We can go live in Pine Mountain, where you came from," he said with a conviction in his voice that Eleanore had never heard before. "We can start our family and make a whole new life together in Georgia."

"I really don't have any family back in Pine Mountain, but I do have good friends where I used to work at the Kountry Kafe. I think that Johnny, who was my boss, would hire me back. There's also a bar in town called Stumpy's. Everybody goes to Stumpy's on Friday night. They look forward to socializing at the end of the workweek. Saturday nights are busy, too. I'd bet anything that the people at Stumpy's would be happy to have someone as talented as you to play music for their customers. It gets boring just listening to the same songs from the jukebox. Live music would liven up the house. I bet you could put together a band to play your saxophone. There's plenty of guys, and girls, around who like to play guitars, fiddles, and sing."

Eleanore paused to remember all the people she forgot about since she left Pine Mountain. After telling Darryl about all the things that she loved about Pine Mountain, she realized that it wasn't such a bad place to live.

"I think I've missed it," she said nostalgically. "I lived there all my life and always thought there was never much of anything to do but work and go home. But, there's fishing on the lakes. On a dark night in an open field, you can look up at the stars and see the milky way. Moonlit nights are nice, too. Rainy nights bring out a chorus of frogs. Still nights, you can hear the whip-o-wills and owls from miles away in the woods. Speaking of woods, all those pine trees and oaks are home to the cicadas. You've never heard an orchestra playing music until you've heard the cicadas in the Georgia woods at night."

Darryl, becoming more interested in Eleanore's description of life in Pine Mountain, leaned closer toward Eleanore as if to soak up the sights, sounds, and smells of the countryside through her words.

The hills, creeks, and wide-open spaces with winds blowing through the trees sounded appealing. He didn't necessarily need to have the quiet solitude of the Gulf of Mexico. A location change would mean a different experience. Still, the peace of living on *The Lucky Two* could be equally matched by living with this beautiful girl anywhere in Pine Mountain.

"It sounds like a wonderful place to raise a family," Darryl said. "It may not have the aqua blue waters of the Gulf of Mexico, which I will miss, but we can always come back and visit Panama City Beach. I can use the insurance money I received for *The Star Chaser* to use as a down payment on a house for us to live in, or I could buy a piece of land on a lake. We can watch the sweet Georgia sunsets together. I think the sunsets and sunrises are the same color, orange and blue, anywhere on the planet. The billions of stars at night blaze alongside the same twinkling planets. This is a day I've been ready, and waiting for, all my life."

Eleanore felt a warm, pleasant rush of blood pumping from her heart throughout her body. "I can't believe you would think of leaving this place that you love so much to go with me to a strange place that I've only described to you. I can't tell you how much I love you for that!" Eleanore blushed, placed her arms around Darryl, and hugged him stronger than anyone she'd ever embraced in her life.

"I'm so sorry for all the trouble I've caused you," Eleanore's voice cracked. "I know I've been difficult, and it must have been so hard for you to understand."

Tears began to roll down her reddened cheeks. She hid her face against Darryl's shoulder. He wrapped both arms around her and cradled her head.

"No apologies needed," Darryl held her tight. "It's been hard for you, too. You've just made me the happiest man. Don't you remember what I told you back at the marina? I told you I'd never make you cry. Now here you are, crying."

Eleanore choked back a sob of happiness. "Okay," she snorted, half giggled the words. "It's probably time for all of us to get rest. We've got time to sort this all out. I'm ready to go to bed and get a good night's sleep. I'm exhausted after all of the commotion tonight and the past week," she said, and then quickly added, "and you'd better get back to *The Lucky Two*. We'll make new plans for our living arrangements tomorrow."

"I was kind of hoping to stay with you tonight when I drove over here. But I agree. It's a little awkward with Casey in the house, and I left the boat in such a hurry, I don't even think I locked it. We should give Casey a night to absorb the shock. Heck, I need a night to absorb the shock," Darryl laughed.

Eleanore winked at Darryl, knowing that there were going to be many nights together soon. "I'll have arrangements for you worked out with Casey by tomorrow!"

Darryl was too excited to go back to the marina right away. After giving Eleanore a hug and kiss goodbye, he drove on impulse to Estelle's Escape, wanting to share the good news with someone else. Sharkey and Estelle were the people he asked for advice about his problems, and now he could tell them the outcome. Tonight, his problem was fixed. He wasn't going to live on another planet. He was going to live his life with the woman he loved. Going to Estelle's Escape seemed like the right thing to do because there wouldn't be many more opportunities to share camaraderie with them.

"I'll have just one beer," Darryl told himself, "then I'll head back to the marina and start packing. Even if Sharkey isn't there, Estelle will be there. She'll be sure to tell Sharkey."

It turned out that Darryl was in luck. Along with Estelle and a few other locals, Sharkey was there. Once they heard the good news, Sharkey and Estelle congratulated Darryl by buying his beers. He ended up staying longer than he planned.

"I can drive. It's only a few blocks back to the marina," Darryl told Sharkey when Sharkey offered to take him back to the marina. "And, I don't think I'll have any trouble remembering where I have to turn," Darryl slurred his words. "I'd rather my truck be parked at the marina than in the parking lot of Estelle's Escape all night. No telling who might notice," he winked at Estelle, laughing at his own joke when he slid off his bar stool.

His mind was occupied with all the wonderful events that had happened, all in one night when he walked out of Estelle's Escape, but he quickly realized his vision was slightly blurred when he turned the truck onto the road. He drove slowly and with extreme care, gripping the steering wheel while holding his head close above it to see the road better.

The noise of Darryl's truck engine echoed across the lagoon as he made his way across the bridge on Thomas Drive.

The sound of Darryl's truck engine woke up Fat Cat.

"That sounds like Darryl's truck," Fat Cat said to himself. "It's late. I didn't think he would be coming back."

Feeling annoyed by the reminder of his failed attempt to take a ride in Darryl's truck earlier in the evening, Fat Cat shook his head hard. He stood up on all four legs, stretched his front paws out in front, and lifted the back of his body upward to stretch his hind legs.

"Time for me to move on and get out of this bed of flowers. I'm going to check up on my cat condo. I should make sure nobody has been snooping around in it since I've been gone. I'll just walk around it, take a few sniffs for foreign scents, and then I'll go check out that new neighborhood. It's not that far from here, from what I've heard. This might be the right time, late at night, to see what all the hype is about."

In reality, Fat Cat felt insecure and undecided about the idea of visiting the new neighborhood. It would be a unique experience, trying to understand the world of domesticated cats who actually lived in a house with an owner. The only domestic cat he'd ever met was Princess, and she had rejected him.

"I've got to think through this a little bit more. It might be better to postpone the visit tonight and plan my strategy for a visit. Where will I go exactly? Who, or what, will I be looking for in the new neighborhood? What do I do if a neighborhood local cat sees me, feels threatened by me, and wants to start a fight? What will I say to the cats who used to be part of the old gang? What exactly do I want to say if I run into Oscar, because, after all, he's claiming to be the gang leader in the new neighborhood?

"If I start fresh, and hopefully with a little more food in my stomach, I'll make a better presentation of myself. Yeah, I'll go when I'm not feeling so weak from near starvation," he thought, agreeing with all his rationale to abort the reconnaissance to the new neighborhood.

He crept slowly out of the flower bed, through the shrubbery, placing his paws in strategic spots to avoid stepping on anything that might be a foreign object or a dangerous foe. He made his way down the slope, through the landscaped flowers and shrub, toward Smith's parking lot. He perked up his ears, listening to the sound of Darryl's truck approaching closer.

Knowing that there would be no food left in the bowls sitting out on the sidewalk, Fat Cat turned his attention to the dumpster behind Smith's.

"I'm pretty hungry. I think I'll stop to see if I can find some morsels of food that may have fallen from trash bags carried to the dumpster tonight," he thought.

Fat Cat began to walk along the edge of the pavement, heading toward Smith's where the dumpster sat behind the building and the kitchen.

Darryl relaxed his grip on the steering wheel once he made the turn off Thomas Drive and onto the road that led to Captain Anderson's Marina parking lot. Feeling more at ease now that he was off the main highway, he didn't have to concentrate so hard on driving straight. He let his mind go adrift on all the details of the momentous night.

"The parking lot is empty," Darryl said to himself, then broke into a grin that spread from ear to ear across his face. Loud laughter quickly replaced the smile.

"Why not? I'm celebrating! The words to a brand-new song are in my head. I'm calling the song *Lucky Us*.

Darryl sang the words to the song with a three-chord melody for the chorus:

We met by chance, or maybe providence
Our hearts were together from the start, and now we'll never part
The stars in heaven will be our guide, for heaven is where the angels fly
In search of you, I found me
With you, I'll always be
The stars in heaven will be our guide, for heaven is where the angels fly
Some days may bring fears, and some days may bring tears
There's always the promise of a rainbow appearing
The stars in heaven will be our guide, for heaven is where the angels fly

You'll be my wife and complete my life
Our baby will seal our future, and we'll share the joy of forevermore

"I need to hurry. I need to get inside the boat and write these words down. I need to try the melody on my saxophone. Tonight, I'll be sitting under the stars on a boat in the marina for the last time in my life. I can't wait! I'm so excited!"

Darryl's mind was in a frenzy on everything but his driving. He raced the truck wildly across the parking lot. Tire rubber screeched loudly when he yanked on the steering wheel, pulling it left and right, driving like he was a kid in a bumper car at the amusement park. He slammed on the brakes and pulled into his parking spot in front of *The Lucky Two,* bumping the front tires against the curb of the sidewalk.

Fat Cat's unfamiliarity with speeding cars caught him unprepared. In one of the rare times in his life, his mind did not work correctly. Fear, indecision, and confusion took hold of his actions. When the truck erratically swerved close to him, Fat Cat jumped in the wrong direction to get out of the truck's way.

The rear wheel of Darryl's truck clipped Fat Cat in the head, sending him flying across the pavement, bouncing off the sidewalk, and near the bushes beneath the windows of Smith's.

Fat Cat limped a few paces, using every ounce of energy left in his body to reach the bushes, where he flopped down to lay on his side. His big head rolled over, coming to a rest on top of his shoulder.

Fat Cat's plan to explore the neighborhood where the new gang of cats lived was never realized. Fat Cat's final, faint meow wasn't heard by a single member of the cat gang. His life was cut short that night.

CHAPTER 30
HONOR AND A PROPER BURIAL

DC was the first to discover Fat Cat's body lying near the bushes beneath the windows at Smith's. DC was out for his regular early morning stroll and checking out the sidewalks in front of the boat slips to see if anyone accidentally dropped some bait before boarding for a day-long Gulf of Mexico fishing trip.

"Something feels strange to me," he mused. "It's tranquil, or maybe it's my imagination. I'm wondering where Fat Cat is. I normally see either his head or his tail hanging over the edge of his cat condo. Maybe he had a bad night, and he's tired. If he's backed up in a corner up there, I'd better not bother him."

Strolling alone, stopping frequently, and turning his head to check for edible moving critters, he headed in the direction of the back door of Smith's kitchen. If he didn't find any tidbits near the door, he'd head toward the dumpster. DC didn't have a bad experience with the notorious dumpster like ST did at an early age. Whenever DC ventured inside the cavernous metal box to claw through the plastic bags searching for something to eat, he usually found a shrimp or piece of fish. To DC, it felt safer to be exploring inside the dumpster than rummaging through fast food bags left in the parking lot.

Once he got closer to the restaurant building, DC sharply turned off the concrete sidewalk to cut across the grass. DC halted and stood on all four paws, poised like a pointer dog flushing out birds for a hunter. Barely exposed but distinctly visible was the orange head of Fat Cat. Fat Cat's head seemed to be twisted into an awkward position lying across his front paw.

DC backed up, turned around, and raced down the sidewalk, past the cat condo where Fat Cat lived. He was on his way to find his parents in the public restrooms but ran into ST when he turned the corner of the fish cleaning house.

"Come help me, ST," DC howled the words like a cat fending off an attack by a barking dog. His grainy, pink tongue panted and curled. The upper lip of his mouth quivered, causing his whiskers to twitch. "Something terrible has happened!"

"Calm down, buddy," ST mewed. "Has something happened to your parents?" ST asked.

ST was returning to Captain Anderson's Marina after spending the night in the new neighborhood. He had just finished feasting on a small bowl of dry cat food left out on the back porch of a house several blocks deep into the neighborhood. ST discovered more suitable places in the new setting to curl up and have a good night's rest than inside Fat Cat's condo. He took a shortcut across the Lighthouse Marina parking lot to get to the docks.

ST was aware of Fat Cat's disappointment when he didn't stay at the cat condo at night, but ST found himself preferring the new neighborhood, day and night. There was food, plenty of bushes and trees for hiding spots, and more cats to socialize with than at the marina.

Despite the many times Fat Cat irritated and ridiculed him, ST still believed it was his duty to be a loyal friend. Fat Cat had been a leader, helping everyone in the gang of cats for years. Fat Cat was family and deserved to be checked on regularly. Most of the cats in the gang had abandoned Fat Cat completely, leaving him to fend for himself when he needed their support. Fat Cat was visibly growing thinner and frailer.

"No, no!" DC bellowed. Tears were forming in his eyes, and he rolled over, down on his side in tearful resignation. "Marouw," DC wailed loudly. "It's Fat Cat. He's dead!"

ST sat down on his haunches and nervously licked his forepaw, trying to keep himself distracted while processing the weight of DC's news.

"Why did this happen? How did this happen?" ST grieved, deeply hurt. "I should have been with Fat Cat last night."

The noise of DC's meowing brought out other on-lookers, humans and cats alike.

His wailing brought out Princess and King, who knew the sound of their beloved offspring. They rushed out of the public restrooms and found ST with DC at the corner of the fish cleaning house. ST began to walk in circles around DC, who, seeing his parents, regained enough composure to share the news about Fat Cat.

ST, Princess, and King ventured together, away from the corner of the fish cleaning house, down the sidewalk together. They stopped short of reaching Smith's. From a distance, they saw the head of Fat Cat lying on the ground, not moving.

"Follow us back to our safe place," Princess told ST. "We must get away from the horrible scene. There's nothing we can do for Fat Cat, now."

When he heard the loud meows inside the cabin, Darryl stepped outside onto the deck curious to see what all the noise was about. He looked down the sidewalk toward Smith's, where he knew the cats usually hung out in the bushes. Seeing nothing, his eyes switched direction and picked up movement at the corner of the fish cleaning house. Once Darryl recognized Princess, King, and the snaggled tooth cat running with a kitten toward the public restrooms, he retreated back into the boat. He had planning, and packing, to do.

"Seems like the cats have settled their problems. That younger cat could be the offspring of Princess and the black cat. That white patch of fur on his chest looks like he's wearing an ascot with a tuxedo. Maybe Eleanore may want to take a tuxedo kitten back to Georgia," Darryl chuckled to himself. "Princess won't come along, but perhaps I could coax a kitten."

Later that day, two kitchen employees arriving early for their shift at Smith's noticed a cat's head sticking out from beneath the bushes as they walked together from the parking lot to the kitchen's back door.

Big Joe asked Geneva to go with him to investigate the scene after being informed by the employees that there was a dead cat on the property. Hoping it wasn't the kitten they nicknamed DC and the one they both had grown affectionate about, they were still distressed when they saw the cat.

"I'll ask for a volunteer to go out with a shovel and scoop the cat up off the ground. It's not good to have the poor animal lying out there. Next thing we'll hear is that some other animal is going after it and tearing it up," Big Joe said. "Maybe one of the busboys will be willing to do it. Put it in one of the black garbage bags and throw it in the dumpster."

"Aww, that sounds terrible," Geneva said.

"Do you have any other ideas?" Big Joe asked.

"I would prefer to see the cat have a proper burial. Putting it in a black garbage bag is okay, but I disagree with putting the cat in the dumpster," she answered. "I hate it. It looks like that cat got hit by a car and got its neck broken. I wonder who ran over that cat."

Big Joe gently touched Geneva on the shoulder. "Yes, it does look like it got hit by a car. It's a shame since I know it survived the hurricane. I've seen that particular cat around these docks for many years. He was one of the biggest, boldest, and toughest. He has lived a long life.

"Let's not worry too much about it, okay, honey?" Big Joe said softly. "I agree with you. I'll ask one of the busboys to bury the cat near the bench, where we've sat and had good conversations."

Geneva was taken aback by Big Joe's kind words about a cat and realized that he used the word honey when he spoke to her. "What's up with that?" she wondered. "He's got a soft spot for cats, or does it have something to do with me? After all the bad stuff he's had to deal with this week, Big Joe is one good man with a big heart. I'm just so glad that the Darryl, Dorinda, Eleanore burden might have worked itself out. Wait until Big Joe finds out the news from Eleanore!"

Dog Ear had also heard DC meowing earlier in the day. He was lying on a pallet below Fat Cat's usual spot inside the cat condo. Dog Ear waited all night for Fat Cat to return, only to find out in the morning what happened. Dog Ear had not been able to force himself to leave the condo or take his eyes away from the bushes by Smith's, where Fat Cat's body lay. From his vantage point inside the cat condo, Dog Ear had watched the activity going on at the marina all day.

Unlike his cousin Oscar, rumored to be his brother from the same litter of kittens, Dog Ear had spent all of his life at the marina. Dog Ear was shy, insecure, and, unlike Oscar, not at all adventurous. "I'll never be able to follow Oscar in the new neighborhood," he convinced himself. "Without Fat Cat, what am I going to do?"

Soon after Big Joe and Geneva walked back inside of Smith's, Dog Ear heard the screen door of Smith's kitchen slam. A young man, wearing a white T-shirt with Smith's logo, and carrying a small shovel typically used to scoop charcoal out of the grills, walked around the corner of the restaurant building. The young man walked slowly, bent at the waist, near the bushes, keeping his head close to the top of the bushes. Suddenly he stopped, squatted, and scooped up the lifeless body of Fat Cat with the shovel.

The young man slipped Fat Cat into a black plastic bag, then carried the bag to the concrete bench. He dropped the bag on the ground and began digging a hole at the corner of the bench. A few minutes later, the young man dropped the body of Fat Cat inside the deep hole, then shoveled the dirt back into the hole.

After witnessing the ceremonial burying of Fat Cat, Dog Ear's emotional state fell into crisis mode. Stunned, filled with anguish, and without thinking, Dog Ear jumped off his perch in the condo, landing flat on all four paws on the concrete sidewalk. He ran as fast as he could to find Oscar in the new neighborhood.

Overcome with grief, exhaustion, and confusion, Dog Ear forced himself to stop running when he reached the first lawn of a house. Dog Ear observed the unfamiliar surroundings.

"Oscar's somewhere in this new neighborhood," Dog Ear said to himself, panting hard from anxiety and the sprint. "But I have no idea which direction to turn."

As was always his habit, Dog Ear began to repeat himself.

"I have no idea which direction to turn," he mourned, turning his head from side to side, looking for Oscar.

He slowly and carefully crept through the first yard, slinking low, allowing the fur on his belly to drag across the soft grass.

"I can't let myself meow. No, I can't meow in this strange place. But, if I don't, how will I find Oscar? I need to find someone to tell me where Oscar is."

"Marow, Marow," Dog Ear, desperate, wailed loudly, unable to control his emotions. He opened his mouth before thinking about it. The wails were loud and constant.

A large black and tan, spotted-striper cat suddenly jumped in front of him from nowhere. It was Purr Baby's father, Fernando.

The glossy, black, translucent pupils in Fernando's eyes grew large, further frightening stressed-out Dog Ear. Dog Ear tried to take a step backward, but his paws froze in mid-step. He couldn't avoid staring back at the menacing eyes attached to the head of a cat so much larger than him.

Fernando growled and hissed at Dog Ear. Fernando held his tail straight up, high above his arched back. His black, striped tail puffed out, doubling its normal size. Every hair on Fernando's body puffed out like he had touched a live wire of electricity. Suddenly Fernando started hopping sideways toward Dog Ear.

In a split second, Dog Ear was running donut holes in the grass with Fernando chasing him. Fernando's muscled haunches vaulted his forepaws forward, high above the ground. Soon Fernando was closing in on Dog Ear, cutting off Dog Ear with each turn Dog Ear made. Fernando quickly caught up to Dog Ear, who suddenly stopped in the middle of the grassy lawn. Dog Ear arched his back. His back haunches were taunt, and he cowered low in a defensive posture. His front paws, claws extended, were ready to swat if necessary.

"Stay back. Do not get near me," Dog Ear hissed at Fernando, followed by loud, continuous growling.

Surprised by the scruffy-looking cat's aggressive temperament, Fernando crouched, growled too, and postured to take a better look and assess the foreign enemy.

"This cat's been in a fight before. One ear is missing. That must mean he has experience fighting. I don't want to mess with him," Fernando thought. "I know he's one of those marina cats, probably kin to one of the many cats who have found their way into our neighborhood. I need to think twice about picking on him. He might be a dirty fighter. I don't want his claws on my face or my ear bitten off."

"I'm looking for Oscar," Dog Ear meowed loudly while Fernando glared at him.

Oscar, who was resting beneath a storage shed on the next-door neighbor's back yard, heard his name. Realizing it was Dog Ear's meow, and surprised to hear it, he bolted out like a flash of lightning to find Dog Ear.

"What are you doing here?" Oscar asked Dog Ear.

Fernando flopped down on his side, relieved to end the confrontation with the strange new cat and eager to find out the cat's connection with Oscar. He eavesdropped on the story Dog Ear told Oscar about the end of Fat Cat's life.

"This is unfortunate news and the end of an era," Oscar said. "I'll coordinate a celebration of Fat Cat's life for all the cats who knew him. We'll have the official funeral ceremony at the marina. I'll even invite cats from the new neighborhood too. They'll understand us better when they find out how we used to live together and support each other when we were a gang before the hurricane disrupted our lives. Fat Cat was our leader."

The welcoming committee for the funeral of Fat Cat consisted of Oscar, Dog Ear, King, ST, and Princess. Many cats from the new neighborhood accepted the invitation to attend the ceremony, curious to see the marina and hear stories about the legendary Fat Cat.

DC, who had discovered Fat Cat lying in the bushes, was first in the receiving line at Fat Cat's funeral. Despite knowing how Fat Cat felt about his parents, and Fat Cat's criticism, DC was impressed with the stories he heard about Fat Cat's leadership.

When it seemed to be an appropriate time DC spoke. "In honor of Fat Cat, despite his snarky attitude about me and most of my family, I'm going to do something today that I know he would appreciate." DC looked around to see if he had everyone's attention, then said. "It would give him an excuse to be the boss, say something to correct me, and puff out his fur and say something like *'I was right all along about that dumb cat.'*"

After making the announcement, DC proceeded to jump, bounce, and repeatedly run around in circles in the marina parking lot, chasing his own tail.

Purr Baby, so proud of DC's humility in honor of Fat Cat and pleased with his animated display, couldn't resist joining DC. Without asking permission from her father, Fernando, she began to mimic DC in his exuberant, energetic prancing.

"That foolish cat will always end up in trouble," Fernando thought, watching his daughter run around the parking lot with DC.

"Next thing to happen, I'll be seeing a new breed of kittens. I know that I can't put a stop to that. I would if I could. The problem is that nearly the whole gang of cats from the marina has migrated to my neighborhood. If I try to get rid of one, I have to get rid of them all," Fernando said intentionally loud enough for all the cats to hear.

Whisperings spread amongst the cats after hearing what Fernando said.

Leo, an older brother of DC's from Princess and King's first litter, was sitting with his own new family of kittens. He calmly approached Fernando and said, "I'm positive my dad, King, and my mom, Princess, don't like hearing those words about DC. I consider what you said as disrespectful to my family and inappropriate to announce at Fat Cat's funeral."

"I've already seen Purr Baby a few times at the marina," Princess spoke up next, in defense of the two playful cats. "We don't have a problem if Purr Baby wants to spend time at the marina. Furthermore, my boy Leo has mentioned that he's seen a certain cat sitting in the window of a house in your neighborhood making eyes at him. Maybe that domesticated neighborhood cat might be interested in joining our gang. Our Tuxedo breed, the offspring of King and myself, possess outstanding qualities."

DC believed it was now his turn to speak up since he was the subject of Purr Baby's affection and Fernando's displeasure.

"For everyone here, I am making this announcement. I will no longer accept that I am a dumb cat. If you call me DC, it will be because I am Da' Captain. There is nothing wrong with living at a marina or as a domestic cat in this neighborhood. The most important thing for me is to be the captain of my future family, or gang, whichever it may be. That's what Fat Cat did, and I'm going to do it too." DC turned to Purr Baby and asked her," Where would you like to live? Would you like to be called Purr Baby or Doll Baby? Anything you want, I'm ready."

Purr Baby walked up to DC and licked his face. "I know you understand that I've never liked others making fun of me for purring all the time. I can't help it if I am so happy. If Da' Captain wants to call me Doll Baby, I like it."

Fernando, upon hearing the two cats discuss their future, snorted. "It won't be long before all the cats at the marina end up in this neighborhood. We'll be sharing our food bowls with a big gang of cats."

Princess retorted. "Doll Baby will never go hungry. I speak from experience. I used to be a domesticated cat, like you, but I learned how to survive quite well at the marina."

"We also have humans who leave us bowls of food, but we have fresh fish from boat captains and restaurant food leftovers. It's not a bad life." King added.

Hearing the pride in Princess and King voices, talking about their satisfaction of living at the marina, humbled Fernando. He spoke solemnly and sincerely, "I've never been to the marina before today. I believe it's not going to be my last visit. I hope you both, Princess and King, will visit me in the future, too."

"What's in our future?" Dog Ear asked Oscar, who was sitting next to him and alternately licking the tip of his tail and the toenails on his hind feet. "I feel lost now. How will I fit into the group of cats in the new neighborhood?"

"I don't know, right now," Oscar replied. "I've been enjoying all my bragging rights in this new neighborhood for over a year, and now I feel like I've just fallen from first place. Da' Captain, formerly known as DC, has moved up a few notches. King and Fernando might take turns bragging. It doesn't matter that much to me, though. The important thing is that we're heading toward a more unified, growing gang of cats."

Dog Ear was unsure if he could believe what Oscar was telling him. He decided to wander over to where ST was mingling with Princess and King's first litter of grand kittens.

"I'll ask ST what he thinks," Dog Ear thought. Dog Ear left Oscar's side and reached ST just in time to overhear him say to the kittens, "I'm going to miss Fat Cat so much. I can say a piece of my heart has died with Fat Cat. I've enjoyed hanging out with him at the marina all those years. But, I have to say that now I'm looking forward to hanging out with you guys in this neighborhood."

ST's words brought comfort to Dog Ear. Dog Ear decided he was going to look forward to visiting the new neighborhood. He was seeing his future with a whole new perspective. He'd grown confident after bravely standing his ground with Fernando. Still, his home would be at Captain Andersons's Marina with Doll Baby and DC.

CHAPTER 31
WELCOME BACK PARTY

Geneva went home after work and tried to get comfortable but tossed and turned in her single bed. Finding the dead cat, a busy night in the kitchen at Smith's, and worrying about her brother Charles kept her awake.

Another night and Geneva didn't get a chance to ask Sue if there was a possibility that she could take on a roommate. "Hopefully, I'll get a chance to ask Sue tomorrow," Geneva told herself. "I have patience, but the big question is do I have time to work this out if Sue isn't interested and says no?"

Geneva also couldn't get out of her mind that Big Joe called her honey when he told her not to worry about the dead cat.

"This big white man, my boss, Big Joe, called me honey. Does that mean something? Is he thinking of me romantically, or is he trying to be my friend? He's a big white man, and I'm a big black woman. He's said to me more than once *I like you, Sista*.

"When I was working at the Elks Club in Altoona, the atmosphere in the kitchen was much different than here. The employees at the Elks were more like family, joking with each other and checking on each other if they thought something was wrong with you. At Smith's, the employees seem to be in their own little world. But, now, Big Joe is talking to me in a way that makes me think he cares about me.

"I remember hearing the servers at the Elks Club come back into the kitchen to get their orders and talk about the women out in the dining room. The servers knew the customers by their names. They were the people who lived in our town and not tourists like at Smith's. The servers at the Elks Club laughed about the women, who were schmoozing with the men, and not always with their husbands. The women liked to call the men, including sometimes the servers, *hon*. It didn't matter if it was a handsome man, an ugly man, or an old man. Those women loved to call everyone *hon*. The true meaning of *hon* should be for somebody you sincerely care about. I'm glad Big Joe called me honey.

"I know who I am, and I like what I do. If Big Joe likes me for who I am, that's all that matters. He doesn't have to be a rich man. Until now, I never thought much about wanting a man in my life, especially with Charles in jail facing prison for murder. All I'd want is a man with a kind heart, just like Eleanore found a kind heart in Darryl. The word honey sounds so much more sincere than the short version."

Geneva hoped she would be able to approach Sue while they were doing their prep work the next night at work. "I don't have time to waste," Geneva thought. "I'll start the conversation before we take our break."

She sided up with Sue in the salad room the next night. Sue was busy chopping lettuce.

"Sue, I have a personal favor to ask," Geneva cautiously started.

Excited to be allowed in Geneva's inner circle, Sue stopped what she was doing, held her knife up in front of her face, and said, "I'm honored to help you. I like working with you. You're a good person. No one else working in the kitchen has ever asked me to help them, even though it makes me unhappy when I see someone do something unkind to someone else. For example…"

"Don't go there," Geneva quickly interrupted, forcing herself not to become irritated with Sue. "I don't want to hear any more names involved in the drama that's been going on around here." Geneva took in a deep breath. "I'm going to ask you right out. My brother, who shared my apartment with me, has suddenly left town. I need a place to rent that I can afford. Do you have an extra room in your house that I could rent? It could be temporarily."

The look of surprise on Sue's face caught Geneva off-guard. She wasn't sure if Sue's reaction to the question was disdain for the idea or if Sue was embarrassed.

Still holding the knife, Sue placed her hand by her side. "I live in a trailer," Sue replied with uncharacteristic simplicity, "not a house."

"I don't have a problem with staying in a trailer," Geneva quickly said, not sure if her request was going in the direction she was hoping.

Sue's face beamed with pride. "It makes me feel bad to hear that your brother left you. It would be an honor for me to help you in your time of need. In my country, where I grew up, we adopt the person into our family if we know someone who does not have a family. I am happy to let you rent a room in my trailer."

Thrilled that she had been approved to move in with Sue, Geneva wrapped her arms around the diminutive woman and nearly cried. "Thank you so much for helping me out in my financial dilemma. I will not be a problem, I promise."

Over three stressed-filled weeks, the employee dynamics at Smith's changed. Dorinda was re-writing the rules of engagement at the hostess stand. Geneva was preparing to move in with Sue. And, Eleanore became the wife of Darryl, leaving Smith's to move back to Pine Mountain, Georgia.

"We want to see that baby grow up," Geneva and Big Joe insisted after Darryl and Eleanore were married at Eden Gardens and left to start a new life in Pine Mountain.

The first summer after the baby was born, Darryl and Eleanore returned to Panama City Beach to introduce their new baby to Casey, Geneva, and Big Joe.

Big Joe reminisced about the fish Darryl used to catch when he went out on his deep-sea fishing charters on *The Star Chaser*. Out of respect, Big Joe honored the memory of *The Lucky Two*.

"Old Earl caught some great fish, too. He was an honest man, and I always felt like he tried his hardest to be successful. There were times near the end, right before Louise wiped out most of the fleet at the dock, that he became a real tough businessman. He tried to drive some hard business transactions with me. I had to push him hard on the price for a pound of fish. Earl had a harder time than most of the other charter boat captains. He wasn't here long enough to build a great reputation, so he had to rely on the restaurant to buy his fish catch. I felt bad for him, but making a profit selling food in a restaurant is just as hard as making a profit catching fish. Earl relied on me for buying most of the fish he caught, and he always caught good fish. Grouper, snapper, pompano, you name it. We served it up to the customers at Smith's, and they loved it!"

Big Joe ended his recitation with the words *those were the days*.

Once hearing those words, Geneva started reminiscing, avoiding the mention of Dorinda, knowing neither Eleanore nor Darryl would be interested in hearing about her. They all knew Dorinda was still working at Smith's.

"I've moved in with Sue right after you left, Eleanore," Geneva started. "Renting a room in her trailer, which helped me out financially. Living in town, and driving over the bridge to work, took a lot of time, not to mention paying rent for an apartment. It was difficult, being with Sue all the time, day and night. Even though she's super sweet, Sue's a chatty woman. I've never met a person more compulsive over their possessions and keeping a clean house. I'm glad I had Big Joe convince me to move out and help me find a new place to stay."

Geneva paused and nodded at Big Joe, who picked up where Geneva left off.

"I told Geneva I had a big house that I would be happy to share with her," he said, trying hard not to laugh at the surprised looks on the faces of Eleanore and Darryl. "It's working out really well, and even Sue thought it was a cool idea for Geneva to move in with me. You should have seen the look on her face when we told her at the break table one night. Of course, when she found out, everyone else at Smith's did too."

"That baby girl is so cute," Big Joe quickly changed the subject.

The beautiful baby girl, with blue eyes just like Darryl's, was alert and attentive.

"Well, we're disappointed that we couldn't see Casey this weekend," Eleanore said. "I would have loved for him to see our little Eve."

"We haven't seen much of Casey around here at the marina," Big Joe answered. "As soon as he got promoted within the Florida Marine Patrol, his days of counting fish at the docks ended. Once he was reassigned to patrol boat duty, he found a new house to live in on the Intracoastal, up near West Bay. Last I saw him, he told me he would rent out his house there off Thomas Drive. He wanted to live closer to his new assignment."

"I know he's happy about all that, getting a chance to be out on the water!" Darryl clicked his tongue and bounced the baby on his knee. "I always felt he was a true fisherman in his heart, just like all of us boat captains. Catching large loads of fish out in the Gulf of Mexico was anyone's dream. I always sensed he hated the limits that were placed on us charter boat captains."

Once his former adversary, Darryl continued to boast praise on Casey.

"Casey always dreamed he would own his own charter boat one day. His dream came true when the probate on *The Lucky Two* got completed. When the keys were turned over to him, for the second time in his life, he knew his responsibilities. We called Casey when we found out that the probate work was finished. Everyone in Earl's family who wanted a share of the money from the sale had to be satisfied with the selling price. Casey was only approved for so much money on the loan, and the bank had to approve his business plan. In order to buy the boat, he was to lease *The Lucky Two* to another charter boat captain. Casey told the bank he wanted to keep the boat and knew enough charter boat captains who had lost their boat in the hurricane who would be happy to lease *The Lucky Two*. His goal is to operate the boat himself when he retires from the Florida Marina Patrol, but we all know when we get older, things can change."

"He told me the name, *The Lucky Two,* would remain painted on the stern as a tribute to us," Eleanore added. "He said we were truly two lucky people in love. Casey said he'd be forever grateful for the boat, and he only hopes that one day he would, in his lifetime, find a love like ours."

After a few years, the ritual of routinely visiting Panama City Beach for a weekend each summer stopped. Darryl and Eleanore settled into work and family life at Pine Mountain.

Darryl formed a three-piece band that included Darryl playing his beloved saxophone, a drummer, and a keyboard player. The band, named *The Pals,* became very popular in the nearby countryside, attracting more customers at Stumpy's than the pool tables ever did. Darryl struck a partnership deal with the owner of Stumpy's. Using some of his insurance settlement money from *The Star Chaser,* Stumpy's interior was expanded to include a dance floor and a small dining area. Part of the deal included allowing Eleanore, using the skills she learned at Smith's, to manage the food side of the business.

With their weekends tied up in their work, and their child going to school during the week, Eleanore and Darryl rarely visited Panama City Beach. They managed to keep in touch with Big Joe and Geneva through an annual Christmas card. Both couples exchanged news about Pine Mountain and Panama City Beach, marking the milestones in their lives.

Darryl and Eleanore were both proud to announce when their daughter finished law school.

Geneva and Big Joe were both proud to announce, each year, that they were still working at Smith's together and enjoying life.

Years passed, until one day Eleanore answered the phone and it was a call from Geneva.

CHAPTER 32
DINNER AT SMITHS

Eve took in all the changes that had taken place at Captain Anderson's Marina as she walked around the parked cars in the parking lot on her way to eat dinner at Smith's. Tonight, Eve was giving herself a special treat.

The most significant change was the renovations that had been made to Smith's restaurant. It was expanded considerably. Additions to the building had been made to include another dining room, an outside patio with a service bar, and a sizable gift shop.

As a very young child, she had eaten at Smith's with her parents. She vaguely remembered it had an elegant dining room and excellently prepared fresh seafood.

She'd made progress in Ricky's case, but the last visit to the prison, and meeting with Charles had tested her instinct abilities. An elusive piece of solid evidence, necessary for her to request the court for a rehearing in the case, was missing in Charles' case.

She was deep in thought about Ricky and Charles when she stepped inside the entrance of Smith's. "Life is not easy for anyone, but I cannot imagine those two men sitting in prison, innocent of a crime, for as long as they've been in there," Eve thought to herself.

The strong aroma of the grill filled her nose and worked on the juices in her stomach, causing a welcome distraction from her serious thoughts.

A polished-looking, elderly woman with bright white hair, dressed in a white, long-sleeved shirt covered in rhinestones, stood at the hostess stand. She looked over reader glasses perched on the tip of her nose at Eve standing in front of her.

"Hello, welcome to Smith's," the hostess said in a well-rehearsed friendly voice.

Eve couldn't help but notice the nose, shaped like a bird's beak, and had to restrain herself from a giggle. The combination of the woman's hair, clothing, make-up, and jewelry screamed, *I love attention.*

"A table for one, please," she said to the hostess.

"We have about a thirty-minute wait for tables. If you don't mind eating at the bar, it's open," the hostess said.

Eve watched the hostess's dark eyes take in the view of the woman standing in front of her. The subtle, unapproving eyes of the woman looking at her unnerved Eve, causing her to momentarily forget her thoughts about the two incarcerated men.

"I don't mind sitting at the bar," Eve said, consciously not allowing herself to feel annoyed by the hostess but wondering why she was being scrutinized. Was it what she was wearing, or did the woman have another reason for the way she looked at Eve? "It might be that's just her nature," Eve thought, dismissing the experience.

The hostess motioned with a wave of her hand to a younger girl standing a few feet away from the hostess stand to come over. "Show this woman to the bar, please." To Eve the hostess said, without looking up from her table chart, "We hope you enjoy your dinner, miss."

Eve was led into a room that appeared to have been recently renovated in a nautical-themed décor. A mirrored wall behind the long oak bar made the room appear to be bigger. Bottles of exotic cordials, brandy, and spirits sat on tiered shelves, lined up in front of the mirror. The dim lights in the room, and various-shaped liquor bottles, slightly camouflaged the image of Eve in the mirror, but she could clearly see her face. She forced herself to stare at the face looking back at her, hoping to find truth in the reason for being in Panama City Beach.

"I'm not here to look good for anyone. However, I have to admit that I do look slightly shabby. Maybe there will be a next time when I can take more time for myself while staying down here on the beach. Take a break from investigating on behalf of other people and investigate on behalf of myself."

Eve looked down at the clothing she was wearing. Her washed-out, loose-fitting jeans, white cotton, collarless shirt, and brown leather strap sandals were casual. She had stopped to change out of her standard business attire to get comfortable for what she hoped would be a relaxing and delicious dinner. Then she would have to go back to the house and pour over her paperwork.

"I suppose I could have put a little more effort into how I dressed before coming into Smith's. It's an upscale, fancy restaurant. I could have touched up my make-up and added a pair of sparkly, big earrings. That would have been easy enough to do. It might energize me if I put more time into my appearance. I've been neglecting myself since I've taken on more than I should for the prisoners," she thought, then turned resolute. "I'm not here to make a fashion statement. Right now, I'm famished, and I'm not going to worry about how I look."

The bartender walked over and stood in front of Eve, ready to serve her.

"I'd like a glass of white wine to start," she said to him, "and I'll need a menu."

"Will there be anyone else joining you?" the bartender asked.

Eve shook her head no.

He grabbed a menu from beneath the bar and handed it to Eve. "Always nice to have a pretty customer eating at the bar," the bartender said, giving Eve a wink and a smile.

"That's ironic," Eve thought. "The hostess gives me a look that makes me feel like a plain Jane. The bartender looks at me and calls me pretty."

When he returned with the wine Eve said, "I'd like the grouper imperial, salad, and baked potato."

"Salad dressing? Sour cream and butter for the potato?" he asked, still looking directly at Eve and smiling.

Eve told him what she wanted, dismissing his friendliness and compliment as fishing for a good tip.

While she sipped wine, she dug deeper into thoughts about her dilemma.

Eve at Peace by Yvette Doolittle Herr

"I feel like I've been sideswiped by a linebacker on the Alabama football team. Why didn't I see this coming? I knew that finding Ricky wouldn't be complicated. What I didn't expect was Ricky's reaction to me. He's eager for me to be a visitor, but he turns into a nervous wreck when I begin to talk about the murder. I can tell that he trusts me because he's been cooperative in sharing information about Vince and the murder site. What I didn't expect was that Ricky would want me to help another man get out of prison.

"It's almost as if Ricky is comfortable with his station in life. He's found purpose being in prison. The guards told me he wants to meet every new prisoner and show them his bible. That's unusual, but more notable is that he's not expressed any interest in getting free. Yet, I do get the sense that he wants the truth to be told.

"Ricky's friend Charles, on the other hand, is bitter about his circumstances and everything that has happened to him. He thought he was framed for the crime, and the framing had everything to do with the color of his skin. Charles would be rushing in a heartbeat, out the gate to freedom, if I told him he was getting freed from prison," she thought and took a long sip of wine.

Eve decided to put the most recent meeting with Ricky and Charles behind her. She needed a break from all of the mental pressure.

"I came here to relax," she reminded herself.

Two other couples were sitting at the bar, laughing and deep in a conversation. Distracted by the laughter, Eve turned her head around and shifted her attention to the windows. Her eyes took in the view out the window, which faced the lagoon. The small waves on the lagoon waters glistened and sparkled from the last golden rays of the sunset. The charter boats, tied to the docks for the evening, swayed with the gentle wind. She gazed at the scene, becoming hypnotized by the beauty and the memories it brought to her mind.

"Ah, yes," she mused. "It all started with a charter boat."

"How you doing here?" the bartender interrupted her trance. "Are you ready for another glass of wine? They're working on your meal in the kitchen. Excellent choice, by the way. When I put in your order, I asked them to move it up since it was for one person."

"That's good. Yes, I would like another glass of white wine, please," Eve said without thinking about her goal to finish dinner and head back to the house she was renting on a month-to-month basis. "I didn't realize I was so thirsty. I drank that first glass of wine too fast. Can you bring me a glass of water too, please?"

"In a short minute," the bartender said and walked away to pour it.

Eve returned to thinking about work to ignore the loud laughter of the other two couples. The glow of the sunset was gone, and looking out the window into the dark didn't interest her.

"Somehow, Ricky's taken control of my visits," she thought, angry at herself for losing control of the situation. "I don't regret agreeing to talk to Ricky's best buddy. Charles' story was more bizarre than Ricky's. The evidence in Charles' case was weak. It shouldn't be that easy to close an investigation, take a man to trial, and put a man in prison. The murdered woman was black. I have a strong intuition that someone of his own color framed Charles. Charles strikes me as a little bit naïve about people."

Ricky wrote down the memories she asked him to share about the day of the Earl's murder, but he also wrote the appeal for his friend Charles. It took Eve by surprise. Ricky could put his thoughts down on paper so eloquently, and Ricky pleaded for another man, not himself.

She didn't want to get involved with Charles' case, but Eve made it her goal as a public defender to fight against injustice. Not getting involved went against her principles. Also, she couldn't shake a strange feeling that there was a connection between Charles and herself.

"I came down here to find justice for a man I repeatedly heard my father talk about. Now I feel a greater need to find justice for another man I've never heard about. I can understand why Charles thinks he was framed. He thinks, as a black man, he wasn't worth the time for the police to bother with a thorough investigation of the murder."

She reflected back on the look of surprise on Charles' face when she asked him to put himself in her place as a woman.

"How would it make you feel," she had asked Charles, "if every time a man looks at you, it feels like he's trying to undress you? Imagine what would happen if I walked through the prison cafeteria today. What do you think most of the men would imagine? Don't you think I've had to deal with discrimination, too? I've studied and worked many hours in my young professional life. I've learned to force myself to stay focused on the important things. I can't allow myself to be troubled every time I know a man is trying to undermine me by getting under my skin with a sneaky look. Charles, I want you to cut back on blaming discrimination for the situation you're in and focus only on the facts. When I come back here, I want you to tell me facts, whatever you can remember, about what happened before, during, and after the night of the Halloween party."

Eve triumphantly lifted up her glass of wine and, before putting the glass to her lips, said a little too loudly, "That took Mr. Charles off his own high horse when I told him to try riding my horse!"

"Are you proclaiming some kind of a victory tonight?" the bartender, hearing what she said, spun around and laughed.

"Oh, not exactly," she said, hoping her face didn't reflect the embarrassment she felt. "Maybe I'll have another glass of wine."

The bartender tilted his head to the side, squinted his eyes ever so slightly, and said, "You're sure you're ready?"

Eve smiled playfully and said, "Bring it with my food."

She continued to rehash her meeting with Charles. It gave her pleasure to remember what he said after she hit back hard with her own feelings of discrimination.

"Then he says to me," 'Yes, ma'am. I think I understand what you're saying. You see me as another man you're not sure if you can trust. Discrimination is complicated. Something I've discovered since I've been here, in this prison, is that it doesn't matter if you're white-skinned or colored-skinned. I've learned that hate is what drives people to do bad things. Hate crosses over many lines. I learned about hate from my father. But I was fortunate to learn the power of love from my mother and Sista. All I really want to do is to see sunsets and sunrises again at my own choosing. It doesn't happen when you live in prison'

CHAPTER 33
CHANCE ENCOUNTER

Geneva and Big Joe left Smith's together, as they had done for many years, through the kitchen door. They immediately noticed a young woman sitting on the concrete bench generally reserved for Big Joe.

Eve was facing the charter boat *The Lucky Two*, singing a song to two cats lying on the ground at the edge of the sea wall. It was a song her father sang to her many times. She slurred the words *The stars in heaven will be our guide, for heaven is where the angels fly.*

"What's that young woman doing over there, sitting on your bench and singing to the cats?" Geneva asked, stopping to pull at Big Joe's elbow.

"No earthly idea, Sista," Big Joe answered. "Let's go over and check on her."

Big Joe and Geneva held hands and walked toward the bench. The sounds of waves lapping against the seawall, and vehicle traffic crossing the lagoon on the bridge, kept Eve from noticing them until they were standing in front of her.

"How is it going tonight?" Big Joe asked Eve, opening up the dialog to find out why she was sitting on his bench alone, late in the evening.

"Well, hello there. I'm a lawyer," Eve said to them. "You two look like a nice couple. What're your names?" Eve's words were slightly slurred. Despite her training in law school to speak distinctly when she was asking questions, she couldn't mask the reality of her drunken state.

Big Joe answered. "We work here at Smith's and just got off. We saw you sitting over here, by yourself, and decided to check on you. We want to see if you are okay. We don't usually see people, or a single girl, sitting out here all by herself."

"I'm actually fantastic," Eve answered, slurring her words more. "Best I've felt in over a month. These cats are enjoying my company, don't you think? Would you all like to sit down, too?"?

"We're ready to go home. The kitchen at Smith's is closed now. I don't think you should be sitting out here by yourself," Big Joe answered.

"I like singing to the cats. And, I like to talk to them, too," Eve said. "Talking's a habit when you're a lawyer. I tend to talk whether I have an audience or not, although sometimes we lawyers also like to listen. We can learn a lot about other people, you know, listening to their conversations. Sometimes I talk, but my audience isn't listening. That often happens in a courtroom, you know. I can be laying down the facts straight out. I think I've got the attention of everyone in the courtroom. Then I look up and see the judge with his elbows on the desk, hands cupping his chin, and his eyes half-closed. I know he's bored listening to me. What am I supposed to do? Stop talking? There have been times I thought I heard a snort from the judge, but I think it could have been a snore."

Eve, laughing hard after telling her side of the story to the two strangers, suddenly closed her eyes. Her head wobbled like a bobblehead doll, then dropped down to her chest. Eve was struggling to be in control of her physical reactions. She was also trying to stay awake.

Just as quickly as her head dropped, Eve jerked it back up. Her eyes squinted at the two strangers staring at her, the white man and the black woman. Eve stopped laughing. She wiped her eyes, filled with moisture from laughing so hard, and wiped away a bit of drool from the corner of her mouth with the back of her hand.

"I bet you two are cooks! This place, Smith's, it's the best restaurant to eat at on the beach. The food is spectacular, and the wine makes me chatty. The bartender was a nice guy, but I can't think of anything good to say about the hostess. Wait. I know. Maybe she looks good for her age. She was all shined up with glittery make-up and clothing. Then I walk in the door wearing faded-out jeans and brown leather strap sandals like Jesus wore."

Eve at Peace by Yvette Doolittle Herr

It was apparent to the perplexed couple that the woman was affected by the consumption of too much alcohol.

Eve laughed, again, much louder. She bent forward and wrapped both arms around her belly. "It hurts to laugh so hard after eating such a big dinner," Eve groaned.

Her head dropped further down to her waist. Her long hair was covering her face and touching the dirt. When she finally regained composure from another laughing spell, she sat up slightly bent at the waist and said, "I can't help my babbling. It's part of my silly genetic code. It helps if you're raised by a father who used to talk constantly. If he wasn't using his mouth to talk, he was using his mouth to play his saxophone."

Big Joe and Geneva turned their heads and locked eyes. Without a word spoken between them, they knew right away this woman had to be talking about Darryl Kay, and this was his daughter that they had not seen since she was a young child.

"I've been trying to help two men at the prison up there in Greenhead. I know that they're both innocent," Eve tilted her head briefly upward to the night sky, then back down. She repeated, "I know it! I know they're both innocent! One man wants to get out of prison, and the other man is content staying in prison. The man who wants out said some things to me. I can't remember his exact words right now because you see the shape I'm in. However, the essence of what he said is that *time is just standing still, but the clock keeps ticking. I have nothing to measure the passage of time except that the days are long, and I'm just waiting for the times to change.* I've never heard anything sadder than those words in my entire career. How can time stand still for someone? I can't seem to find enough time in my day to get all my work finished."

The expression on Eve's face changed from hard, compassionate conviction to sincere compassion. "It brings peace to my heart to help people, "she said, speaking the words more soberly. "He said something about missing watching the sunrise and sunset. That man doesn't have any hate in his heart. He told me he'd never kill a woman. He loved his mother and sister. I believe him."

Eve fell silent. She looked up at Big Joe and Geneva with slightly bloodshot eyes and made an effort to stand up from the bench. At first, her legs wouldn't cooperate; she lost her balance and clumsily sat back down. Gripping the concrete bench with both hands wrapped around the bottom of the bench for support, she was able to press herself up to a standing position.

"Can we help you get back to your house?" Big Joe asked. "I think the bartender might have been nice to serve you all the drinks you asked for, but he didn't do his job right if he allowed you to drink too much. It's dangerous to let you drive. You're are driving a car, right?"

"Yes," Eve replied. "I think you're right. I could call a cab and leave my car here."

"We can help you," Geneva offered immediately. "Is it very far from here where you live?"

"No, it's just a few blocks from here. The house I'm staying in is on Sunset Avenue, a few blocks off Thomas Drive. Maybe I could make it if I drive slow and carefully," Eve said. She tried to take a few steps toward the parking lot and felt her legs buckle below her knees. She plopped back down on the concrete bench.

"Let me drive your car. You can ride. He can follow us," Geneva nodded her head toward Big Joe, "Sunset Avenue is not far from here. It's not an inconvenience for us since we ride to work together. After I drop you and your car off, I'll just get into his car. I'd rather not hear about someone getting into a car crash after leaving Smith's restaurant."

"Are you sure you guys want to do this?" Eve asked as she felt each one of her hands grabbed to help her stand up.

Big Joe and Geneva each took an arm and helped Eve walk to her car.

After Geneva escorted Eve to the front door of the house, where Eve directed her to drive and saw that she was safe inside the house, she slid into the front seat of Big Joe's car. Sitting next to Big Joe, Geneva said, "If I didn't know any better, I'd have to say I'm almost certain that this house is where Eleanore stayed with Casey."

"I think we should give Eleanore and Darryl a call," Big Joe said. "Find out what's going on. There's no doubt in my mind that the girl is the daughter of Darryl."

Geneva reacted, "It would be nice to talk to Eleanore. It's been a long time since we've talked. If this is her daughter, I have some questions I'd like to ask her myself."

"Charles?" Big Joe asked.

"Uh-huh," Geneva said quietly, then turned her head to stare out the passenger window and focus her eyes on the stars in the night sky.

CHAPTER 34
JONNIE MAE

When Jonnie Mae turned sixteen, she learned she had a father in the Florida State Prison in Chattahoochee. A woman who claimed to be a friend of Jonnie Mae's mother from many years ago approached her at the annual downtown Halloween party.

"Are you Lucille's daughter?" a woman tapped Jonnie Mae on the shoulder and asked.

"Yes," Jonnie Mae timidly answered, not sure if she should talk to the woman. "Who are you?" Jonnie Mae asked.

"I knew your mother, Lucille, way back in the day when we were young. We used to work together," the woman, acting slightly nervous, cleared her throat. "I doubt that she would remember me, though. I moved away. I have to say you look like your mom and your dad."

"I don't know my dad," Jonnie Mae stammered, shocked by the boldness of the stranger.

"No, you probably wouldn't," the woman quickly responded. "He's been gone a long time, just like me. I left about a year after that terrible hurricane Louise hit Panama City. You've heard of hurricane Louise, right? "

Not sure whether she should continue a conversation with the woman or walk away, Jonnie Mae simply nodded her head yes. She stared at the woman in wide-eyed shock.

"I came back this week to visit some family and an old friend. I came to this Halloween party with my friend. He nudged me and told me you were Lucille's daughter, so I had to come over and say hello."

Recognizing the look of distrust in Jonnie Mae's eyes, the woman quickly reached into her purse. "I have something I want to show you," she said, holding a wallet and nervously pulling out a photograph. The color in the photograph was slightly faded. Still, it was apparent that a man and woman were together at a Halloween party. "This is a photograph of your father, John."

"Why are you carrying a picture of my father, and who is the woman standing next to him in that costume?" Jonnie Mae curiously asked, becoming unnerved but intrigued that the woman who showed her the photograph also knew her father's name.

"I don't remember the name of the woman in the picture," the old friend of Jonnie Mae's mother, Lucille, lied. "I had a camera with me, and your father asked me to take a photograph when he was attending the first Halloween block party after hurricane Louise. I don't know why he asked me to take it. I think that woman was someone visiting the town."

The woman started to put the photograph back in her wallet, but Jonnie Mae stopped her.

"Can I keep this photograph?" Jonnie Mae quickly asked, reaching out to touch the paper. "It would mean a lot to me to have it. I've never seen a picture of my father."

The woman tried to think of something to say, a reason to not give the girl a photo of a father she never met. Her instincts told her no, but her compassion told her to provide the photograph to the girl. She had carried the memory in her wallet a long time. The memory wasn't dead but in her mind the man she used to know as John was.

"I knew your father quite well. He was friendly with all women. He had a bit of a reputation for being a ladies' man, but I know he loved your mother just as much as anyone else. It's best that you don't show that photograph to your mother, though. She might get jealous seeing him with another woman. Just know that everyone in this town knew your father. He had a good reputation until he lost his mind and then his job. No one knows what caused him to lose his mind."

"Lost his mind?" Jonnie Mae stammered, struggling to comprehend and absorb the information flowing from the woman's mouth. "Is he still alive, then?"

Eve at Peace by Yvette Doolittle Herr

The woman answered, "I don't know if he is still alive. I only heard, after I left, that he was sent to Chattahoochee. That's the state hospital for people with mental problems."

"I wonder if I can go see him there," Jonnie Mae half-whispered to the strange woman while she stared at the photograph the woman had handed to her. Jonnie Mae felt a weakness like she'd never felt before flow through her body.

"If he's still alive, he's a man possessed with mental problems. You probably don't want to see him in that state of mind," the woman said. "Just look at the man he was in that photograph. That's the man to remember. Handsome, proud, confident, and a lover of the ladies," she said. "I hope you'll leave it at that. Listen, you look like a young woman who stays away from trouble." The woman's dark eyes met Jonnie Mae's, expressing the intentional seriousness of her following words of advice." Stay away from that place, Chattahoochee. It might bring demons into your life."

The stranger turned her back to Jonnie Mae and quickly shoved through the crowd of Halloween party-goers. Jonnie Mae's eyes wanted to follow her, see where she went and find out her name, but she couldn't take her eyes off the photograph of her father.

Jonnie Mae was too confused to know what to do but, tried to reason through the facts.

"My mother never wanted to talk about my father. That woman said he had the reputation of being a ladies' man. My mother told me about how she met my father. He came up to her at a dance and asked her if she wanted to shine up his belt buckle, and that's how it all started. All my mother told me about my father was his name was John and just one night can change your life forever. She named me after him, and added Mae because I was born in the month of May. She told me adding Mae made my name sound more feminine."

Jonnie Mae went home and stayed awake all night thinking about the strange encounter with the woman who gave her the photograph. She couldn't forget or dismiss the woman's words about not showing the photo to her mother.

"I remember my mother once telling me that she thought I might have somewhere near twenty-three siblings, brothers and sisters, but I don't know any of them. Maybe that's why my mother never wanted to talk about my father. She never kept a photograph of him," Jonnie Mae thought. "Now I know why. I think the woman was right about not showing the photograph to my mother."

Jonnie Mae kept the photograph, which became a prized possession, hid inside her own wallet, never showing it or asking her mother about it.

At the tender age of sixteen, the hard facts of her background troubled her. By the time Jonnie Mae was twenty, she had possessed a bitterness in her heart about the unfairness of life.

Jonnie Mae had no idea that her father was so handsome. It worried her that he ended up in a mental hospital. "Will that happen to me, too?" she often wondered.

CHAPTER 35
BOMBSHELL NEWS

Eleanore and Darryl immediately left to drive to Panama City Beach after receiving the phone call from Geneva. They promised Geneva they would come down for a couple of days, but they would have to return to Stumpy's by the weekend. Darryl's popular band, the Pals, needed him to play his saxophone, and the busy restaurant needed Eleanore's supervision.

It was different visiting Panama City Beach without their baby girl, who was grown, graduated from the University of Georgia and was busy working as a lawyer, but they knew they'd get a chance to see Eve, too. After she moved away from home to go to the university, Eleanore and Darryl mostly only saw her on special occasions. They had wonderful memories of the family fun times visiting the beach with their baby daughter, watching her play in the sand and water. This visit to the beach would be adding a much different kind of new memory.

After receiving her law degree, they wondered whether their daughter would ever consider pursuing the case of who really murdered Earl. Like her parents, Eve had a passion for justice. Many times, Eve said to her parents, *my peace is found in knowing that the truth is told, and lies are destroyed.*

Her intelligence, and passion, didn't surprise them, but sometimes her decisions did.

"She's finally living her dream," Eleanore said with pride to Darryl near the end of the drive on the impromptu visit to Panama City Beach. "I always wondered if she would find the time to work on the case. You're the one who always talked about those two crazy men visiting the marina, looking for Earl. How many times did you tell her that story about how it seemed implausible that the runty, jumpy, quiet one committed the murder," she laughed. "Now what seems implausible is that Eve's down here working on the case and is accidentally discovered by Geneva and Big Joe. After all these years, I'm finally getting the opportunity to help Geneva. I can't wait to see Eve's reaction when she sees us and finds out why we are here. How coincidental! I wonder if it really is Geneva's brother Eve was talking to them about?"

"What's more coincidental is of all the houses Eve finds to rent, it turns out to be Casey's house," Darryl interjected. "I wonder if she called him? We've talked about him in the story about Earl's murder, so I wouldn't put it past her to use her sleuth skills to find Casey and ask him for assistance finding a cheap place to rent for a month or so. It would be just like Casey to rent her his house as a favor. I'm a little surprised Eve didn't mention her plans to us but, knowing her, I suspect she was going to tell us about it after she found information on the case."

Darryl changed the subject as soon as he made the turn into Captain Anderson's Marina parking lot. "Hey, would you look at this?" he exclaimed. "There's *The Lucky Two* tied up at the docks."

Darryl swung the car into a parking space close to *The Lucky Two*. They quickly exited the automobile and walked directly to stand in front of the charter boat that was the beginning of their history together. Eleanore and Darryl stole a loving look from each other and held hands for a few moments.

"We'd better get going," Eleanore said, "and not keep them waiting too long."

Geneva and Big Joe, who were waiting inside Smith's to have dinner with them, anxiously stood up from their table to greet Eleanore and Darryl. They watched the couple being led by the hostess to their table.

"I think we're too late to watch the sunset," Eleanore commented after the four exchanged hugs and greetings before sitting down. "I can still remember all the times I sat at this table looking out this window."

"This table has always been a favorite of the customers'," Big Joe smiled. "The boss said we can sit here all night if we want. When he found out Eleanore was coming into town, he told me that he wanted you to eat here tonight and to have this table. He also insisted that Dorinda escort you over here. You were always one of his favorite waitresses, you know. I remember him, more than once, calling you a breath of fresh air in the dining room. Did Dorinda say anything to either of you?"

Eleanore and Darryl nodded their heads no.

"She barely glanced at either of us above her reading glasses," Darryl reported.

"I was surprised to see her. I'm just as happy that she didn't say anything to me," Eleanore said. "If she had, I'd have to say something to her, and I would have had a hard time saying anything nice."

Like the times before, when they visited many years ago, their conversation with Big Joe and Geneva covered many of the employees from the past who used to work at Smith's, but tonight there was a new person that they needed to talk about.

"You remember Sue, the salad girl who worked with me, right?" Geneva asked Eleanore.

"Yes! How could I forget, sweet Sue?" Eleanore answered. "Didn't you end up renting a room from her?"

"Let's not bring that up," Geneva laughed. "The short time I spent living with her was a disaster for me."

Geneva continued, "Not too long after you left, Eleanore, Sue decided that she needed someone to help her in the salad room. She claimed that Big Joe was working her too hard," Geneva said sarcastically and rolled her eyes. Geneva and Big Joe shared a brief laugh together.

"We knew that wasn't the case," Big Joe interrupted. "Sue was just compulsive about the salads she made as she was about keeping her trailer clean for the few months Geneva tried to live with her. Sue wanted everything cut up perfectly-sized to fit on a fork and into a person's mouth. She wanted the salad to be good. Everyone who eats at a restaurant rarely talks about the salad. It's mostly the meat or side dishes. On the other hand, no one complained about the salad. Hence, I couldn't dismiss Sue's point. However, Sue's production was getting slower and slower, as if she was intentionally doing it to force me into hiring an extra person to help. Eventually, I did bring in someone else to assemble the salads and decided to keep Sue in the salad room. I wanted her to cut up all the ingredients and train the new girl."

Eleanore tried to suppress a giggle, and Big Joe shook his head in disbelief about his decision to go along with Sue's demands.

Geneva continued to tell the story for Big Joe.

"This young woman walks into the restaurant one day. Told Big Joe that she had no experience working in a restaurant but needed a job. Said she'd do anything and promised us that she was a hard worker. She had a one-year-old baby girl." Geneva abruptly stopped talking and turned her head away as if to hide her feelings. "You go on and tell the rest of the story, Big Joe."

Darryl loved watching Big Joe and Geneva interact with each other. "If I didn't know better," he said, "I'd believe you two are acting like an old married couple."

Big Joe laughed and picked up the story where Geneva left off. "I caved in and thought that this might be the perfect person to work with Sue. Maybe, I thought, Sue could teach the young woman how to cut up the salad ingredients. Hopefully, she would be a fast learner and faster worker."

As if collecting his thoughts, Big Joe stopped for a moment.

"Lucille was her name," he said in a quieter voice. "I hoped she might be able to do the entire job in the salad room. I thought I could place Sue in another area of the kitchen where I could use her good knife skills. Maybe, I thought, Sue could learn how to filet fish. People were starting to come back to the beach after hurricane Louise and business was picking up. It turned out that it didn't hurt to have an extra person in the salad room."

"Lucille was a real nice woman," Geneva interjected, "just like you, Eleanore. She worked with us for several years, then decided to take a job working in town. She didn't want to be so far away from home, working nights on the beach. Her daughter was growing older, and Lucille wanted to be closer to home to keep an eye on her daughter."

Geneva began to rock back and forth while sitting in her chair, like a person who is not ready to hear bad news when their sick loved one is admitted to the hospital.

Big Joe looked at Geneva, appearing concerned and worried, but he continued. "Seems like the father of Lucille's baby got himself into some kind of trouble very soon after she was born. Lucille needed someone to talk to about raising her baby, and she trusted Geneva. It was kind of like when you, Eleanore, went to Geneva and told her about your baby." Big Joe cut his eyes quickly, glancing at Darryl, who winked back at Big Joe, taking no offense at the comparison, and nodded.

"You mean you knew about the baby before I did?" Darryl sarcastically asked. "Why, that doesn't seem right to me. Somebody else knew about Eleanore's baby before the father even found out. I'm pretty sure Eleanore wanted to tell me first."

All four people laughed hard for a few minutes at Darryl's comment, enjoying the levity. They all remembered how Geneva played a considerable role in supporting Eleanore and getting her to go back to Darryl. Sensing that the story they were about to hear would not end up as good as their fairy tale, Darryl was glad to see Geneva laugh and stop her nervous body rocking.

"Fast forward to a year ago." Big Joe said in a conspiratorial tone. "Geneva comes up to me in my office after work one night. She softly knocks on the open door, as if she doesn't want to interrupt me and needs permission to come in and visit me," Big Joe paused and glanced at Geneva, who was nodding her head for him to continue on with the story.

Big Joe said, "Geneva says to me, *"I need to talk to you about something, but you can't tell anyone else. This new girl you hired, Lucille's daughter, showed me a picture of her father."*

"Uh-huh," Geneva murmured and began rocking her body again.

"I'm thinking to myself," Big Joe continues, "what's the big deal about that. Anyway, Lucille's daughter, the baby girl, all grown up now...."

"Just tell them her name," Geneva impatiently interrupted. "She named the baby girl Jonnie Mae because the father's name was John, and the baby was born in May."

"Yes, Geneva," Big Joe obediently said and continued. "Last year Lucille shows up here at Smith's with her daughter, Jonnie Mae, at the beginning of summer season," Big Joe turned his head toward Geneva. "Lucille asks me if I could give her daughter a job. I didn't really need another girl in the salad room, but Lucille wants her daughter, Jonnie Mae, to work with Geneva. Lucille says to me that she thinks Geneva is the right person to teach her daughter the kitchen skills she needs to open her own restaurant one day, but she needs to learn life skills, too. Lucille tells me that Geneva is the only person she would trust to coach and train her daughter. I liked Lucille, and having a little extra help in the busy summer months is nice, so I hire Jonnie Mae.

"Ahem," Big Joe cleared his throat, took a deep breath, and paused.

"As soon as Jonnie Mae starts working here, she's asking Geneva for advice. She wants to find her father," Big Joe cut a glance at Geneva, then continued. "Seems as if an old friend of Lucille's gave Jonnie Mae a picture of him. That's the first picture she's ever seen of her father, but the friend told her not to show it to her mother, Lucille."

Eleanore and Darryl were listening, trying to comprehend the story. Their quizzical facial expressions were not lost on Big Joe.

Big Joe began talking faster. "Been about five or six years ago that the old friend of Lucille's was in town to see some family. The old friend saw Jonnie Mae at that Halloween party they have every year in downtown Panama City. The friend tells Jonnie Mae some background about her father and finishes by telling Jonnie Mae the last she heard was that her father was sent to the Florida State prison in Chattahoochee. That's where the criminally insane people are sent to complete their sentence if they've been found guilty of committing a crime.

"Jonnie Mae says to Geneva that she wanted to visit her father, but that the friend told her that her father didn't know her, and she probably wouldn't want to know him. The friend told Jonnie Mae that before her father ended up in Chattahoochee, he was a nice-looking man with the reputation of being a lady's man.

"The girl is understandably upset that she never got to know her real father, and blames her mother. She has some issues to work through. She's been holding on to that picture, never telling her mother, Lucille, that she has it."

"That whole story sounds so sad and awful," Eleanore moaned.

"The story gets better, or maybe not, if you think about it," Big Joe said.

"One night Jonnie Mae, a few weeks near the end of the summer season, asks Geneva if she has time after work to talk about something. She needs advice. She can't decide whether or not she should go see her father in Chattahoochee. Seems like Lucille was right about trusting Geneva with her daughter's training and more."

"Yep," Geneva said. "She came up to me just like you did. I talked with her on that famous bench you and I sat on together, Eleanore. I was prepared to tell her that her father would not be the person she saw in that old photograph. After this many years, he'd be changed. He probably wouldn't have any idea who she was. I was prepared to tell her that maybe it was best to keep that image in her mind and not the one she'd see in Chattahoochee.'

"Who's telling the story?" Big Joe asked. "You, or me?"

"No, you go on," Geneva said solemnly. "I just didn't know if you were going to mention the bench. You and I have had some good conversations on the bench, too, Big Joe."

"That's true," Big Joe said.

"Wait a minute," Darryl said. "I've never sat on the bench. Where is it? I want to see it!"

Eleanore, Geneva, and Big Joe groaned in united exasperation.

"Quiet. Let him tell the story, Darryl," Eleanore said, forcing calm control in anticipation of hearing something that she wouldn't like.

"When they meet on the famous bench," Big Joe said, continuing the story, "Jonnie Mae takes the picture out of her purse and shows it to Geneva."

Big Joe paused and looked at Geneva for a moment. The expression on Geneva's face was clearly a combination of anger and hate. She was sitting stiff as a statue, her legs firmly planted on the ground, and her eyes staring into space above everyone's head, as if in a hypnotic trance.

The story gripped the attention of Darryl and Eleanore. Neither said a word and turned their heads to watch Geneva's reaction to the story.

"Don't stop," Geneva said. "The story doesn't end there."

Big Joe, in a measured voice, continued. "It turns out that the woman in the photograph is dressed up in a Halloween costume. She's not wearing a mask, so it's easy to identify her if you know her. John is not dressed in a costume, but he has one arm draped around her shoulder, holding her close to his side. He was obviously attending the Halloween party with her."

Big Joe stopped talking, turned his head to Geneva, and asked, "You want to finish?"

The gruff, sharpness in Geneva's voice surprised Eleanore; she didn't recognize the Geneva she heard now.

"Someone found that woman in the photograph dead on the day after she went to a city-wide Halloween party dressed up in the costume she's wearing in the picture. She was discovered by a woman walking her dog in the morning on the beach in St. Andrews. The newspaper printed a thumb shot photograph of the murdered woman on the front page, along with a story that the killer had slit her throat. The thumb shot came from a police file when she had been arrested for something before. I've never forgotten her face. I recognized it, even though she is dressed in a Halloween costume in the photograph Jonnie Mae showed me," Geneva said, adding angrily, "and my brother Charles was sent to prison for her murder. Prison for life. My brother would never do anything like that to another human being. Everyone he worked with at the construction company pointed the finger at my brother. Those people were laying down poison for the detectives. If someone digs a little deeper now that we've seen this photo, I'd suspect they would discover that Jonnie Mae's father, John, worked at that construction company too."

Eleanore and Darryl, stunned and shocked by the story, said in unison, "I'm so sorry, Geneva."

Eleanore stood up, took two steps forward, wrapped her arms around Geneva, and whispered into Geneva's ear, "I'm going to help you, just like you helped me. One day, somehow, we're going to get your brother Charles out of jail. I remember you telling me about him being in trouble, but you kept it to yourself, knowing that you didn't need to add to the burden of my troubles. You are one strong, special woman, Geneva!"

"I always wanted to find another lawyer for my brother. I think I've found the one who is going to get him out of that prison," Geneva said with tears in her eyes.

CHAPTER 36
LUCKY BREAK

Charles sat at the table, carefully watching Eve as she walked into the room. Who was this woman gliding across the floor, smiling at him? She seemed to be behaving entirely different from the woman he had met before.

The last time they were together and talked about Charles' case, he sensed her aloofness. Even though she tried to engage him in a conversation about his life, he could tell that her mind was on something, or somebody, else. She acted indifferent about the details in his case, asking very few questions about the crime he was in prison for. She sat in her chair like a mannequin, hardly showing any signs of life. Because she barely moved, Charles had wondered if she was in some sort of a trance, away somewhere else.

On this visit, Eve's mannerisms were completely different from the get-go. She seemed to possess an energized excitement that she couldn't contain or control.

Eve yanked the wooden, slatted-back chair away from the conference table and slid into the seat with a controlled but animated plop. She slapped a thick file folder on top of the table and tapped on the file with her forefinger several times. When Eve stopped tapping the paper file, she waved her hands over the file, like she was a magician about to pull the rabbit out of the hat. She sucked in a long breath of air through her opened mouth, puffed out her cheeks like a blowfish, then blew out the air between her lips, mouth like she was ready to blow up a party balloon.

"I am so glad you agreed to talk with me again," Eve gushed, acting like a young woman going out on a second date with a man who gave her thrills.

Charles was so surprised by this new Eve person that he involuntarily scooted his chair back, away from the table, a couple of inches. The wood legs made a screeching noise, but no one seemed to notice. Charles's eyes followed all of

Eve's movements. He began to wonder if the woman had gone a little crazy in the last month. "The heat in Florida can do that to anyone," Charles thought to himself.

"Why did you come to see me again?" Charles wanted to ask her. Why was this woman, who was only a stranger in his life, interested in meeting him again? The last time he met with seemed super non-productive.

He began to second guess Ricky's recommendation and insistence that he meet with her a second time. He remembered feeling skeptical about her being able to help him at all, but didn't want to hurt Ricky's feelings. Ricky was his friend.

"I agreed to meet with her because I didn't want to hurt Ricky's feelings," Charles thought. "On the other hand, I don't like being around some crazy lady."

As if she'd read his mind, every thought he just had, Eve said, "I've got some great news to share with you," vigorously nodding her head up and down several times as if to convince him. "I've been doing research and found some new evidence about your case. That woman you supposedly murdered led a shady life. Her name was Rose. I bet you didn't even know her name. I remember you telling me that she wouldn't even talk to you when you wanted to dance with her, and after all these years, you still refer to her as Fallen Angel. When the case came to court, her name was on the docket, but you still think of her as Fallen Angel."

In Charles's mind, the Fallen Angel's real name didn't matter as much as the look of crazed excitement in Eve's eyes.

"It's all in here," Eve tapped harder on the file with her forefinger, then flipped open the cover. Stapled to the front cover was a picture of Rose. "The thumb-nail mug shot is a copy from a police file when Rose had been previously arrested, on more than one occasion. Apparently, she was involved with drug trafficking and other vices."

"Why am I wasting my time?" Charles wanted to say to Eve but instead interrupted her to ask, "By the way, what did you say your last name is?"

"Oh my, did I forget to tell you?" Eve answered with less animation. "I thought I left you my business card."

"Maybe you did," Charles said coldly, "But I forgot."

"Kay," Eve quickly answered.

"Okay?" Charles asked.

"No, K-A-Y. Kay," Eve answered without losing her enthusiasm.

Charles said to Eve, in a flat tone of voice, "Nice, good name. Thank you." To himself, he thought, "Two first names. Another reason to think she might be crazy."

Eve continued talking. Like her father, she didn't hesitate to say what she was thinking. She believed that her ability to talk incessantly was a good quality; talking is what make a good lawyer.

Charles felt highly uncomfortable and began to wish, again, that he had refused to meet with her. His own attention was starting to drift when he became aware she was talking about things that were making sense to him.

"Eleanore and Darryl came to Panama City Beach to see me. They're my parents. They're the ones who always thought that your friend, Ricky, was not guilty of killing a man who my mother knew quite well. Then, by some chance, they show me a photograph of...," Eve stopped in mid-sentence. "Wait, I'm getting ahead of myself."

"She's going to lay down a bombshell," Charles immediately thought to himself. "Whatever that is, I have no clue. I've only talked to this woman once before in my life. However, I recognize the signs when someone is acting like they've got an ace up their sleeve."

Eve also inherited the tendency of her father Darryl to talk in tangents. Those who listened would eventually find the connections between all of the subjects.

"So, I came to Florida to spend a few months down at the beach, take a break from working. I just finished a year working on a case in Georgia. Pocketed enough money from that case to take off a few months.

"While I was down here, I thought I would do some investigation into the murder case that sent Ricky to prison.

Eve at Peace by Yvette Doolittle Herr

My parents have a friend named Casey. He's been a friend of theirs for years and agreed to let me rent his house. My parents, and Casey, all share a history with a charter boat, *The Lucky Two*." Eve paused and closed her eyes to think about the sentimental love story of her parents. She sensed she was talking more to herself but was enjoying the moment of exhilaration. "Well, you probably don't know about the story about the charter boat, *The Lucky Two*. It's hard for Ricky to communicate, but the charter boat is the beginning of the story. It's partly the reason why Ricky's in prison. Ricky is such a sweet man. I'm glad that you're friends."

The moment of exhilaration was coming for Charles.

"It turns out that my mother, Eleanore, and your sister Geneva, are very good friends," Eve blurted. "I had a chance to meet with Geneva, the woman you call Sista."

Eve smiled, knowing ahead what to expect Charles' reaction to be.

"That's unbelievable," Charles said, his eyes popped out, wide open in amazement. He scooted the chair forward, leaned both arms on top of the table, and lowered his head to get more direct eye contact with Eve. He said again, breathlessly, "That's unbelievable."

Charles now felt an urgent need for Eve to get to the fine points about his case. Because Eve met his sister, Geneva, who had rarely visited him in prison in the last twenty years, there had to be so much more Eve was about to tell him. There was much more to the story. He was finding it difficult to control his excitement.

Acting like Ricky, Charles began to shuffle his feet. He held both hands above the table and tapped the five fingertips of each hand together. He maintained eye contact with Eve, finding it challenging to sit still in his chair. It became apparent to him, watching the excitement in Eve's eyes, the animation of her hands when she talked, and the speed of her words, that she was about to tell him something spectacular.

"The photograph I started to mention a minute ago is here in this file," she finally said, flipping over to another page in the folder.

Charles could see the photo lying on top of several other sheets of paper. He observed that the picture was old, color-faded, and the paper wrinkled at the edges from the few feet across the table.

Eve carefully picked up the photograph with her thumb and forefinger at the corner, then stretched her arm to place it on the table in front of Charles.

She watched Charles' reaction as his eyes squinted and his head tilted to the side, like a person unsure of what he was seeing, and not happy about it, either. Charles pursed his lips together tight and lifted his head up to look squarely in the eyes at Eve.

"I recognize this man with that woman you named Rose," Charles said. His face expressed anger, hate and shock. He gravely shook his head side-to-side in disbelief, deeply hurt by a vivid reminder of his past. "I used to work at a construction company before I was sent here for the murder of that woman he's standing with. This is unreal. This isn't some kind of joke, is it?" Charles choked on his words as raw emotion swelled up in his throat.

"Take your time, Charles," Eve said sympathetically. "I thought this would be good news, but obviously, it also brings back a bad memory."

"This man worked with me at the company. I think his name was John," Charles said in a quiet voice. "Where did this photograph come from? Why didn't someone show it to the authorities after the murder? How did you get it? What does this mean? What are you trying to tell me?"

"I think it means we can get you out of this prison," Eve said, with a broad smile plastered across her face. "I have all of the background evidence in this folder. It takes some time to file the paperwork with the courts, but I am sure that I have enough evidence to overturn your conviction and can get you out of here in a few months. What do you think?"

"I think I'm living a dream," Charles choked on his words, and tears welled up in his eyes. "Did my Sista do all this?"

"She did have a part," Eve said. "There was luck and coincidence. The biggest part that brought all of this together was that your Sista helped my mother when my mother had a need. My mother was finally able to return the favor of helping your Sista. I love that you still call her Sista!"

Charles covered his face with his hands and sobbed. When he collected his composure, he faced Eve with a look of genuine concern.

"What about Ricky," Charles asked.

Eve laughed and said, "That was another stroke of luck for me. I have the DNA evidence that will help me argue before a court that Ricky did not commit murder, either. It will take his case longer than yours to clear him, but you can be waiting for him, ready to help him like he helped you. Get yourself set up with a job and a place to live. Be ready for the day Ricky gets out of prison, too. You both can be roommates in a better place."

"There's something I want to ask, though, before you leave today," Charles said. "How did you get that photo?"

"You probably don't want to know the story right now," Eve said. "I'm sure when you get reunited with your Sista, she'll fill you in on all the background, including the night I first met her and Big Joe."

"My Sista hangs out with a man named Big Joe?" Charles asked. His mind was filling up with speculations of surprises to come.

"Oh yes," Eve chuckled, sounding like her father. "That's another story."

EPILOGUE

Both of Eve's parents impressed upon her to seek the truth, and justice, where ever the path of life took her.

"Never forget to do something good for someone else whenever you have the opportunity. The rewards will be greater than the sacrifice," they both repeatedly reminded her. "There are givers and takers in this world. The givers are the happiest people by far. Their pleasure comes from the feeling they've been able to help someone. The good memories stay forever."

With her mission to secure Charles's and Ricky's release from prison finished, Eve knew she needed to eat at Smith's one more time before heading back to Georgia. Her purpose was twofold. One last good seafood meal was important, but redeeming her reputation was more important. If there was a chance for gossipy talk about her now that Charles and Ricky were working in the kitchen, her ego wouldn't allow any chance that the bartender might slander her reputation. Although she had over imbibed, she remembered everything that happened the night she ate dinner at the bar and connected with Big Joe and Geneva. She was going to make sure the bartender had his facts straight.

She declined the offer by the hostess to sit by the window overlooking the lagoon and asked to be seated at the bar.

The bartender never forgot the night he met Eve, and was genuinely happy to see her again. After apologizing for serving her too many glasses of wine, he asked about her lawyering career, interested in knowing more about how she put the evidence together to free the two men from prison, especially the one who couldn't talk. He'd already heard the story about Geneva's brother Charles going to prison for murder.

Eve briefly explained the discovery of Earl's body in the truck; relayed the arduous task of pulling information out of Ricky; the day she spent at Pine Log Forest State Park searching for a wallet; and waiting for the DNA results to come back linking Vince to Earl's death. The visit to the Florida State Hospital in Chattahoochee was more demanding. Armed with a tape recorder and the photograph of Fallen Angel together with John, Eve explained how the man kept looking away from the photograph, and covering his eyes with his hands. After hours of talking to him, Eve finally solicited the confession when John said, *"Rose, why did I kill you?"*

After hours of talking, and drinking iced tea refills, the night ended with the bartender asking Eve if she'd consider riding to Eden Gardens State Park with him the next day. He planned to do some hiking along the paths on his day off. He promised the park with acres of flower gardens would be a much more interesting park to visit than Pine Log Forest State.

She had never visited the park where her parents were married, so she accepted the invitation, but didn't tell him about her parents.

Listening to Keith Urban during the thirty-minute drive back to Panama City Beach, put Eve in a nostalgic mood. Recalling the story of her parents' serendipitous encounter, she wondered if the music of one of her favorite country music artists, spending the afternoon with the bartender at a place of special significance to her, were portending of something more to come. When he took Eve back to her car parked at Smith's, where they agreed to meet, the bartender asked if she would be willing to go out with him on a dinner date before she left town.

Eve had no doubt she would take a chance, since the man came with a good recommendation from Big Joe and Geneva, who she also went to visit the day before, telling them of her plans to eat dinner at the bar. She wanted to see them, too, before leaving town. They reported the changes already in the making at Smith's. Big Joe was hanging up his apron and turning the kitchen responsibilities over to the Sous Chef. Geneva planned to continue working with Sue, and keep an eye on Charles working side-by-side with the Sous Chef. Ricky would be the best-loved dishwasher Smith's ever hired. Ricky never complained. Ricky and Charles became like birds of a feather, looking out for each other at work, and going to their nest after work, renting Casey's house.

Somewhat nervous about a second date, Eve mulled over the idea of going to a spiritual advisor, like her mother once did. Agreeing to go out with the bartender on a dinner date, who she decided was more handsome than she remembered from the first night, was taking a big step. Flipping through a magazine filled with beach business advertising, Eve found an advertisement for Madame Star on Thomas Drive. Wondering if this was the same woman her mother visited, she called her mother, who was surprised to hear Madame Star was still in the business of giving spiritual advice. "Go have a little fun before you come back to Georgia and dive into work," her mother also advised.

Eve was even more surprised when the woman informed her that her name also was Eve.

"When you called to make your appointment, I thought it was interesting that we have the same name," Madame Star said to Eve. "My real name is Evelyn, but my siblings used to call me Eve."

Less interested in having her palm lines or Tarot cards read, Eve asked Madame Star if she had a crystal ball. "I've always been intrigued by the idea of someone looking into a crystal ball and seeing the future. I'd like to look into one, if you have it."

"I have a hereditary condition in my left eye," Madame Star answered brusquely, throwing a dart into Eve's anticipatory night of having fun with a spiritual advisor.

Madame Star promptly raised her eyebrow, cocked her head, shut one eye, and stared at Eve for a long minute with the other eye. "Light refracted through crystal interferes with my eyesight. I get a burning, tingling sensation. I can't imagine any good visions of someone's future in a crystal ball," she said while gently moving her head closer to Eve's face.

Eve saw the distinct outline of a crescent-shaped spot in Madame Star's eye. It seemed to be flash.

"Shall we get started?" Madame Star opened both eyes and cut them toward a door. She tossed her long gray hair over a shoulder with one hand, motioning to the door with her other hand.

Eve suddenly felt worse than uneasy. Something about Madame Star, besides the spot in her eye and sharing the same name, made her start rethinking the whole idea of being with the woman. "Can you just tell me a little bit about yourself first?" Eve asked. "I made an appointment and I want to pay you for your time. I've changed my mind. I'm not interested in the Tarot card experience. I thought you would have a crystal ball."

Speaking fast, like the trained lawyer, Eve continued, "To be fair, maybe you'd be interested in knowing a little about me first. My mother was pregnant with me and came to see you. You made such an impression on my mother that she decided to marry my father after you read her Tarot cards. So, in a nutshell, that's how I got here. How did you become a spiritual advisor, if you don't mind me asking."

"Well," Madame Star let the word roll off her tongue and clucked. "I suppose that's fair. I will have to charge you for my time even if I don't read the cards. It's very rare for me to hear a story like the one you just told me, so I'll indulge you for a few minutes and tell you about me."

Madame Star relayed a short version of her family history. A mother in jail in Georgia for shooting her husband; a long-haul truck-driving father who moved back home to Alabama; siblings placed in foster homes in Alabama; and the youngest sibling, a brother, who came to Florida to go deep-sea fishing with a friend but ended up dead.

"I came down here to bury my youngest brother," Madame Star said in a deep, but silky-smooth voice. "I didn't want Vince to be forgotten, like some nobody, so I stayed in Florida. After a few years of cocktail waitressing, I took a weekend trip to New Orleans with some of the girls from work. I brought a pack of Tarot Cards from one of those Voodoo souvenir shops. Once I studied the cards, I knew I was meant for this calling. It's a lot easier than serving drinks to people who tend to drink too much and forget to tip. Many of my customers are only looking to have a little fun, but some are searching for answers to their problems. I don't make any guarantees."

"I can't imagine you could," Eve commented, adding "I'm sorry to hear about your brother."

"The way I see it, every day brings a new story," Madame Star said. "We're finished now. In an hour I have to be at a bachelorette party for a group of women staying at the Lamp Lighter Motel on the beach. The girls want their fortune told. My house is too small to accommodate all of them, so I have to collect my tools and get ready."

Eve hoped it didn't look too obvious that she was anxious to leave when she hastily opened the door and rushed out of the house. She hyperventilated for a few minutes once she was safe inside her car. After processing the story Madame Star told her, Eve knew that she had just met the sister of Ricky's best friend, Vince. Eve couldn't shake off the feeling that she'd been struck by a bolt of lightning.

Made in the USA
Columbia, SC
28 February 2023